PRAISE FOR VEILED FREEDOM

"Jeanette Windle is the kind of storyteller other writers want to be when they grow up. If you've never been to Afghanistan, *Veiled Freedom* will put you there so vividly. But be prepared: this novel pulls no punches—your comfortable sense of American cultural logic will be stripped away as Windle exposes the thorny issues that plague this ancient land. The result is a brutal but fascinating portrayal of life as it really is in this crossroads between east and west, and nobody can describe it like Jeanette Windle. She's like a painter so skilled that her artwork is indistinguishable from a photograph. It's fiction, but just barely."

Chuck Holton, former U.S. Army Black Beret; author of the Task Force Valor series and of *American Heroes* with Oliver North.

"Windle's storytelling in *Veiled Freedom* is so vivid that I could practically feel the dust from Kabul's streets on my skin as I turned the pages. Windle's use of intricate details, intriguing characters, and important themes teases our imaginations and makes us wrestle with profound spiritual truths. This book is for the casual reader and the deep thinker alike."

Abdu Murray, author of *Apocalypse Later: Why the Gospel of Peace Must Trump the Politics of Prophecy in the Middle East* and president of Aletheia International.

"The technical aspects of the book are spot-on. Jeanette has the gift of making the complex cultural, political, and personal issues understandable and believable. She really understands how the multitude of subplots that are the central Asian states make life hard for both the citizenry and those trying to help."

Joe DeCree, retired Army Special Forces major & private security contractor. Completed two combat tours with the Army in Kosovo and Afghanistan and one as a PSD operative in Iraq.

Veiled Freedom

VEILED FREEDOM

J. M. WINDLE

Tyndale House Publishers, Inc.
Carol Stream, Illinois

Visit Tyndale's exciting Web site at www.tyndale.com

Visit Jeanette Windle's Web site at www.jeanettewindle.com

TYNDALE and Tyndale's quill logo are registered trademarks of Tyndale House Publishers, Inc.

Veiled Freedom

Designed by Beth Sparkman

Edited by Lorie Popp

Published in association with The Knight Agency, 570 East Avenue, Madison, GA 30650.

Library of Congress Cataloging-in-Publication Data

Windle, Jeanette.
  Veiled freedom / J. M. Windle.
    p. cm.
  ISBN 978-1-4143-1475-4 (sc : alk. paper) 1. Afghanistan—Fiction. I. Title.
  PS3573.I5172V45 2009
  813'.54—dc22   2009000014

Printed in the United States of America

15 14 13 12 11 10 09
 7   6   5   4   3   2   1

To those I hold dear—
you know who you are—
who offer yourselves unhesitatingly
as hands and feet and heart
of Isa Masih
to shine the light of his love
into dark places.

"You will know the truth,
and the truth
will set you free."

ISA MASIH

PROLOGUE

"Land of the free and the home of the brave."

The radio's static-spattered fanfare filtered through the compound wall. Beyond its shattered gate, a trio of small boys kicked a bundle of knotted rags around the dirt courtyard. Had they any idea those foreign harmonies were paying homage to their country's latest invaders?

Or liberators, if the rumors and the pirated satellite television broadcasts were true.

Scrambling the final meters to the top of the hill, he stood against a chill wind that tugged at his light wool vest and baggy tunic and trousers. Bracing himself, he made a slow, stunned revolution.

From this windswept knoll, war's demolition stretched as far as his eye could see. Bombs and rockets had left only heaps of mud-brick hovels and compound walls. The front of an apartment complex was sheared off, exposing the cement cubicles of living quarters. The collapse of an office building left its floors layered like a stack of *naan*. Rubble and broken pavement turned the streets into obstacle courses.

But it wasn't the devastation that held him spellbound. So it was all true—the foreign newscasts, the exultant summons that had brought him back, his father's dream. Kabul was free!

The proof was in the dancing crowds below. After five long years of silence, Hindi pop and Persian ballads drifted up the hillside. Atop a bombed-out bus, a group of young men gyrated wildly. Even a handful of women in blue burqas swayed to the rhythms as they bravely crossed the street with no male escort in sight.

Nor was blue the only color making a comeback against winter's brown. To his far right, a yellow wing fluttered skyward. There was an orange one.

A red. Scrambling on top of a broken-down tank, two boys tossed aloft a blotch of green and purple.

Kites had returned to the skies above Kabul.

Another tank moved slowly down the boulevard. Behind it came a parade of pickups and army jeeps, machine guns mounted in their beds. A staccato rat-tat-tat momentarily drowned out the music. But the gunfire was celebratory. The dancing mobs were not shrinking back but tossing flowers and confetti, screaming their elation above the noise.

He shouted with them, the fierceness of his response catching him by surprise. He'd hardly thought of this place in long years, the warm, fertile plains of Pakistan far more a home now than this barren wasteland. Yet joy welled up to squeeze his chest, the watering of his eyes no longer from wind and dust.

"Land of the free and the home of the brave." Down the hillside behind him, the radio blasted a Dari-language commentary. But the words of that foreign music still played in his mind. The sacred anthem his American instructors had taught their small English-language students in the Pakistani refugee camps.

As they'd taught of their homeland, America. A land where brave and honorable warriors guarded peace-loving and welcoming citizens who lived freely among great cities of shining towers and immense wealth. A land of wheat and rice and fruit trees, grape arbors and herds of livestock that offered to all an abundance of food. The very paradise the Quran promised to the faithful.

And Afghanistan? Land of his birth, his home? Brave, yes. No one had ever questioned the courage of the Afghan tribes. Not the Americans and Russians who were history's most recent invaders. Nor in turn the British, Mongols, Persians, Arabs, all the way back to Alexander the Great, whose armies were the first to learn that Afghanistan could be taken with enough weapons and spilled blood but never held.

But free?

He blinked away the sudden blurring of his vision. When had Afghanistan ever truly known freedom? Not under all those centuries of alternating occupations. Certainly not when the *mujahedeen* had finally brought the Soviet empire to its knees because then they—and the Taliban after them—had turned on each other. The rockets of their warring factions had rained down on Kabul in such destruction that his family was driven at last into exile.

"Have faith," his father had whispered into his ear. "Someday Afghanistan will be like America. A land of freedom as well as courage. Someday we will go home."

Even then he'd known the difference between wishes and painful reality. And yet, unbelievably, there it was below him. Today the liberators' anthem, his father's dream, had come true at last for his own country.

Yes, *his* country.

His people.

His home.

He'd missed dawn's first call to prayer. Now he stripped his vest to spread it over the dirt. Prostrating himself, rising sun at his back, he began the daily *salat*: "*Bismillahir Rahmanir Raheem.* In the name of Allah, the Beneficent, the Merciful."

The memorized Arabic prayers were rote, but when he finished, he whispered his own passionate plea against the ground: "Please let it be true this time. My father's dream. His prayers. Let my people know freedom as well as courage."

Standing, he shook out his vest. Beyond shattered towers of the city's business center and compounds of the poor lay a quiet, green oasis. The Wazir Akbar Khan district, home to Kabul's upper class. Its high walls, spacious villas, and paved streets looked hardly touched by war.

His sandaled feet slipped and twisted in his haste down the hillside. At street level, his old neighborhood proved less untouched than he'd thought. The walls were scarred by rocket blasts, sidewalks broken, poplar trees lining these streets in his memory now only stumps.

He headed toward the largest compound on the street, its two-story villa built around an inner courtyard. A brightly patterned *jinga* truck indicated the others had already arrived. The property differed so little from childhood memory he might have stepped back a decade. Even the peacock blue house and compound walls showed fresh paint. The Taliban officials who'd commandeered his home had at least cared for their stolen lodging. Or perhaps it had been his family's faithful *chowkidar*, who'd stayed when his employers fled.

Music and cheerful voices drifted over walls along with a hot, oily aroma that brought water to his mouth. Frying *boulani* pastries. He quickened his steps. He'd be home in time for the midday meal.

At first he thought he heard more celebratory gunfire, but when the unmistakable explosion of a rocket-propelled grenade shook the ground, he broke into a run. A mound of rubble offered cover as he reached the final T-junction.

His mind reeled. Surely he'd seen this victory convoy from the hilltop. But why were they firing on his home?

Even as he crouched in bewildered horror, the distinctive rat-tat-tat of a Kalashnikov rifle crackled back from a second-story window. Down the street a fighter rose from behind a jeep, an RPG launcher raised to his shoulder. A single blast. Then a limp shape slid forward over the window-sill and toppled from view.

The action unfroze his muscles, and he sprinted toward his home. A shout, the whine of a bullet overhead told him he'd been spotted. Apple trees edging the property wall offered hand- and footholds.

His feet touched brick, then ground on the other side. The acridity of gunfire and explosives burned his nostrils as he raced forward. He stumbled across the first limp shape facedown on the lawn. Turning the body over, he fruitlessly tried to stem a red sea spreading across white robes. Their faithful caretaker would never again tend these gardens or paint these walls.

An explosion rocked him as he raced around the side of the villa. Just inside the main entrance, the painted wooden frame of the jinga truck was burning. Behind it, the blast had blown the metal gates from their hinges. Invaders poured through the breach.

But he only had eyes for another huddled shape on the mosaic tiles of the courtyard and a third sprawled across marble front steps. The second-story gunman had fallen across a grape arbor. Through tears of smoke fumes and grief, he noticed the Kalashnikov rifle that had dropped from a dangling, bloodied hand.

Before he could snatch it up, a boot kicked the AK-47 out of reach.

Another smashed his face into the grass. Hot metal ground into his temple. He closed his eyes. *Allah, let it be quick!*

"Don't shoot! We need live prisoners. Here, you, get up!"

As the gun barrel dropped away, he struggled to his knees. Except for the poorly accented Dari and a shoulder patch of red, white, and blue, the man—with a flat wool cap, dark beard, hard, gray gaze, tattered scarf over camouflage flak jacket—could have been as Afghan as the *mujahid* whose weapon was still leveled at his head. He knew immediately who this tall, powerfully built foreigner was. For weeks Pakistani news had been covering the American elite warriors fighting alongside the mujahedeen Northern Alliance.

Our liberators! His mouth twisted with bitter pain.

"Where are your commanders? Mullah Mohammed Omar? Osama bin Laden?" The American must have taken his blank stare for incomprehension because he turned to his companion, shifting to English. "Ask him: where are the Taliban who had their headquarters here? And if any of these—" a nod took in the sprawled bodies—"are bin Laden or Mohammed Omar. Tell him he just might save his own neck if he cooperates."

"There are no Taliban here!" he said in English. He pushed himself to his feet and wiped a sleeve to clear dampness from his face and eyes. It came away with a scarlet that wasn't his own. "This is a private home! And you have just murdered my family! Why? The fighting was over. You were supposed to bring peace!"

"Your home? With a house full of armed combatants?" The American's boot nudged the Kalashnikov rifle now fallen to the grass. "You were firing on our troops."

"They were defending our home. They weren't soldiers. Just my father and brothers and our caretaker and his sons."

"You lie!" A blow rocked his head back as the mujahedeen translator snapped in rapid Dari. "You speak to me! I will translate!"

"I am not lying!" He spat out blood with his defiant English. "This has been my family's home for generations. Any neighbor can tell you. Yes, the Taliban stole it from us, but they have been gone for days. We only came back from Pakistan this very day."

He threw a desperate glance around. The last pretense of fighting was over, the mujahedeen drifting off except for those making a neat, terrible heap of limp bodies like laundry sacks near the broken gate. Wailing rose from a huddle of burqas and small children being herded out into the street. Were his mother and sister among them? Or had caution left them behind in Pakistan?

Then his gaze fell on a face he knew. A mujahid in full battle fatigues instead of the mismatched outfits of the others. The mujahid turned and stared at him indifferently.

Yes, it was he. Older, gray-streaked beard and hair. But it was the family friend who'd supplied his father's business with imported goods. Who'd been in this home countless times before their exile. Who'd brought him and his siblings small gifts and strange foreign sweets.

"Ask him. He will tell you who I am. He knows my family. He bought and sold for my father when I was a child."

"Who? The *muj* commander?" For the first time he saw a crack in the American's disbelief.

The family friend walked over. His cold, measuring appraisal held no recognition as the translator intercepted him for a brief conversation. Then, unbelievably, he swung around and marched up the marble steps into the villa.

The translator spread out his hands to the American. "The commander says he knows neither this youth nor his family. And it is well-known that all in this house have served the Taliban."

"No, it isn't true! Maybe he does not recognize me. I was only a child when we left. But he knows this house and my family. Please, I must speak to him myself."

Another foreign warrior emerged from the villa, clipped yellow hair and icy blue eyes shouting his nationality louder than curt English. "All clear. Body count's six male combatants. Minimal damage except the gate. This one's the only survivor minus a handful of female dependents and kids. From what the muj told us, I expected more bodies on the ground. They must have been tipped off."

"Maybe. Or the muj were fed some bad intel." The foreign soldiers moved away, and he missed the rest of their low-voice exchange.

Then the yellow-haired American waved a hand. "We followed the rules of engagement. They were armed and shooting."

"A handful of AK-47s. The kid's right—that's practically home protection around here. And the prisoner—he's no combatant. I saw him come over that wall. Should I turn him loose?"

"You know better than that. The interrogators are screaming for live ones up at Bagram. Besides, you've no idea what else he might know. If he's just in the wrong place at the wrong time, they'll sort it out and let him go."

A radio on the yellow-haired American's belt sputtered to life. "Willie? Phil? Either of you available? We've got brass touching down at the airport. They need an escort to the embassy."

"Okay, we're out. The muj will finish here and deliver the prisoner. They've got a load of Arab fighters and al-Qaeda types heading to Bagram this afternoon."

The translator snapped his fingers, and a knot of mujahedeen stepped forward to take his place. The translator hurried after the yellow-haired American, now marching toward the gate.

But the other foreign warrior hesitated. "Be there in a minute."

He braced himself as the first American walked over. He didn't allow himself to imagine sympathy in the foreigner's gray eyes.

"Look, I've got no choice but to send you up to Bagram with the other battlefield detainees. But if you aren't al-Qaeda or Taliban, you've got nothing to be afraid of. We don't shoot prisoners. And the muj commander's a stand-up guy. If there's been an intel error, he'll make things right.

"I can at least report that you arrived after the fighting was over and never raised a weapon. If I can find something to write on." The American dug through the interior pockets of his flak jacket and pulled out an envelope, removing a folded notepaper, then what looked like a snapshot of a yellow-haired young female surrounded by too many children to be her own.

A tiny, olive-colored volume fell into the American's palm. Western script read *New Testament*. "I wondered what I was supposed to do with this." Taking out a pen, he scribbled inside the cover. "Here. I've explained what I witnessed and given my contact info if Bagram needs confirmation. It might at least make a difference in where you end up. If you're telling the truth." The foreign soldier dared to offer a smile with the book.

Fury and hate rose in an acid flood to his throat. With a scream of rage, he struck at the outstretched hand. "You think this makes up for murdering my family? once again stealing our home? You call this freedom? How are you any better than the Taliban or the Russians?"

A rifle butt slammed him again to his knees. The blow scattered not only the olive-colored volume but the envelope and its other contents. The folded note fell into a sticky puddle, white rapidly soaking to scarlet.

The American made no attempt to retrieve it but scooped up the envelope, snapshot, and book. Above the dark beard, his mouth was hard and grim as he tucked the small volume into the prisoner's vest. "I really am sorry." Then he too headed toward the gate.

The foreigner was hardly out of sight when a bearded figure in battle fatigues emerged from the villa's columned entryway, an honor guard of mujahedeen at his heels. The one-time family friend strolled over. This time his survey was no longer indifferent or unrecognizing. But nothing in the unpleasantness of that smile, the merciless black eyes above it, renewed hope.

"So you are the offspring of—" His father's name splashed in spittle across his feet. "You've grown tall since you abandoned your people. And now you think you can simply return to claim this place?" The mujahedeen commander pulled free the American's offering. Its pages drifted in shreds to the grass. Then a rifle butt slammed into the prisoner. No one called for it to stop.

He closed his eyes, his body curved in supplication, forehead touching the ground. But this time he didn't bother to pray. His father had been wrong. The dream was over. It would take far more than dreams, a few impassioned prayers to Allah, before his homeland could ever be called land of the free and home of the brave.

"So who's the blonde chick? Picking them a little young, hey, Willie?"

The two Americans had commandeered one of the convoy's pickups and a jeep for the airport run along with a volunteer posse of mujahedeen. Their translator was at the wheel of the jeep. Willie, the only name by which their local allies knew the twenty-two-year-old Special Forces sergeant, and his companion clambered in to brace themselves behind the roll bar.

Willie glanced down at the retrieved correspondence still clutched in his hand. The girl who'd drawn his teammate's suggestive leer did indeed look very young, a pack of preschoolers crowded around her. "Nah, just some kid Sunday school teacher who pulled my name out of a hat. Like we don't have enough to do looking for bin Laden and taking out Taliban, we've got to answer fan mail."

"Why do you think I don't bother picking mine up?" As the jeep engine roared to life, his companion plucked away the photo for a clinical scrutiny. "Though maybe I should. Cute kid. How about I take this one off your hands? The way things are shaping up over here, she'll be old enough to date before we rotate home. So what's she got to say?"

Willie didn't bother explaining. But the accompanying note had been brief enough he had no problem recalling its contents:

> *Dear Sergeant Willie:*
>
> *My Sunday school class picked your name to pray for. We're so fortunate to be living here safe in the land of the free and home of the brave, and we're so proud of how you all are fighting to bring freedom to the people over there. I'm enclosing a class picture and a New Testament if you don't have one already. Someday when the fighting's over, I'd like to go to Afghanistan to help make the kind of difference you are. But since I'm only sixteen, I guess I'll stick to praying and writing for now. Anyway, we're praying for you to be safe and that you'll win this war soon so Afghanistan can be as free as we are.*

The jeep jolted out onto the street. Willie turned his long body to run a swift appraisal over the rest of their convoy. The mujahedeen volunteers were still scrambling on board as the pickups moved into line behind the jeep. They didn't look like men who'd reached the finale of a brutal military campaign. They were laughing as they jostled playfully for a position at the mounted machine guns, flower garlands from the afternoon's victory parade draped across bandoliers, wrapped around rifle barrels, even tucked behind ears.

But Willie had witnessed these local allies charging suicidally into enemy entrenchments, even with American bombs crashing down all around them. If he was so sick of this war after a few weeks, what had it been like for them to live decades—for many, an entire lifetime—of unrelenting fighting and death? Simply to have survived in this country required courage and fortitude seldom required of Willie's own compatriots.

Freedom was another matter.

Catching Willie's eye, a fighter barely into his teens raised a flower-festooned AK-47 from the next pickup. "Is it not glorious? We have won! We are free!"

Willie had divested himself of sentimentality before he'd ever made it through basic training. So it had to be the cold winter breeze that stung his eyes, dust gritting in his teeth that made him swallow. Willie had never doubted the value of his current mission. Nor even its ultimate success. Serving his country was a privilege, spreading freedom an honor worth these last difficult weeks.

But not even his rigorous training had prepared him for the brutality and ugliness of combat. The ragged chunks of flesh and bone that had once been human beings. Even worse, the screams from broken bodies that still held life. Too many of them his own comrades.

Yet scarcely two months since plane-shaped missiles had slammed into the heart of his own homeland, the people of Afghanistan were taking to these very streets to celebrate their liberation. Even now his countrymen were touching down to raise the flag over Kabul's long-abandoned U.S. embassy compound. Okay, so everything hadn't run as smoothly as their mission training. Maybe there'd been mistakes. Maybe even today. But at least those raucous dancing mobs with their music and kites and the battle-wearied fighters in the pickups behind him finally had a chance for real freedom.

A chance he'd helped to give them.

You can tell your kids their prayers have been answered, Willie composed a mental reply to that bright, smiling young face. *It's all over but the mopping up.*

The thought prompted him to lean forward, tapping the driver on the shoulder. "You're heading back over here after the embassy run, right? Do me a favor and check on that kid for me. Make sure whoever's hauling them up to Bagram delivers him in one piece. Some of the muj are a little trigger-happy."

The translator turned his head after he maneuvered between a rubble heap and a pothole. "I am sure the commander will have given orders for anything you have asked. He is very happy with you."

"Happy?"

"But of course! Because of the property you have secured for him. The finest residence in the Wazir Akbar Khan. The commander has desired it for his own possession since before the Taliban. And now because of your weapons, it is his at last. We will move our headquarters here this very day."

Willie went rigid in furious comprehension.

"Hey, easy, man!" The blond soldier's arm was an iron-hard barrier, his voice low and warning. "Back off. It's not his doing."

Willie's grip tightened to white knuckles on his M4 assault rifle. "We've been had!"

"Hey, it's not the first time, and around here it sure won't be the last. Are you that naive? This is war. *Their* war. We're only advisers, remember? And that doesn't include refereeing property disputes."

That his teammate was right didn't temper Willie's mood. The crinkle of paper reminded him his fist wasn't empty. The envelope was a crumpled mess, and only now did he notice the rusty smudge blurring what had been a return address. He wouldn't be answering this fan mail. Which was just as well.

Willie tossed the wad of paper over the side of the jeep, the adrenaline rush of this afternoon's victory draining to intense weariness, his earlier elation as acrid in his mouth as the smoke rising from a burning truck just inside the wrecked gates. It was going to take a whole lot more than wishes and a few kids' prayers before Afghanistan could ever be called land of the free and home of the brave.

Baghlan Province, Afghanistan
Present Day

A day from the past.

No, a day for the future.

The farmer stood proud, tall, as he shuffled down the crowd-lined drive. A switch in his hand urged forward the mule pulling a cart piled high with huge, swollen tubers. They looked like nothing edible, but their tough, brown hide held sweetness beyond the sucrose to be squeezed from their pulp. The firstfruits of Baghlan's revitalized sugar beet industry.

In a long-forgotten past, when the irrigated fields stretching to high, snow-capped mountains were not known best for land mines and opium, the farmer had worked his family's sugar beet crop. He'd earned his bride price stirring huge vats of syrup in the sugar factory, Afghanistan's only refinery and pride of the Baghlan community. Until the Soviets came and Baghlan became a war zone. For a generation of fighting, the sugar factory had been an abandoned shell.

But now past had become future.

The massive concrete structure gleamed with fresh paint, the conveyor belt shiny and unrusted, smokestacks once more breathing life. By the throngs packing both sides of the drive, the entire province had turned out to celebrate the factory's reopening. In front of the main entrance was a dais, destination of farmer and cart.

The token harvest followed on the stately tread of regional dignitaries making their way toward the dais. Students, neat in blue tunics, offered pink and white and red roses to the distinguished arrivals. Among them the farmer spotted his grandson. No smile, only the flicker of a glance, a further straightening of posture, conveyed his pride. Too many sons and brothers and kinsmen had died in the war years. But for his remaining grandson, this day presaged a very different future.

On the dais, the factory manager stood at a microphone. Behind him, chairs held the mayor, regional governor, officials arrived from Kabul for the inauguration ceremony. "The government has pledged purchase of all sugar beet. Our foreign partners pledge equipment to any farmer who will replace current crops. So why plant seed that produces harvests only of violence? On this day, I entreat you to choose the seed of peace, of a future for our community and our children."

The procession had now reached the dais. But it wasn't the dignitaries' arrival that broke off the factory manager's speech. The roar of a helicopter passing low overhead drew every eye upward. Circling around, the Soviet-made Mi-8 Hip descended until skids touched pavement. Crowds scattered back, first from the wind of its landing, then as the rotors shut down, to open passage.

The government minister who stepped out was followed by foreigners, the allies who'd funded the refinery project designed to entice Baghlan farmers from opium poppies to sugar beet. The newcomers leisurely moved through the parted crowd. The minister paused to speak to his foreign associates, then turned back toward the helicopter.

The explosion blasted through the factory, blowing out every window and door. A fireball erupting from the open entrance enveloped the dais. A panicked swerve of the mule placed the heavy cart between farmer and blast, saving his life but burying him in splinters of wood and beet. He could not breathe nor see nor hear. Only when the screams began did he realize he was still alive.

Pushing through the debris, he staggered to his feet. Shrapnel had ripped through the crowd where the fireball had not reached, and what lay between dais and shattered cart was a broken, bleeding chaos. Those uninjured enough to rise were scattering in panic. The farmer ran too but in the opposite direction. Ignoring moans and beseeching hands, he scrabbled through the rubble. Then with a cry of anguish he dropped to his knees.

The school uniform was still blue and clean, a single white rose fallen from an outflung hand. The farmer cradled the limp form, his wails rising to join the communal lament. For his grandson, for so many others, the future this day had promised would never come.

Kabul International Airport

"Oh, excuse me. I am *so* sorry."

Steve Wilson barely avoided treading on heels as the file of deplaned passengers ground to a sudden halt. A glance down the line identified the obstruction. In pausing to look around, a female passenger had knocked a briefcase flying.

The young woman was tall enough—five foot seven by Steve's calculation—to look down on her victim and attractive enough that the balding, overweight Western businessman waved away her apology. Platinum blonde hair spilled in a fine, straight curtain across her face as she scrambled for the briefcase. A T-shirt and jeans did nothing to disguise the tautly muscled, if definitely female, physique of a Scandinavian Olympic skier. Though that accent was 100 percent American.

Steve had already noted the woman several rows ahead of him on the plane. With only a handful of female passengers, all discreetly draped in head shawl or full-body *chador*, her bright head had been hard to miss, face glued to the window as the Ariana Airlines 727 descended through rugged brown foothills into the arid mountain basin that was Kabul.

Now as she handed the briefcase back, Steve caught his first clear glimpse of her features. It was a transparently open face, hazel eyes wide and interested under startlingly dark lashes and eyebrows. The candid interplay of eagerness, apprehension, and dismay as she turned again to take in her surroundings roused in Steve nothing but irritation. *Wipe that look off your face or Afghanistan will do it for you.*

As the line moved forward, Steve stepped out of it to make his own survey. Next to a small, dingy terminal, only one runway was in service.

Down the runway, a red and white-striped concrete barrier cordoned off hangars and prefabricated buildings housing ISAF, the NATO-led International Security Assistance Force. Dust gusted across the runway, filling Steve's nostrils, narrowing his gaze even behind wraparound sunglasses. He'd forgotten the choking, muddy taste of that dust.

The taste of Afghanistan.

Beyond the 727, a guard detail was loading passengers into a white and blue UN prop plane. Steve recognized the bear paw and rifle scope logo on their gear. Private security contractors. He'd done contracts for that company, and if he dug binoculars from his backpack, he'd likely spot guys he knew. But the wind was picking up, the other passengers disappearing inside the terminal, so instead Steve lengthened his stride.

He needn't have hurried. The immigration line was excruciatingly slow, the Afghan official scrutinizing each passport as though he'd never seen one before. The single baggage conveyor was broken, its handlers dumping suitcases onto the concrete floor with complete disregard for their contents. Air-conditioning was broken as well, the lighting dim enough Steve pushed sunglasses to his forehead.

But Steve had endured far worse. Besides, he was already on the company clock, so it wasn't his loss if he wasted half the morning in here. With a shrug, he peeled a trail mix bar from his pack and settled himself to wait.

"Worse than Nairobi, isn't it?"

Steve swung around on his heel. "Maybe. But it sure beats Sierra Leone."

The man offering a handshake sported the same safari-style clothing Steve was wearing. The resemblance ended there. Half a foot shorter and twice the circumference of Steve's own lean frame, he was bald, by razor rather than nature from the luxuriance of that graying red beard, a powerful build sagging to fat.

Though there was nothing soft in his grip. Nor in the small, shrewd eyes summing up Steve in turn. Cop's eyes. Steve could read their assessment. Caucasian male. Six foot one. Dark hair. Gray eyes. Tanned. Physically fit.

"Craig Laube, logistics manager, Condor Security. Call me Cougar. And you're Steve Wilson, security chief for our new PSD contract." The file with attached photo in his hand explained why his statement included no question mark. "If you'll come with me, our fixer's made arrangements to fast-track your team. The rest came in on the New Delhi flight. They've already left for the team house."

The fixer evidently referred to the Afghan in suit and tie who plucked Steve's passport from his hand, tucking a local currency note inside before moving to the front of the line. On the nearest wall, a sign advised passengers to report any requests for bribes to airport security. Not that Steve suffered any qualms of conscience at following on the fixer's heels. In his book, a bribe involved paying someone to break the law. Tipping local bureaucracy to speed up what they should be doing anyway was a survival tactic in every Third World country he'd known.

At least fast-track was no exaggeration. The line had barely inched forward when they left the security area, entry stamp in hand. The scene was repeated at customs, where Steve's two action packers and duffel bag were waved through without a glance. A grin tugged at Steve's mouth as he took in a bright head still far back in the first line. The woman from the plane looked frustrated, one small boot tapping impatiently, and only too conscious of the stares her wardrobe choices were attracting.

Dismissing the hapless blonde from thought, Steve followed Cougar across a parking area to a black armored Suburban. The Afghan driver already had the engine running. Though an unnecessary swarm of porters had accompanied the baggage trolley, Steve counted out a bill into each outstretched hand. *"Tashakor."*

Steve's thank-you engendered beard-splitting grins as the porters scattered.

Pulling his head from inside the Suburban, Cougar raised bushy red eyebrows. "So you speak Dari. I'd understood this was your first contract in Afghanistan."

"It is." Steve sliced into one of the action packers. The tactical vest he strapped on was not the screaming obvious black of a private security detail, where you wanted unfriendlies to know you were on alert, but a discreet utility vest style. "But I was in Kabul during liberation. And after. Picked up a fair amount of Dari and Pashto along the way. I assumed you knew that's why I pulled this contract."

"Sure, your bio says Special Forces. So you were Task Force Dagger, first boots on the ground, all that. That must have been a trip." Cougar studied his taller companion's clipped dark hair and deep tan. "Your coloring, I'll bet you pass as a native if you grow a beard. Gotta be useful in these parts. When did you make the jump to the private sector?"

"I was in Afghanistan about eighteen months. Got tired of being shot at and switched to a Blackwater private security detail. Then ArmorGroup embassy detail. Back to PSDs. Most recently Basra in southern Iraq. That was Condor Security, and when this came up, they gave me a call."

Steve could have added, "And you?" But his contact info had included a bio. Craig "Cougar" Laube had done an Army stint a lifetime ago, then put in twenty years with NYPD, more of them behind a desk than on the street. A second career as a security guard hadn't proved lucrative enough to support an ex-wife and three kids because he'd jumped at the post–9/11 boom in the private security industry.

Strapping on his own tactical vest, Cougar retrieved M4s and Glock 19 pistols for both from the back of the Suburban before handing Steve a manila envelope. So the guy had his priorities right.

The SUV's air-conditioned interior was a far more comfortable ride into Kabul than the dust and jolting of an Army convoy. As the Afghan driver eased past a mounted Soviet MiG fighter jet that marked the airport entrance, Steve rifled through the manila envelope. Mini Bradt Kabul guide. Dari-English phrase book. List of embassy-cleared restaurants and lodging. An invite to an open house Thursday evening at the UN guesthouse. It was a welcome packet! Underneath were some blueprints and a city map.

"The diagrams are your two primary security zones." Cougar carried his M4 unslung, looking out the double-paned windows as he spoke. "How much did they fill you in?"

Steve stuffed the material back into its envelope, retaining the blueprints and a personnel data printout. "Just that CS picked up a private security detail for some Afghan cabinet minister, and they want me to pull together a team ASAP. So who is this guy, and what's the big rush?"

"Our principal's the new minister of interior. He figures he's got a bull's-eye painted on his back. Which isn't such a stretch when you consider what happened to his predecessor."

"You're talking the sugar factory bombing." Steve straightened up with sudden alertness. Bombings had become a dime a dozen lately in Afghanistan, but that incident had been significant enough to make international news. Reopening a sugar factory in the northeastern province of Baghlan was the crown jewel in an alternative development program intended to soften the impact of the U.S. counternarcotics campaign against Afghanistan's proliferation of opium poppy. A number of dignitaries had been on hand when a bomb went off inside the factory. With more than fifty killed and hundreds wounded, it had been the largest single-incident civilian death toll since liberation.

"Sure, I saw the minister of interior on the list of VIP casualties. And weren't there Americans involved too? But that was more than two weeks ago."

"It's taken this long to get all the ducks in a row. There weren't any American casualties, but a helicopter load that included embassy and DEA reps had just touched down for the ribbon cutting when the bomb went off, one reason the incident got so much international press. In fact, the chopper belongs to the current minister. If he hadn't forgotten his briefcase in the chopper and just happened to turn back, there'd be two dead ministers instead of one.

"What makes this more interesting is that the late MOI had just been in office a couple of months himself, appointed when his predecessor was removed for gross corruption and incompetence. Only after plenty of pressure from the West, I might add. The MOI's by far the most powerful cabinet seat, just short of the president himself. It oversees the Afghan National Police, counternarcotics, the country's internal security, *and* provincial administration. Which includes appointing the governors and regional law enforcement officials."

Steve let out a low whistle. "So what's left for the president?"

"There's a reason they call our friend in the Presidential Palace the mayor of Kabul. Not that anyone really runs the provinces except the provinces themselves. A lot of people point to the MOI for Afghanistan's current security failings. Not that there isn't plenty of blame to go around, but the Afghan National Police are a joke, and too many provincial officials are former warlords up to their own ears in drug trafficking. Our late MOI had made it his mission to clean house and rein in the regional warlords."

That drew Steve's sharp glance from the data sheets. "You don't think—"

"The sugar factory bombing could be payback—or just the local opium cartels trying to stamp out competition. But the new MOI's taking it personally. He asked for a personal security detail as soon as he nailed the promotion. No local bodyguards, either. They might be infiltrated. Western. And since Khalid's a former muj commander—"

"Khalid!" Steve interrupted. "Khalid Sayef?"

"That's right." Cougar looked at Steve. "Hey, come to think of it, Khalid was part of the coalition that took Kabul. Any chance you ran across him?"

"Yes," Steve responded. "Though when I left Afghanistan, Khalid was up to his neck in local politics, nothing like this."

"Sure, as a matter of fact, Khalid's still governor of his home territory up in Baghlan. But like most of the muj commanders, he picked up a cabinet seat when the new government was signed in. Minister of commerce, originally. But he's played his cards right, and when the minister of counternarcotics threw in the towel a couple years back, Khalid was in the right place and time to take over there. In fact, since counternarcotics is also the biggest department within the MOI itself, most locals figured Khalid would move up to minister of interior when his predecessor got the boot. But with the West screaming for a housecleaning, they brought in a complete outsider."

Cougar's shoulders hunched under his tactical vest. "Well, Khalid's got the job now, and it's our responsibility to keep the guy alive. The contract's a level one, three-month renewable personal security detail. We should have on hand most equipment you'll need. Ditto, transport. Scrambling a team wasn't as easy on such short notice. But the bunch that flew in this morning are pretty decent. Their bios are in that packet. All Special Ops, all with security detail experience. Navy SEAL. Ranger. Delta. SAS."

Steve's attention shifted from data sheets to the windshield as the militarized airport zone gave way outside to bustling streets. Kabul had changed since he'd last passed this way—and it hadn't. Steve wasn't sure which was worse.

The biggest change was congestion. Vehicle traffic must have multiplied ten times over without a corresponding expansion of the street system. If there were traffic lanes or even sidewalks, no one was taking them seriously. Toyota Corollas, wood-framed trucks, motorcycles, and mule carts oozed through swarming pedestrians and street vendors. Late-model SUVs, mostly white, bore acronyms on doors and roofs. Agency vehicles of the numerous Western government and aid organizations now making Kabul their home.

"The two security zones are Khalid's personal residence and the Ministry of Interior," Cougar continued. "The residence's already in a high-security district, but the MOI building's smack downtown."

City limits too now crawled much farther up the mountain flanks. Construction was still largely mud brick, but the glitter of Kabul's new business skyline thrust itself like misplaced jewels above a haze of dust and smog. The Mashal Business Center, all futuristic blue glass and chrome. The five-star Serena Hotel rising like a sultan's palace on a busy intersection. The Safi Landmark shopping mall where, according to the welcome packet, any number of trendy restaurants offered foreign cuisine and forbidden alcohol.

Who in this dirt pile has disposable income to support this kind of infrastructure?

Cougar pointed at another new glass-and-brick department store. "Kabul isn't the hardship post you all rolled into. Anything you want, some Afghan will have started an import outlet. The expat social scene's pretty decent too. Mostly in what we call the green zone—Wazir Akbar Khan, Shahr-e Nau, and Sherpur districts—where security's tight enough you don't have to worry about locals crashing the party. Or some mullah screaming over Jack Daniels or bikinis. Stay here awhile with all those burqas, and you won't believe how good any woman in a bikini starts to look."

Steve grunted. Astonishingly, the burqas hadn't changed. He spotted numerous headscarves, many of them expatriates by their features, as well as the more enveloping black chador. But the burqa remained the female norm, flitting like silent white or pale blue ghosts through an overwhelmingly male pedestrian mob, the face panels thrown triumphantly back when he'd last been in these streets now firmly in place.

9

The commercial district wasn't the only construction boom. Steve counted the third rounded dome and tall minaret the SUV had passed in the space of five minutes. This one was a massive complex, gleaming with sparkling new mosaic tile. Behind it rose a series of five-story buildings Steve had assumed to be a housing development until he saw that the mosque's perimeter wall enclosed them.

Cougar caught his stare. "Really something, isn't it? That's a new Shiite madrassa built by Iran. Bigger than the university. New mosques have been going up all over Kabul, mostly donations from other Muslim governments."

"Useful outlay of aid funds," Steve commented sardonically.

Cougar shrugged. "We build malls; they build mosques."

For all the city's new infrastructure, the acute poverty Steve remembered seemed little diminished either. They'd passed miles of hovels clinging to hillsides like human-size termite cells. How did people live without running water, sewage, or electricity? As for that apartment complex mujahedeen rockets had ripped open, Steve could swear it hadn't been touched in all these years. Then he spotted plywood and plastic tacked down across a concrete cubicle, a burqa hauling a bucket up a shattered staircase. People were living in that ruin!

Beggars remained everywhere. Men missing limbs squatted on sidewalks or negotiated traffic on wheelchairs crafted from bicycle tires. Women in burqas exposed a cupped palm at intersections, small, ragged children at their skirts. Nor in the glut of automatic weapons and armed vehicles did Steve see any indication of a country at rest from war. It wasn't just the ISAF convoys with their armored Humvees and turret guns. A dozen different uniforms belonging to the Afghan police, army, or hired security firms roamed sidewalks, stood guard at intersections and outside buildings, and crouched behind sandbags on the tops of walls.

And I thought we'd freed this place.

Just what did those war victims in their wheelchairs and burqas scrabbling for a daily food ration, the shopkeepers and street vendors with their watchful eyes think of the new Afghanistan he'd helped create? or of the Westerners flooding their city with new cars and shining towers and shopping malls and restaurants few Afghans could ever afford to enter? for that matter, of those equally ostentatious new domes and minarets that did nothing to put food on their tables?

Steve felt a sudden weariness that was not from jet lag. *Why did I come back here?*

Because it's safer than Iraq, and the money's even better. I was tired of being shot at, remember? After all, who was Steve to sneer when his own latest contract would net him five times what he'd ever earned as a proud member of his nation's Special Operations Command?

2

A city of dirt and mud.

Such was Amy Mallory's first disenchanted impression as the Ariana Airlines flight banked above a wide, dust-brown mountain valley. A dirty haze blurred a maze of lines and rectangles that crawled up barren flanks of encircling foothills. As the plane dropped, the maze resolved itself into endless mud-brick compound walls and flat-roofed houses the same dun hue as unpaved streets. Only in the basin's center could be glimpsed brick and glass and concrete of modern construction.

Kabul.

First impressions were not improved by grit whipping across face and eyes during an interminable march from plane to terminal. Or the hot, bumpy drive into the city. Dust as fine as talcum powder seeped around window- and doorframes, drifting through the mesh grille that covered Amy's face to clog her throat and nostrils. She reached under shiny polyester to wipe at sweat trickling down her face, and her hand came away muddy.

Swallowing dryly, Amy tried not to think of the bottled water she hadn't bothered to pick up at the airport. Instead, she glanced into the reflective surface a coating of dust had made of the nearest window. It showed a blurred, pale blue outline as though Amy Mallory were no longer an individual—capable, independent, world traveler, international aid worker—but a shapeless, anonymous blob.

A burqa. The women's prison that to the twenty-first-century West had come to symbolize Afghanistan.

So get a grip and stop whining. I've been dreaming and praying about coming to this place for years. Where's my sense of adventure—and humor?

The latter had withered badly under the driver's glare in the rearview mirror. *Drop Amy Mallory into any back corner of the planet,* her long-suffering father often joked, *and you could count on her emerging unscathed, chattering a new language, a fresh project under way, and a host of new friends in tow.*

If an exaggeration, Amy's communication and people skills had proved useful. But neither her sunniest smile nor the Dari phrases she'd memorized on the long flight over had made any visible impression on the turbaned, bearded Afghan who'd picked her up at the airport. The flight had been at least half expatriate but overwhelmingly male, and Amy's unease began as she'd witnessed one passenger after another whisked through immigration into recent-model SUVs.

Several such groups screamed private security contractor. All male, all physically fit, in the safari-style clothing, heavy boots, and wraparound sunglasses that seemed to be the community's international uniform. And though they appeared unarmed, the catlike aggression of their stride bristled invisible weapons. Amy had been going through the first checkpoint when one such pair walked by unchallenged, the tallest sliding a cool, gray gaze over Amy as they passed. Not as though noting a young and presentable female. More like assessing a threat level.

Meanwhile Amy found herself in one endless line after another. When she finally emerged, it was to her current escort holding up a hand-lettered sign to a steady chant of her last name. The large, burly man in pajama-like tunic and baggy trousers had stared at her as though she were martian. Only when Amy held up her passport, matching her name to the sign, had he herded her to this ancient Russian army jeep.

Then without a single word, he'd pulled out a bundle of shiny blue cloth. Shoving it at Amy, he'd stood there expressionless, unmoving, giving no indication of understanding her protests, until with exasperation Amy tugged the tight cap piece of the burqa over her head and allowed the voluminous material to drop around her. A strong odor of perspiration and sandalwood talc indicated regular use. The driver's wife? Okay, so the handful of other expat women climbing into those SUVs had been farsighted enough to include long sleeves and a head shawl in their travel wardrobe. Still, if it weren't for that sign with her name on it, she'd wonder if she were being kidnapped.

Now she was being paranoid. But Amy didn't allow tense muscles to relax as a dissonance of car horns, blaring radios, and vendor cries swirled around her. Through the burqa's mesh grille, the accompanying shapes were such a dizzying kaleidoscope, she found it easier to keep her eyes shut. The worst was that neither mesh nor polyester allowed air to flow easily, so that between dust and dryness and recycled carbon dioxide, Amy found herself gasping for breath. She was growing desperate enough to yank the burqa away when the jeep slowed, then stopped. A moment later, the back passenger door opened. Groping for her shoulder bag, Amy scrambled out.

Now that her world was still, Amy could make out a paved street, the construction concrete and brick instead of sun-dried mud. A high wall in front of Amy had once been peacock blue, faded now to the color of her burqa. A black, metal pedestrian gate and a wider vehicle gate farther down completed a match with the JPEG she'd received. Her surly escort had, after all, conveyed Amy safely to her destination, the Kabul headquarters of the NGO—nongovernmental organization—that had brought her here: New Hope Foundation.

A small panel in the pedestrian gate slid sideways; then the gate opened. An elderly Afghan man stepped out, beard long and white, assault rifle hanging by a strap over one shoulder. The driver headed up a cobblestone path, leaving Amy to shoulder her bag and follow. As the gate clanged shut behind her, Amy seized the opportunity to yank off the burqa. A late morning sun felt deliciously cool after the sauna inside the burqa, and Amy felt no shame as she used the polyester to wipe away sweat and grime before balling it up under one arm.

But now that she could see, Amy found herself swallowing back disappointment as well as dust. In the JPEG the gate's black metal hadn't shown itself rusted enough to fall off its hinges. The cobblestone path led to a courtyard with a fountain. Behind the fountain, marble steps rose to a columned portico and into a two-story villa.

But the fountain wasn't running, the courtyard's tiled mosaic broken, windows on both floors boarded over. Though the lot was several acres, only tree stumps, broken trellises, and sun-baked dirt remained of what had once been extensive gardens and orchards. Alongside the path, a cinder-block partition divided the property from pedestrian gate to main residence. Over this wall, the sun glinted on a metal shed roof. Banging, thuds, and men's voices indicated some kind of manual labor.

A similar cinder-block divider on either side of the villa effectively cut the property into four. In the quadrant where Amy had entered, stacks of bricks, tiles, sawed lumber, and piled-up cement sacks suggested repairs. But these were thick with dust, and Amy saw no workmen in sight.

Nor anyone else. Where was evidence an international nonprofit organization occupied these premises? Amy's escort had disappeared up the marble steps. Little though she welcomed his company, he was Amy's only contact here, so she quickened her steps. Debris propped massive wooden doors permanently open. Amy walked through into a wide hallway. Her escort had already reached the far end, where doors were missing altogether. In compensation, double doors to either side were not only closed but locked, a tentative wiggle of door handles confirmed. To the left of the back entrance, a staircase curved upward.

Tap-crunch. Tap-crunch.

The footsteps whirled Amy around. A man had stepped onto the broken mosaic of the courtyard. Amy's first thought was the watchman, but this man was far younger, closer to Amy's own age. He'd stopped to look around, his head tilted back to take in the boarded-up windows, giving Amy the opportunity to look him over thoroughly.

He was bareheaded, with the curly dark hair and beard, high forehead, and wide-spaced, espresso-brown eyes of a movie-screen Jesus that had startled Amy the first time she glimpsed such features in real life here in this part of the world. Behind him, the pedestrian gate now stood open, the elderly watchman shuffling inside. No mystery then. The newcomer too had just come in off the street.

Ahead in the far doorway, Amy's driver-escort had paused to look back. As his unsmiling gaze rested on her naked face and arms, Amy again felt unease, acutely aware of being not only foreign here but female and alone. She was beginning to understand the rationale of tugging that blue polyester back on. A burqa could be as much a shield as a prison.

No, now I'm not being paranoid. Where is this boss of mine who's supposed to be here?

Then the watchman disappeared into a guard shack beside the gate. Her driver-escort stepped forward through the missing exit doors. At that same moment, a shadow at the base of the staircase coalesced into a black chador, the less-confining women's covering that left eyes and nose exposed. A straw broom in the wearer's hands slid over the tiled floor as silently as she'd emerged from the shadows. The presence of another woman gave Amy the fortitude to return to the entrance to confront the young man.

"Who are you? What do you want?" Amy dredged up her laboriously memorized Dari to repeat the second question. "*Che mekhaahed?*"

The young man looked startled, whether from her atrocious accent or because he hadn't noticed Amy inside the hallway. His gaze rested everywhere but on Amy as he responded hesitantly, "You are an American, yes? I am looking for the—how do you say it?—the boss who is in command of this facility. I was told I might inquire as to employment."

"Oh, you speak English."

The young man certainly looked like he needed a job. At this closer vantage, Amy could see that he was very thin even for his slight build, cheekbones protruding above beard and mustache, shoulders bony under the tunic. His dark eyes were sunk deep into their sockets and somber.

Amy shook her head. "I'm sorry. I just got here myself, and I'm looking for my own boss. But you might try over there. I heard men talking on the other side of that wall."

"Mallory?" The driver reappeared in the far doorway. "The American will speak with you now."

So Amy *did* have a new boss around here somewhere. And surprise of surprises, her escort could speak quite passable English when he chose.

The driver's gaze fell on her new acquaintance. "*Tu!*"

Amy caught none of the rapid Dari that followed, but the driver's peremptory gesture needed no translation. The newcomer obediently hunkered down on his heels in the passageway. At the jerk of her escort's head, Amy followed him through the missing doors. The woman in the black chador drifted out behind them, still sweeping.

Once outside, Amy could see that the villa was actually three wings that formed a square with the rear property wall around an interior courtyard. A colonnade around the three sides of the house supported a second-story balcony. Huge stone pots had once held flower shrubs or potted trees, and in the center was another fountain.

But here, too, the fountain held no water, its basin cracked. Missing tiles exposed crumbling concrete, and a wrought-iron balcony railing was rusted to brick red. *It must have been so beautiful. How could they let it be destroyed so?*

Maybe it was just the consequence of war, though one would think that would be repaired by now. Amy abandoned her inspection as her escort tapped his foot outside a door on the right-hand colonnade. When Amy obeyed his gesture to go inside, he didn't follow but strode away across the courtyard.

The salon Amy entered was as dilapidated as the rest of the premises, plastic bags tacked over windows instead of glass, plastered walls stained and peeling. The only furnishings were a card table and plastic chairs. The woman hadn't penetrated with her straw broom—Kabul's powder-fine dust lay thickly over everything.

Almost everything.

The exception was behind the card table. A stocky Caucasian man in his forties with thinning sandy hair. Fingers drummed restlessly on a closed briefcase. Black dress shoes tapped impatiently.

All that mattered to Amy was that he was obviously, gloriously, expatriate. Relief liberated Amy's smile as she crossed the room with outstretched hand. "Mr. Nestor Korallis, New Hope Foundation. I'm so glad to see you. Amy Mallory."

The man made no effort to rise or take her hand, which offended Amy less when she glanced down to realize how grimy it was. Instead, he was staring at Amy with the same stunned incredulity with which her escort had greeted her at the airport. "*You* are A. M. Mallory?"

Amy surreptitiously wiped her hand on the blue polyester ball. "That's right. Amy Margaret Mallory. Why? Is there a problem?"

"The problem is, I was expecting a man." He checked his watch. "And you're eighteen hours late."

Indignation dimmed Amy's smile. "Mr. Korallis, I'm sorry, but—"

"I'm not Korallis. He couldn't make it. I'm Bruce Evans, New Hope's chief financial officer."

"Mr. Evans, then. If there's been a mix-up, I apologize. As to the delay, I reached Dubai on schedule, but the Ariana flight was grounded for an engine repair, so I spent the night in the terminal. I tried to e-mail, but the wireless connection was down."

"Call me Bruce. We aren't that formal at New Hope." The man was still staring at Amy as though he couldn't quite believe what he saw. "Unfortunately, I have to be at the airport by noon to fly to DC. Which gives us, instead of a full day to line you out here, barely an hour."

He pulled his stare from Amy to open his briefcase, then looked up again, blinking rapidly. "Are you aware of just why you're here in Afghanistan and what your duties will entail?"

Now it was Amy's turn to stare. Was this some trick question? "I originally applied for your earthquake relief project up in Kashmir, if that's the confusion. But I've always had an interest in Afghanistan. So when Mr. Korallis called to say you'd had a personnel emergency and needed me here for a few months, I told him I'd be willing to fill in wherever you needed me."

"Then you spoke to Nestor personally. He knows you're a woman and a young one."

"I'm twenty-four. That's hardly young in the aid community. I've been in the field for three years and have experience in project administration as well as disaster relief."

This was not Amy's first time at this particular conversation. While volunteers of all ages could be found in the NGO community, they tended toward youth, so it was not uncommon for field personnel to find themselves in management positions at an age when back home they'd still be making coffee.

"I'm aware of your résumé. Miami-raised. International business degree from Florida International University. You've spent the last three years working with a volunteer NGO called Christian Relief. Honduras. Peru.

India. Philippines. Indonesia. Africa. Any place some natural disaster called for cleanup. Nestor forwarded your credentials to me when this situation arose. Age and gender were little tidbits he left out."

"So you just assumed I was a man?" Amy said slowly.

"I assumed that Nestor understood Afghanistan is hardly a work-friendly environment for a young and single American woman. At least not in our current situation." Bruce unearthed a satellite phone from his briefcase. "If you'll excuse me a moment." He rose from the table, hurrying across the room to step outside onto the veranda.

Amy could hear his voice but not the words. With some annoyance, she glanced around. If he wasn't going to offer a decent welcome, she'd just have to make herself at home.

Wiping a chair with the blue polyester, Amy pulled it up opposite the briefcase. Then she noticed the small cooler sitting on the floor under the table. As she'd hoped, it held bottles of water. The first order of hospitality in expat travel. Amy suppressed an unladylike moan of pleasure as the dust and thirst washed down her throat.

"I'm sorry. I should have taken care of that." Bruce was back. "This has all caught me so off guard, I wasn't thinking. Do make yourself at home." He sat down. "Nestor confirms you are the A. M. Mallory contracted for this position, and he informs me he not only was aware of your gender but considered it a bonus in the hiring. We've been lacking gender balance in our overseas hires." His tone was as dry as the dust filming the table. "So now that everything's in order, let's get the paperwork started."

As Bruce unloaded files from his briefcase, he added belatedly without glancing up, "I trust your trip was uneventful other than the delay. Rasheed collected you, no problem? We've got a lot of ground to catch up, so may I assume you've arrived ready to hit the ground running?"

What a question. With no new boss to charm, Amy was irritated enough to trade diplomacy for frankness. "Actually, it was the longest twenty-four hours I've ever sat straight up in coach. After eighteen hours' delay, Ariana still didn't transfer my luggage, which added another hour filling out forms at the airport. As to your driver, he seems to have a major attitude problem. Would you believe he made me wear a burqa?"

Okay, enough honesty for one dose. Letting shoulder bag and blue polyester ball slide to the floor, Amy wrinkled her nose in a rueful grin. "But I made it, and that's what constitutes a good flight, right? As to getting started, I'm ready when you are."

Bruce looked taken aback. He blinked again as he pushed a sheaf of papers across the table. "Good, then you can start with these. The contract's standard three-month probationary with automatic renewal if both parties are satisfied. Just sign every place you see an X."

Now it was Amy who was blinking. The salary listed was more than she'd been led to expect, while the project budget—*Wow, if we'd had this in Mozambique . . . !*

"As for Rasheed, he's a devout Muslim, and he was expecting a man. If you arrived like that, well, just be glad he handed you a burqa instead of ditching you at the airport. With your credentials, I'd have assumed you'd know long sleeves, loose clothing, and head covering are a minimum here even for expats. Women, that is."

"You have *got* to be kidding." Amy set down her pen hard. "How many years has it been since the Taliban skipped town? I'm aware of local sensibilities and have every intention of wearing culturally sensitive clothing when mixing with locals. One of those missing suitcases has an entire wardrobe. But I sure didn't expect to fly from Miami that way. And certainly not inside New Hope's vehicles or quarters."

"Yeah, well, the big NGOs run their own vehicles and drivers. New Hope prides itself on working through the locals. In fact, you'll be our first expat living on-site. So I trust you'll accommodate their cultural prejudices."

This time Amy opted for diplomacy. "Actually, New Hope's commitment to work directly with the Afghans was a major selling point. . . ." Then what he'd said sank in. "Wait, you're saying I'm your first expat? Who's been running the project? I must say I expected a little more infrastructure than I've seen so far. What size staff do you run?"

"Actually that's the emergency." Bruce looked uncomfortable. "I don't know how much Nestor told you of how New Hope works. It's a foundation that partners with local NGOs in developing nations. Funding comes mostly from Korallis Enterprises, an investment firm founded by Nestor

Korallis's grandfather. Nestor's been administering the foundation since he retired from the corporation.

"Since 9/11, Afghanistan has been the largest focus of international aid. About two years ago, Nestor decided to jump on that bandwagon. The foundation was approached by an Afghan NGO with impeccable connections to the current local government and international community. New Hope contracted the project. A dozen regional centers offering employment, nutrition, shelter, education, and health to be set up over a two-year period."

Amy didn't like where this was going. "So who oversaw the project?"

"Nestor or I would fly over for a few days every two to three months. That's how we got to know Rasheed. One of the other NGOs recommended him as a driver-slash-translator. The project was going well. Unfortunately, when we published pictures in our promo literature, NGOs began coming out of the woodwork saying those were their projects, not ours."

"And the project funds?"

"Gone. Along with our local Afghan project manager as soon as he found out the whistle had been blown. And all the staff, who it turned out were family members."

"That's terrible. Poor Mr. Korallis," Amy exclaimed. "Why am I here then? If there's nothing left, wouldn't it be easiest to just shut down the project and walk away?"

"That's not an option," Bruce said. "The IRS doesn't take kindly to vanishing funds, and we're scheduled for an audit. Either there's a documented project here by the end of this calendar year, or the monies will have to be reimbursed."

"But this is already September," Amy said, aghast. "And you've no personnel."

"Just our new country manager. You did say you'd do whatever was necessary. And may I remind you that you've just signed a contract."

"Which I wouldn't have if I'd known the situation." Amy rubbed her face. "This is crazy! I've done project management, but not completely on my own. I don't even speak the language. And what could Mr. Korallis possibly expect anyone to do in three months that your Afghan personnel couldn't do in two years?"

"On the contrary, the project itself shouldn't be a problem," Bruce said coolly. "I signed a lease on a major chunk of this property for New Hope's new country office. Rasheed's lived on-site here as caretaker for years. He'll serve as driver and translator; his wife, Hamida, to do housekeeping. The budget's a generous one, so hiring further personnel is only a matter of finding them. As to aid recipients, this country's crawling with starving widows and children. How hard can it be to get a few of them in here, clean them up for a few decent photo ops? The right person should have no difficulty turning this around."

Bruce began stuffing papers back into his briefcase. "All that to say, I hope you understand now my consternation at finding out just who A. M. Mallory really is. Nothing personal, believe me. I have no doubt you are a very capable young woman. Nestor Korallis certainly seems to feel so. But as you've already found out, Afghanistan is a man's world."

In other words, a man could pull this off, but I can't.

Bruce pushed a manila envelope across the table. "Here are your lease papers and banking arrangements. Nestor is a generous employer. If you feel this is all beyond you, there's the option of breaking the contract you just signed. I'm assuming you took a careful look at the penalty clauses. Under the circumstances, we could work out a waiver. Make your decision, though, because I'm leaving in five minutes."

"And if I broke the contract?" Amy asked slowly. "Mr. Korallis told me he had no one else to take the position on such short notice, that Afghanistan was a hard slot to fill."

He shrugged. "That's true. But that's New Hope's problem, not yours. If I know Nestor, he'll make good out of his own pocket if he has to."

"But that could be millions." Amy fell silent, her feelings conflicted. None of this had turned out as she'd envisioned. She didn't like to think of letting down that sweet old man she'd spoken with on the phone. But how in the world was she to do what was demanded of her in a strange country without language skills, staff, or existing infrastructure?

On the other hand . . .

The smallest flame of excitement burned at Amy's dismay. How many times in the last three years had she dreamed of having enough funds and a free hand to carry out a project properly? to do away with the incompetence and bureaucracy she'd battled so often?

So now the chance was falling into her lap. She'd been dropped into a strange country without a soul she could count on, but she had a base and money. *Time to see if Papa is right!*

Amy straightened up to look directly across the table. "I have no intention of breaking the contract. I'm ready to start today."

3

"Ministry of Interior's on the next block. There's no parking, so I'm figuring a drive-by just to give you an overview. We've got a lunch date with the minister at his residence at 2 p.m. There won't be a lot of down time at the team house."

The SUV had just turned a corner, and Steve saw what Cougar meant about parking. They were now on a major boulevard, traffic inching forward several vehicles abreast. Sidewalks were swallowed up by the bright awnings and ambling vendors of an open-air bazaar.

Steve shook off unpleasant reverie. "If there's any way we can give the ministry a walk-through, I'd rather not waste time."

"You're the boss. I suppose Ahmed could drop us off and circle back when we're ready."

Cougar leaned forward to speak to the driver, and Ahmed immediately hit the brakes. Ignoring angry honks, Cougar climbed out, waited for Steve to follow, then led the way toward a high, army green wall topped with concertina wire. That Steve hadn't immediately noted a barricaded gate or armed guards in blue gray uniforms of the Afghan National Police could be blamed on the market bustle hemming it in.

While the contractors' own armed status was hardly unusual in these streets, their dress broadcast not only foreigner but PSD. Steve's back crawled under a battery of turned heads and unsmiling stares. Just inside the MOI entrance, new arrivals were being patted down, bags searched.

Steve expected some protest, but a guard barely glanced at the credentials Cougar showed him before waving them through.

"Khalid's offices are this way."

Steve matched his surroundings with the blueprints he'd scrutinized as he followed on Cougar's heels. The compound was larger than he'd anticipated with several buildings. Lines of people waited to squeeze into government offices. Others wandered the grounds or rested against walls. A loud honking outside sent a man in a blue gray uniform scurrying to open a gate for two green police pickups.

There is so much wrong with this picture I couldn't begin to list it.

Cougar steered the way to the largest building, where a clerk led the two on a tour of offices with male secretaries bent over antiquated computers, classrooms of police recruits watching training videos. Khalid's work space was on the fourth and final floor, an entire suite filled with imported furniture and clerks in Western business suits.

The tour ended up a short flight of stairs to the roof. Concertina wire had been added to the low parapets, and though sandbagged observation posts were not in use, several men in uniform crouched around a tall clay hookah, assault rifles balanced casually across their thighs. As their guide abandoned the two contractors for a drag at the water pipe, Steve leaned gingerly over the barbed wire.

This side of the building formed part of the perimeter wall, second- and third-story balconies jutting out over a narrow alley that separated the MOI compound from the neighboring apartment building. Market vendors had commandeered the alley as a storage dump, leaving room for only a single vehicle to squeeze through.

"So is it doable?" Cougar asked.

Steve took cover behind a sandbag fortification as he dug binoculars from a vest pocket. A useless precaution considering he could count a dozen buildings tall enough for a line-of-fire view of his position.

Still, he didn't allow himself to be hurried as he completed a methodical survey of surrounding skyline before lowering the binoculars to answer Cougar bluntly. "Anything's doable. But this site's got major problems. From what I've seen, anyone with a badge or uniform can waltz right in without any serious challenge. The place is a sniper's heaven, not to mention grappling hooks over those railings could have a sizable task force up here in five minutes.

"Number one, we move the minister's offices out of here to his own residence or somewhere else we can control access. Second, we go low profile. No marked vehicles. No in-your-face expat Secret Service parades for the media. We keep the guy under the radar and don't let hostiles know we're coming."

At the mention of snipers, Cougar edged behind the sandbags. "You've got to be joking. You might be able to do something about Khalid's work habits. But low profile? As far as Khalid's concerned, the whole point of this is big and obvious."

An Afghan in the Western dress of a government clerk emerged from the stairwell. Their original guide jumped up from the hookah circle to meet the newcomer.

Cougar lowered his voice. "There're politics involved. Why settle for MOI when presidential elections are coming up next year? Khalid may be worried about death threats, but expat muscle also happens to look good on cable news and makes the West take him seriously."

"There're *always* politics involved," Steve said. "Or maybe the actual threat level's a whole lot less than our new principal's been saying."

"In any case, it's not our job to secure the entire MOI. Only our own principal. This building's tighter than it looks. All exits are solid metal and secured from the inside. No one's allowed past the first floor without MOI credentials."

Their original guide crossed the roof to hand Cougar a folded note. The logistics manager scanned it. "The minister's running late for that lunch meeting. He flew to his home district yesterday for a wedding and isn't back. He'll host us for dinner to discuss details of his PSD. Like I said, really worried about those death threats."

"He's not on our nickel yet, so it's no worry of ours." Steve shrugged. "Meanwhile, I've got what I need here. If we can't adjust the op, we deal with what we've got. But the extras are going to cost. I'll get the prelim assessment written up this afternoon."

"Good. I'll give Ahmed a buzz then, and we'll head over to the guest-house and get you settled."

As Cougar pulled out a cell phone, Steve raised his binoculars again, shifting position to train them on the crowded boulevard fronting the main gate. Angry shouts drew his focus to a personnel carrier sandwiched between two armored Humvees just emerging from a side street. The ISAF convoy sped onto the boulevard fast enough to stampede pedestrians and vehicles alike into opening a path. Steve sighed as raised fists and a hail of rocks greeted the convoy. That kind of local ill will just made his own job that much harder. Not that he could blame the ISAF. With a recent spat of IEDs—improvised explosive devices—targeting foreign armed forces vehicles, they were simply following standard operating procedure.

Steve's binocular-sweep across the scattering crowd paused on a darting pale blue figure. He focused in. A burqa. And running not to escape the oncoming juggernaut but straight into its path.

Steve's knuckles turned white against the binocular casing as the explosion tore into the convoy. The lead Humvee skidded through a row of market stalls into a light pole. The personnel carrier couldn't stop in time. It slammed the Humvee forward with a screech of metal and burning rubber.

The street was pandemonium, the bazaar a chaos of smashed stalls, screams, and blood. On the rooftop, the guards abandoned their hookah party to crowd along the parapet. Steve spotted a pale blue and scarlet heap before it disappeared under the stampede. Man or woman? Woman suicide bombers were rare, but there'd been reports of militants donning burqas for disguise.

"Steve, we've got to pull out! Ahmed says he can get us out, but it's got to be now."

Cougar was right. Steve was no longer a Special Ops master sergeant but a civilian, and this wasn't his gig. Stowing the binoculars, he jogged down the stairwell with Cougar.

The convoy was moving again by the time the two contractors made it out into the street, the personnel carrier using its bulk to push aside the wrecked vehicle as helping hands yanked the Humvee's contingent aboard other vehicles. Again, SOP. ISAF troops were neither paramedics nor ambulance, their sole responsibility to remove their own wounded and the aggravation of their continued presence before a nasty situation turned into all-out war. A single spat of a turret gun, aimed deliberately high, pushed the converging mob back enough for the convoy to pick up speed.

Steve would have given much to swing aboard. This wasn't the time and place to be obvious foreigners in these streets. As Steve and Cougar pushed quickly through the crowd, the M4s in their hands maintained a bubble of personal space, but glances their way were now openly hostile. *Just one more block.*

The mob began to settle as soon as the convoy turned a corner. Across the street, people helped groaning victims, doused the flames of a burning car. Afghans were supremely resilient and experienced at reacting to disaster.

A few meters away a small boy huddled on the sidewalk sent up a terrified wail. Steve hesitated as he saw that the child was alone. Then he spotted a woman in a burqa weaving swiftly through stalled traffic, a youngish man with dark hair and beard at her heels. The woman scooped up the child. Parents, presumably.

Steve had scarcely relaxed when he stiffened again. *Wait.* That was no Afghan woman under the burqa. It was something in the walk. The awkwardness with which the polyester material settled over head and shoulder. Feet tripping on the hem instead of gliding with practiced grace. And yes, those were hiking boots, not sandals, under the blue folds.

Cougar had stopped and turned toward the woman as well, his body tensed. So the cop-turned-security-guard wasn't totally devoid of the right instincts. "Another bomber?" he mouthed.

With a furious babble of Dari, hands snatched at the blue folds, others grabbing at the boy. The woman in the burqa stumbled, almost dropping the child. The little boy screamed hysterically.

"The child! Put the child down!"

Steve had time only to register that the urgent call was in English when a burly man snatched the child from the woman's embrace. The angry mob was still closing in. A fist came up. Then the cloaked figure collapsed into a puddle of blue. Hands pulled at the polyester, exposing the clothing underneath. Steve's swift search did not locate the woman's male escort.

Steve's strides took him toward the woman. Now the mob grabbed at him, jostling bodies and scowling faces close enough to reek of rancid beard grease. Steve didn't slide the safety from the M4 but instead snatched the Glock from the small of his back. A single shot in the air restored the bubble of personal space.

Steve heard quickened, raspy breathing under the mound of blue material. The figure sat up, trying to push away the netlike face grille.

Steve's mouth tightened to a furious line as he pulled back the burqa's veil. "You!"

4

Ideas spun in Amy's brain. "You said you'd signed a lease on part of this place. Which part? And you mentioned Rasheed was caretaker. If he's not the owner, who is? Do they share the premises? Also, what are my living arrangements?"

"The owner doesn't live here," Bruce said. "He's some big-shot government official. Minister of interior, whatever that entails. After the Taliban, he built himself a new place, then rented this one out. Some German NGO ran a school here for quite a while. After the kids trashed the place, it was subdivided for piecemeal rent."

That explained the villa's dilapidated abandon.

"When Rasheed told me this place was available at a discount in its current condition, I grabbed it. New Hope's lease is for this back court-yard with the two wings on either side. I'm told that used to be women's quarters. I'd assumed our new project manager would live on-site. There's plenty of room."

Amy shook her head. "Not acceptable. A respectable woman doesn't live alone in a Muslim community. I'll book a guesthouse room until I can look over the situation."

Bruce frowned. "It's up to you. Just be aware that will come out of your living allowance."

"That's fine," Amy agreed. "Now that lease. There's no access to this courtyard from the street. If we're to have any meaningful aid project, women and children can't be walking through someone else's rental. I'd like to have access to the front courtyard, preferably the entire house."

"That you'll have to negotiate with the owner. Rasheed can direct you to his offices. Just remember you've got a budget."

"Yes, Rasheed!" Amy's next point of concern. "Hiring staff will be my first priority. The best starting place for that will be the local expat and NGO community. Meantime, I need someone with whom I can communicate and who can communicate to the locals on my behalf. Which means more than speaking a bit of English. At minimum, if I'm to exercise any authority as project manager, I need someone who doesn't look at me as though I were an insect underfoot."

Bruce reached under the table for his cooler. "That isn't so easy. With all the expat organizations here, English speakers and drivers are at a premium. Rasheed may not be to your taste, but he's the best we could get at such short notice."

Amy's enthusiasm dimmed. She *couldn't* find herself alone with that turbaned, bearded misogynist, even if he did have a wife in that drifting black shadow. "Just a minute. There was a man out in the courtyard who said he'd been sent here to look for work. He had good English, too."

"Then let's take care of both your problems so I can get on the road. Rasheed!"

The driver-escort appeared so suddenly he must have been lurking outside the door. To Amy's surprise, the young man she'd seen earlier stepped into view behind Rasheed.

Bruce jerked a thumb. "That the guy?"

At Amy's nod, Bruce announced, "Rasheed, I've just signed Ms. Mallory on as our new country manager. I've explained to her she can count on you for anything she needs."

The caretaker nodded, a hooded glance sliding to Amy, then away.

Bruce went on. "Now, Ms. Mallory here tells me this man speaks English and is looking for work. Do you know anything about him? Is he available for hire?"

Rasheed inclined his upper body with a respect he hadn't shown Amy. "Yes. Jamil is a distant relative. I can assure you he is honest and hardworking and speaks much better English than my own."

"Oh, really?" Bruce said skeptically. "If he's as good as you say, why's he unemployed?"

"Jamil has been living in Pakistan for many years, where everyone with education speaks English. Finding a good job there is difficult, especially for Afghans. So, like many others, he has returned here, where such skills are more in demand."

"A sensible decision. Jamil, would you be interested in a job with New Hope Foundation? It would involve doing translation for Ms. Mallory here, guiding her around the city, anything else she requires."

Amy noticed Jamil glance at Rasheed, saw the older man's slight incline of his head, before he nodded. "Yes, that would be acceptable."

"That settles it, then. And I'm late." Bruce headed toward the door, briefcase in one hand, cooler in the other. "You can work out the details with Ms. Mallory. Rasheed, the airport's calling. Amy, any questions that can't wait till I'm back in the DC office tomorrow?"

"Could you have Rasheed check for my luggage at the airport? They told me it would be on the next flight. Here are the two baggage claim tickets."

"No problem." Bruce took the tickets. "And speaking of the airport, you *did* think to get your MOI card when you came through?"

"MOI card?"

"Ministry of Interior. As in your new landlord. They also handle immigration. The latest red tape is an expat ID card. They should give you the form at the airport, but they never do unless you ask."

"But I've got a visa," Amy exclaimed. "None of my info mentioned an ID card."

"Get used to red tape changing here every time you turn around. Keeping you updated on local bureaucracy will be part of Rasheed's duties."

Except he hadn't bothered on this occasion. An oversight or deliberate punishment for those bare arms and head?

"In any case, you should be able to pick up a form at MOI. From arrival you've got forty-eight hours to register before your visa's revoked, leaving you in this country illegally. I don't think you'd get deported, but it could be expensive to sort out." Bruce hesitated in the doorway. Then he dug into his briefcase, pulling out his sat phone. "Why don't I leave you this? You'll need it more than I will." As he handed it to Amy, uncertainty flickered in his eyes. "I just hope we're doing the right thing here."

"I'll be fine," Amy assured him as she took the phone. "And thank you. Please give my greetings to Mr. Korallis."

Then they were gone, leaving Amy alone with her new assistant. Jamil stood rigidly just inside the door, eyes on his feet. Amy, who'd chosen jeans and T-shirt as both practical and amply modest for the long flight from Miami, felt conscious of her body, of bare arms below short sleeves and exposed face, in a way she hadn't since her teens.

Well, she'd always found directness the best approach. Amy didn't make the mistake of crossing the room to shake hands but said firmly, "Hi, Jamil. I'm Amy Mallory, country manager for New Hope Foundation here in Kabul. Are you going to have a problem working for me? Because I can promise you I won't be wearing a burqa."

This time he glanced at her, and the somberness might have even lifted a little. Moving farther into the room, he said simply, "I need this job. I will do what I am asked for whoever pays me to eat and live, man or woman. As for the burqa, my mother was an educated woman. She did not cover her face to work."

His English had a musical, somewhat stilted cadence Amy knew well from Pakistani and Indian colleagues in other relief projects. Its familiar lilt and his slight build, only two or three inches taller than hers, made him far less threatening than the tall, burly Rasheed. This had been a good idea. "In Pakistan or here in Afghanistan? Do you still have family here?"

A flash of emotion restored somberness to his dark eyes. "My family is the past. I am concerned only with the future."

Amy kicked herself mentally. After all the horror stories she'd heard and read of the war years, she should know better than to ask a personal question. Hastily she pulled the lease information from the manila envelope Bruce had given her. This had been typed up in neat English, but the official-looking heading at the top and signatures at the bottom were all in the curlicue Arabic script. "Can you tell me where this address is? How hard would it be to get there?"

Jamil drifted over to the card table. "The Ministry of Interior? It is not far from here. See?" He pointed to a piece of meaningless calligraphy. "It is near Shahr-e Nau Park on the other side of the King's Palace. Perhaps two kilometers walking."

Amy considered. It could be hours before Rasheed was back with the jeep. What better way to spend those hours than attending to Bruce's final directive? Maybe even touch base with her new landlord if he was in his offices? Walking would stretch her legs and let Amy get a feel for her new habitat at the same time.

"Good, then if you can show me the way, I'd like to walk to this address. I'll probably need you to translate as well. I don't know how much English your government offices usually have."

But not as she was currently dressed. Digging into her shoulder bag, Amy pulled out an oversize cardigan she'd tucked in for warmth on the plane. It was uncomfortably hot, but at least it covered her arms and any pretence of shape. Reshouldering her bag, Amy started for the door.

Jamil made no move to follow. "I am sorry, but you cannot walk the streets uncovered."

Amy spun around, annoyed. "Look, I'm sorry if it offends you, but I am not an Afghan woman. I want to respect your culture, but if you're going to work for me, I need you to respect mine as well, and I hope I've made it clear I will not be pushed into a burqa!"

Jamil spread his hands wide, but there was no yielding in his expression. "It is not for me. In Pakistan I have seen many women not of my family with uncovered face. But I know the men of this city, these streets. You will not be able to walk in peace if you appear so."

Oddly, his intransigence gained Amy's respect. With exasperation, she snatched up the burqa. If nothing else, it would be an opportunity to better understand the culture—the women—with which she'd come here to work. "Fine, just this once. But if I trip and fall, it'll be your responsibility."

It wasn't quite as bad as she remembered. The shoulder bag held the burqa tentlike away from her body, allowing for reasonable air circulation. As Amy followed Jamil out onto the street, she quickly learned to use her hands underneath to keep the grille positioned over her eyes. In some bizarre fashion, it reminded Amy of her favorite umbrella as a small girl.

Also blue, it had curved below her shoulders with a small plastic window through which to see. *Like walking around in my own little castle.*

The burqa offered some of the same sense of privacy, along with protection from wind and dust and prying eyes.

On the negative, the burqa's mesh grille proved a far inferior window than the umbrella's plastic. Within blocks, Amy was developing a headache, a dizzying pattern of lines dancing in front of her eyes even when she closed them. She couldn't see the ground, her peripheral vision only a few feet on either side, so she was constantly tripping. Without Jamil's thin shoulders to focus on just ahead, she'd have soon been hopelessly lost.

Or run over. Amy stumbled back as a bus barely missed her. How did countless Afghan women do this every day?

There were plenty of burqas drifting through market stalls, begging at car windows, as well as the black chadors Amy had glimpsed at the New Hope compound. But other women were less constricted in enveloping headscarves but bare faces, long-sleeved tunics over pants, and ankle-length *chapans*, embroidered, button-up overcoats. *As soon as I get my luggage.*

Amy swerved to avoid two burqas squatting on a street corner, skeletal hands outthrust, several small children huddled close. Bruce's snide comment sprang to her mind. *"This country's crawling with starving widows and children."* Had she just stumbled over the first candidates to revive New Hope's mission?

"Jamil?"

Amy almost collided with her escort as he spun around. Jamil had remained a stride ahead with only the occasional gesture to indicate when there was a street to cross. It seemed women were expected to be mute as well as anonymous. Now his tone was taut with irritation as he snapped, "What is it?"

"How much farther?"

Jamil was suddenly too close. "Be silent!" he hissed near a cloaked ear. "Do you wish the entire world to know you are a foreigner on foot?"

Only that Jamil was right, the note of fear in his voice, excused his harshness. Though Amy's English had hardly been loud, it had attracted unwanted attention, the narrowed stares turned her way ranging from interest to hostility. From somewhere a globule of spittle landed on the mesh grille.

"*Kafir!*"

Infidel.

Amy hastened to follow as Jamil started forward again.

"The place you seek is over there." The jerk of his head indicated a long army green wall topped with concertina wire across a wide, busy avenue. "We can cross here, but you must be careful. No, wait!"

An armored convoy was coming down the boulevard fast, soldiers in body armor at gun turrets, others braced in open hatches, lethal-looking weapons cradled in their hands. *ISAF* was lettered across door panels. Then Amy spotted a pale blue form sprinting toward the convoy instead of away. She had time to wonder how a woman in a burqa could run before the explosion knocked her from her feet.

Amy was blind, the burqa twisting in her fall so that she was choking too. Around her, angry shouts had become panicked shrieks, the thud of running footsteps. Short bursts of gunfire spattered the screams. Amy scrambled backward until she felt a wall behind her. Not caring anymore who should see her, she pushed the burqa up until her face was free.

The street was pandemonium, traffic jammed to a stop, the armored Humvee leading the convoy now twisted metal. Despite a bloodied face here and there, its contingent didn't seem seriously injured. The shooting Amy had heard must have been in the air because the only still shape was the pale blue and scarlet heap that had been the suicide bomber. But there were plenty of gashes and abrasions, blood-splattered clothing and cries of pain. A yellow Toyota Corolla was in flames.

"Go, go, go!"

The damaged Humvee's contingent had clambered to safety among the other vehicles. And now, Amy realized incredulously, they were leaving. The stalled traffic made maneuvering easier, but more than one vehicle was simply pushed aside by the weight of an armored personnel carrier before the convoy disappeared around a corner.

I don't believe it.

Hers was not the only furious response. Raised arms and voices chased the departing convoy.

Amy looked for her guide. She couldn't spot Jamil anywhere, but across the street was the gated entrance to her original destination, and without traffic she could cross freely. With tensions calming, Afghans were shooting glances at her exposed face, so Amy dropped the blue polyester back into place.

A high-pitched and very young cry altered Amy's route. Down the block, a toddler no more than two years old was huddled alone on the curb, wailing fear and abandonment at the top of his lungs. Amy couldn't have even said what motivated her swift weaving through stalled traffic and crowds. Certainly the terrified anguish of those screams. Perhaps too some subconscious image of the empty rooms and dusty courtyard that were now hers to fill. Was one of those begging women in burqas the mother? *Maybe even the suicide bomber?*

The child came into Amy's arms willingly until he realized she was a stranger. His shrieks redoubled, and if Amy couldn't understand the words, others could because she was now drawing more than hostile glares. Turbaned, bearded, and very angry faces closed in on her. Hands snatched at the burqa, tugged at the child in her arms.

"The child! Put the child down!"

It was Jamil's voice. So he hadn't abandoned her. Amy would have happily put the toddler down now. But his small, wiry body was struggling so hard, she didn't dare loose her grip for fear he'd fall.

Then she didn't have to worry anymore. Amy felt the boy yanked from her arms, saw through the burqa's mesh grille a tall, burly man scooping the toddler close. She made no protest. From the child's clinging embrace, the man was no stranger.

But it wasn't over. Amy glimpsed only an upraised fist before a blow to the side of her head knocked her to the ground. She didn't even try to get up as sandaled feet made contact with her ribs, drove the air from her lungs. Burying her face against her shoulder bag, she tried to curl her body into a protective ball.

A single gunshot released her. The masculine voice calling out a curt order into sudden silence was deep and authoritative. Rolling over painfully, Amy struggled to a sitting position, her breath rasping in her ears.

Her hands clawed at the polyester entangling her. Before she could pull it away, the burqa was yanked from her face.

Amy blinked her surroundings into focus. Her attackers had moved back out of arm's reach. A man bent over her, the metallic gleam of a pistol still in his right hand. The face only inches above her looked as furious as her assailants', but it was clean shaven. Wraparound sunglasses were pushed up onto ruthlessly trimmed dark curls to reveal a furious gray gaze above a grimly compressed mouth, a jawline taut with anger.

Still gasping for breath, Amy managed to speak at the same instant her rescuer chose to do so. "You!"

Stepping back into the cover of a toppled stall so that none could note his interest, he surveyed the disaster scene with disapproving satisfaction. The *shaheed*, the holy martyr, had challenged the invincibility of the infidel leviathan. But the damage inflicted was insignificant, and though a cheering mob already swarmed over the disabled vehicle, not one of the foreign occupiers had joined the shaheed in death.

Allah's judgment because martyrdom had come in the unheroic form of a woman? And those screams of anguish, the bloodied garments and smashed merchandise. Did they not belong to fellow Muslim brothers? Did Allah truly reward with paradise such senseless incompetence? Besides, however unwelcome, the foreigners were not the true enemy of his people.

Or his own mission.

He swayed on his feet, exhaustion warring with his urgency. Nearby a toppled food stand had spilled the bright saffron yellow of *pilau* across the ground, the redolence of garlic and spice and fried bits of meat twisting at his stomach. He hadn't slept since he'd been released to his task, and his few afghanis had evaporated on transport, so he hadn't eaten since the day before.

When and where he'd next eat or sleep, he did not yet know. Nor how he would achieve the commission to which his life was now committed.

But he thrust away hunger and weariness and apprehension with the discipline of long practice as he straightened up and moved away. The hell of these last years had taught him to be patient.

To endure.

To hate.

"Are you okay? Can you get up?"

At the young woman's nod, Steve flipped the veil down again, concealing that exasperatingly bright hair and expat clothing. His Glock remained raised in his right hand, but his left reached down to take hers. She gasped as she scrambled stiffly to her feet. As Steve tugged her close enough to feel her quick breathing under the blue polyester, the corner of his eye caught Cougar's approach, unslung weapon melting away a path.

Tucking his Glock into the small of his back, Steve spread his hands palms outward, his Dari fluent and regretful. "Please accept my apologies. There has been a misunderstanding. The woman was frightened and confused by the noise."

Turbans and flat wool *pakul* caps bobbed in comprehending nods. Who, after all, did not understand the hysterics of which a woman was capable?

"She is your woman? You accept responsibility for her behavior?"

Any need to respond was disrupted by a loud drone approaching fast and low. Heads shot up as the drone modified to the throp-throp of rotor blades. Steve expected an ISAF aircraft dispatched to assess the damage. But this was no Black Hawk. Russian-built Mi-8 Hips were Soviet leftovers the mujahedeen and Taliban and now the new Afghan government had snapped up for transport. This one hovered over the roof Steve and Cougar had vacated, scattering men in blue gray uniforms leaning over the parapet. Khalid had returned earlier than expected.

Steve had no doubt who was in that chopper. He'd ridden in it himself with the current minister of interior. That it still flew paid tribute to Soviet engineering. A discreet commute it was not. A single RPG would blow the chopper through the ministry roof.

As the Mi-8 hovered above the flat roof for passengers to disembark, Steve debated turning back. But only fleetingly. Dragging along a stray expat female was hardly a propitious introduction to this contract. The necessity of that decision roughened his tone as muffled noises beneath the burqa could now be heard above the departing chopper.

"Be quiet! Haven't you caused enough trouble? Follow me and don't say another word. Cougar, you've got the rear."

If they didn't understand his English, the gathered crowd approved of his harshness.

"Beat her well for causing so much trouble!"

The suggestion was followed by laughter, expressions no longer hostile but interested.

Steve didn't bother to disillusion them but strode off, making sure only that the pale blue shape was obeying his orders.

Cougar plucked at his sleeve. "We can't take an Afghan woman with us. You trying to get her killed—and us?"

"She's expat," Steve tossed curtly over his shoulder.

Cougar made no further protest. Nor did the woman in the burqa, both staying close on his heels, though the woman stumbled repeatedly until Steve slowed his pace. As traffic began to inch forward again, Steve scanned the crowd. Where was the Afghan man he'd thought to be accompanying his new charge? Their retreat was hardly inconspicuous, so if the man had made himself scarce, it was by choice.

As they entered the alley where the black Suburban had pulled over, Ahmed jumped out, a raised arm halting traffic. Or maybe it was the unslung M4s in the two contractors' hands. Steve gestured for Cougar to take the front passenger seat. The woman needed no urging to scramble into the backseat. Steve got in after her, Ahmed easing forward into traffic as Steve slammed the door shut.

Beside him, the burqa was already coming off. From the front passenger seat, Cougar twisted around, recognition dawning on his broad face. No, Steve hadn't been mistaken. The disheveled flaxen hair definitely belonged to the woman from the plane.

She wiped whatever was left of makeup from her face with the blue polyester before giving both contractors a smile bright with gratitude. "Boy, it feels good to be out of this. I can't thank you enough for getting me out of there. I'd hate to think what might have happened if you hadn't come along."

"Exactly!" The uncompromising bite of Steve's response offered no encouragement to her eager friendliness. "You want to tell me what possessed you to go out into the middle of a suicide bombing dressed like that?"

Warmth immediately drained from her expression, and Steve found himself under a cool survey. He could have counted to five as she shook her shining curtain of hair back into order and unloaded the polyester bundle and shoulder bag onto the seat beside her. A hazel gaze rising to clash with Steve's was a little too composed and impenitent for his taste.

"I saw you at the airport this morning, didn't I? Let's start over. I'm Amy Mallory, country manager for New Hope Foundation, a nonprofit working with women and children at risk here in Afghanistan. I really do appreciate your intervening back there. I know it wasn't the smartest move, but there was this little boy who looked like he might be in trouble—"

"Hey, no harm done. Perfectly understandable. Glad we could help," Cougar said, trying to mollify her.

But Steve wasn't so easily conciliated. "Next time you're looking to add to your client base, you might check to see if the kid's already got parents. Even in Afghanistan people get antsy about strangers snatching their children off the street. And that hardly explains what you were doing there to start with, an expat woman alone and on foot. Or didn't you bother reading the current security alert before getting off that plane? Oh yes, I noticed you, too. As to masquerading in a burqa, even the greenest newbie might have guessed that's asking for trouble."

The SUV's air-conditioning wasn't enough to keep Amy's annoyance from burning at her cheeks. She was still feeling shaken, her ribs sore enough for nasty bruises. And where was Jamil? His urgent shout when she'd picked up the child reassured Amy he wasn't seriously hurt. Why hadn't he caught up with her?

As for her rescuer, Amy met his uncompromising stare with raised chin, her initial glow of gratitude fading fast. In the vehicle's confined interior, her seatmate seemed much larger than he had at the airport. The terse drawl of his English answered the question of nationality, while apologetic glances from his companion made it clear who was in charge.

The polished metal in his hands didn't intimidate Amy. In the places she'd spent the last three years, armed guards were the norm, and by his casual handling, he knew what he was doing. But the palpable warmth of his long, muscled frame and a musk that was both perspiration and cologne were claustrophobically close. When Amy shifted her shoulder bag so that it was between them, the twitch of his mouth held malicious understanding. But he didn't speak, and it was clear he was still awaiting an answer.

"You think I wanted to wear this stupid thing?" Amy burst out. "I only put it on because people keep yelling at me for not being covered up enough. You'd think I was strolling through Miami in a bikini. No, I wouldn't get half this attention if I were. And I didn't go down there alone. I don't know where my translator went. I just hired him. I hope he didn't think I dumped him when you dragged me off."

"Rescued you," her seatmate corrected, but this time the twitch of his mouth relaxed almost to a smile. "And you're probably right. About the bikini in Miami, I mean."

"Whatever! As to why I was there, I was trying to get to the Ministry of Interior. My new landlord's the minister in charge of the place, and I was told I had to fill out some form down there right away."

"That's right, the new MOI card. A reminder we'll need to run those down for your team, Steve." The shorter, older man in the front seat swiveled around. "Wait a minute. Are you saying Khalid Sayef is your landlord?"

"The minister of interior is," Amy answered cautiously. "You know him?"

"Well, that would be Khalid. As a matter of fact, he's our current principal. Client, that is." The front seat passenger shuffled his weapon to offer a handshake over the seat back. "I guess it's time we introduced ourselves. I'm Craig Laube, logistics manager for Condor Security. My friends call me Cougar, and I hope that'll include you. My colleague here is Steve Wilson, detail leader for Khalid's private security."

Ignoring her seatmate, Amy turned a brilliant smile on the older contractor. "Then I'm so glad it was you I ran into. If you know this Khalid, maybe you could advise me how best to get in touch with him."

"Actually, that was his chopper you just saw coming in. We'll be meeting with him later today—"

"He should be in his office tomorrow," Steve interrupted. "If not, I think you'll find that the main office can make any arrangements you need. And may I suggest that you consider taking along a reliable Afghan employee? This country holds a lot of pitfalls for newbies. Now, is there somewhere we could offer you a ride?"

Steve's statements were courteous enough, but Amy caught his glance at his watch. Outside the tinted windows, traffic flowed with as carefree lawlessness as though death hadn't just exploded a few blocks away. The driver spoke up in rapid Dari, his gesture inquiring which direction to turn.

Amy bit her lip, realizing she had absolutely no idea what answer to give. "I only arrived this morning, and, well, due to a mix-up, I don't yet have a place to stay. I guess the best thing would be to go back to New Hope."

Except that without Jamil, Amy had no clue how to get back there. With a pointed glance in Amy's direction, the driver began another turn around the block. Amy wrinkled her nose ruefully as she admitted, "I'm so sorry to have put you to all this trouble. But I'm totally lost. Maybe you can take me to the embassy if it's anywhere on your way?"

Something about the complete lack of expression on Steve's face made Amy flare up. "Look, I don't know how many times I can say I'm sorry. But if you hadn't dragged me away without my translator, I wouldn't be in this mess. If it's such a problem, just leave me on a corner."

"That wouldn't be advisable," Cougar intervened hastily. "I wouldn't leave another man out there without security, much less an expat woman. We'll make sure we get you somewhere safe. It's absolutely no trouble and our pleasure, right, Steve?" He didn't wait for a response. "I know Khalid's properties. If you could describe the place, maybe we can figure out where you were."

"Well, it's a big, two-story house in a pretty nice neighborhood. Blue green walls with black gates."

"Khalid's Wazir property," Cougar said. "That's only a mile or so from here, and it's practically walking distance from the CS team house. We're headed right that way."

A few minutes later, the Suburban pulled up outside a black metal gate.

"That's it! Oh, thank you so much." Though Amy reached for her shoulder bag and the wad of blue polyester, she made no move to get out, anxiety squeezing again at her stomach.

Steve leaned across her to stare out the window at the high, faded blue wall, the movement bringing him so close Amy could feel the even exhalation of his breathing, the brush of his shoulder against hers. "This is your headquarters?" he demanded sharply. To his companion he added, "This isn't Khalid's primary you mentioned?"

Cougar looked surprised. "You know this place? No, Khalid's primary residence is over in Sherpur district on the edge of Wazir, and it makes this one look like chicken feed. Khalid's got a couple rentals around the city."

"He's certainly done well for himself in the new Afghanistan." Steve straightened, pulling away from her. "Well, Ms. Mallory, is this where you wanted to go?"

Amy didn't respond as she clenched the burqa material. "Let me guess. Your guard doesn't speak English either."

"I don't know. I was wearing the burqa when I came. I'm not sure he'd even recognize me. The man who brought me, Rasheed, drove my associate to the airport. I don't think he'd be back yet." Amy was mortified at the helplessness of the gesture with which her hand came free of the polyester.

Steve climbed out of the SUV and spoke briefly through the security window, then came back to yank open Amy's door as the metal gate creaked open. "If 'a woman with hair like spun sunlight' rings a bell," he said with irony, "it seems your guard did catch a glimpse of you. He says you're welcome to come in and wait, that Rasheed should be home shortly, Rasheed's wife is here, and that you will know where to go."

"Yes, I do. Thank you." Amy turned to offer a grateful smile to Cougar, who despite the quietness of this side street, had his weapon up and ready, head and eyes roving. "And thank you. I can't tell you how much I appreciate this."

Cougar removed a hand from his weapon to waggle his fingers. "Our pleasure."

A sentiment his companion wasn't likely to echo, Amy told herself sourly as she got out. Leaning into the SUV, Steve took Amy's shoulder bag and burqa before she could grab them, then emerged with a manila envelope. Amy hadn't donned the burqa as she followed Steve through the gate, but when the elderly guard hurriedly averted his eyes, she rebelliously draped the polyester shawl-style over head and shoulders, feeling like a fool under the contractor's sharp gaze.

But Steve's survey had shifted immediately to the interior of the compound. Turning slowly on a boot heel, he made a 360-degree scan of his surroundings. What did he find so interesting in a dried-up garden, construction materials, and dilapidated ruin of a house? "You sure you feel comfortable being left alone here? If you'd feel safer waiting with other expats, I'm sure my associate would have some suggestions."

Amy wasn't too excited about the empty courtyard, elderly guard, a babble of men's voices across the cinder-block wall. If she'd seen any flicker of real concern on Steve's face, she might have wavered. "I'll be fine. I'll wait with Rasheed's wife until he gets back. He'll be able to help me make housing arrangements."

"Then you can probably put this to better use than I would." Sliding a few folded sheets from the manila envelope, Steve handed Amy the rest.

Amy skimmed through the envelope's contents. English-language city guide. Folded map. Kabul business directory. Even a list of expat guesthouses. "Why, this is wonderful. Thank you."

"Don't thank me. That's Cougar's doing. Make sure you read the security info packet. He'll blame himself if you end up in some embassy incident report."

Unlike you. To Amy, there was mockery in Steve's tone, and once again, her initial flush of gratitude evaporated abruptly. He headed back to the gate. Fury gave Amy the boldness to take a step after him. "What is your problem?"

Steve stopped, swung around.

Amy could feel the burning in her cheeks as she went on hotly. "I don't know why you're so down on me. I've tried to be nice and polite. I've apologized again and again for interrupting your mission or whatever you're doing here. It's not like I did this to inconvenience you or even asked you to step in. So why are you acting like the whole thing is somehow my fault? I mean, it's not like I asked for any of this to happen."

Steve's eyebrows knit together as he looked at Amy. Then he took a long step toward her, his tall frame looming over her so that she retreated a step.

"No, of course you didn't ask for this," he said evenly, bitingly. "You didn't have to. It was a logical outcome of your decisions and actions."

Steve raised a hand to cut off her protest. "My problem is people like you waltzing into this country as though you were on some adventure cruise. You don't do your homework. You don't plan for security. You don't have backup in place. Inevitably you get in over your head and start screaming for help. Then it's up to those who *have* done their homework to waste time and effort and money—even risk lives—to get you out of whatever mess you've gotten into. People who don't come prepared shouldn't be allowed here—" He broke off, looking away from Amy.

Amy seized the pause to choke out her fury and humiliation. "You don't even know me. Who are you to judge? But don't worry. You'll never have to bail me out again. Or speak to me either."

Then Amy realized that Steve hadn't broken off because he'd finished or thought better of his tirade. He didn't even look as though he'd heard her retort. He was staring somewhere past her left shoulder, the color under his tan draining to an odd gray white, his jaw tightened with as much stunned incredulity as though he'd just seen a ghost.

6

Steve gave his head a slight shake, and the memory he was staring at slid back into the present. This was no teenager running through winter-barren gardens with a scream of anguish and rage. Just a man who'd swung himself lightly down over a cinder-block interior wall added to the property since Steve was here last. The jolt of familiarity was because Steve had seen this same man earlier at Amy's heels.

"Oh, there he is!" Amy had turned to see whom Steve was staring at. "I'm so glad you got back okay, Jamil. You must have run the whole way."

The Afghan paused among stacks of construction material some ten meters away, breathing quickly. A slight build and underfed gauntness had given Steve that first illusion of adolescence, but the somber bearded features and wary gaze were closer to his own age.

"Then you know him?" Steve confirmed.

"Yes, that's my translator. The one you left behind." Amy's annoyance still burned in her cheeks, the fire of her gaze. "And now that Jamil's here, you don't need to bother about me anymore. You can go do whatever you were doing when I interrupted you."

"Then good-bye." Two strides carried Steve to the open gate, the elderly guard stepping hurriedly from his path.

Amy took a step after him, that ridiculous head covering slipping from her hair as she held up the manila envelope. "I want to thank you again for this. And for everything. I understand what you're saying. In fact, I agree. But that's not really me—being unprepared and risking other people's lives. Today just happened. It won't happen again. If you knew me, you'd believe that." A tentative smile invited a friendly response.

Instead Steve dismissed himself with a curt nod. "You're welcome. And you're right. I don't know you well enough to judge. I apologize if I was rude." He'd stepped through the gate when he turned back. "By the way, you might want to rethink your security. Your guard didn't even turn his head when your friend there hopped the wall. Next time it might not be someone you know."

Steve wasn't sure why anger still burned in him as he slid into the SUV. Amy or the idiot of an employer who thought it ethical to send a kid that green to a place like this? Though maybe Amy Mallory was older and less unworldly than Steve's assessment. She'd almost have to be for her current position of authority.

Of greater interest was the property where he'd just left her. What coincidence had Amy's new rental turning out to be the site of that final skirmish in the liberation of Kabul? Or for that matter had brought Khalid Sayef back across Steve's path? Would the muj commander even remember Steve? The twenty-two-year-old sergeant had been the most junior of the Special Forces unit embedded with Khalid's fighters.

Khalid had hardly crossed Steve's own mind in years. His furious indignation over Khalid's commandeering of the Wazir compound had faded in the roller coaster of ongoing combat. Especially since investigation bore out that the entire neighborhood was indeed a hotbed of Taliban and al-Qaeda. If bin Laden never turned up on the property, a compound down the street proved to house one of his wives. Nor was it just the mujahedeen who'd seized on recently abandoned properties. Steve had returned that day from his airport run to find his team leader supervising the Special Forces unit's move into another Wazir compound. Who'd occupied their new living quarters before the Taliban wasn't raised.

"There're not a lot of property deeds around here. Possession's nine-tenths of the law." Steve's lieutenant had shrugged. "You can bet those people who stayed in this country through the worst of the war aren't going to move when refugees start trickling back and laying claim to properties. Especially all those former aristocrats who fled this country when things got tough. And why should they?"

A valid question. Did the traditional aristocracy deserve to move back into their lives of leisure, privilege, and wealth, benefiting from a war others had fought while they'd built new and safe lives in exile? Or did the actual combatants and survivors of that war, who'd suffered terribly, deserve to pick up the remaining crumbs? even become the new aristocracy, as victors had done for thousands of years?

Not that it was Steve's call.

Still, Steve felt it was a shame that the man who commandeered the place had let it fall into the ruin he had just witnessed. And the civilian casualties that day, however unintentional, even inevitable in the heat of war, still left a bad taste in Steve's mouth. If the kid had been telling the truth . . . *Whatever happened to that kid?*

Like Khalid, he hadn't crossed Steve's mind in years. His team had been transferred out of Kabul immediately after liberation to hunt down remaining al-Qaeda and Taliban on the Pakistan border. He'd inquired about the boy the next time he passed through Bagram Air Base north of Kabul, but the civilian interrogators had made it clear they didn't hand out info to just any uniform wandering by.

"Our team house is on this next street."

Ahmed pulled up at a lowered red and white boom pole. Concertina wire and sandbagged machine-gun nests atop walls plus concrete blast barriers blocking driveways marked the street as an expat sanctuary.

"This whole street's PSD lodging, so no through traffic." Cougar showed a badge out the window to a uniformed Gurkha. The small, wiry mercenaries, once a keystone of the British Indian army, were now Nepal's chief export and a staple of the PSD industry. The boom rose, and the SUV drove on. "Makes security easier for everyone. DynCorp and Blackwater both have team houses in here, so we can keep our security to a minimum."

Like its neighbors, the CS team house had once been some Kabul aristocrat's personal residence. Indoors, downstairs salons had been converted into communal living quarters complete with cafeteria, workout gym, lounge. It might have been some exclusive bed-and-breakfast except for the communication stations, situation maps, and conference table that converted the largest salon into a command center.

Someone hit the Mute button as Cougar and Steve walked into the lounge, laptops and gun parts pushed aside as half a dozen men hoisted themselves to their feet. Steve matched introductions with the bio data Cougar had given him.

"Mac." A huge former Army Ranger with tangled blond hair and beard, Mac wasn't short for any given name but a Mack truck.

"Rick." Another American, Ricardo Calderon had been a Navy SEAL.

"McDuff." Retired British Special Air Service, Jamie McDuff was the oldest of the group with a formidable résumé: counterterrorism in Ireland's civil war; parachuting into Kuwait in the first Gulf War; more recently, Kosovo and Iraq; and who knew what else since little of SAS service records ever saw the light of day.

"Ian." Kiwi SAS Ian Grant's Polynesian features indicated his Scottish forebears had fraternized with New Zealand's original residents.

"Bones." Though Wyoming native Timothy Bonefeole had no Special Ops experience, Steve had personally requested his addition to the team.

The last of the six, tall with a blond crew cut and cool, blue eyes, pounded Steve on the back. "Willie! Hey, great to see you, man."

Steve hadn't heard his nickname with that particular flattened drawl since he'd last been in Afghanistan. "Phil, glad you could come to the party."

His ODA teammate hadn't stayed in Special Ops as long as Steve. Less than four months after Kabul's liberation, Philip Myers had been the sole survivor when his reconnaissance patrol hit a booby-trapped cave. Phil had lost a foot and partial vision in one eye. Discharged, he'd dropped out of Steve's life. But Phil had skills worth more than an intact body and shooting eye, and when Steve had come across Phil's résumé in the system, he'd bumped the name to the top of his wish list.

Only a limp hinted now at an artificial extremity, and from his powerful embrace, the Special Forces sergeant hadn't allowed the rest of his brawny frame to lose its conditioning. In fact, the whole team looked good, all fit, alert, and matching reasonably in age and muscle to their ID photo, not always a given.

"And I'm Steve Wilson. Detail leader for Khalid's PSD. I'll be calling a team meeting shortly. Cougar, how long before we go on the clock with Khalid?"

"ISAF's been running a security team since the sugar factory bombing, and I'm counting on manpower from them for tonight's shift. But Khalid has a 10 a.m. photo op with a congressional delegation at the embassy, and by then he'll expect to parade his personal security." Cougar checked his watch. "Khalid won't be expecting us for dinner before seven. Which gives us at least six hours. How about lunch, siesta, then team meeting around five?"

"Make that the other way around. We've got serious planning to do. We'll worry about a siesta if there's time."

Cougar's cell phone shrilled. The others waited as the CS manager interjected an occasional *balay* and *nay*, Dari for yes and no. Cougar looked unhappy as he snapped the phone shut. "Khalid's had some major blowout with ISAF—seems they weren't too happy with his chopper excursion—and they're staging a walkout at the end of the day. He wants us there stat."

Team members were already reaching for laptops and M4s when Steve held up a hand. "No."

Everyone turned to him.

Steve told Cougar, "Call back and tell Khalid we'll be there in two hours."

"But he's asked—"

"Khalid's asking a lot of things. We might as well get off to a good start. If he could blow us off till tonight, he can wait a couple more hours."

Cougar looked worried. "Khalid isn't going to like that. He's not the patient type. His deputy sounded pretty ticked off."

"So what's he going to do? Send us away and turn down his pretty expat detail? Khalid may be our principal, but he's not the one picking up our tab. We start letting him jerk us around now, and we've already lost our leverage to control this mission."

After pushing Redial, Cougar exchanged a few Dari phrases.

When he hung up, Steve went on. "Give me fifteen minutes to shower and change, and we'll have that team meeting. Cougar, if you'd ask your kitchen to rustle up something we can eat while we work. Meanwhile, the rest of you might want to get some gear together. When we leave, I expect us to be ready to step into this detail."

His new teammates were nodding agreement, Steve noted with approval. Contrary to Cougar's solicitous concern, they were all big boys who hadn't come here for a vacation. Hungry, thirsty, or sleep-deprived, their training was to get on with the mission. If they couldn't handle that, they had no business on his team.

Upstairs, bedrooms held multiple cots and bunk beds, most of them in use by the footlockers and tacked-up photos. Two closed doors read, "Keep Quiet. Sleeping."

"Night shifts. We've got convoys heading out at midnight, our best bet for catching the Tallies asleep." Cougar pushed open a door to a small room holding a single bed. The perks of team leader. Steve's luggage was unloaded in a corner. "Bathroom's down the hall. Real flush toilets and hot water. We run our own generator."

As promised, the water was hot and ample, and Steve was back downstairs within fifteen minutes. The others had already shifted to the command center, maps and blueprints spread out on the table.

Steve grabbed a sandwich from a nearby platter. "Okay, let's see who and what we have. Phil, thanks for pulling up stakes to join us on such short notice. Phil was my ODA's medic when we were deployed here," he added.

Nods signaled comprehension. So this was why a guy short one limb had been invited to the party. Special Forces medics were the best in the world at combat zone trauma.

"Phil, I'd like you to go over the medical kit and make a wish list. Now, Bones—well, let's just say I did time with Bones on my last two contracts, and I'd take a pay cut myself to keep him on my team." That got everyone's attention. PSCs didn't joke about pay scales. "Why don't you tell them why, Bones?"

"Well, back on the ranch they call me an engine whisperer." The Wyoming native's drawl was quiet and placid. "They kinda talk to me about what's wrong with 'em. There's nothin' that drinks gas or diesel—car, truck, Zamboni—I cain't fix. In the Army I fixed choppers, so if you got one of those, I'll keep it flyin' too."

"You might mention your other skill," Steve prompted.

"I was demolition derby champion in Cheyenne till I joined the Army. And if there's a fight, I can still pick off a gopher with a headshot at two hundred yards."

The lanky cowboy was now receiving respectful looks. Next to a good medic, a PSC valued no one more than the mechanic who kept overloaded, overstressed vehicles from breaking down in hostile territory.

"Bones'll handle our transport. Mac, Ian, Rick, you've all worked PRS." Primary ring security was the innermost circle of defense protecting the principal. "Any of you do much driving?"

Ian raised a hand.

"We need more drivers. In fact, we need more personnel across the board. We've got two stationary security sites, and I want primary ring on at least every shift to be Special Ops. Add convoy duty and miscellaneous, and let's say minimum two dozen more Special Ops and a hundred third country nationals for support. And gear and transportation for all the above. Cougar, what all do you have in the pipeline?"

The logistics manager looked unhappy. "I'm afraid it's not so easy. There are budget considerations."

"What does that mean?" Mac demanded.

"What it means, I'm betting," Ian cut in sardonically, "is that Khalid screamed loud enough to get his PSD, but that's about all he's got. Are these 'budget considerations' the reason Condor walked off with a level one PSD instead of DynCorp or Blackwater? I've been wondering."

"We did come in with a bid the embassy considered commensurate to this mission," Cougar answered stiffly. "DynCorp and Blackwater declined to tender a bid. That was one reason Condor obtained the contract."

"And the other?" Mac challenged.

"For that you'll have to ask your team leader. Khalid himself put in the deciding vote when he saw Steve Wilson was our proposed detail leader."

So Khalid did remember him. Steve answered the battery of eyes with a shrug. "I did liaison work with Khalid's muj militia after 9/11. So did Phil. Haven't seen or heard from the guy since. Have you, Phil?"

At the medic's head shake, Steve went on. "Bottom line, then: what do we have?"

"If we go easy on transport, we might squeeze out another half-dozen Special Ops." Cougar shuffled through a sheaf of papers. "For TCNs, Condor has about a hundred Guats and Sals on contract from Central America, including a few officers trained by our own Special Forces. We've got Gurkhas too and can get more.

"Vehicles—that Suburban out there's the nicest for limo duty. We've got quite a few armored Hummers at our main base for convoy protection. Weapons, ammo, comm gear—we've got some stock. And once you get your wish list together, we've got a cargo flight chartered from Jordan next week."

If not particularly happy with Cougar's summary, Steve was philosophical. There was always a disconnect between what the team on the ground considered essential to carry out a mission and what HQ was willing to shell out. Too big a disconnect and the team walked—or someone got killed. As team leader, you pushed for the optimum, then made do with what you got.

"Okay, let's see those blueprints of Khalid's place."

7

As the pedestrian gate clanged shut behind Steve, Amy let out a breath she hadn't realized she'd been holding. Never could she remember feeling such a fool. An incompetent fool, at that.

She conjured up a composed expression before facing Jamil. "I'm sure glad to see you safe."

"Yes, I saw you leaving with the two foreign men." Jamil's glance took in Amy's unorthodox head shawl as he closed the distance between them. "I hoped they were bringing you back here. I didn't know where else to go."

"No, that was exactly the right decision. But how did you get in?" Amy looked past Jamil to the cinder-block partition over which he'd swung himself. "Did you just climb over the wall from the street?"

"Please forgive me. I did not wish to explain to the *chowkidar* how it was I had come to lose you."

"No, that's okay, except if you can hop the wall that easy, so can anyone else. We'll have to do something about that." Amy hated to admit that Steve Wilson was right about anything.

Jamil was still breathing rapidly, and he swayed slightly on his feet. Then Amy saw that a blood-stained bandage was thrust into one of his cheap plastic sandals. "What happened? You were hurt in the explosion!"

"It is nothing. I stepped on some broken glass."

"Well, it's going to need to be cleaned at least. Come on. Let's get you out of this dirt."

The woman in the black chador, presumably Rasheed's wife, Hamida, drifted after them as Amy led the way into the villa and across the interior courtyard. By the time they reached the salon where she'd met with Bruce, Jamil looked paler than before, and he sank without protest into a plastic chair. Hamida paused in the doorway.

Digging out a spare T-shirt, Amy used it to dust off the card table. "Would you please ask her to bring some water?"

Jamil roused himself for a quick phrase. As the woman disappeared, Amy pulled out her first aid kit and began sorting its contents. A roll of gauze. Antibiotic cream. Antiseptic swabbing wipes. Tweezers. Hospital tape.

Jamil's dark eyes showed a glimmer of life. "You are a doctor?"

"No, just a few first aid courses required to work in the refugee camps. Here, let me take that off."

The bandage looked clean and new, a headscarf or carrying cloth snatched up perhaps from a market stall in the chaos of the bombing. Amy didn't pursue ethical questions because the wound itself was more extensive than Jamil had intimated—a deep, jagged slash that must have been excruciating to run on.

By now Hamida was back with a plastic bucket filled with water.

Amy dredged up a thank-you from that Dari phrase book. "Tashakor." She dipped an unstained portion of the bandage into the water, but Jamil lifted the wet cloth from her hand. "No, please, you should not have to do this."

Competently, Jamil wiped dirt and blood from the wound. By the time he was done, sweat beaded his forehead, and he offered no dissent when Amy broke out an antiseptic wipe to clean the gash. He flinched as Amy used tweezers to pull out two lingering slivers of glass but made no other sound. Nasty though the gash looked, it wasn't going to need stitches. Spreading antibiotic cream generously, Amy reached for a roll of gauze.

But here she hit a snag. Amy had neither scissors nor other means to cut the gauze. Of course! Airline regulations had necessitated her moving that piece of her first aid kit into checked luggage.

Producing a knife from somewhere in his baggy attire, Jamil leaned forward to slice the lengths of gauze Amy measured off. He was breathing hard again by the time he'd finished, and he closed his eyes, slumping back into the chair, as Amy taped the new bandage into place.

Amy spun around to where Hamida was watching silently from the doorway. "Tea? Chai?" The latter at least was the same in Dari as it had come to mean in English. Amy made drinking and eating motions. "And some food too if you have it."

"I am sorry." Jamil opened his eyes and pushed himself up. "It is nothing."

"No, no, sit!" As he subsided, Amy busied herself cleaning up, rolling debris and discarded bandage into the dirty T-shirt. She was stuffing it into an outer pouch of her shoulder bag when Hamida came back with a teapot and two cups. The steaming brew she poured was green tea boiled with milk and cardamom, strong and bitter and very sweet. Life returned to Jamil's eyes as he drank thirstily.

As Amy sipped her own drink cautiously, she shook Steve's manila envelope out onto the card table. However disagreeable Steve had been, Amy appreciated his parting gift, especially the list of UN–approved accommodations. With this she could arrange housing and even transport without leaving the security of New Hope.

Amy was familiarizing herself with the sat phone when Hamida reappeared to unroll a length of oilcloth across the floor tiles. Removing the water bucket, she returned carrying two plates of steaming yellow rice. Amy understood her hesitation. A foreign guest deserved the highest honor. But Amy was female, and men and women didn't eat together. When Hamida finally set the food on the oilcloth, Jamil resolved the problem by retrieving a plate and retreating to a corner.

Amy carried her food to the card table. No utensils had been supplied, but she expertly molded rice into a ball with her right hand, popping it into her mouth. The yellow rice contained shredded carrot and raisins and bits of meat Amy couldn't identify. *Palau. Palaw. Pillau.* The transliterations were as wide-ranging as the variations of the rice dish traditional throughout the Middle East and not dissimilar to the Spanish paella Amy's mother prepared in Miami.

So it wasn't the taste that stopped Amy's eating. Sitting on his haunches, back to the room, her new assistant was eating with voracious concentration, his plate empty before she'd managed half a dozen bites. Amy noted again how thin Jamil was, shoulder blades and ribs standing out starkly under the threadbare material of his tunic. How long had it been since he'd eaten a decent meal? How many others in Afghanistan could not on this day dream of such a mound of food?

Appetite gone, Amy unobtrusively returned her plate to the oilcloth, digging out a hand wipe to clean her hands as she returned to her work. The accommodations list was arranged alphabetically, and Amy had just connected with a guesthouse called Assa when out of the corner of her eye, she saw her barely touched plate disappear to be silently replaced by the empty one.

A male receptionist answering Amy's call switched to English as soon as she spoke. A good beginning, but he regretfully informed Amy the guest-house had no vacancies. She'd worked through B's Place, Gandamack Lodge, and Kabul Inn when Jamil rejoined her at the card table.

Hamida had X-ray vision—or was peering through the window—because she was immediately there with a basin and a pitcher of water to rinse hands. As Hamida cleared their meal, she added the wadded burqa to her load.

Jamil translated her apologetic murmur. "She says she'd been missing this since visiting the bazaar with her husband. She misplaced it when unloading his vehicle. She apologizes that it was not clean for your use."

So Rasheed didn't keep the thing stashed for offending female passengers. "No, please tell her it was perfect and tashakor for its use."

Jamil was complying when heavy footsteps, thuds, and a raised male voice signaled Rasheed's return.

Emerging, Amy was delighted to discover her luggage deposited on the veranda. The chowkidar also handed over a three-by-five card covered with inscriptions Amy couldn't read.

"Mr. Bruce asked me to acquire this for you."

"The MOI card!"

"You will need to take it to the Ministry of Interior to be filled out and have a picture taken."

"Now?"

Rasheed shook his head. "You have not heard? There was a bombing outside the ministry. It will not be open again today nor tomorrow either. When it is open again, I will find out for you."

"But it has to be done in forty-eight—"

The chowkidar was already walking away.

Amy turned to her luggage, her first act to dig out a change of clothing. The outfits she'd collected in India and Kashmir were female versions of the *shalwar kameez*. Conscious of Afghan sensibilities, Amy had forgone the filmy silks of India's hot plains for Kashmir's elbow-covering sleeves and heavier synthetics. The outfit Amy chose now was deep burgundy, its only ornamentation gold stitching around the neck and cuffs. The matching scarf Hindis draped over the shoulders would do as a head covering.

But another need was more urgent on Amy's mind. She was going to learn Dari, if only so she didn't have to rely so heavily on a translator. Gathering up the burgundy outfit and shoulder bag, Amy turned to Jamil, choosing her phrasing with delicate care. "Could you ask if there is a place where I might take care of personal needs?"

Amy didn't know what Jamil said, but as she followed Hamida to a door at the far end of the veranda, she was relieved to discover she'd been led to the right place. An indicator of the original owner's wealth, floors and walls were tiled in intricate mosaic. A marble sink boasted brass fixtures and a gilt-framed mirror, though like so much else, the gilt frame lacked most of its glass, and the sink had no water.

Amy took her time wiping away dust and perspiration, restoring the minimal makeup she wore in a fragment of mirror, brushing her hair until it shone again. A futile exercise once she tucked every shining wisp under the burgundy scarf.

Still, the effort improved Amy's spirits, and despite the indignity of her headscarf, the outfit was comfortable. Amy had come to love the loose, easy feel of shalwar kameez. Lose the headscarf, and the calf-length tunic over drawstring pants had to be the most comfortable women's clothing on the planet.

Her change in dress certainly made a difference to Rasheed and his wife. It was as though Amy had suddenly become visible as a human being. When Amy returned to the sat phone and guesthouse list, the two were gone, perhaps to their own meal, but they reappeared just as Amy was informed that Naween Guesthouse was full. Hamida greeted Amy's makeover with an excited twitter, and for the first time she let her chador slide down from her face as she patted the burgundy material and fingered the gold embroidery. Amy saw green eyes, the light-skinned Slavic features of northern Afghanistan, and several missing front teeth. Hamida was at least a decade younger than her grizzled husband and must have been pretty before hard work—and maybe Rasheed—had worn her down. Did she have a family somewhere? children?

Rasheed himself might never have been the stern, censorious man who'd forced Amy into a burqa. With an expansive smile, he lifted the sat phone from her hand. "Please you do not need to occupy yourself so. I will fix all."

It wasn't Rasheed's first time with a sat phone; he quickly punched in a number. Finished, he beamed at Amy. "The Sarai Guesthouse is where Mr. Nestor and Mr. Bruce stay when they are here. They have a room for you. I will drive you there when you are ready."

And what's your commission? Amy wasn't sure she liked the new jovial Rasheed or the satisfied glance resting on her new outfit. *He thinks he's won. He's exercised his will over me, a female, and gotten away with it.* But Amy was going to need the man's connections and knowledge of the local system that Jamil wouldn't have.

At her request Rasheed took Amy on a tour of her new rental property. Downstairs, a single large salon on each side opened onto the inner courtyard. To either side, a tiled staircase wound up to the second-story balcony. Upstairs, the rooms were smaller with two on each side. Amy was pleased to find a second bathroom directly above the first.

Rasheed nodded when Amy explained her interest in expanding to the front courtyard and at least part of the main wing, waving aside her suggestion that she negotiate personally with the landlord. "That is not necessary. I will speak with Khalid myself tomorrow. I am sure all can be arranged. Whatever you should require I have already informed Mr. Bruce I will fix it for you."

Amy would have liked to survey the entire property from this upper level, but the only windows in the women's quarters opened onto the interior courtyard. In contrast, the main wing had no windows facing inward through which visitors might catch a glimpse of female residents. At the top of each outer staircase, a door led into the main wing's second story. But like those locked salons in the hallway, these doors were in good repair and locked.

"Hamida will clean all of this when you require it," Rasheed said.

His wife and Jamil had both trailed at a discreet distance during the tour. Hamida pulled her chador back over her face as she stepped out onto the second-floor balcony.

So even in the prison of their own quarters, they've got to worry about men looking over the back wall. Amy rebelled.

"Hamida is not educated, and she is barren. But she is a hard worker, and she is not stupid. She can learn whatever you wish for her to do." Turning to his wife, Rasheed broke into Dari.

Repeating his directive, Amy guessed, and by Hamida's apprehensive expression, not kindly. At that moment Amy hated Rasheed for the way he spoke of his wife and how he was grinning at Amy as though he'd just offered her a housewarming gift.

Her indignation warmed Amy's smile as she stepped toward the other woman to acknowledge the halfhearted introduction. "*Salaam aleykum,* Hamida. Please call me Amy."

Hamida's fingertips barely brushed Amy's offered hand.

Pointing to herself, Amy repeated with clear emphasis, "Thank you so much—tashakor—for a delicious meal and all your help."

"Ameera." Rasheed nodded, shaggy beard wagging as though Amy had been speaking to him. "Yes, that is a much better name. An Afghan name. Ameera."

Under the expectant pleasure of his beard-splitting grin, Amy gave up being angry. She wasn't here to bang her head against countless genera-tions of cultural attitudes. By Afghan standards Rasheed might even be a decent husband. Hamida looked well fed, adequately clothed, with a roof over her head despite the barrenness that entitled any good Muslim husband to a divorce.

Stay focused. I'm here to help women and children, not try to reform macho jerks. Her mind flashed to a tall, lithe form. *Of any nationality.*

Just so the chowkidar didn't treat Amy like that. Amy infused author-ity into her voice as she continued to smile at Hamida. "This property is much too large for one person to clean. Would you ask Hamida if she knows of a few other women who need employment and would like to help?"

"Of course," Rasheed agreed, though he didn't add a translation to his wife.

Amy let it go because she'd just remembered another undone item on her to-do list. She turned to Jamil. "What about you? Do you have a place to stay?"

Again Rasheed intervened. "That is not necessary. There is a place for him to sleep in the mechanics yard. It will be useful to have another guard at night."

That explained the trucks and noises Amy had encountered over the cinder-block partition. "The other side of the property is rented out?"

"The business belongs to Khalid." Rasheed led the way downstairs. "But you need not be concerned. There is no entrance into this side of the property."

Amy would have inquired further, but an undulating cry split the air. It was followed by another more distant cry, then another. The city mosques issuing the third, or midafternoon, of the day's five calls to prayer.

The effect on her Afghan companions was electric. As one, Rasheed and Jamil unwrapped the light blanket, called a *patu*, that Afghan men wore draped around their necks to spread it out on the courtyard tiles. Amy's presence was forgotten or ignored, their flow of speech so rapid Amy caught only the occasional *"Allahu Akbar."* "God is great." They bowed, hands dropping to their knees. Then they were prostrate on the ground, foreheads pressed against the material that separated them from the ground.

Hamida had drifted away, perhaps to her own prayers.

After an awkward moment, Amy slipped unobtrusively back into the original salon and sank into a chair at the card table, feeling as though she'd been spying on something intensely personal.

These people have things to teach us about prayer and devotion. How many Christians stop everything to pray five times a day?

To Amy it was a gentle rebuke. For the first time since she'd stepped off the plane she pulled her thoughts from all that needed to be done. *I'm here, heavenly Father, as I've dreamed for so long. Thank you for bringing me this far, for keeping me safe from my own stupidity. Thank you for this unbelievable opportunity to do something new here. It's all so much bigger than I expected, and I'm not sure I know what I'm doing.*

Against the inside of Amy's eyelids, a mental image sprang to vivid Technicolor, then another. A terrified toddler lost on a crowded sidewalk. The passionate relief on a man's face as his son's arms closed around his neck. The indomitable grin of a grizzled old man propelling his legless body in a homemade wheelchair. The skeletal hand and hopeless slump of a woman in a burqa wailing *baksheesh*. The somberness of remembered grief turning a young man's eyes old. A black veil falling away to reveal a gap-toothed smile of unexpected sweetness. Even the furiously twisted faces of her own attackers, their anger birthed not of hate but of fear.

But even without really knowing them yet, I care about these people. You made them, and I know you love them. They've suffered so much. I want to show them your love.

"Miss Ameera?"

Amy opened her eyes. Jamil was standing in the doorway, patu back over his shoulder, a puzzled expression knitting his eyebrows together. "You wish to sleep?"

"I wasn't sleeping. I was praying."

Her assistant looked unconvinced as his glance touched her seated position. "Rasheed is sending me to the bazaar to purchase paint and cleaning supplies. He wishes to know your desires in regards to window glass."

"I'll be right there." Rising, Amy went out to embrace Afghanistan.

8

Steve raised the Motorola hand radio to his mouth. "Let's roll."

And right on schedule, though Steve was still adjusting the Velcro straps of his tactical vest as the reinforced Hummer that was the convoy's lead vehicle nosed out onto the street. Bones was at the wheel, Mac's huge shape emerging from the roof hatch to man the turret gun. Steve, Cougar, and Phil followed in the Suburban. Behind, Ian had the wheel of a double-cab pickup. Rick and Jamie McDuff brought up the tail in a Mitsubishi Pajero. A dozen troop hires were divided among the vehicles.

The convoy exited via the opposite checkpoint from where Steve and Cougar had entered. A few blocks later the streets turned abruptly to dirt. They were now out of the Wazir district and into neighboring Sherpur. This had been a modest mud-brick district when Steve was last in Kabul. No longer.

"Wow, what happened here? Barbie meets Arabian Nights? Vegas on Ecstasy?"

Phil's stunned analogy was appropriate enough. Mansions sprouted two, three, even four stories above the unpaved streets. A bewildering fusion of domes, peaks, cupolas, and turrets were trimmed in even more bewildering combinations of pinks, oranges, yellows, greens, and blues. Only concertina wire and the occasional row of blast barriers spoiled the effect of confectioners gone wild.

"The latest in Afghan architecture," Cougar said. "They call it Pakistani wedding cake. Or poppy palace, depending on the funding. The spoils of war. This little subdivision's been a media hot button since President Karzai's cabinet—all former muj commanders—bulldozed over the existing residents and parceled out the land among themselves."

The street ended in a cul-de-sac fronting the largest wedding cake. The Humvee curved left to park along a row of blast barriers. The Suburban pulled up behind it, pickup and Pajero following suit. Climbing out, Steve stared upward in consternation as Cougar hurried his way. This was what they'd been contracted to secure?

The villa was only three stories, its walls a mustard yellow. There modesty ended. There must have been a dozen roof levels in blue, orange, purple, and chocolate. The perimeter wall rose a prudent ten feet, but the architect wasn't thinking defensive depth because a second-story terrace ran right out over a canary yellow pedestrian gate. Just off the terrace, an onion-domed, four-story tower glittered blue glass and chrome.

"The guy's sure come up in the world since we were air-dropping MREs for him and his muj." Phil had emerged to join Steve. "And from the looks of it, he's rolled the dice on the Americans keeping the peace. Imagine an RPG on that."

It was certainly impressive enough to understand why Khalid had chosen to relocate. But the Wazir compound was at least built like a fortress. All that exposed glass made even Steve itch to loose his M4 on it.

The contractors threaded through blast barriers toward the front gate. The rest of their force fanned out in defensive positions around the vehicles. Afghan sentries behind the barricade and ISAF troops patrolling balconies and terraces had been alerted to their arrival, because they showed no alarm at the invasion of a couple dozen armed men.

"Like I said, the minister isn't interested in low profile," Cougar told Steve. "This is Khalid's palace, and he isn't going to budge out of here, so we'll just have to roll with it. You did say it was doable."

"Sure, and those blueprints you gave me didn't tell the whole story. Who in blazes did the advance assessment?"

Cougar's expression displayed guilt. "Are you saying you can't carry out the contract?"

"I'm not saying anything," Steve gritted, "except that if we're going to do this, I need to start hearing more than what Khalid wants or doesn't want."

The ISAF detail was a Dutch unit. Their commander met the Condor party just outside the yellow gate. The ISAF officer spoke excellent and furious English. "Now that you are here, I will remove my men within the hour. I will not expose them unnecessarily to further threat."

"What exactly is the threat?" Steve asked.

"Judge for yourself. Khalid wishes to speak to you immediately. He is waiting inside."

Inside the compound, the perimeter wall ran back twice the depth of surrounding lots, where land must have been at greater premium than money because the gaudy mansions were built to completely fill their surface area. Helicopter rotors thrusting out past the curve of the glass tower indicated what Khalid had done with the extra footage. His own heliport.

By contrast, a narrow drive between the house and right perimeter wall allowed room for no more than three or four vehicles. They wouldn't even be able to get the convoy vehicles inside, Steve took in with annoyance.

The Dutch officer led the way through an arched colonnade that supported the second-floor terrace and into a foyer so five-star Steve looked around for bellhops and a reception counter. To the right, an arch opened into the glass tower, padded with rugs, cushions, and bolster pillows that were the Afghan version of a sitting room. Across the foyer, a broad marble staircase rose to higher levels.

Steve paused as a white-robed attendant emerged through double doors. The room beyond was sparkling blue from tiled walls and columns to vaulted roof. An indoor swimming pool? Steam rose from at least three water surfaces. Not a pool but a private *hamam*, the bathhouse that was an integral part of every Muslim community.

Men were everywhere. Lounging in Afghan dress on cushions. Perched in Western suits on sofas and chairs. Laughing. Talking. Eating.

"Who are they?" Steve asked the ISAF officer. "And how do you process them for a decent security check?"

"We don't," the Dutch officer said flatly. "It seems it's an insult to have

Kafir infidel hands patting them down. Khalid's own people check over the lower ranks. But the VIPs no one can touch. I'm just waiting for one to show up rigged to blow. It's all we've managed to enforce a weapons check. At least for those we can see."

Steve, Cougar, and Phil followed the ISAF commander up the staircase. Steve had not yet seen armed presence indoors, but as they entered the second floor, two flaxen-haired, uniformed men moved aside at their commanding officer's signal.

"We've at least convinced Khalid to move his personal reception area back here, but he doesn't like the view." The Dutch officer stopped outside a door where two more ISAF troops stood watch. "Khalid's waiting for you. Be aware we're pulling out at 1700 hours on the dot. When you're ready to walk through security procedures, let one of my men know."

Cougar pushed open the door. The salon into which they stepped was big and airy, its decor an eclectic mix of Afghan cushions and rugs along with burnished leather sofas and chairs. But floor-to-ceiling windows explained Khalid's complaint. They overlooked a concrete slab supporting the gray green bulk of Khalid's Mi-8 helicopter. Beyond a rear perimeter wall, the neighborhood reverted back to mud-brick hovels and dirt alleys.

"Willie! Salaam aleykum." The former muj commander was as changed as his living conditions, at least thirty pounds heavier, hair and beard styled and suspiciously free of gray. An Italian suit replaced combat fatigues, and if the watch he wore wasn't a Rolex, it was an expensive facsimile. Steve received a whiff of pricey cologne as Khalid kissed him enthusiastically on each cheek. "I am so happy you are here. I feel safer already."

Then he took in Phil's presence and repeated the embrace. "Phil! I did not think to see you here. I had heard you were wounded and had left my country. I am glad to see the reports were exaggerated. And now you have come to defend my life again. Come, friends, let us converse."

As they moved into the room, Khalid waved at a tall, lean man who'd lingered silently at a distance during Khalid's effusive welcome. Steve recognized him as the translator who'd been their team's personal driver and liaison with Khalid and his men.

"You remember Ismail, my comrade and yours against the Taliban. He is now my deputy minister."

Steve had seen Ismail minimally since the liberation of Kabul. In fact, the last time had been only a couple of days later. He'd asked about the prisoner transfer. Ismail had assured Steve all had gone well. The next day their team had flown out to prepare for the Anaconda campaign.

The deputy minister followed Khalid's lead with hearty kisses and salaams. Unlike the former muj commander, Ismail still clung to traditional dress. But a richly embroidered chapan and turban were of expensive silk, curly dark hair and beard ruthlessly trimmed and oiled.

"So, my friends, what do you think of the new Afghanistan you have helped to create? Much change, no?" Khalid settled himself into a leather chair with a gingerness that betrayed he wasn't yet comfortable in the constriction of Western dress. "Allah has prospered us greatly since you and I fought jihad together."

"You certainly have a beautiful home here," Steve agreed evenly.

"Yes, I designed it myself. Just like America, no? There are those who criticize this beautiful neighborhood we have created. But all these houses were built from the private pockets of Afghans. It is our prayer that one day all Afghanistan will be beautiful like this and that all the poor too will have such houses." Khalid lifted his hands toward the ceiling. "But everything belongs to Allah, does it not? And is it not he who chooses who should be blessed and who should not? Allah gave this land to those who fought on his behalf."

For all the exigency of his earlier summons, Khalid seemed content to reminisce indefinitely. But his affability evaporated when Steve steered the conversation to the purpose for their presence. Steve soon understood why the ISAF commander had opted out. He didn't remember Khalid being so intransigent. Of course back then the MOI had been a ragtag warlord in desperate need of the firepower and money Steve could call in for him. Now he plainly considered the shoe to be on the other foot.

"No, no, no, no, no! My people must be free to see me. I must be free to come and go. You may post all the guards you wish, but I will not change my manner of living to satisfy barbarians who think to terrorize me. Nor offer insult to men who once risked their lives fighting at my side."

"It's just standard security protocol." Cougar was endlessly patient and cajoling, Phil silent.

Steve stood up abruptly. "I guess that leaves nothing to discuss. Khalid, we're prepared to do everything possible to minimize impact on your daily life without compromising security. But our contract is with the U.S. State Department, and we answer to them for the success of our mission. I will simply report that you've declined our protection. I'm sure they'll be happy to redirect those funds elsewhere."

Steve heard Cougar's muted noise of dismay and knew the millions CS stood to make—or lose—were passing through his mind. But Steve's hard gaze did not waver from Khalid's, and it was the former muj commander who at last flung up his hands.

"I am happy to make whatever arrangements you require. Is it not, after all, my life you seek to protect? Let us sit and reason together."

An hour later Steve walked out onto the second-story terrace that overlooked the front gate. Down the street the ISAF troop transport was disappearing around a corner. TCNs patrolled balconies and hallways. Khalid's own guards had been relegated to outer perimeter lookout duty. Cougar, Bones, and Ian had taken the convoy back to the team house to prepare for tomorrow morning's embassy expedition.

On the lower floor, a departing tribal delegation had thinned out the crowd. The European diplomats with their entourage were now holed up with Khalid. Mac and Rick had peeled off two Guatemalans, both former Kaibil officers, feared elite unit of that country's past military regimes, to form a provisional PRS detail. Phil and McDuff were sorting through comm and camera gear.

From the cover of a marble column, Steve turned slowly to examine each crazy curve, angle, and jutting roof surface Khalid had dreamed up to complicate his job. Then he began the same painstaking inspection of the panorama outside the perimeter walls.

Beyond those Crayola box mansions, visibility was so poor Steve could barely make out the city's encircling mountains. The dust he remembered well but not this oily gray haze so thick Steve could taste diesel in his mouth. A low rumble beneath his feet gave away the biggest culprit, the private generators with which anyone who could afford it supplemented Kabul's uncertain electricity.

From somewhere a whiff of hot oil and garlic and sizzling meat over-powered the diesel. The kitchens were working on the evening feast. Elsewhere servants were readying an upstairs suite for CS headquarters. No one had ever faulted an Afghan for hospitality, and once he'd capitulated, the minister had been effusive in his accommodation.

We can do this.

After all, despite Steve's frustration on basic principle, every statistic showed that Kabul was relatively safe. Sure, there was the occasional IED or suicide bomber like this morning. Random street crime and kidnappings were on the rise. But none of the constant insurgent attacks or rocket barrages they'd faced in Iraq.

Steve zoomed in on a scurrying movement below in the cul-de-sac. Animal or human? The cul-de-sac wasn't a solid one. The poppy palaces had gone up haphazardly on their parceled lots so that compound walls didn't actually adjoin, leaving a narrow access on either side of Khalid's property leading off into the mud-brick squalor beyond. Construction debris abandoned in that no-man's-land blocked Steve's scrutiny. Something else he was going to change.

The scurrying movement ducked behind a blast barrier. A moment later Steve spotted it farther down the row. His hand went to the M4, then dropped as a small, dark head poked cautiously above the concrete. Another flurry of movement, and now Steve had a clear view. A dirty, ragged child was crouched down outside the barriers, scooting to evade the Afghan sentries standing guard outside the perimeter wall.

The child had something in his hands, and again Steve tensed. A grenade? Insurgents had used children to carry out attacks. But as the child scribbled across the concrete with a black marker, he relaxed. Steve recognized the diagonal line. Then a curve with a dot underneath. *A* and *B* in Dari script. A dare from other kids?

The child glanced up to meet Steve's gaze, and a grin lit thin features to a flash of white. He cupped hands in the unmistakable gesture of baksheesh. Despite the grime, the kid was cute enough Steve was tempted to dig into his pocket. But he hardened his heart. Giving to a street kid was like tossing sugar to a single ant. If Steve dropped an afghani, the local currency, into those hands, there'd be a hundred such kids here tomorrow. So he shook his head firmly and stepped out of sight of that pleading gaze.

"You, get away from there, you thieving son of a dog!" The shout came from one of Khalid's militia doing sentry duty at the front gate.

The child's grin froze. Scrabbling away on all fours, he got to his feet and ran.

The sentry raised his AK-47. A terrified scream rose above the staccato of gunfire.

"Stop it!" Steve didn't waste time on the stairs but swung over the parapet, dropping lightly to the ground. His shouted command had stopped the shooting. Steve refrained from snatching the AK-47 and slapping it across the guard's face only because he'd glimpsed the child race sobbing but unhurt into the gap between compounds. "Are you crazy? You just fired on an unarmed child."

"This area is prohibited to loiterers. There are signs." Sure enough, the concrete barriers bore graceful Dari script the kid probably couldn't read any more than Steve. "I was not shooting to hit, only at the ground. Our orders come from the minister himself. If we do not do this, such delinquents will be everywhere like the thieving rats they are."

"And if a bullet ricochets and hits the child? You do not shoot again unless you are being shot at."

"But the minister—"

"I will deal with the minister." Steve was so furious he waited a full five minutes before speaking to another human being. This was the side of Afghanistan he'd let himself forget, the side he'd come to hate. The casual cruelty despite all that surface hospitality that was almost a reflex, as though a generation or perhaps even centuries of incessant aggression had hardened these people against anything but their own survival and perhaps that of their closest family.

Steve banished a lingering image of those tearful, frightened childish features. You didn't have to like your principal or even approve of his lifestyle. You simply did the job you were paid for. And Kabul promised to be an easier gig than Basra.

Meanwhile, you didn't get personally involved. It wasn't just that saving these people from themselves was a hopeless job. As far as Steve was concerned, Afghanistan just plain didn't deserve to be saved.

The American was an easy shot, the sentries too apathetic to bother clearing out the rubble that allowed him to inch close. He'd recognized the American soldier and his companion among the infidel mercenaries. But then they all looked alike, these foreigners with the merciless brawn and stride of warriors even when they did not wear the clothing. Just like those in the prison camp. He didn't worry that he might be recognized in turn. In his gaunt frame and hollowed eyes remained no vestige of the soft-skinned, well-fed student he'd been.

Still, even if he'd had a weapon, he wouldn't have raised it. There'd been a time when he would have gladly. But he'd had too long to think, too long to determine who were the true infidels whose actions, if not words, were a blasphemy against Allah. And invaders though they were, these foreigners brought benefit to his people. As long as they were willing to pave roads and build schools and feed the hungry, let the infidels remain.

The child hadn't finished his task before being frightened off. For which he could also thank the guards, since he lacked the promised payment. He settled himself to wait. Evening darkened to full night, stars and moon dimmed by the haze of smog, the only lights twinkling above high walls where diesel generators labored, so at street level the guards across the cul-de-sac were shifting shadows against darkness.

Patience had given way to restiveness, then apprehension, before the pedestrian gate creaked open. An entire party, black silhouettes against light spilling through the open gate, moved down the cul-de-sac toward parked vehicles. One detached itself to saunter toward no-man's-land, a moving red glow marking its progress. A man out for an evening stroll, lit cigarette in hand.

He waited until the red glow moved close to announce softly, "I am here."

The scent of cigarette smoke grew stronger. The red glow disappeared as the man cupped a hand to draw on his cigarette. Then a voice spoke quietly. "You were to have drawn the sign on this wall. Children playing—"

"I did not think you could see it. The opportunity arose—"

"Obedience is as essential as success." A rustle marked a folded piece of paper dropping beside his prone body. "Your instructions are there. You will find what you need waiting at the marked location. I will contact you when preparations are ready. And do not ever return to this place."

The man took another drag on his cigarette, then pivoted around to saunter back out into the cul-de-sac. He paused to commend the sentries as they sprang to open the gate. "You are performing your duties of protection most impressively. Continue on."

9

Now to fill the ark—if I can ever get myself legally in this country.

Two more days had passed since Amy's arrival in Kabul before Rasheed informed Amy that the Ministry of Interior was again processing paperwork. Not that the intervening time had been wasted. From a second-story window overlooking the roofed entrance, Amy surveyed her new kingdom with a glow of accomplishment. Cantankerous misogynist Rasheed might be, but the man got things done.

If Amy's suggestion of women workers had never materialized, a wave of the chowkidar's hand had produced an army of laborers to clean, paint, and carry out debris. The front courtyard was now free of construction materials, the tiles and fountain patched. Grass would take until spring. But along the perimeter wall, workers were replacing stumps with a row of apple and cherry seedlings.

Others were up on scaffolding replacing windows. Glass was on a waiting list in the city's reconstruction boom, but Rasheed had scrounged a reasonable substitute. Amy rapped on the transparent plastic sheeting in front of her. She had insisted on one other modification that left Rasheed shaking his head. A double panel of plastic sheeting now rose above the inner courtyard's rear wall, allowing sunlight to pass through but not prying eyes. No woman inhabiting that inner sanctum was going to be asked to cover up ever.

Best of all, Rasheed had approached Amy with keys to the left half of the main wing. "No, no, the minister is not asking for greater rent. He is pleased to have tenants dedicated to helping the people of Afghanistan. It is *zakat*, charity, the third pillar of Islam."

Her new holdings on the main wing's second floor included two living suites with functioning bathrooms and several smaller rooms. The one where Amy stood was now an office, Rasheed conjuring up desks and a filing cabinet. Below her off the entry hall were two more salons divided by a wooden partition that could be folded to create one large room. French doors at the far end revealed what lay beyond that cinder-block partition Jamil had hopped—a vegetable garden, an outdoor bread oven, and a row of rooms that were Rasheed's housing.

Amy's new keys didn't encompass the French doors, though she wouldn't in any case intrude on the chowkidar's privacy. Hamida moved back and forth to clean and serve meals through a door under the stairs in the inner courtyard.

Nor since that first day had Rasheed shown Amy less than respect. *Maybe I didn't need to hire Jamil after all.* Though if the younger Afghan hadn't proved necessary as a buffer between Amy and the chowkidar, he'd shown himself amply useful, following silently on Amy's heels to translate for Hamida or a workman, shouldering debris, or grabbing a paintbrush without prompting when Amy didn't need him.

Amy answered the shrill of a phone from her bag. "Jamil?"

"Rasheed says that it is time to go to the Ministry. Your vehicle is ready."

"I'll be right down." The small cell phone Amy tucked back into her bag wasn't Bruce's sat phone but a more economical local phone Rasheed had obtained. She'd planned to purchase phones as well for Jamil and Rasheed to simplify communication. But Rasheed had his own, and if Jamil had arrived with few other possessions, he'd produced a phone from the baggy folds of his tunic.

Amy checked that passport and MOI card were in her bag, then adjusted her headscarf in a decorative mirror. Dressing one's best to deal with local bureaucracy signaled respect, not ostentation, and she'd chosen the nicest of her India outfits, a soft green-blue silk embroidered with stylized flower patterns in emerald, lilac, sapphire, and ruby red glass beads and sequins. Long amethyst earrings and matching sandals completed the outfit.

Like an Arabian Nights princess. Amy approved her reflection, then spoiled the effect by wrinkling her nose as the scarf slipped from her hair. Tightening it ruthlessly, she scooped up her bag and hurried downstairs.

"Salaam aleykum, Wajid," Amy greeted the elderly guard as he emerged from his shack. Stepping through the gate, she stopped in surprise. Rasheed wasn't waiting at the curb with his ancient Russian jeep. Instead Jamil stood next to a yellow and white Toyota Corolla.

Amy had last glimpsed her assistant painting balcony railings, a streak of black down one cheek and two more splotching the tattered "pajamas" in which he'd arrived. But Jamil had found time to visit the bazaar with his salary advance, because he was now resplendent in sky blue shalwar kameez topped with a vest and matching cap stiff with rich embroidery. He'd bathed, too, his hair and beard still damp from washing.

Wow! Amy tamped down the appreciative word that rose to her mind. Commenting on male appearance was undoubtedly some major cultural faux pas. Instead she asked, "Where's Rasheed? And whose car is this?"

"Rasheed ordered me to drive you to the Ministry of Interior. This vehicle belongs to his cousin who runs a taxi service in the city. But it is for sale."

A hint? Well, it certainly looked more comfortable than the broken-springed ride that had been taking Amy back and forth from her guest-house. As Jamil held the door open, Amy slid into the backseat. "I didn't know you could drive. This is a nice surprise."

"It has been a long time, but Rasheed tested me yesterday in this vehicle to ensure your safety in my hands."

Jamil kept his eyes averted as he climbed into the driver's seat. Amy had read up on local customs enough to understand the reasoning. Afghan women did not raise their gaze to men, especially those not of their own family, while a man staring at a woman was at minimum insulting. As a foreign woman alone, Amy recognized that Jamil's air of what she could only term polite invisibility was undoubtedly for the best. Still, it went against the grain for Amy to treat another human being as little more than a piece of office equipment.

"To the MOI then."

As Jamil maneuvered the car through heavy morning traffic, he seemed competent enough. It was with dismay that Amy recognized the army green wall and concertina wire of the MOI compound ahead. Bombing debris had been cleared away, the street again crowded with market stalls and pedestrians. Concrete barriers now closed off the entire block from vehicle traffic.

But that bomber was a pedestrian.

Amy had waited until after lunch in hope that lines would have dwindled. But by the time Jamil found parking several blocks away, tossing a coin to a street urchin to guard the sedan, and they walked back to the MOI entrance, a multitude waiting to get inside still stretched far down the block. Amy forced herself not to glance across the street where a burned-out taxi had inexplicably not yet been removed.

Suicide bombers like lightning never strike the same place twice.

The oft-repeated truism seemed to Amy more wishful thinking than scientific fact, and she was thankful when the line finally crept up to the entrance. While security guards patted Jamil down, Amy stepped behind a canvas screen. The female guard offered a cursory body search, then peered into Amy's shoulder bag. Amy didn't dare protest when the guard confiscated a pack of chewing gum, tucking it into her utility vest before waving Amy through.

Inside, the compound held several buildings. Amy waited while Jamil made inquiries, then followed him down a hallway into a large room that was crammed with people. Amy trod forward until she reached a desk.

Picking up her U.S. passport, the immigration officer switched to reasonable English. "Please open to the correct visa page."

And there progress stalled.

"I *know* it's been more than forty-eight hours. But the office was closed because of the bombing. I couldn't get the card stamped. No, please! I've already been in this line more than an hour. There has to be *something* we can do! What about all the others who've arrived in these last two days?"

Jamil's urgent plucking at her sleeve as much as the official's peremptory gesture moved Amy reluctantly to a huddle of people standing against a wall. Only then did she realize the immigration officer's glare wasn't only because of her paperwork snafu. Yanking her headscarf back over her hair, Amy tightened the ends around her shoulders.

Did the guy expect a bribe? Was she simply to stand here the rest of the day? Amy's desperate glance landed on a shaved head and stocky frame in safari clothing just entering the room. The older of the contractors who'd rescued Amy was accompanied by an Afghan man Amy recognized vaguely as having been with the two men at the airport. They walked straight through a door beyond the desks.

Almost immediately they reappeared, heading back toward the exit. Amy could see a sheaf of passports in the contractor's hand. Amy looked around for Jamil. He had his back to Amy, cell phone to his ear. Detaching herself from the wall, Amy threaded swiftly through the throng. The two men had reached the hall before she caught up. "Cougar?"

The man turned. "Why, it's Amy. What are you doing here?"

"I've been trying to get my MOI card. Thanks to that bombing, I'm past the forty-eight hours, so they're saying I'm out of luck. Is—uh, Steve here to do his?"

"And waste time in all this? Whoever's giving you advice, I hope they told you it's not necessary to come down in person. Just send in your passport and photo with your fixer." Cougar's nod indicated the Afghan beside him as he waggled the passports in his hand. "He'll settle the overdue issue too, though it may cost you a bit extra." Then he was gone down the hall.

And if you have no fixer? Amy wanted to wail after him.

Furtive stares alerted her she'd lost her head covering again.

"Here, honey, let me show you how to do that so it won't fall off." The woman who reached up to shake Amy's headscarf loose around her face was several inches shorter than Amy and plump. Graying brunette wisps escaped a flowered cotton scarf. Under a matching tunic, she wore jeans.

"The trick is heavier material. These synthetics just slide right off." A few deft tugs and tucks secured Amy's scarf. "I'm guessing you're new in town. Let me introduce myself. Debby Martini, New York."

"Oh, thank you, I've been fighting with that ever since I got here three days ago." Amy could have hugged the American woman—or burst into tears on her shoulder. "I'm Amy Mallory, Miami. I'm country manager for New Hope Foundation, an NGO looking to set up projects for women and children at risk here in Kabul. That is, if I can ever get myself legally registered." She held up passport and MOI card. "Are you here for this too?"

"Oh no, I've been down the hall trying to cut some red tape for a project of my own. Unsuccessfully, I might add. But you shouldn't be fighting with that. Where's your fixer?"

"I didn't even know there was such a profession. Is that why people keep jumping to the head of the line? That doesn't seem a very fair system."

"Fair or not, it's the only way you'll get anything done. Everything here runs on having the right contacts—or at least being able to pay for them. If I can't cut my own red tape, I can certainly help with yours. My fixer can have you in and out in no time. Najibullah?"

Only then did Amy realize a tall Afghan in Western dress lingering nearby was with Debby. The New Yorker plucked passport and MOI card from Amy's hand with as little hesitation as she'd adjusted Amy's head covering.

Within minutes, Najibullah was waving them in front of an immigration official.

Before Amy could follow Debby's fixer through the door, Jamil intercepted her, narrow features frantic. "Miss Ameera, I turned to look for you, and you had disappeared. I was afraid I had lost you again—"

"I know. I'm sorry," Amy broke in. "I should have told you where I was going."

Then they stepped into a much less crowded room where two officials stamped and signed cards at a rapid pace. Najibullah positioned Amy against a wall while a clerk snapped a digital camera. In five minutes, she had her card complete with photo and stamp.

"I can't thank you enough," Amy told Debby fervently. "I just wish there was something I could do to return your kindness. I'm so sorry your own paperwork wasn't successful. Do you work with an NGO here in Kabul?"

"I'm heading back stateside in a few days. I've been in town the last couple of months dealing with a project over at the women's prison. Which is what I'm doing here. MOI oversees the police and the local prisons."

"The women's prison? Then you're in law enforcement?"

Debby chuckled. "Back home I run a beauty salon. But I've got a friend who did a stint here after liberation as consultant for the new Ministry of Women. When I came over to visit, she took me to the women's jail." She shuddered. "It was like going back to the Middle Ages. A bunch of women in rags huddled in what was basically a dungeon. No heat. No sanitation. No medical care. Whatever food the prison guards didn't siphon off for their own families."

The two women started walking down the hall, the male escorts at their heels.

"When I got home, I raised enough money to come back and paint, clean some rooms, and add real bathrooms. We bought space heaters and blankets, set up a fund with a local NGO to get food and milk for the kids into the jail. We even brought in some pedal sewing machines and cloth so the prisoners could make clothes for themselves and learn a trade. Then I headed home, thinking I'd solved at least one of Afghanistan's problems."

"I remember something about that," Amy said. "Wasn't there some CNN special on the place?"

"Oh yes, there was a lot of interest, but it didn't last. There's always a fresh news story. Anyway, a few months ago, I was able to come back. I thought maybe we could do a similar project in another city.

"Instead, I found the jail we'd fixed up here totally trashed. There were three times as many prisoners crowded into a couple of unfinished rooms. So I've spent the last two months fixing the place back up. This time no improvements that can be physically carried off. And at least now some other NGOs are getting involved in things like classes for the children."

The story was sounding depressingly familiar to Amy. "I'm surprised Kabul even has a women's prison. As restricted as women are here, I wouldn't think they'd have the chance to get into any real criminal activity. Is that why the prison's grown so much—because women have more freedom of movement than under the Taliban?"

Debby stopped dead in her tracks to stare at Amy. "You really don't know, do you?"

10

Amy and her new companion had reached the MOI compound's front entrance.

Debby eyed Amy. "Didn't you say you were setting up projects for women and children at risk? I'm heading over to the jail right now. Why don't you come with me and take a look to see what you think of the possibilities?"

Female criminals were not on any project list Amy had remotely considered for New Hope. On the other hand, Debby had been enormously helpful, and thanks to her kindness, Amy was freed from those endless lines. "Well, I suppose I could. But I've got my driver with me and a car parked down the street."

"Bring him along. That way you can leave any time you're bored." Debby turned to address Jamil. "Do you know the Welayat, the prison?"

He hunched his thin shoulders. "Everyone knows the Welayat."

"Then how about I meet you there in a half hour? The women's section is around back. Look for a green door. Here's my card with cell phone number if you can't find me."

Feeling as though she'd been caught up by a benevolent whirlwind, Amy took the card. Out on the street, Debby bustled away, Najibullah lengthening his strides after her.

Amy followed Jamil in the opposite direction to the Corolla. Was she imagining that her assistant seemed even more somber and silent than usual?

Their underage guard was still on duty, the vehicle intact. Amy dug out another coin as reward.

Jamil was pulling out into traffic when he spoke up. "I must beg your forgiveness, Miss Ameera. I have failed you. Rasheed will be angry."

"For what?" Amy demanded, puzzled.

"Your papers. The foreign woman is right. I have been gone too long from this city. I do not have the proper contacts or knowledge to be an adequate assistant to you."

"That isn't true. I didn't hire you for this fixer job," Amy responded vehemently. "You've done a wonderful job translating for me and now driving and everything else. I'll make sure Rasheed knows that too. And if we really do need someone to deal with red tape, we'll just have to see about hiring someone."

Jamil nodded, but his expression lightened fractionally. His knowledge of city layout was at least adequate because he showed no hesitation in following Debby's directions. The Welayat proved to be another tall wall topped with concertina wire, though the compound behind this one was much larger, covering several city blocks. Amy spotted the green door as Jamil turned into an unpaved parking lot.

Debby and Najibullah emerged from a white Land Cruiser lettered *USAID* across the door panels. Only as the Corolla pulled into the adjoining dirt patch did Amy realize they weren't alone. Two other women were climbing down from the SUV. One was a petite Asian in pantsuit and high heels, her headscarf the scantiest Amy had seen in Afghanistan.

"I'm so glad you could make it," Debby greeted Amy cheerfully. "This is Alisha Chan with USAID." Which explained the Land Cruiser. "She's been spearheading a children's project at the women's prison. Alisha, this is Amy."

Debby gestured toward the second newcomer. "And this is Soraya from right here in Kabul. She'll be translating for us."

The guidebook Amy had perused on the plane covered Afghanistan's ethnic tapestry. The northern Uzbeks and Tajiks were as fair as many Europeans. Hazaras, an often persecuted minority group, were descendants of Genghis Khan's invading Mongolian hordes. Pashtuns, Afghanistan's largest ethnic group, were related to the Pakistanis. Somewhere in her later thirties or forties, Soraya looked Pashtun. Dark, curly hair escaping under her scarf. Smooth, olive features with a high-bridged nose. Elongated dark eyes with impossibly long lashes. Her chapan, an ankle-length buttoned-up robe, looked like real silk, and she carried herself with authority Amy had not yet seen in an Afghan woman.

"I am pleased to meet you," Soraya murmured, her gaze cool as she leaned forward to kiss Amy—left, right, left—as though rebuking these foreigners for the paucity of their welcome.

"Soraya just finished her master's in defense law at Kabul University," Debby announced. "She was one of only three women. Finally some new women's lawyers here."

"But I will not work as a lawyer," Soraya stated.

Debby stared at her in dismay. "Why not?"

Soraya's shoulders rose and fell. "The Women's Ministry offers perhaps fifty euros a month. Far less than a translator. My family is accustomed to my earning a higher wage. And there is no other call in Kabul for women lawyers."

"Isn't that the way it always is," Debby muttered. "We invest money on training, and the graduates still all end up working for NGOs because they're the only ones who can afford a decent wage."

Catching a flash in Soraya's dark eyes, Amy spoke up quickly. "You speak very good English, Soraya."

Soraya turned an unreadable gaze on Amy. "Yes, I studied in the university before the Taliban came. And I have been working for foreign companies since they left. I speak Dari and Urdu and French as well as Pashto and English."

Which explained the proud lift of the head and air of authority. Afghanistan's small professional class lived on a different planet from its illiterate peasant majority.

"In time things will change," Alisha Chan said. "Afghan women will be able to hire their own lawyers. Meanwhile, I'm thankful you've been available to me these last months."

Soraya said nothing as Debby steered their party across a plank foot-bridge laid over a trench to the green door.

Amy looked back along the tall wall, any number of buildings visible above the concertina wire. "All this is a woman's prison?"

"Thank goodness, no," Debby said quickly. "The Welayat includes a good part of the judicial system—courts, legal offices, administration, and the men's prison. We're just this wing."

Debby knocked on the green door. It swung open, a small, round woman, head wrapped in a bright red shawl, peering out. Suspicious eyes and hard expression dissolved to a smile at the sight of her visitors.

"Geeti, so nice to see you again," Debby effused. To Amy, she added, "Geeti is the women's warden."

The warden led her visitors down a dark corridor and through another metal door. As they emerged back into daylight, Debby demanded, "What happened to the electricity? It was working the other day."

"The lighting tubes are burned out," Soraya translated Geeti's indifferent shrug. "They have been switching them from other rooms, but now there are no more. Besides, the electricity only comes a few hours a day."

The women's prison was laid out like the New Hope compound, if on a much bigger scale, three wings around a central courtyard. Green paint was peeling and dirty, but walls and roof tiles had been recently patched.

"That wing belongs to the guards," Debby pointed out as they followed Geeti across the courtyard. "That one's offices. The prisoners are over here."

Amy hadn't needed that final identification. All windows had shutters and bars, but where Debby gestured, the bars were newly painted and set solidly in fresh concrete. The courtyard was empty, but behind those bars, silent, draped shapes stood watching the newcomers. Amy spotted a small, pale face pressed up to one window. At Geeti's irate shout, the face abruptly disappeared.

"Why don't we see the children first? That's Alisha's USAID project," Debby explained to Amy. Then her glance moved past Amy, and she frowned. "Great. What's he doing here?"

Najibullah had stayed outside with the vehicles, but Jamil had followed on Amy's heels as automatically and noiselessly as always. Her shadow, Amy was beginning to think of him.

"I should have warned you to leave him outside. Male visitors are hardly appropriate in here."

"Oh, nonsense." Alisha waved a dismissive hand. "I bring male reporters and State Department personnel through here all the time. The prison officials have never said anything."

"Yeah, well, I'll bet they never asked the women. With everything else, the last thing they should have to endure is a bunch of men traipsing through staring at them. Anyway, no big deal." Debby turned to Jamil. "You can stay with the kids while we visit the women."

They'd reached the other side of the courtyard. Geeti lifted a heavy key ring from her waist to unlock a metal door. Another unlit corridor led to a large room that was bright and cheerful, daylight streaming through open shutters to reflect from daffodil yellow walls, green matting alleviating the chill of concrete underfoot. A curious decorative pattern to shoulder height proved on closer examination to be the dirty prints of myriad small hands.

On the matting, several dozen children sat cross-legged, chanting as an elderly Afghan woman tapped a series of swirls and dots on a blackboard. The Dari alphabet. One small body clad in a pale pink tunic stood against the far wall, hands clasped behind her back. Amy recognized the face at the window.

"These are the school-age children," Alisha explained. "We offer a kinder-level class in the mornings with a locally hired teacher. They're all pretty well on that level, regardless of age."

Amy had already noted the students' wide age span from preschool up through eleven or twelve. "So how many kids are in the jail altogether?"

"About seventy or eighty. Almost as many as the women prisoners. Though only half are old enough for classes."

The single teacher had maintained admirable control of such a large class—until the children spotted their visitors. They surrounded the newcomers, hugging, patting, tugging. The small girl from the window chose this moment to overcome bashfulness, rushing forward to throw her arms around Amy. There was time for a hug before the teacher scolded and shooed the children away. The girl in the pink tunic burst into tears, holding out her arms to Amy as she was led away.

"Sorry about that," Alisha said. "They do that with any visitors. Inexperienced aid workers are always amazed the kids seem so loving. In reality, it's not a good sign. An emotionally healthy child doesn't offer affection to random strangers. That's what parents are for. Most of these kids get so little emotional support; they crave human touch from anyone."

The small girl's wails wrung Amy's heart. The destroying of a childhood was perhaps the worst evil for which a place like this had to answer. Still, the kids looked better fed than the waifs Amy had seen begging on street corners and probably lived better than a good percentage of Kabul's poor. Amy had been bracing herself for much worse and was beginning to wonder why Debby had dragged her here. However much sympathy she felt, New Hope wasn't in the market for a project another NGO was clearly doing well.

Alisha stepped away to talk with the children's teacher, Soraya at her side to translate.

Debby's own Dari was enough to manage a simple exchange with Geeti. Then she beckoned to Amy. "While they're busy, let me introduce you to some of the prisoners. Oh, and tell that driver of yours to stay here. We'll be back soon."

Jamil rested his shoulders against a wall as Amy followed Debby. The room into which Geeti led next was as gloomy as the schoolroom had been cheerful. It took Amy a moment to puzzle out that this wasn't due to the furnishings. The walls were painted the same hand-printed yellow. Green matting was lined neatly with *tushaks*, the flat cushions Afghans used for both sofa and bed. Open shutters let in a dusty breeze, the window bars laying a striped pattern of light and dark across the floor.

Gloom came from mounds of cloth huddled silently against the wall on each tushak. Only when a mound stirred, a head turning to reveal eyes glittering above a tightly drawn scarf, did Amy recognize that each mound was a woman. A hook above each cushion held a bag. The prisoners' personal belongings.

Gloom came too from the smell. A depressing stench of unwashed bodies and urine and illness. Even more, of hopelessness and despair. Amy was beginning to understand Debby's fervor. Even the worst criminal deserved better than this.

"So what are they all in for?"

A few women raised their heads and turned their eyes to the visitors. Others hadn't moved. The closest to Amy clutched a tight-wrapped bundle, its surface rising and falling in gentle rhythm. A sleeping child.

"*Zina*, mostly. That means unlawful sexual contact."

"Prostitution, you mean?"

"Actually, it could mean anything from adultery to simply sitting down next to a man unrelated by blood. Or on the flip side, defying male authority, especially in connection to marriage. Take Meetra here, for instance."

Lowering to a crouch beside the woman with the sleeping bundle, Debby dug into a large handbag and produced a handful of Baggies filled with dried fruits. She offered one first to Geeti, who snatched it, before turning to the prisoner. "Salaam aleykum."

"At fourteen Meetra was married off to her cousin in Pakistan. She had a son and was pregnant with her daughter when a neighbor kidnapped her and sold her over the border to an Afghan. She's never seen her son since. Her new husband abused her. When the baby was two, he got so enraged, he beat the little girl to death. Meetra was brave—or heart-broken—enough to go to the authorities. The man ended up going to prison for murder. But Meetra was handed a six-year sentence for adultery, even though she was a kidnap victim. By then she was pregnant again. Her son was born here in the prison. The man who killed her daughter has already paid his fine and will be out before she is."

Meetra had shown no reaction to Debby's gift, so the New Yorker laid the dried fruit beside the woman. Her eyes, all Amy could see above a shawl pulled across her face, were beautiful, dark and long-lashed, but they held a blankness that didn't see the dirty yellow of the wall in front of them.

"Then there's Farah."

Unlike her neighbor, Farah had straightened up immediately at the intrusion of visitors. Her scarf hung free to reveal a fair-skinned teenager with blue green eyes and a mass of brown curls spilling over her shoulders as she snagged Debby's offering.

"Salaam aleykum, Farah." Debby looked over her shoulder to Amy.

"They get enough food of sorts these days, but I still like to bring them a treat. Something they can eat before the guards walk off with it."

The teenager munched the fruit as Debby continued. "Farah was thirteen when her guardian sold her off to a sixty-year-old neighbor in settlement for a gambling debt. The man had already beaten one of his other wives to death. She's got some real spunk, so she pilfered a few afghanis for bus fare, dressed as a boy, and almost made it to Iran before she was found out. She's been in here almost three years.

"Zaira didn't have the gumption to run away when her husband and his mother and sisters beat her, so she did what many women here do to escape. She set herself on fire with kerosene."

Zaira's scarf slipped as she reached for her treat, and Amy saw that her face was a mass of burn tissue.

"When she survived, she was arrested for defacing her husband's property—herself. As for Aryana over there—"

Most of the women were now roused, hands outstretched. But not even Debby's gentle greeting raised the head of an olive-skinned Pashtun girl with a toddler curled up on her lap.

"Aryana was married off to a distant cousin at fourteen. The guy seems to have been pretty decent from what she says. But when her son was two months old, her husband died and her brothers-in-law accused her of poisoning him. No autopsy and no trial. But some judge wrote up a guilty verdict, and she was arrested for murder. Aryana's husband was the oldest brother, so there may have been some family inheritance at stake.

"Najeeda's mother-in-law started passing her around for money. When she got pregnant, the husband couldn't be sure whose child it was, so he beat her badly. When she still didn't lose the baby, he accused her of adultery. She's been here almost seven years. Her six-year-old son is in here with her. She'll be twenty this summer."

Najeeda would have been pretty, except that a broken nose had healed crooked and all but a few teeth were missing.

The kindergarten class must have finished, because just then the door banged open. As a dozen children rushed in, the room came to life. A small, thin boy climbed onto Najeeda's lap, and she hugged him tight, murmuring against his hair.

"Theoretically, the boys have to leave the women's prison when they turn six, the girls when they turn twelve, but if they have no place to go, even the hard-nosed prison officials haven't yet tossed them out. Now Roya is probably the only woman who'd be considered a criminal back home. Ironically, here no one figures she should be in prison. She's only in as a gesture to the Americans."

Perhaps what appalled Amy most of that horrible biographical litany was the youth of the prisoners. Most were far younger than Amy. The Pashtun woman snatching the last bag from Debby's hand was an exception. Thin, stooped, with work-worn features, she might be anywhere from forty to eighty. Probably closer to forty, Amy amended, considering that the life expectancy for women here wasn't much beyond that.

"Roya was caught scraping opium gum in the poppy fields. On her husband's orders, of course. Around here, that's little more than weeding potatoes. But they're supposed to be getting tough on drugs, and since the big landlords who actually own the poppy fields are off-limits, they grabbed a bunch of peasant labor. Roya hoped her husband would buy her freedom. But just last week she found out he's divorced her and married a sixteen-year-old cousin of theirs. It was cheaper. Her two younger daughters live here with her."

By the time Amy and Debby reached the end of the room, Amy could no longer look at one more silent mound or beseeching hand. Stepping thankfully into the corridor, she drew in a shuddering breath. It wasn't that Amy hadn't read the reports, even known of such happenings Debby had been describing. But putting dry statistics to those hopeless faces and despairing eyes was worse than anything she'd encountered since arriving in Kabul.

"Debby, these stories are terrible! My grandfather was Cuban and spent years in prison, his crime being an outspoken Baptist pastor in Havana. I used to think nothing could sink any lower than Castro. But these women have suffered even worse outside of prison than they are in there."

"It's how too many Afghan women live. Human rights studies estimate upwards of 70 percent suffer some kind of abuse, a lot of it from their own families or in-laws. Back when I first came, journalists and film crews were always coming in here to collect the prisoners' stories. We all figured

95

the notoriety alone would push the new regime at least into stopping this kind of arrest."

Debby grimaced. "Now there are four times as many prisoners, plus kids stacked in here like sardines. I was over at MOI this morning to see about opening another wing. So far, it's no go. Still, for a country this size, I used to wonder why so few in jail. I mean, eighty women out of an entire city? Then I learned these were the lucky ones. Most women in their circumstances don't end up in jail. They just disappear. Or prove more successful than Zaira in ending it themselves."

"So maybe, for all the injustice of it," Amy said slowly, "they're better off in here than back home. Those kids have more opportunity with what you're doing than they would on the streets."

"Exactly. Which is why I wanted to bring you here." Debby faced Amy, determination on her round face. "Take Farah. She's still only sixteen years old. When she gets out, if she goes home, she'll be handed over to that sixty-year-old neighbor. And Aryana. No one will allow an accused murderer into the house. Not to mention, I wouldn't give an ice cube in the Sahara for that little boy if he goes home to claim his daddy's piece of the pie. And Roya. No one's going to keep an elderly field-worker in jail forever. Especially with two kids to feed. But now she's divorced, so where can she go?"

"And—?" Amy asked.

"I've been talking to every NGO I know about some kind of half-way shelter for these women when their sentence is up so they aren't forced to go back to the homes that abused them. Except the only thing my pushing's done is make the prison administration agree the place is overcrowded. So they've ordered a bunch released, including the three I mentioned. They'll be out next week."

"What about Alisha and her program?"

"Their funding is tapped out. Besides, USAID is a State Department program, and it's not PC to interfere, however deservedly, with local culture or family structure."

Amy had listened with half-incredulous dismay, but Debby's last statement roused her ire. "I am so sick of politically correct. What about right and wrong? It's bad enough there are judges who'd put these women in here—"

Amy stopped as Alisha and Soraya emerged with the children's teacher into the hall. Geeti had been listening to Amy and Debby with blank incomprehension, but now she broke into voluble speech as she waved the other women over.

Debby turned back to Amy. "We've got to discuss some accounting issues before I turn over this project. Are you in a huge hurry? It'll just be a few minutes."

"No problem. I'll wait with my driver in the schoolroom."

11

Not all the children had returned to their mothers; at least a dozen remained in the schoolroom when Amy entered. They sat in a circle on the floor, playing duck, duck, goose.

More disquieting was the silence, a girl's bare feet moving noiselessly around the circle, the others tensed expectantly, as though engaged in some illicit pursuit. Was play also forbidden in this horrible place?

Jamil didn't look as though he'd moved from where Amy had left him. His back was to the children, cell phone again to one ear, eyes focused on the nearest wall.

As the circling girl tapped her "goose"—the small girl in the pink tunic Amy had first spied in the window—Amy stepped into Jamil's line of vision to say quietly, "It'll be just a few minutes more."

At her voice, Jamil's head shot up, his cell phone flying from his hand, and for an instant Amy caught a play of conflicting emotion across his face—unhappiness? fear? uncertainty?—so strong she was startled into silence. Then a thud and a startled yelp spun Amy around.

The clatter of phone to floor—and perhaps Amy's own interruption—had distracted the runners so that they'd collided, the older girl's weight slamming the smaller child into the matting hard enough to knock the air from her lungs.

Amy hurried over to them. "Oh, sweetie, are you okay?"

The girl in the pink tunic hadn't moved. But just as the older girl was giving her playmate a panicked tug, the smaller girl drew in a gasping breath. She rolled to a sitting position. Then she caught sight of bloodied palms, scarlet soaking through the ripped knees of her pink pants. Even the little girl's wail was no more than a mewling kitten, the other children crowding close with anxious murmurs.

"Shh, don't cry. It'll be all right." The child wasn't pacified by Amy's English litany, and holding the writhing little body while digging the first aid kit from her bag proved no easy task. Amy had managed to extract scissors to cut open a bloodied pant leg when a hand stopped her.

"Excuse me." Jamil's expression held nothing but solicitous courtesy as he lifted the scissors from Amy's grasp, his expression so composed Amy wondered if she'd imagined that earlier distress. "Her mother will not wish to lose the clothing."

Jamil proceeded to work the pants gently down over the scraped knees. Even for Afghanistan, the little girl's tunic was long enough to offer decency. Jamil sorted through the first aid kit. Bemused, Amy watched him swab hydrogen peroxide and smooth on antibiotic cream, the deft experience of those long, thin fingers so clearly greater than her own, she made no effort to intervene. Amy had no idea what he said to the little girl as he taped gauze into place, but she was smiling through her tears before he was done.

"And to think I was patching you up," Amy exclaimed as Jamil closed the first aid kit. Her own dressing still swaddling Jamil's left foot looked clumsy next to the little girl's neat bandages. "Why didn't you tell me you'd had first aid training?"

"I was once a medical student." It was the first personal comment Jamil had ever made, and as though he regretted it, he got to his feet immediately. "And you did a very competent job. I was thankful." He nodded toward the little girl. "The child should remain still so she does not pull off the bandages."

Easier said than done. The girl had attached herself to Amy like a limpet, and when Amy tried to peel off clinging arms, the little girl's wail rose enough that the other children looked worried, their hushing murmurs anxious. Were they afraid of that hard-faced warden out there?

Amy looked up at Jamil. "Tell her if she'll let me go, I'll tell her—all of them—a story."

It worked. By the time the girl released Amy, the others were squatting down, their soft chatter holding excited anticipation. Amy glanced around. The room's only furnishing was a blackboard, but among the donated supplies was a bright rainbow of colored chalks. Amy drew a navy blue circle, then reached for sunshine yellow. Few tales from her own childhood made sense to children who lived without electricity, books, toys, pets, TV, DVDs, computers, or even running water. But the refugee camps had taught Amy which stories offered universal delight.

"In the beginning God created the heavens and the earth. Now the earth was formless and empty. Darkness was over the surface of the deep, and the Spirit of God was hovering over the waters. Then God said, 'Let there be light.'"

Amy was no Picasso, but she could draw the sun and moon, sky and clouds, trees and flowers, birds and fish. The children whispered excitedly with each new picture, those close enough reaching up to touch a leaping whale, a dubious lion.

"Then God said, 'Let us make man in our image, in our likeness, and let them rule over the fish of the sea and the birds of the air, over the livestock, over all the earth, and over all the creatures that move along the ground.'"

Human figures emerged discreetly behind green bushes. The very cadence of the biblical narrative was the rhythm of Eastern storytelling, the Dari into which Jamil was translating a dialect of the Persians whose fabled princess Scheherazade had staved off death with her tales for a thousand and one nights.

"And every day in the cool of the evening, God came down to walk and talk with Adam and Eve in the garden. They ate the fruit and played with the animals. And God saw all that he had made, and it was very good."

The small faces upturned to Amy were far from clean, but they were rapt with wonder, eyes wide with delight, and to Amy they were all beautiful, even the spiky-haired boy who crept close enough to rub a dirty face against Amy's tunic.

But now Amy could hear voices approaching down the hall. Grabbing the eraser, she wiped away the garden and creatures. "I have to go, and you need to find your mothers."

The children's unhappy protests as they straggled reluctantly to their feet were high praise. A girl of seven or eight tugged imperiously on Amy's arm.

Jamil translated. "She wishes to know what happened to the beautiful garden and why we can no longer play with the wild beasts."

Amy bent down to look into the girl's face. The girl's long-lashed gaze met hers with fearless interest. A bigger boy jostled her deliberately, stepping in front to seize Amy's attention, but the younger girl pushed him out of her way, eyes intent on Amy's as she waited for her answer. Life had not yet cowed her spirit, bowed her head and shoulders into submission, as it had the women huddled silently in those dark dormitories.

Dear God, let it be different for her. May she grow up in a different world than this.

"What is your name?" Amy asked. *"Nametan chist?"*

"Tamana." The girl pointed to the boy she'd shoved. Amy caught the meaning of her words without translation. *"Baradar"*—"brother." "Fahim"—his name.

"That is a story for another day," Amy said gently.

"Then will you come back to tell it?"

Amy didn't have to answer because at that moment Debby, Alisha, and the others entered the schoolroom. At a harsh phrase and sharp clap from Geeti, the children scampered off.

Debby hurried over to Amy. "Sorry about the wait. Alisha and I have to run over to the men's prison. But I wanted to ask if you've had time to think about what I've shared."

"Actually, I enjoyed the wait," Amy answered sincerely, but she was shaking her head. "I've got to be honest. I sympathize with these women and kids. But this isn't the kind of project New Hope had in mind for Kabul. And though I may have room and budget, I don't have personnel. I have two translators, but they're both Afghan men. I don't think these women are likely to get much sympathy from them."

Debby's round face showed her disappointment. "I understand. It just seemed so perfect when I ran into you. Especially since I'm out of time."

Alisha, in conversation with Geeti and Soraya, beckoned to Debby.

Hurriedly, Debby added, "I have to go. Geeti will show you out. But

I'd sure like to chat a bit more, maybe answer your concerns. Are you hitting the Thursday circuit tonight? If not, I'd be happy to pop by your guesthouse."

"I'm staying at the Sarai. You're welcome to drop by." Amy's eyebrows came together. "I did see a mention on the guesthouse bulletin board of an open house tonight. Is that what you mean by Thursday circuit?"

Debby chuckled. "If you don't know, you'll find out soon enough. The Sarai has one of the biggest Thursday bashes in town. I'll plan on dropping in when I get away from here. Is it a date, then?"

"It's a date."

"Go right! Go right! No, left! There're unfriendlies approaching. A mob of them. Just protesters, but it's looking ugly."

An armed phalanx advanced warily across the sand. Four men formed a diamond at compass points around a fifth. Four more ranged out to form a square around the diamond. All wore tactical vests, and all but the center cradled unslung M4s.

"Okay, you've got shooters there. Get him out! Get him out!"

The square's two forward points dropped to one knee and began firing. Behind them, the diamond collapsed, hands grabbing at the center figure and rushing him backward. This would have been easier if he hadn't been six and a half feet tall and upward of two hundred and fifty pounds. Halfway back, the big man slumped to the sand. The square's rear points jumped in to haul the man to a concrete walkway.

"He's safe! He's safe! Break contact!"

Firing stopped. Half a dozen firing targets lay riddled with bullets. The entire phalanx retreated to the concrete.

As Steve joined them, Jamie McDuff ran a pen down a clipboard. "Not bad. You got the principal out. But you lost both shooters and took out a civilian. This isn't the Marines. You don't stay and fight it out. Break contact and get out of there just as soon as the principal's safe. Mac, good simulation. Good thing Khalid isn't your size. Let's try it again. Julio, you take center this time."

Steve offered McDuff a thumbs-up as he headed downfield where Phil, with no medical emergencies on hand, was putting two dozen assorted TCNs through "scoot and shoot" runs, half the group prone on the sand laying down imaginary fire while the rest retreated, then vice versa.

"Lock and load. Fire. Cease fire. Okay, I think we're ready to hand out ammo."

The sand wasn't local but had been trucked in to create an artificial dune a hundred meters long and twice a man's height, an effective if inelegant bullet trap for firing exercises. The training facility itself might have been mistaken for a military base. Rows of armored Humvees and personnel carriers. A helipad. Prefabricated Army "hooches" for housing TCNs. A high concrete perimeter wall topped with guard towers and machine-gun nests.

"So how are they doing?" Steve asked as he reached Phil's side.

"More spraying than aiming." The medic shrugged. "But the Romanians can handle a convoy run, and the Guats are ready for secondary ring security. The Chilean bunch are former Pinochet secret police and know what they're doing. Khalid's own militia have the most actual combat experience."

"And are most likely to be infiltrated. We'll keep them on outer perimeter—and no ammo."

The advantage of TCNs or third country nationals was that they were cheaper and endlessly available. So for a high-value contract like Khalid, you did exactly what Condor Securities had done. You surrounded your principal with an inner defense "diamond" you personally could trust, preferably all tier one Special Ops.

Then you started sorting out your second tier of TCNs, finding out who had real combat training, who could be trusted for basic guard duty or convoy ride-along. The best you elevated to supervisory capacity. But you never let them inside your inner defenses. It wasn't that these guys would necessarily take a bribe, sell off their equipment, steal supplies, turn weapons on civilians, or just throw them down and run when trouble came. It was that you couldn't count on them not to do any or all of the above.

"Give McDuff your evaluations. As of tonight we go three shifts, let everyone start getting some decent sleep."

"And R & R. Cougar brought by an invite to another open house this evening. I think that makes a round dozen."

"No thanks. Schmoozing bureaucrats and aid workers hardly falls into my CS contract. But, hey, you're off shift with the new schedule."

Phil shook his head. "My first evening off? Nothing doing. I'll be spending it with my wife and kids. I've got Skype and a webcam set up. You, on the other hand, my friend, have no family restrictions. Go have some fun. Give some poor Peace Corps volunteer a thrill. Better yet, pick one, settle down, and have some babies. I mean, what's the point of making all that dough if you've no one to spend it on?"

"And end up separated three weeks out of four? Not interested." Steve wished he could bite back his words as he caught the stricken look on Phil's face. "Hey, I didn't mean it that way. I'm just not in the market. Though if I ever come across a gal as special as yours, I'll reconsider."

An unlikely scenario in his current profession. Which was just as well. Despite Steve's retraction, bottom line, this job was murder on relationships. Maybe Phil could make it work. For his friend's sake, Steve hoped so. But Steve had seen too many Special Forces and PSD buddies go through the misery of divorce to do that to any woman.

Not to mention his own family.

Steve headed toward the administrative modules that made up a small town near the compound entrance. The last three days had been a scramble, but things were coming together. Cougar had squeezed another six tier one operatives out of CS, not all Western Special Ops, but the two Russians and German looked good. Former KGB, Steve would hazard.

Khalid's embassy run had gone smoothly, his handshake with the U.S. Senate majority leader making cable news. The minister's ensuing good humor allowed Steve to push through a solution to their guest flow problem. When a local German beer garden was liquidated for ignoring Ministry of Vice edicts, Cougar had snapped up a metal detector gate they'd installed for security. This now formed a trellised archway just inside Khalid's pedestrian gate.

Now if they could do the same for the Ministry of Interior. Absolute security was never attainable. But the place was just too big, too open, too crowded—and too much a part of Khalid's regular pattern—for even minimal security.

Which was the motivation behind Steve's current quick stride. Dyn-Corp, one of the largest private security companies, had the contract for training the Afghan National Police as well as a recently formed separate counternarcotics task force, placing MOI squarely within their sphere of operation. Combining resources could be a win-win for both sides. A blast of air-conditioning welcomed Steve into a large module. A bored-looking Aussie, feet up on his desk, M4 balanced across a paunch, barely glanced at Steve's CS credentials. There any pretense of helpfulness ended.

"What do you mean, you can't give out that info? Then who does have the authority to discuss this?" Steve looked around the long room with its empty desks and blank computer screens with exasperation. "Where is everyone? This place was full yesterday."

"It's Thursday. Everyone leaves early to hit the showers and open house circuit."

Steve needed no further explanation. Friday was the Muslim day of worship, making Thursday equivalent to a Saturday back home. In Basra, a large Western base, the local calendar had been ignored. But here it seemed bureaucrats and aid workers weren't the only expats who'd made a conscientious effort to adapt, at least when it came to playtime.

The DynCorp contractor managed not to topple weapon or chair as he stretched an arm to grab a Post-it pad. Scribbling name and number, he shoved it toward Steve. "Here. If it's urgent, you can try our country manager. Or come back Saturday after the weekend."

Steve pulled out his cell phone.

"Jason Hamilton." The DynCorp manager's voice was barely audible above a babble of voices and roar of engines. "I'm out at the ISAF hangar. Then I'm heading over to an open house in Wazir. If you want to come on down there, I'll be happy to discuss details."

"I'd rather—" A background whine rose to a roar of rotors; then the connection broke. Steve slapped his phone shut with a grimace. Like it or not, he was in for some R & R after all.

12

Small faces popped up at window bars to watch Amy and Jamil trail Geeti back across the courtyard, though the girl in the pink tunic was not among them.

"The story you told the children, it is a beautiful story," Jamil told Amy. "The story of paradise, is it not? I did not know you were a follower of Muhammad."

The green door slammed shut behind them, the prison warden's key ring jangling as she locked them out.

Amy followed Jamil across the plank bridge. "Yes, that was the story of paradise—the creation of earth and the Garden of Eden. But I'm not a follower of Muhammad. I'm a Christian, a follower of Jesus Christ. Isa Masih, as you would call him. And the story of Creation isn't just a Muslim story. It's from the Bible, the first chapters of the Old Testament."

"Your Christian holy book."

"Not just Christian. The Old Testament was the holy book of the Jews, and a lot of its stories are taught also in the Quran."

"I did not know that." Ushering Amy into the back of the sedan, Jamil slid into the driver's seat.

Amy's smile met his fleeting glance in the rearview mirror. "And I didn't know you were a medical student. I feel especially privileged now to have you on board at New Hope. Are you planning to go back to finish?"

But her assistant wasn't giving out any more personal data. "That was another life. To begin again, no, it would not be possible. Now where do you wish to go next? Back to the New Hope compound?"

Amy considered as Jamil pulled out of the unpaved lot. Between MOI and Welayat, her afternoon had evaporated, the sky still light overhead, but the sun already dropped behind the mountain peaks. "No, it's too late to start anything else at New Hope. I think I'll head back to my guest-house and type up those reports. Do you know how to get to the Sarai?"

"Yes, Rasheed showed me your lodging when he was testing my driving. Then you will not be needing me to drive again today? Rasheed has requested that I transport you anywhere you require to go."

The questions held the neutral courtesy of an employee. But Jamil's hands were tight on the steering wheel, something of his earlier conflicted expression back in the rearview mirror.

Amy was taken aback. She and Jamil hadn't discussed his hours, though the generous salary by local standards presupposed a certain flexibility. "I don't expect you to be on call 24-7. I'm not planning on going out tonight, but if I do, I'll make my own arrangements or call a taxi."

She leaned forward. If commenting on appearance was a cultural faux pas, she was about to compound it. But her assistant looked so desolate. "Is everything all right?"

His face went blank. "Yes, everything is as it should be. It is just . . . I had thought to go to the bazaar if you did not require me. I do not have a proper *musallah* for the mosque tomorrow. But it is not important. And you must not seek transport with strangers. It is not safe. Should you choose to go out, you need only call. If not I, then Rasheed will retrieve you."

"I'll keep that in mind." Unconvinced, Amy studied Jamil with covert interest as he maneuvered between a mule cart and a swaying, top-heavy city bus. In just three days, Jamil had lost some of the gaunt exhaustion that had first moved Amy to compassion. He was a good-looking man, and in his new finery, even the set of his shoulders seemed straighter and more self-assured. He'd been a medical student, of an educated family by his account, so he hadn't always lived like this. Had Jamil transformed himself only to go to the bazaar? Or did he have evening plans he felt no obligation to share with his foreign and female employer?

It was a reminder of how little Amy knew of her assistant beyond the convenience he afforded her. Did Jamil have a life outside the New Hope compound? What dreams and hopes and aspirations did he have beyond dogging Amy's heels?

A sudden impulse to ease Jamil's somberness, a rebellion against treating another human being as an invisible prop whatever the cultural dictates, prompted Amy to speak. "The University of Kabul has opened again. I've heard they have a medical course of study. I'd be happy to work something out with your employment at New Hope if you'd be interested in finishing your studies. It's never too late."

"For me it *is* too late! Please, I do not wish to speak of it again." It was not a request but a harsh command, and as though immediately regretting the force of his reaction, Jamil added in a milder tone, "Miss Ameera, I have wanted to ask. This 'date' of which your friend spoke. And 'bash.' I know the English words, but perhaps my understanding is not so good."

Jamil's gaze touched Amy with limpid candor in the rearview mirror. "How does one have a day of the calendar? Or is it the fruit you speak of? And to bash—is this not an act of violence?"

At least he was talking, and if Jamil's change of subject was intended to deflect intrusion on his personal life, that was his prerogative. "No, in this context a bash is just a big party. And a date is an activity you plan with another person for a certain day and time. Sometimes a friend, like Debby, though it usually means a man and a woman doing something special together."

"Special?"

"Yes, like going to a party or out to a movie or a restaurant. To get to know each other better and have some fun."

"Unmarried? Alone?" Amy wasn't sure whether Jamil's shocked exclamation held disbelief or disapproval as he glanced in the rearview mirror at Amy's finery, then quickly away. "Yes, I have heard of such things. Then this date of which you spoke, it is a party? With men and dancing and alcohol, as in the movies? This is permitted in your country for two women without brothers or father or husband to protect them?"

Amy turned pink, only now recognizing the pitfall into which she'd stepped. "Things are done a little differently in my country. But tonight isn't that kind of date. An open house is just a gathering of other foreigners."

Amy hoped Jamil's nod indicated comprehension. They'd reached the wide, paved streets of Wazir Akbar Khan. Amy slid forward across the seat as Jamil slammed on the brakes.

"Miss Ameera, is this not the proper direction of your lodging?"

For a moment, Amy too thought they must have taken the wrong turn. Like many of Kabul's guesthouses, the Sarai was an aristocratic residence refitted for the expat trade on a quiet side street not far from the New Hope compound. At least it had been quiet when Rasheed picked Amy up this morning.

Now barrel-shaped movable barriers blocked the street. A red and white security bar rose for a white Land Cruiser. Beyond it, SUVs filled both sides of the streets.

A Gurkha guard strode over to the Corolla, tapping his automatic rifle against the driver's window. As Jamil rolled it down, a blare of reggae spilled into the car.

"Only foreign passports permitted. Please reverse the vehicle."

"I live here." Amy handed him her passport.

The Nepalese soldier frowned at Jamil. "You may proceed, but due to the presence of alcohol, Afghan citizens are not permitted entry."

"He's just dropping me off." Amy winced as the crash of steel drums over the wall morphed into mariachi brass.

Jamil's expression was closed again, his hands so tight on the steering wheel his knuckles were white. After all she'd said, was he getting the wrong idea about her evening plans? Or was something else on his mind?

"I'll walk in from here," she said quietly. "You go on and enjoy your evening. I'll see you in the morning. No, Friday's your day off, isn't it? Then I'll see you on Saturday."

As the car backed away, Amy allowed the Gurkha to probe her shoulder bag, then detoured the red and white security bar. The Land Cruiser had found parking, and a Caucasian man in a Hawaiian shirt and jeans headed toward the guesthouse gate. Recognizing Amy, a guard waved her through as a companion ran a metal detector wand over the Hawaiian shirt.

Inside, unroofed parking was also crowded with vehicles. Amy followed the music into the two-story residence's communal lounge. French doors opened onto a veranda, beyond which stretched the rosebushes and grape arbors, lounge chairs and swimming pool of an extensive backyard. Had she just stepped through a space portal from the streets of Kabul, the New Hope compound, that awful women's prison?

People swarmed everywhere, splashing in the pool, eating around tables, stretched out on lounge chairs, gyrating on a makeshift dance floor in the middle of the lawn. Under a thatched shelter, tables held food and meat sizzled on several grills.

Amy hadn't dreamed Kabul held so many expatriates. The chatter around her encompassed English, French, German, and Italian. She noticed tall, blond Scandinavians and small-framed Asians, Africans with Nigerian and Kenyan accents, and East Indians.

And every one of them dressed for the perfect September garden party—back in Miami.

It was no sin of his employer that consumed Jamil as he drove away but his own. He did not like to tell lies. Not only because the look in the foreign woman's eyes was the trusting one of an Eid lamb, but because with each, he added another grain to the scales of Allah's justice already weighed damningly against him. Still, what choice had been left him? At least Ameera had been easily distracted from his doings.

Medical school. Those days were so long in Jamil's past, he'd thought them forgotten, as his fingers had forgotten their skill until he'd touched the child. Now Islamabad's finest university rose up around him, the laboratories and computers, the white-robed professors, the books.

A carefree existence it had been, even privileged despite the deprivations of war, with no greater concern than the results of his latest exam. There'd been companionship. Debate. The excitement of intellectual challenge. The warm, noisy safety net of family. And more freedom than he'd recognized until it was taken away.

Freedom, above all, from shame and guilt.

It had seemed so simple then, to be pure before Allah such an all-consuming aspiration it hardly required thought, the five pillars of Islam giving framework to every hour of life.

The *shahada*—the declaration of faith made over and over on every occasion since the moment of birth. *Illaha illa Allah. Muhammad rasul Allah.* There is no God but Allah, and Muhammad is his prophet.

The *salat*—the five prayer times that divided each day into its rhythm: the sun's first rays, its zenith, the western arc of afternoon, sunset, the coming of night.

The *zakat*—almsgiving that the poor and widows and orphans might share some small measure of Allah's bounty.

The *sawm*—the Ramadan fast that could be onerous on a growing, young body and yet so purifying and uplifting in the challenge of its discipline.

The *hajj*—the pilgrimage that outweighed in merit all other acts but one of submission. As his father and his father's father and his father's father's father had earned merit, so he too had planned one day when life was not so pleasurably full.

And within the framework of those five pillars, countless other requirements of Jamil's faith studied and memorized in careful emulation of that most righteous of lives, Allah's apostle Muhammad. The proper cleansing ablutions so that one's prayers were not nullified. Which foods to eat. How to sit cross-legged with the right foot above and soles carefully inward. How to brush one's teeth. Which hand to use for eating. Which *rakats* to recite at each succeeding cycle of prayer.

Until in time the smallest detail of daily life became a habitual act of submission to Allah.

And each act an offering piled up into the scales so that at the end of life they might outweigh the stray loose thought. The glance of lust at a woman's bared ankle or eyes. The unintended defilements that lurked when one was not attentive. Even willful disobedience.

The mullahs stressed that in Allah's implacable sovereignty even the most untainted could not be assured of divine favor. But as long as the scale was safely tipped toward purity and submission, there was no need to lose sleep over one's eternal destination. Was not his very choice of vocation—to mend the bodies and souls of his fellow men—a daily meritorious offering of zakat?

Had the Creator, the Mighty One, the Reckoner of Deeds, who humbled and exalted at his own unfathomable pleasure, laughed at Jamil's blind arrogance? taken away his present, his future, his hope, his confidence as punishment for such overwhelming presumption?

The car slid into a courtyard opening, the bazaar closing around Jamil as he continued on foot. A musty sweetness of dried fruits. Pungent spices in red, yellow, green, orange mounds. Meat sizzling in vats of sesame oil. Bamboo cages fluttering with noisy parakeets and budgies and fighting partridges. Threading a narrow alley of canvas-covered stalls, Jamil ducked his head to enter a carpet shop, then followed its bearded merchant through neatly rolled cylinders to a door in the rear.

No, the foreign woman Ameera meant well. He'd seen it in her eyes. And there'd been a time when Jamil still clung to hope, believed that he could one day step back into that life, the future once laid out in front of him as wide and clear and inevitable as the Kabul-Kandahar Highway.

Even that hope was so long ago he'd forgotten the feel of it.

It was dangerous to let such thoughts return. To let so much as the memory of hope rear its head. Or of freedom. His future, his family, his eternal destiny lay now in the grip of the man who'd summoned him here tonight.

For himself all that remained was the expiation of sin.

13

"*Ay, querida,* you must be new. Did no one send you the memo about Thursday night dress code?"

Amy's face burned as a young woman in a bikini with Mediterranean coloring offered Amy a pitying smile. Women in strapless cocktail dresses, tank tops, and shorts were wandering by. Amy let her scarf slide from hair to shoulders, its exquisite blue green silk making her feel less a princess now than the court jester.

I can run upstairs and hide or go out there looking as much an idiot as I feel!

Or Amy could lift her head high and walk out there as though there was absolutely nothing out of place in her wardrobe. *Mallorys don't run away. Besides, I promised to meet Debby Martini.*

Tilting her chin, Amy stepped forward carefully because her ridiculous high heels weren't made for the veranda's ornamental tiles.

"Amy? Amy Mallory, is it not?"

The hail came from the nearest table. At first Amy hadn't recognized the graying blonde in tank top and shorts. The fortyish German was the only other woman currently boarding at the Sarai. "Elsa Leister, right? We met at supper the other night."

"Yes, you are the American. I have been visiting with one of your countrymen. Come join us. You have met Peter, *ja?* And give no attention to Marleni." Elsa waved toward the retreating bikini. "There isn't really a dress code. It is just Thursday nights are when we all let loose and forget we're stuck in this godforsaken end of the earth."

"Yes, and thumb our noses at all those screaming mullahs and their ridiculous rules. No women. No pork. No booze. Speaking of which, I'm off for another round." Peter lumbered to his feet, barbecued rib in one hand and empty margarita glass in the other. "Amy, what can I get you? A margarita? Rum cola?"

From empty glasses around his plate and slurred words, he'd amply sampled both. Amy took an empty seat with some reluctance. "Nothing for me, thank you."

She wouldn't have responded so eagerly to Elsa's hail had she noted the German woman's companion. Peter Dunsmore worked for an American mineral consortium and was one of several reasons—all male—Amy preferred to escape to her room in the evenings.

As Peter wandered toward the bar, Amy turned to Elsa. "It *is* nice to lose the head cover. To think I'd never heard of 'chador hair' when I came here. But I must say I'm a little overwhelmed. I'd seen mention of an open house, but this wasn't what I pictured."

"On Thursday nights you will find parties like this all around the Wazir," Elsa explained. "All very tight security, of course."

"The Thursday circuit," Amy hazarded.

"Ah yes, I have heard it called such. The objective is to see how many parties one can hit before the police start cracking down on curfew. A game for the young and undignified. Though one I will play myself tonight as I must make my good-byes. My contract here is complete, so this will be my last Thursday in Kabul."

"Oh, really?" Amy said with disappointment. It seemed like every contact she made was on her way out of Afghanistan. "So what type of project were you working with?"

"A work-study on the advances women have made here since the Taliban in comparison to the considerable aid my government has invested on their behalf."

"I see." This was at least of interest to Amy. "So what is your evaluation?"

"Hey, I thought we weren't in Kabul tonight." Peter was back, swaying slightly on his feet, a cup of beer in one hand and a margarita in the other. Though his plate was across the table, he dropped into a chair beside Amy. "Let's leave the poor, victimized Afghans at the office."

"It is better conversation than your ex-wives." Elsa snagged the margarita from Peter's hand before turning back to Amy. "I will certainly mention progress. Still, my report will not be completely positive. Those women who work for a Western organization are most fortunate because they bring valuable income to their families. But then they are of the educated class, so their families are more enlightened. For the rest—"

She shrugged. "What good does it do to build girls' schools when a majority of fathers still do not permit them to attend? to remove the burqa from some small part of the population when women as young as seven or eight are still forced into marriage? when the abuse within their own homes is not addressed?"

"Yes, I wanted to ask about that," Amy said. "I visited the women's prison this afternoon with Debby Martini. It was a bit of a shock. I understand you can't change cultural attitudes overnight. But it's been years since the Taliban were tossed out. With democratic elections and a new constitution, one would think at minimum the current justice system could refuse to arrest women on such ridiculous charges."

"Unfortunately there is little that can be done," Elsa said. "As long as *sharia* law makes women the property of their male relatives, these prisoners are legally criminals. At least these days they are only sent to jail, not whipped or executed."

"Sharia law?" Amy's brows knit together.

"The Islamic legal code," Elsa explained. "Sharia is the basis of law in all Muslim countries."

"No, I know what sharia law is." Amy's hands clenched in her lap, indication of a shock and bewilderment she hoped didn't show on her face. "Forgive my ignorance, but I wasn't aware Afghanistan was under sharia law. Wasn't the whole point of a new Afghan constitution to guarantee basic human rights?"

"It's not so bad." Peter took a long swallow of beer. "From what I've read, the new Afghan constitution includes the International Bill of Rights."

"Yes, where those rights do not contradict sharia," Elsa retorted. "The two are not always compatible."

"Now wait a minute." Peter looked bored. "If Afghanistan chooses sharia law, that's what we call democracy, isn't it? I mean, they did have elections."

"And now you see why we do not permit office talk on Thursday nights." Draining the margarita, Elsa pushed back her chair. "I am off to the UN open house. Are you still offering me an escort, Peter?"

Peter raised his remaining beer. "No, I've got a little more business here."

"I can see that," Elsa replied. "Then I will look for a companion who will not fall flat on his face in the street."

As Elsa headed through the French doors, Amy turned to scan the garden. Had Debby Martini arrived while she'd been distracted? No, still no sign of the New Yorker.

Nor was she among a new influx of people spilling out onto the veranda. But one tall figure in khaki shirt and pants striding across the garden caught Amy's eye. She couldn't place his vague familiarity until she realized that the difference was an absence of body armor and weapons.

Was it business or play that brought private security contractor Steve Wilson to Amy's lodging?

The guesthouse was more crowded than Steve had expected. Well, there was one quick way to locate his contact. Flipping open his cell phone, Steve hit Redial.

Under a thatched shelter, a Hawaiian shirt at an outdoor bar raised a hand to his ear.

Flipping the phone shut, Steve headed through the celebrating mass. He spotted a flaxen head at a table on the veranda, his lips twitching as he took in the long sleeves and dress. But he approved of the proud lift of that small, determined chin, the straight-backed poise that announced she wasn't out of place.

Amy Mallory's got backbone. Maybe she'll make it after all.

The Hawaiian shirt, cell phone still in hand as Steve reached the open-air bar, was big and blond with the packed muscle of a regular workout regimen. Definitely PSC.

"Jason Hamilton? Steve Wilson."

"Ah yes, Condor Security," the DynCorp country manager said. "So you've got the new Khalid detail. You wanted to discuss joint ops."

"That's right. Khalid is hosting a delegation of provincial police chiefs over at MOI as we speak. I'm sure you're aware the place is as leaky as a sieve. You've got expat training personnel and police recruits in and out of the place. I'm guessing they can use field experience, and we could sure stand to tighten security over there. And anywhere else Khalid goes. He *is* their ultimate boss."

"I'm sure we can work something out." Jason raised his voice over the music blasting from two waist-high speakers at either end of the bar. "I'll put you in contact with our security people."

"And I'm told you have K-9s." Steve raised his own voice higher. "I'd like to turn a couple loose on the ministry building. If you've got extras, I'd give a lot to kennel a team up at Khalid's residence."

"That's another contract. I'd have to talk to the trainers. If I'm not mistaken, they're running a demonstration over there tonight for your police chiefs—" Jason broke off as his phone vibrated on the bar counter. Snapping it open, he listened, then shook his head. "I can't hear a thing in here. If you'll excuse me, I'll be back as soon as I take this."

As the DynCorp manager stepped away from the thatched shelter, Steve commandeered an empty barstool. His gaze found Amy across the garden. What was it about that flaxen head, the particular tilt of that determined chin? Something was nagging at him, had nagged since the first time he'd seen her on the plane. And not just because she was an attractive young woman.

The older woman he'd noted at the table had left, leaving Amy alone with her final companion. A man, chair pulled close, head bent intimately above hers. Then she wasn't as friendless here as Steve had thought.

"So, *mi amor*, what is it you do here in Kabul?"

Steve turned his head to meet a coy smile. An attractive brunette in a bikini slid a shapely body onto the next stool. Steve glanced around for his contact. The DynCorp manager had finished his phone conversation, but instead of heading back toward Steve, he was moving swiftly through the crowd toward the French doors. Something somewhere was going down. *And whatever it is, it's not my gig!*

A long nail ran gently up Steve's forearm, the invitation unmistakable.

But Steve didn't even turn his head, his survey caught on its return swing by that cameo duo beyond the pool. "Sorry, lady, I don't speak Spanish." He got to his feet, jaw clenched and mouth compressed to a hard line. Ignoring a disappointed pout, he pushed with furious strides through the crowd.

14

Amy had noticed the bikini snuggling up to Steve Wilson. *Typical,* she'd dismissed in the fury of her own thoughts. In the short time since her arrival, twilight had set in. The dust that so plagued Kabul residents had in recompense caught the failing light to create one of the most spectacular sunsets Amy had ever seen. Though Amy's gaze had shifted to flaming pinks and oranges laced with pale green and mauve streaks, her hands didn't ease in her lap.

"So it's down to you and me."

Amy hadn't heard Peter's chair scraping closer. The arm sliding around her shoulders was an unpleasant surprise. She couldn't turn her head because that would put her in contact with that slurred voice. A hand squeezing her shoulder was damp and hot even through the silk material.

She spoke impersonally. "If you don't mind, Peter, I'd appreciate it if you'd move back a bit."

"Why so unneighborly? We Yankees should be sticking together. Believe me, I can be *very* good company."

As his hand slid down to her arm, Amy took in with disgust the gold of a wedding band. "I'm going to do you a favor and assume this is too much beer talking. But if you don't remove your hand and move away, I'm going to scream."

"Now we wouldn't want to make a scene, would we?"

If that hot, rank breath didn't remove itself from her ear, Amy wasn't sure she was going to be able to resist that scream. "I don't know about 'we,' but *I* have no problem making a scene."

"And neither do I."

The grim declaration punctuated the abrupt removal of Peter's unwelcome bulk. Amy looked up to see Steve Wilson. He not only had removed Peter from contact with Amy but had him on his feet, and if the mineralogist was heavier, the security contractor was taller and strong enough that Peter's attempts to twist away were not proving successful.

"Your party's over—" Steve grabbed the man's wallet and flipped through it with his free hand—"Peter Dunsmore. When I let you go, you're going to head for the door, find your driver, get yourself home, and sleep it off."

"For your information, I live here." Peter stopped struggling, but his glare was belligerent. "The lady and I are just having a little—"

"The lady isn't interested." Steve's interjection had the sharpness of a whip. "And may I suggest you pack up and find other lodging? If you don't head out, I'll let site security take over, and then it'll be official, not this friendly little conversation. Somehow I doubt your company hands out awards for getting drunk and tossed out on your ear for making a pass at a lady."

The image obviously penetrated Peter's sodden imagination because when Steve released him, he snatched back his wallet and with a final glare lurched across the veranda.

"That wasn't necessary." Amy was on her feet. "I didn't need to be rescued. I could have handled him."

Steve studied Amy. Then the jawline eased and the firm mouth relaxed into the amused quirk Amy had come to recognize as the security contractor's version of a smile. "I know," he said unexpectedly. "But you shouldn't have to. I just figured taking the guy out quietly might suit you better than having to scream your head off. But do forgive me if I've deprived you of that pleasure. You want an apology, you've got one. Or I can go invite him back, if you prefer."

He had a point, Amy admitted unwillingly. "Of course you don't need to apologize. I appreciate your discretion. I just don't want you to get the idea I run around needing to be rescued on a regular basis."

His laugh transformed the stern features, making them much younger than Amy had first thought him, not so many years older than herself, and for the first time Amy understood the attraction that had drawn the bikini like a bee to a dessert cart.

"The thought hadn't even crossed my mind," Steve said dryly. "Actually, I was thinking I'd have hardly recognized you." His gaze left Amy's face to rest on embroidered silk and amethyst sandals. "You look—"

"Out of place?" Amy's nose wrinkled ruefully. "You don't have to tell me. I just can't seem to get the dress code right."

"Not at all. You look—well, certainly more appropriate to local weather conditions than—" Steve glanced toward the bar area. "You know, I've been wanting to ask, have we ever crossed paths before?"

He's floundering. The incongruity of it humanized the tall, formidable contractor, and Amy laughed. "I'm going to assume you weren't referring to the plane or dragging me out of downtown Kabul, or that's got to be the worst pickup line I've ever heard. And no, I think I'd remember if we'd met elsewhere. I've got one of those faces, I guess. Blondes do all look alike and all that."

"That didn't come out so well, did it? I'm afraid I'm a little rusty at the social thing. Here, let me start over. Hi, Amy. I'm Steve. Glad you could make it this evening. You and that silk whatever-it's-called look absolutely stunning tonight." He grinned.

At least he could poke fun at himself. "And it's a pleasure to see you again, Steve," Amy said, a smile playing at the corner of her mouth. "I just love what you've done with your own look. I hardly recognized you without body armor and a gun."

His bark of laughter acknowledged her hit. "That settles it, then. I don't know about you, but it's been a thirsty afternoon. How about I scrounge some drinks to settle the dust? I see some food over there too."

Amy's glance flew instinctively to a stocky figure still stumbling toward the French doors.

"And don't look so worried. I'm no Peter Dunsmore. In my line of work, there are three things I need to be able to do at all times. Think straight. Drive straight. And shoot straight. And you can't do any of them when you're seeing double."

A reminder of just who and what Steve Wilson was. "But you're off duty now."

"I'm never off duty," Steve contradicted. "Not when I'm on the ground in-country. I learned the hard way a long time ago that alcohol and guns don't mix. I watched a contractor mow down a taxi in Baghdad. If he hadn't been partying so hard the night before, he'd have noticed the car was full of women and children. That's when I switched to Coke. But I can get you something stronger."

Amy shook her head. "When I first started working in this part of the world, I made a commitment that my Muslim coworkers shouldn't have to smell alcohol on my breath."

Steve gestured to the dancing crowd. "I'm guessing that makes us both the oddballs in this group. Two sodas then? Coke? Sprite?"

Amy hadn't totally forgiven Steve's incivility on their last encounter. But at least he was a known face, and at the moment she just didn't feel up to crashing another table of strangers. "A Coke would be nice." She couldn't resist adding, "If you're sure your girlfriend isn't missing you. I didn't mean to break up your party."

Even in the last of the twilight Amy could see red rising to Steve's cheekbones. "There was no party to break up. I popped in to meet a fellow contractor. Business. But he disappeared. Meanwhile, why don't you settle in here, and I'll be right back."

Steve waited courteously for Amy to resume her seat before walking away. Amy's expression lost its animation as soon as he disappeared into the crowd. She was deep in thought, hands curled in her lap, when two Coke cans dripping with condensation plunked down onto the table, followed by two paper plates piled high with barbecued ribs and finger foods.

"Dunsmore won't bother you again," Steve said quietly, adding a stack of napkins. "I've already dropped a word to your manager. He'll be out tonight."

Only then did Amy notice Peter through the French doors. He was arguing with the Sarai's manager behind the reception desk, and even as Amy watched, he disappeared up a staircase toward the guest quarters. So that was why Steve had bothered lingering here with Amy. Despite his disavowals, he somehow still felt she needed a keeper.

Well, that was certainly more in character with the man who'd chewed Amy out on their last encounter. But Steve had misread Amy's thoughts, because Peter had been nowhere near Amy's mind.

Lifting a Coke can, she popped the tab. "Thanks. But I was actually thinking about my driver. Jamil had this crazy idea I was off to some wild Hollywood movie of illicit drinking, dancing, and partying. I told him I was just visiting with some expat colleagues. But I can't help wondering what all this would look like through his eyes. And what it must feel like to be told he can't enter a building in his own country because foreigners have freedoms he doesn't. The idea that expats here have a choice and he doesn't—well, I know how I'd feel."

Putting down the Coke without drinking, Amy demanded abruptly, "Is it true that Afghanistan's new constitution makes this an Islamic state under sharia law?"

Steve's intent look dissolved, and again his grin made him young. "You don't bother much with small talk, do you?"

When Amy showed no response to his teasing, his expression grew serious. "It's not the expats but the local Ministry of Vice that enforces liquor laws on Afghan citizens. Foreign entities that don't check for passports have been getting kicked out of the country."

Steve picked up a barbecued rib. They looked and smelled wonderful, a reminder Amy hadn't yet eaten supper. But she didn't trust them near her silk attire, so she reached instead for a cucumber sandwich.

"You're in what is officially the Islamic Republic of Afghanistan. And yes, sharia law is the basis of its jurisprudence. That's nothing new. It's been several years since the new constitution was ratified."

"And Iraq? What about their new constitution?"

"Ditto, though not quite so long ago." Steve chewed thoughtfully, a quizzical gaze resting on Amy's face, her hair spilling over her shoulders without the confining scarf. "I'm surprised you need to ask. I'd have assumed that would be one of the no-brainers included in your field briefing. Or that you'd have researched it yourself before getting on a plane."

Steve laid down the half-eaten rib. As abruptly as Amy's earlier query, he demanded, "Do your parents approve of their daughter galloping around a war zone? I'd think they'd be sick with worry."

"I'm not a child," she said sharply. Sometimes possessing the youthful look of a teenager was a definite professional disadvantage. "And since my parents are to blame for my being here, they hardly have grounds to complain."

An eyebrow shot up as Steve reached for a napkin. "Enlighten me."

Amy dropped her sandwich back to her plate. "You want my whole life story? It's hardly screenplay category."

"On the contrary, who you are determines what really motivated you to come here. And that does interest me."

"Fine then." Amy had done this often enough on the expat circuit to have her bio down to a rapid patter. "I grew up in Miami. My father's Anglo, pastor of a pretty big church, mother Cuban. Her father was a pastor too in Havana, jailed by Castro. After he got out, they made it to Miami when my mom was about six. A lot of people helped when they came as refugees, and my parents taught us to pass that on. When they weren't helping refugees in Miami, they were taking church teams on overseas humanitarian stints. I was sixteen the first time I went on a short-term missions trip doing hurricane relief in Honduras. There's an adrenaline rush to helping people smile again when they've lost everything. I got hooked."

"You said *us*. You've got siblings?"

"A brother with World Vision, sister in Peru with USAID, two more in college. Anyway, I was overseas every summer until I graduated from Florida International University. Since then I've been in so many countries I've lost track. Mainly with Christian Relief, a volunteer NGO our church sponsors."

"But you're not with them anymore. Why the switch to this New Hope Foundation? And why Afghanistan?"

Amy felt no surprise that Steve had remembered. By the sharpness of his gaze and tone, he rarely forgot much of anything. "New Hope's easy. School loans. Volunteer relief doesn't pay Wells Fargo. I've wanted to come to Afghanistan ever since liberation back when I was in high school."

Bio complete, Amy firmly dragged the subject back to her own disquiet. "But I never had a field briefing. I was asked to come here at the last minute. Naturally I googled some country reports, bought a couple guidebooks. But I didn't read anything about sharia law.

"The media and politicians are always talking about how Afghanistan's a democracy now. The way they talked, I assumed it was like India or Turkey, where you've got Hindu or Muslim majorities. And of course one expects those beliefs will dominate the local culture. But since it's a democracy, people are at least theoretically free to decide what they want to keep of their cultural beliefs and philosophy and faith—and what they themselves might choose to change."

Amy wasn't sure why she was spilling this out to a sardonic-looking contractor who was at her side only because he felt a certain guilt—except that the questions were burning inside her.

"But if sharia is still Afghanistan's governing law, then how can this be called a democracy? Under sharia, you're not allowed to think or do anything that's considered contrary to Islam. Forget political choice or women's rights. There's no freedom of speech. No freedom of religious or philosophical expression." The horror of it was in Amy's voice. "Sharia means it's still a death sentence for an Afghan to so much as choose their own faith in God."

"You've got that right," Steve said. "It wasn't too long ago the local Islamic council put a Christian convert on trial. That made the international media. There's no doubt the purpose and timing was to challenge whether sharia or some foreign code of human rights was going to carry the day here."

"And which did?" Amy demanded. "I remember hearing something at the time, but I was in India then, away from the news. I'm sure I'd have heard if they actually executed the guy."

Steve shrugged. "In the end it was mutual face-saving. After enormous international pressure, the mullahs declared the man mentally incompetent, therefore ineligible for the death penalty. He was whisked out of the country and is living in Europe."

"So in other words, they got out of it without anyone having to take an actual stand on religious freedom. Including our government. I thought we were in Afghanistan to help bring democracy and freedom. I cheered when we came over here, no matter how horrible it was, because I believed that it was worth the guns and the bombs. Not just for us but for the Afghan people. But if we haven't even given them basic human freedoms, then what are we doing here?"

Amy had started out calmly, keeping her voice below the rowdy hip-hop now playing. But tears were stinging her eyes, and her fingernails bit into her palms to keep them from spilling over. The outrage that had gripped her since Elsa Leister dropped that single, overlooked bombshell compelled her on. "People keep talking as though what matters is whether women have to wear a burqa or get to go to school. But every freedom we have is based first on the fundamental freedom to believe in your heart and worship God according to your own conscience. If you don't have that freedom, how can you ever have freedom over what you say out loud, much less what you do?

"You were a soldier, right? At least I know most PSCs were. You know the local language, so you must have served around here somewhere. Tell me, how could this have happened? How could you all have *let* it happen?"

"That's where you're wrong." The harshness of the statement cut Amy off as much as its finality.

Steve's expression was no longer affable but as hard as chiseled stone, his gaze chips of gray ice. "Sure, I was a soldier and I served in Afghanistan. But my teammates and I came here with one very simple mission: to take out al-Qaeda and their Taliban support and prevent them from attacking our country again—period. We carried out our mission well, if you haven't noticed."

"Look, I wasn't trying to disparage our troops. I know they're not the ones who make those decisions. But—" Amy hesitated, appalled at the misunderstanding, but the words burst from her. "Their superiors back in DC are, and they've had plenty to say about democracy and freedom. Besides, don't we owe something to the Afghans after coming over here and turning their country on its ear? Okay, so there're still people who want sharia law. But there must be plenty of ordinary people who really believed we were bringing them something better. I just can't help thinking those people must feel we've betrayed them."

"The question is—who's betrayed who?" Like Amy, Steve kept his voice low, but its harshness bit through the music so clearly Amy couldn't have ignored it.

"Unfortunately only too many Afghans share your crazy idea that America can and should bring them a better life. But that's where they and you are dead wrong. They want *us* to bring them freedom, *us* to make changes. But America doesn't have the power or the will to bring freedom to Afghanistan or any other country. Or frankly the responsibility. And it never did."

15

"I didn't mean—" Amy subsided as Steve's sharp gesture cut her off.

"Bottom line, you can't give freedom to people at the point of a sword—or gun—any more than you can give faith. And for much the same reason. It's got to come from inside. You'd think we'd have learned that by now. Oh yes, I can testify the Afghans believed when we came here that we were powerful enough to whistle the warlords to heel, wipe out corruption, and restore stability with all the precision and speed of our guided missile system. They know better now.

"But let me tell you what *we* expected. We expected that when we took away the excuses for these people to keep fighting and abusing each other that they would stop. That we could roll in with our money and heavy machinery and good intentions, have everyone shake hands, and get to work rebuilding this country."

Steve crushed his now-empty Coke can under his fist with a force that sounded like a gunshot. "Now you've been here—what, three or four days? And I'm betting you've already made the same snap judgments they all do. With all the troops and weapons and aid, why aren't things getting any better?

"I have no real issue with the aid crowd. Salt of the earth and all that, but they've got to be some of the dumbest smart people I know. I'll never forget one of my Basra PSDs. A twenty-six-year-old woman with a master's in international relations contracted to lecture Shia and Sunni leaders on religious reconciliation—as though she'd any experience."

Amy opened her mouth with a biting reply. But a memory of a college roommate with a fresh law degree heading to Baghdad to raise gender awareness among Iraqi generals closed her jaw. Her friend's security budget alone could have underwritten a tsunami refugee camp. "We don't all run those kinds of projects. Some of us do practical things like feeding people and meeting survival needs."

"I'm sure you do. All I'm saying is you should try looking at it the other way around. Enough money's been poured into this entire region to turn it into the Garden of Eden. *If* the locals would stop trying to kill each other and us. Or lining their own pockets instead of working for the good of their country. After all, who's to blame if the bulk of the aid money has to be wasted on security?"

The jerk of Steve's head encompassed the noisy, dancing crowd. "Do you think these people *like* spending their days locked up behind barbed wire and sandbags? that they wouldn't prefer to be out there doing a whole lot more for this country than they are? The Afghans had a choice for a future, and they've been their own worst enemy."

"That's not what I—"

Steve wasn't done. "You have to understand sharia isn't just law to these people. It's the way to God. More accurately, to the Afghans or any Muslim, there's no difference between the two. And if you really believe, as they do, that enforcing Allah's law—sharia law—not just on yourself but your family and community is the only way to heaven, then standing up for it against all your new, powerful infidel allies not only makes sense but is downright laudable. I'll give our State Department credit they weren't dumb enough to persist. They wouldn't have won, believe me."

"I can't believe you're defending them!" Amy pushed her plate away. "Are you saying it's okay to put someone on trial because of his belief in God? to force people to follow a religion, not by personal choice but on pain of death?"

"Not at all," Steve said evenly. "I agree that freedom of personal faith is so basic a human right there can't be any other real freedom without it. And that sharia is an oppressive system. But I also believe any real change has to come from the Afghan people themselves. You can't have it both ways. Either it's our right and responsibility to ram democracy and freedom down these people's throats. To make them be good and get along. In other words, to stop acting like they have for a thousand years. And you're talking powerful people with a lot to lose. We'd need Saddam or Taliban tactics and a whole lot more troops than we've got. Or if we're really going to give them freedom, then they—not we—have the responsibility of stopping the killing and corruption and abuse. And for that matter, living with the consequences if they won't. All we can hope to do is ensure they don't become a launching ground against our own country again."

"Except that as long as the mullahs run the show, that change has no chance. What you're really saying is that it's hopeless. That it's always been hopeless. For the Afghans if not for us. So why are we still here?" Amy didn't like the despairing note that had crept into her low appeal.

"You tell me. I'm just doing a job I've contracted. When I'm done, I'll head home or take another gig elsewhere. What I *won't* do is take it personally. How do you think these people get by?"

It was now full night overhead, any stars or moon hidden behind the smog and dust, the only illumination a dim white gray of fluorescent tubing along tree branches and verandas. But the party was going strong, the dancers moving with fresh energy to an impromptu karaoke competition, the pools heaving with wet bodies.

"They come. They do the job they're hired to do the best they can. Some better than others," Steve amended dryly, and from his ironic expression, he too was thinking of a certain mineralogist. "Then they go home. If you can't do that, you're not going to make it here. Why do you care so much, anyway? You don't know these people. And one way or another, you've got more freedom than under the Taliban to feed the hungry and take care of women and children and whatever else you came here to do."

"Because I came here to make a difference. I really believed I could make a difference." Amy raised her chin high, but the fluorescent lighting overhead wavered as if underwater. "I guess that sounds pretty naive."

"Not naive. Passionate." As though surprised at his own words, Steve straightened abruptly.

A cell phone rang. Steve snatched it from his belt. "You're where? You're kidding. . . . I'll be there as fast as I can." Slapping the phone shut, he pushed himself to his feet. "That's my contact. Got to go."

But the security contractor didn't move immediately. Roughly, he said, "There's nothing wrong with caring enough to be passionate. Passion is the only way great things get done. Believe it or not, I was once young and dumb enough to feel that way. But caring can get you hurt, especially in Afghanistan. Just watch your back, okay?"

Steve had taken two strides away when he turned around. "By the way, if you're really looking to make a difference, there're some pretty needy kids in that neighborhood just past Khalid's new palace."

What a strange man Steve was. One minute hard and cold as ice, the next almost kind. Amy watched him swiftly retreat with relief. At least now she could discreetly wipe away those unshed tears.

Amy wished she could be angrier. But she was too honest not to recognize at least some element of truth in his harsh lecture. She swallowed back a lump in her throat. Why had that man's words, that simple piece of data she should have known, hit her so hard?

Because all these years she'd dreamed of coming here and sharing God's love with these people. All those years in Sunday school of praying for the door to be open to the Muslim world. And she was so sure that the invasion, however ugly for both sides, was worth it in part because it meant that door cracking open.

Amy had given credit to her own country for achieving that freedom. Like other Americans, she'd cheered those purple-thumbed Afghan voters, the signing of that new constitution. *How is it possible that was wrong? How could I not know?* And why had so little been said on cable news or anywhere else of what democracy really entailed in Afghanistan beyond those triumphant elections, a few unveiled spokeswomen judiciously trumpeted across the TV screens of the world?

Amy had always been a forthright person. Passionate, Steve had called her, and it was a fair adjective. What was in her, for good or bad, spilled forth, dissembly so alien to her nature she wouldn't know where to start. Especially that which was most important to her, the greatest treasure she had to offer—her faith. Amy had never doubted that the love of God she'd been privileged to experience could in turn transform the world, even while the very strength of her faith impelled courtesy for others' differing beliefs.

But if she couldn't even share that love?

In Hindu India, the Muslim camps of Kashmir and Indonesia, that had never been in question. The very name of the organization for which she'd worked made it abundantly clear in whose name Amy's hands offered their aid. If in her current position Amy had reconciled herself to a certain circumspection, it was because she no longer worked for a faith-based NGO, not because the law of the land made Amy's very essence, all that truly mattered to her, a crime. A crime punishable by death to any Afghan she might influence.

A sudden horror seized Amy. Could she have brought danger on those children in her careless retelling of paradise? But no, as Jamil had been so quick to note, the creation account was one that varied little between Christian and Muslim versions.

Why did you bring me here if the door is still shut? Did I hear you wrong? Was it my own passion to love that drew me here and not yours as I believed?

Not that it mattered. Amy had signed a contract and was committed at least for the next few months. She looked around drearily. Somewhere in this jostling crowd were undoubtedly the contacts, even the personnel, she needed to do that job well. But she was too disheartened to pursue them further this night.

"Amy! There you are!"

Amy turned. Inside the French doors, a plump female shape waved wildly as she liberated her hair from its scarf. Debby Martini. Amy hurried over.

"Amy, I'm *so* glad I caught you. Sorry to be this late. And I can't stay. But I've got wonderful news. Turns out Soraya had a contact at MOI who was able to give us authorization for our halfway shelter."

The New Yorker's anxious, beaming face lifted Amy's spirits. Debby too had passion. A passion that had impelled her to keep trying to help the women of this country despite all the obstacles and setbacks thrown in her way.

Amy's smile banished that sheen of unshed tears. "That *is* wonderful."

"*If* we can find housing and funds. I promised not to push you, but you mentioned that personnel shortage was your major obstacle to taking on such a project, and I think I may have a solution. Would you mind terribly a short walk down the block? I'm still with Alisha and Soraya, and Soraya can't come through the security checkpoint."

"I'd be happy to."

"We're parked on the next street." As Amy followed Debby through the guesthouse to the front gate, the New Yorker went on. "As I mentioned earlier, Alisha's USAID contract is up in a few days. Which leaves Soraya looking for a new position. I thought of you."

Najibullah jumped out to open a passenger door as the two women reached the USAID vehicle. Alisha and her translator were in the back-seat. Climbing in, Debby waited until greetings were exchanged before recapping her earlier discussion in a few sentences.

"That's a great idea," Alisha enthused. "Soraya would give you a female translator. And she knows the local bureaucracy and prison personnel. What do you think, Soraya? I've been concerned about your job ending when I rotate out. That is, if you're interested, Amy. We sure don't mean to jump the gun here."

"No, this could really work," Amy said slowly. The very seriousness with which the USAID project manager was taking Debby's proposition had begun to kindle Amy's enthusiasm. "Soraya would solve the communication problem, especially if there's both Dari and Pashto speakers among the prison women. And her law experience would be invaluable." Her mind flashed to those empty upstairs suites. "Soraya, how would you feel about a live-in position?"

Soraya was sitting so still Amy wasn't sure she'd followed the entire English exchange, her bright red lipstick curved in a polite smile that didn't reach wary eyes. "Live-in means to live with you, yes? Is this live-in a condition of employment?"

"No, though it would certainly be helpful," Amy said honestly.

"And the wages?"

"I can guarantee what USAID is paying. On top of room and board if you choose to live in."

"Then I accept," Soraya said immediately.

Amy's smile grew wide as she looked around at the other three women. "Then so do I. Let's do this!"

Debby climbed out to walk with Amy back to the Sarai. "Honey, I can't begin to tell you how much this means to me. The thought of leaving these women to their fate has been eating me up inside. You're the angel I've begged God to send."

"I can't promise miracles, but at least I can offer those women a man-free sanctuary until *they* decide what they want to do with the rest of their lives."

"A one-woman revolution." Debby grinned at Amy. "Good for you!"

"Yeah, well, I'm not feeling very happy with men at the moment."

"Oh, come on, there're some decent ones, even here in Afghanistan." As though Amy's enlistment had rolled a load off her shoulders, Debby's step was newly light and free. She offered Amy a knowing look. "That was a winner you were talking with when I walked in."

Amy waved away the distraction. "That's what everyone says. There are a lot of decent men. There are a lot of decent Afghans. There are a lot of decent people everywhere. So why is this country in such a stinking mess? Or the entire planet, for that matter? If most people are decent, why can't they act more decently to each other?"

Debby shook her head. "People may be decent. But they're also selfish and out for number one. Yours truly included. Haven't you learned that yet? To change it, you'd need Jesus Christ himself to come back and wave a magic wand. And even one of his disciples betrayed him, if I remember the story right."

Jesus Christ.

The one person Amy could not introduce into this equation.

16

Steve had gone cold inside at Amy's challenge, then hot with fury. This was why he and other PSCs preferred to stay with their own kind and away from civilians. Especially the bleeding, do-gooder types like Ms. Amy Mallory with their stupid misconceptions formulated from a TV screen instead of hard reality under their boots. Even the appalled look in her eyes that made it clear she hadn't meant to denigrate every uniform with the courage to come here failed to mollify him.

Flashing ID at the Gurkha guard, Steve waited impatiently for the red and white checkpoint boom to start its rise before gunning the Suburban savagely down the street. He hadn't planned to linger once it was clear the DynCorp manager wasn't coming back. But something about Amy had drawn Steve. Some nagging reflection of his own youthful naiveté and passion?

Steve remembered only too well when he'd believed in his country, in his mission. Even in these people, the men beside whom he'd fought and for whom he'd been as willing to die as for his own countrymen. He'd been confident that this time would be different from the Taliban and the muj and the Russians and all the other invaders responsible for Afghanistan's woes. That the hand of friendship could accomplish what the despotic tread of conquerors had not.

Then had come the gradual, terrible recognition that this was not so. That the failing came not from without but from something deep and ugly within. Steve remembered because his night dreams never let him fully forget, just when naive and youthful passion had hardened to disillusion.

To betrayal.

It wasn't just the lying and corruption at every level. The village leaders demanding compensation for a hundred flattened houses where only twenty had stood. The bogus toll ropes slung across freshly liberated roads to bleed passing transport. The newly formed police force demanding bribes instead of justice. Their greed Steve could understand, if not condone. Desperation for survival turned men hard. But if he'd learned to dismiss Khalid's land grab and its like as an inevitability of war, his disenchantment was back tenfold before the fighting wound down as muj commanders and local leaders scrambled not just for a slice of the aid pie but their own pet coalition official into whose ear they could whisper their version of local affairs.

Steve's ODA had been the one to call in an air strike against a Taliban unit on the word of a trusted Northern Alliance commander. Only to discover the "insurgents" were a delegation of tribal leaders on their way to offer allegiance to the new president. And, coincidentally, the strongest opponents to that particular commander's local power grip.

The very next week had seen Phil's patrol wiped out when their local guide walked them into an ambush. Al-Qaeda? Taliban? Or locals taking a potshot at the latest occupiers? No one would ever know since said guide had conveniently slipped away just before things blew.

Steve had come to feel completely paralyzed in doing his job because he couldn't know who was lying. Who really were the good guys and the bad. He'd almost envied the fresh young troop arrivals with their ignorance of the language and faith in their mission and local liaisons. By the time his unit shifted to the Iraq theater, Steve was more than ready to put Afghanistan behind him. All he'd taken from this place was vastly improved Dari and Pashto and a deep disenchantment, if not with his profession, certainly with the viability of his current mission.

Steve pulled up to the MOI security checkpoint, raising his ID even as he flipped open his cell phone. No, he was right in giving Amy Mallory the heads-up she should have had before ever coming here. If Steve had his way, such a lecture would be required for every expat heading this way. Let them walk into this mess with their eyes open at least.

As his call had arranged, DynCorp country manager Jason Hamilton was walking toward Steve by the time the Suburban pulled through the vehicle entrance. Though MOI offices were long shut for the day, the compound was an uproar of people.

Mac, evening shift leader for Khalid's detail, met them inside the main building. "Principal's secure. I've called in the next shift for backup just as a precaution."

"So where is it?" Steve demanded as the two CS contractors followed Jason down the hall. In contrast to outdoors, this at least was empty. "And how in blazes did it get past security?"

Jason led the way upstairs. "How the perp made it inside, we're still trying to shake out. As you're undoubtedly aware, the minister of interior—your principal—had the K-9 unit over here showing off for those visiting police chiefs. The demonstration zone was the bottom floor of the MOI headquarters. The exercise involved both C-4 and narcotics, so no one thought anything of it when the dogs started going ape. Except they kept going ape even outside the containment area. So they turned the dogs loose on the whole building."

The three men emerged on the top floor where the minister of interior had his offices.

Jason didn't head toward Khalid's suite but up the final stairwell to the roof. "That's when I got called away from the party. They should have evacuated the entire compound, but Khalid insisted it would be an insult to send all those police chiefs packing. Not as big an insult as getting someone blown up. Still, even I wrote it off as a false alarm. Then the K-9s stumbled over this baby. That's when I figured you'd appreciate a heads-up."

Portable floodlights had been set up to blaze into every corner of the building's flat roof. Dead center lay the dynamite sticks, duct tape, and wiring of a suicide vest.

"It's been disarmed," Jason assured quickly. "We wouldn't have let Khalid up here otherwise. Or at all if I'd my way. But this is his turf, and he insisted."

Unlike the sealed-off corridors below, the rooftop swarmed with activity. Steve had already noted with disapproval that Khalid was among a huddle gathered around that ugly, dark blotch. At least the minister's CS detail was tight around him, Rick and Ian among them.

As Jason joined the huddle, Steve swung around on Mac. "So why didn't *you* call?"

The huge Texan didn't back down an inch. "Because there was nothing you could have done that wasn't being handled. Believe me, when there's something worth dragging you away from R & R, you'll hear about it."

"Fair enough. But since I'm here, let's take a look." Steve pointed to an Afghan news crew holding a caterpillar mike over Khalid's hunkered-down position as he talked into a camera, his animated gestures indicating the explosives at his side. "Great, now who let them up here?"

Mac grinned. "That's a local TV station here to film tonight's demo. Khalid insisted on bringing them. Don't worry. We patted them down good."

"And so you see how the enemies of our country persist in their attacks on my person and this ministry. But they will not intimidate us—" Khalid stopped as Steve approached, straightening up so that the news crew had to take a hasty step back. As always on MOI business, the former muj commander was wearing a Western suit, making his squatting inspection as awkward as his rising. His deputy, Ismail, hurried forward to offer a supporting arm.

"Do you see how they are trying to kill me?" Khalid sounded more triumphant than aggrieved. "Did I not say the sugar factory bomb was intended for me? Now they will have to listen."

"We don't know yet what the intended target was here," Jason cautioned.

Khalid waved that away. "Who else would be a target?"

Steve knelt beside the vest. The duct-taped explosives looked no less deadly up close.

Rick glanced up. "We're thinking the bomber was going for the chopper. Security was just too tight to get anywhere near Khalid and his guests downstairs. But Khalid and his team flew over tonight."

An unnecessary ostentation designed only to impress the police chiefs with their new boss, neither contractor commented aloud.

"If the bomber was targeting the chopper, he'd figure it would be back to pick up its passengers. All he had to do was wait here." Rick poked cautiously at the vest, using a handkerchief to glove his finger. "This is what sent the dogs ape. That's not just dynamite. There's C-4 in there. Which means we don't have an ordinary suicide bomber."

"Except that so much has been pilfered from our bases the bazaars are awash with it," Mac countered skeptically. "And all over the Internet there're schematics to build this thing. Anyone with basic mechanics could put it together."

"What I'd like to know is how he got up here wired like a Christmas tree," Steve demanded. "Or left again afterward."

"I double-checked everything myself," Mac put in defensively. "Every person coming in or out went through a metal detector wand and pat-down. There's no way they missed something like this. And there was no serious danger to Khalid because we swept the roof before the chopper touched down and would have swept it again before it came back."

"I think we may have part of an answer." The voice belonged to Jason, who was leaning over the parapet that overlooked the alley and neighboring apartment building.

The brightness of searchlights outlined what had drawn their attention. Two sandbags removed from the nearest observation post had been heaved side by side onto the concertina wire, flattening the sharp barbs enough for an agile person to climb over them. Below, the third-story balcony would be an easy drop, Steve judged with an experienced eye. Ditto from there to the second-story balcony, then the alley. Or from the end of the balcony into the compound itself.

"He might have gone down this way. Climbing up's another matter." Mac shook his head. "Besides, those dogs were going crazy long before they got up to the roof. I'd swear the bomber was inside the building."

"What interests me," Steve mused, "is why the perp didn't carry out his mission. Did he get tired of waiting for the chopper? Or did something spook him? Maybe the dogs raising the alarm? And why leave the vest here? Why even let us know he's been here? Some kind of warning?"

"Or taunting," Mac suggested. "Like he's saying, 'I can hit you anytime. I just chose not to tonight.'"

"Well, if that's what he's thinking, he's out of his skull," Steve said calmly. "Forewarned is forearmed. Jason, we've got some coordinating to do. We'll need to scramble a search of the entire compound, just to make sure there isn't a repeat of this somewhere else. Oh, and the chopper's out for tonight. We don't know if the bomber had backup, maybe even an RPG. Call up Bones and tell him to get a convoy over here. Meanwhile, get Khalid off this roof before someone decides to take a potshot."

Khalid was already heading for the stairwell with the camera crew and his security detail scrambling to take up position ahead and behind.

Steve hooked a thumb toward the dark blotch spotlighted on the concrete. "Jason, any chance you can have your trainees process the vest and do some dusting for fingerprints? And send a few over to that apartment building to interview the residents. Maybe someone just happened to be looking out a window."

He was looking out a window, though it no longer held glass panes or even wooden framing. From it, he could still see the foreign mercenaries, thanks to those bright lights and the binoculars he'd been provided. This war-blasted, abandoned apartment building had been the drop site on his instructions, the ruined cubicle in which he now huddled so high and difficult to access even the most desperate of squatters had not seized on it.

He'd found the equipment where indicated, concealed under the rubble. He'd followed every instruction. Made himself ready. Steeled mind and body to finality.

So why was he still here, breathing acrid dust, shivering under the chill fingers of a wind that whistled across the shattered walls?

He waited until the floodlights blinked off and the searchers went away. His body, hunkered down and unmoving, had gone numb before he heard a stealthy tread on the broken stairs. He stilled his breathing to the same frozen wariness as his limbs.

"It is I."

He relaxed as he recognized the voice, the shape, taller and heavier than his own, though it was too dark to make out more than a silhouette against a glimmer of city lights filtering through the broken openings.

"Why did you not let me carry out the mission? I was ready. I was in position. And why leave evidence of my passing? I was not detained in my leaving, and now it must be prepared again."

"It was necessary, and this was not the right time."

"What do you mean, the right time?"

"You must be patient. There was purpose in tonight." The voice in the darkness hardened. "If only to prove you can follow orders. And we have now probed the efficiency of the infidel mercenaries. Many things must be in place to assure this is a strike worth making. Trust me."

Trust! There was no trust in these debris-choked ruins, only expediency. "It is just that I had thought it would be over tonight."

"It will be over soon enough. And when it is, it will be as glorious as you have dreamed; that I can promise you."

"I do not care for the glory, only that your promises are kept."

He turned back to the jagged opening that had once been a wall, but this time he didn't raise the binoculars. Against the black of night, his mind's eye saw the panorama spread out below. Not as it was nor even as it had once been. But as he'd dreamed it could be. A sweet scent of ripening fruit and grain and the lowing of fattened sheep and goats. The sturdy bulwark of compound walls and homes huddled together for warmth and comfort. Children with full bellies curled up in a father's embrace. Men's faces and fists relaxed in pleasure and kindliness, not hard and raised in anger. Music and feasting and laughter.

The sights and sounds and smells of peace.

Could it be that there were even now such pockets he was too blinded by hate to see?

A shudder shook him, a pang thrusting into him like air striking a freshly opened wound. Or a heart beginning to beat again. He bit hard on his lip until he felt pain instead.

He could not allow himself to feel, to find reason again on this earth to live and love.

He turned swiftly to the shadow beside him. "Soon then. I cannot wait much longer. It must be soon."

17

And now the ark was full.

Stepping out onto the marble front steps, Amy accepted from Wajid the package a courier service had just delivered. As he hurried back to his post, she lingered, smiling at the music floating across the front courtyard. The laughter and joyous squeals of playing children.

A dozen of them squatted in a circle on the packed dirt that had once been a lawn, engaged in a lively game of duck, duck, goose—and no longer in silence. Catching sight of Amy, they stopped the game to swarm up the steps. "Ameera-jan! Ameera-jan!"

It hadn't taken the children long to learn her name with the "jan" ending denoting affection, while hugs and kisses needed no translation. Detaching herself reluctantly, Amy sent them scampering back to their game. Though she'd seen it again and again in the disaster relief camps, Amy continued to be astonished at the resilience of children, who with minimal food in their bellies and protection from heat and cold could find reason to play and laugh in the bleakest of circumstances.

Heading back down the hall, Amy walked through the open double doors into the inner courtyard.

"Salaam aleykum, Miss Ameera."

"Salaam, Farah."

The Tajik teenager and a Hazara woman were directing several older children in the cleanup of the noon meal, served on a long oilcloth under cover of the colonnade. Two women rinsed dishes in plastic tubs. Others were scattered along the three sides of the veranda, mending worn clothing, twisting yarn on wooden spindles, chatting idly, or resting silently against the wall, a toddler or two curled up in their laps. From inside the communal kitchen drifted music and dubbed drama from a Bollywood soap, courtesy of New Hope's latest addition, a satellite dish on the roof for broadband Internet and television.

Satisfied all was running smoothly, Amy took the outside staircase to the second floor. Two full weeks had passed since Amy's visit to the women's prison, the first few days a madhouse of purchasing supplies, visits to government offices, conference calls to DC. A pair of gas grills and wooden shelving had turned the downstairs salon next to the bathroom into a communal kitchen. Tushaks and more shelving converted the other inner courtyard salons to dormitories.

Alisha Chan and Debby Martini had rearranged their flights to be on hand when Geeti released the first wave of Welayat prisoners into Amy's custody, twelve women and twenty-six children in all. More had been released, but they either chose or were compelled to return to their own relatives. Which was just as well, since thirty-eight new residents was as full as Amy liked to see even in a property this size.

Moving the group into their new quarters was made simple by the scantiness of their possessions—some well-worn clothing, blankets, a few personal mementos. Amy's original idea was to erect some kind of partition so each woman had a space to call her own. But the women vetoed this, and Amy recognized they weren't accustomed to privacy, sleeping as poorer Afghan families did in a single room on tushaks rolled out at night.

Even so, the women had divided into distinct groups. The largest family group was a Hazara widow and two adult daughters, who like Roya were not in jail for zina but a roundup of poppy field harvesters. They had a dozen children among them, ranging from babies to ten- and twelve-year-old boys who were uncles to most of the others. They'd staked out the downstairs salon opposite the kitchen.

Meanwhile, Roya, Aryana, and Najeeda, all from the same Welayat cell with five children between them, chose the salon beside the upstairs bathroom. Farah and two women from other cells with their four children moved into one of the two upstairs salons on the other side of the court-yard while the final three women and their five children took the other.

The divisions were understandable. Roya's group were Pashtuns. Farah's Tajiks, her neighbors Uzbek. Amy didn't like perpetuating the ethnic divides that had caused so much trouble in this country. Yet she'd opened this sanctuary with the premise of offering these women choices, and since the living arrangements seemed to be working, she hadn't interfered. At least the neutral ground of kitchen and courtyard required the women to mingle as their children played happily together.

Communication hadn't proven a problem. Though each tribal group had its own language, the women all spoke some Dari, a *lingua franca* in Kabul, and it would seem in the Welayat as well. Many words were similar to the Urdu that Amy had learned in Kashmiri relief camps, and thanks to dogged study, she was already understanding much of the chatter floating up the stairs.

The final and smallest upstairs salon had been turned over to the two older Hazara boys along with four others above six years of age. Sooner or later, the problem of young males in this female sanctuary would have to be addressed. But not for a year or so. By then Amy could hope other opportunities would have opened for these women.

Entering the upstairs main wing, Amy stopped first by the apartment suite she now shared with Soraya. Two bedrooms were furnished scrupu-lously the same with twin bed, wardrobe, desk and chair, and bookshelf. The living area between was fixed up Afghan style with tushaks and floor rugs. Two cinder blocks and a board propped a TV against one wall. Amy had lingered with the children longer than she'd realized because when she'd hurried downstairs to retrieve her package, Amy and Soraya's noon meal had been spread out on an oilcloth. Now the oilcloth was cleared away, Soraya gone.

Already Amy couldn't imagine what she'd do without her new house-mate. If Amy had settled the women into their new home and provided for their needs, it was Soraya who organized them into work teams to cook and wash and sweep. Soraya who'd helped Amy collect personal data from the new residents, no easy task since Afghans rarely recorded birth dates or possessed a surname. Soraya who'd taken over the new office computer after Amy discovered the keyboard was in the Arabic script Dari used.

Though if it weren't for Soraya, Amy would probably have joined the Welayat women's meals in the courtyard.

"No, that is not your place," Soraya vetoed firmly. "You must maintain a proper distance to maintain authority."

Though the distinction troubled Amy's democratic soul, there was something to be said for the clout of aristocracy. Soraya had only to walk into the courtyard and raise her voice for the women to end arguments over chores or meal choice.

Amy tore open her parcel as she continued down the hall to the project office. The package was from New Hope headquarters, and Amy knew its contents because Bruce had called to tell her. She shook out a small camcorder, no bigger than the palm of her hand. An advantage for filming discreet footage outside the compound. Nestor Korallis had been pleased enough at Amy's progress reports to postpone the rigors of travel and jet lag. Instead, Amy was to send video of the new project for its corporate donors.

"Soraya?"

But Soraya wasn't in the office either. Her computer was off, and when Amy glanced out the window, she saw her housemate hurrying down the walk toward the gate.

The Muslim weekend consisted only of Friday, most Kabulis working a six-day week. But last Thursday, the first since her arrival, Soraya had asked if she could take early leave after lunch. A family emergency, she'd murmured. *So maybe she thought I meant every weekend.*

"Miss Ameera, you called?" Jamil appeared in the office doorway. "I am finished with the infirmary if you have need of me."

"No, I just was looking for Soraya. But let me see what you have."

Amy followed Jamil into the next room. After the Sarai open house, Amy hadn't seen her assistant until he'd picked her up for work Saturday morning. He'd shown Amy his new Friday mosque prayer rug as though he believed she might doubt his word.

But his communication thaw hadn't proved ongoing. If anything, Jamil was more silent than ever. Amy hoped uneasily he was being fed properly.

The improvement she'd perceived that first week hadn't continued any more than his communicativeness. Where Jamil ate, Amy had no idea. He disappeared whenever Hamida carried up Soraya and Amy's meals.

I'm paying a food allowance. I wonder if I should talk to Rasheed, see how he's being fed. But Rasheed will be sure to think I'm interfering. Or accusing him of starving the help.

How these social and gender divisions complicated things. It would be so much simpler to run one big cafeteria for the compound. Amy looked around the room. A locked metal cabinet for medicines. A long, sturdy table for exams. Two foldout cots. Shelving held rudimentary medical instruments, bandages, gauze, hydrogen peroxide, and other supplies.

"It looks perfect. Did you find everything you need?"

"I purchased everything on their list." Jamil held up a copy of *Where There Is No Doctor*, the useful humanitarian handbook translated into dozens of languages around the globe. For major emergencies, Kabul had a hospital. But this infirmary would handle the usual childhood ailments, cuts and scrapes, of which twenty-six children were already keeping Jamil in business as resident paramedic.

For their mothers something else would be needed. They'd never allow a male medic to touch them. *I wonder if any of the NGOs have a female nurse or doctor who'd be willing to come for an occasional clinic. I'd like to see the Welayat women get a thorough checkup.*

As she mused, Amy turned back to her package, shaking the rest of its contents onto the exam table.

Jamil looked over her shoulder. "What is it?"

"It's a video camera. See, here is the foldout screen. And here's where you turn it on. There, you can see the medicine cabinet. It takes still photos too."

"But it is so small." Jamil's expression was alight with the first enthusiasm Amy had seen on him. Picking up the camera as Amy laid it down, he turned it deftly and carefully in his hands. "And where are the tapes?"

"It's digital. That means it can be uploaded right onto the computer." Amy looked quizzically at Jamil. "You've used a video camera before?"

"When I was a student, I had a friend who worked for a news station in Islamabad. But his camera was big with very big cassettes." Jamil set the camera down, then made a motion with his hands as though measuring a fish.

"Maybe you can try your hand at this one. If I can just figure out the manual." Amy frowned over a page of diagrams and the usual incomprehensible techno-gibberish. "I'm trying to figure out how to shift from video to still shots."

"But that is easy." Lifting the manual from Amy's hand, Jamil studied it, then picked up the camera again. "You see this? The screen works like a computer monitor. You push this button as a mouse and choose this menu option."

To Amy's open mouth, he added, "It is no more difficult to comprehend than a computer manual."

Amy closed her mouth with a snap. "I could never figure those out either. Does this mean you know how to use a computer?"

Jamil spread his hands. "Not for many years, but if it has not changed too much, perhaps."

"Then come with me." Scooping the camera components back into their box, Amy led the way next door to the office. She handed a stack of printouts to Jamil. Translation was one of the biggest office needs; red tape needed translating from English to Dari for appropriate government offices and vice versa for New Hope headquarters. "Could you translate these?"

Jamil shuffled through a few sheets and nodded. "You need them today?"

"Only that MOI project approval I promised to fax Mr. Korallis. The rest can wait for Soraya to finish Saturday."

Amy had wondered how Jamil and Rasheed would take the addition of an Afghan female colleague. It proved simpler than expected. Both men ignored her existence as Soraya ignored theirs, all parties dealing directly with Amy. Which was fine with Amy. What mattered was how quickly—and successfully—it had all come together. Included in that courier package was a glowing commendation from Nestor Korallis.

It's not so hopeless. There are people here willing to work together, to change this country, even if it's one small project at a time. Why had she allowed a single jaded opinion to discourage her so much?

A screech broke into that exultant thought.

At first Amy thought it was the TV. But as the screech rose to a wail, she rushed down the hall. If her multiethnic experiment was proving successful, it was not without snags. For the first days, her new residents had seemed too dazed at their good fortune to do more than reiterate gratitude and scramble silently and eagerly to do as they were asked. But though enforced intermingling had pushed the women out of their shells, a side effect was the quarrels.

Amy could guess at some of the tension, though Soraya proved reluctant to translate their bickering. In the eyes of their countrymen, Roya and the Hazara women were guilty only of economic disadvantage. The older Hazara was an honorable war widow, she'd informed Amy through Soraya. Why should her offspring associate with criminals?

Amy had been forced to make a stern announcement that anyone was free to leave. The Hazaras had chosen to stay, but *bad women* and *immoral* were Dari words Amy now knew.

A man's angry voice rose above the woman's cries. Rasheed. Amy groaned, her steps quickening. If she'd been foolish in assuming that as mutual victims these women would automatically empathize, it hadn't even occurred to Amy that the caretaker might have a problem with New Hope's new project. Her own burqa experience should have been a warning.

If Rasheed had been cooperative in readying the New Hope compound, even producing an elderly cargo truck to transport their new residents, his bearded face had darkened to fury when he recognized where Amy was directing him.

"They aren't criminals; they're abuse victims," Amy insisted. "And our authorization is from the landlord's own offices."

The MOI seal on the release papers ended Rasheed's objections, but he'd maintained a sullen distance from his new tenants—except when outbursts spilled over into the chowkidar's quarters. Two days earlier when a fight degenerated from name-calling to actual hair pulling, Rasheed had burst into the courtyard before Amy or Soraya could interfere, separating the women by tossing them apart. No one was hurt, but Amy had felt it necessary to ask Rasheed not to interfere again.

No, to order him. Not without trepidation, because the look on

Rasheed's face carried Amy back to her original burqa episode. But with a curt nod, he'd acquiesced.

So why was he back? Amy hurried to the balcony railing as the shouting rose to a crescendo, anxiety twisting at her stomach. She didn't want to confront the burly chowkidar again.

But the woman Rasheed was harrying furiously by the arm toward his side of the compound wasn't one of Amy's charges. It was Hamida. This wasn't the first time Amy had seen her slipping in to sit with the other women in the courtyard. How isolated Rasheed's wife must feel all day in her own quarters.

A slammed door under the stairs cut off stifled sobs. Down in the courtyard, the women returned to their activities, cheerful chatter now muted.

Amy turned to Jamil, who remained standing in the doorway. "Why is Rasheed so angry?" she demanded as she trailed him back down the hall. "Hamida served his meal before mine, so it wasn't like she skipped out on his lunch."

"His wife did not have permission to visit these women," Jamil said dispassionately over his shoulder. "She should have been in her own home working, not mixing with troublemakers and immoral women."

"Is that what you think of these women?" Amy asked incredulously. "You know their stories. You know how unfairly they've been treated. And Rasheed—how can he treat his wife like that? She's not a child to be told who she can speak to."

They'd reached the office again. Jamil looked at Amy, his expression perplexed. "But I have told you what Rasheed said, not what I think. Still, he is right to chastise his wife. How else will he maintain discipline in his home? The Quran says women are to be silent and obey. And it is only natural he would not wish his family to mix with such women. You say they are not truly criminals. But they were in jail because they were not obedient."

"Seen and not heard, you mean." Amy swallowed back disappointment. Had she thought because Jamil was younger and educated, he couldn't be as prejudiced? "I guess I should be glad he doesn't treat me like his wife and the other women."

"But you are not a woman." Even as Jamil said the words, an apologetic glance slid to Amy, then away.

Amy didn't let it go. "What do you mean by that?"

"I only meant that you are a foreigner, not an Afghan woman. You speak, you think, you walk like a man. You are—" The hunch of Jamil's narrow shoulders was expressive. "What is permitted for you is not permitted for Afghan women."

Like some kind of third gender, neither woman nor man. Amy understood perfectly the logic, infuriating as she found it. Afghan men *knew* what women were supposed to be and do. But that conflicted with accepting generous salaries from Western women.

So they just turn us into some kind of asexual creature rather than admit they're wrong about women to start with. And someone like Soraya they just ignore. Fine, I'm not a woman, so let's forget about being bashful.

"What do you think? You said your mother was an educated woman."

Jamil was silent, and at first Amy thought she'd pushed too hard. Then he said slowly, "That was long ago. Before the Taliban. She studied under the Russians, and they were godless, as all know. Even so, she was a good Muslim woman. She would not answer back to a man or dispute what my father ordered her to do. Besides—" contempt flared in his dark eyes— "these women are ignorant and unruly. Rasheed is right. It takes discipline to keep them in order and properly subject to men. As my mother was to my father."

"And what about love?" Amy demanded, outraged. "I have no problem with women being respectful to their husbands. My faith teaches that too. But men are also supposed to love their wives like they love their own bodies. And take care of them. And treat them kindly if they want their prayers to be heard."

Jamil's eyebrows knit together. "That is not in the Quran."

"Maybe not, but it's in the Bible. That is the Christian holy book."

"I know it is your holy book. But I did not know it contained such sayings. May I see it for myself?"

Amy hesitated. Jamil had been talking so freely for a change, she might have been in one of the frequent philosophical discussions Hindu and

Muslim and secular, as well as Christian, colleagues enjoyed back in the refugee camps or even in Miami. *Not an Islamic fundamentalist regime,* she reminded herself.

At her hesitation, Jamil added, "I have seen the book you read during the calls to prayer. That is your holy book, is it not? I have wondered what it contains. I would like to see this *hadith*—this teaching—about marriage for myself."

"Of course, if you'd like." Amy took out the Bible she kept in her desk. Now that she was living submerged in Afghan life, the calls to prayer had become part of her own daily routine. The interruptions weren't as burdensome as Amy had expected, the memorized Arabic prayers repeated so swiftly the whole process took only a few minutes.

Until Soraya's coming, Amy had wondered if the prayers, like so many other rituals here, were only for males. Her housemate not only religiously followed the salat—schedule of prayers—but superintended the other women's observance, descending to the courtyard each time the high, undulating call rang out from a neighborhood minaret.

"They must be taught to be good women, moral women," she'd told Amy decisively.

Though Amy didn't like the flavor of coercion, the other women seemed to take it for granted, so she'd left it alone. As a Christian and infidel, Amy knew she wasn't expected to follow suit nor indeed that it would be appreciated were she to mimic their actions. Instead, she sat at her desk, praying and reading her Bible until Soraya returned to the office. Amy hadn't realized Jamil had taken note.

"I just wouldn't want to get you into any trouble if reading the Bible isn't permitted in your culture," she finished diplomatically.

Jamil's face darkened, his voice sharp as he answered, "If you think the foreigners can forbid us to read your holy book as they forbid us to drink their alcohol or enter their buildings, we are not children. We do not need you to choose for us what is right and wrong."

"That's not what I meant. And I don't think it's the foreigners who make those rules. I've been told on pretty good authority that it's your own Ministry of Vice that makes those laws."

Jamil considered, then seemed to accede to the justice of that because he went on more mildly. "There is nothing in the Quran forbidding the reading of the Christian holy book. It is simply not customary. I have never seen them available to be purchased. But Isa Masih, your Jesus, is one of our prophets, and Muhammad himself spoke of your holy book as containing the word of Allah. Of course, it is said that which the Christians use has been corrupted. That is why it was necessary for Allah to send Muhammad a new holy book."

"I can promise you that isn't true," Amy said decisively. "There are manuscripts today of the Bible that predate Muhammad, some of the Old Testament from even before the time of Christ. What's in my Bible certainly hasn't been corrupted. But why don't you read it for yourself and see what you think? Here are the passages I was talking about." She flipped her Bible to Ephesians 5, then 1 Peter 3. "See? God won't even hear all those prayers if a man doesn't treat his wife kindly."

Jamil read again, his lips moving silently as he sounded out the English words. "So it does say. But this book is in English. The Quran is in Arabic alone, the sacred words exactly as they were given to Muhammad. If this is not in the original language, how can you know what has been corrupted?"

"The Bible has been translated into hundreds of languages, including Dari and Pashto. But the original languages and old manuscripts still exist, so anyone can go back and see if it's been translated truthfully. You don't have to take my word for it. Check it out on the Internet."

Amy glanced at Jamil as she put the Bible away. "I didn't realize you spoke Arabic. But if the Quran is in only Arabic, how do most Afghans who don't speak that language know what it says?"

Jamil's shoulders rose and fell. "I do not speak Arabic. But we memorize the *surahs* and the hadiths in school. And the mullahs tell us what they mean."

"So you can't be so sure either what the original really says." Amy's wry grin robbed the comment of any offense.

Turning suddenly to her desk, she rummaged through her shoulder bag. "You know, if you'd really like to see what our holy book says for yourself, I can give you this. It's only the second half of the Bible that tells about the life of Jesus and his teaching and his disciples, but you're sure welcome to it. Please, I'd like to give it to you as a thank-you for everything you do for me."

The olive green volume extended in the palm of her hand was a pocket-size New Testament Amy kept in her bag in preference to lugging around her larger study Bible. Jamil looked at it but didn't touch it, showing as much reluctance as though the book contained a cobra's venom.

As the moment extended to awkwardness, Amy let her hand drop. "That's okay. It was just a thought. Here, let me turn the computer on, and I'll see if I can pull up the program Soraya was using to do that translation." As she spoke, Amy discreetly turned to slide the New Testament back into her bag.

But before she could do so, Jamil snatched it, tucking it into his vest. "No, wait. It is a fine gift. I . . . I wish to read it. Thank you."

Jamil walked swiftly back toward his quarters. It had taken the rest of the afternoon to finish the translations Ameera had requested, so long was it since he'd read or written the Western script. His evening meal awaited retrieval in the guard shack, but Jamil had chosen to fast. The food Rasheed's wife set aside for him and the elderly Wajid was nourishing enough, better than he'd eaten in years. But the acid twisting unendingly at his stomach did not permit him to enjoy it.

And now confusion tore at his insides as well. Jamil had told Ameera she was like a man to him. But it was not true. However he might try to pretend it wasn't so, her femaleness troubled him in its closeness. The flower scent of her hair, a shimmering gold he'd thought artificial when he'd seen it in photographs or on the satellite television channels. The shape, definitely not male even under the enveloping attire she now adopted.

But the directness and contemplation and fire with which Ameera spoke was not female. Or so he'd always been taught. There'd been female students in Jamil's classes in Islamabad. Not many, but women too needed doctors. They kept to their own corner of the classroom, eyes lowered, not offering opinions. Not like the vociferous, argumentative male students. Did they have such discussions as Ameera offered among themselves when men were not listening?

And the things Ameera had to say. The things she did. These were more troubling to Jamil's peace of mind than her undeniable womanhood. His pace quickened as though the propelling of his body would thrust aside unwelcome thoughts. Jamil didn't bother with the front gate. Wajid's slumber never roused unless someone thundered against its metal. Hoisting himself onto the partition wall, he dropped easily to the other side. Two mechanics hammering inside an open hood looked up but showed no reaction. They'd grown accustomed to Jamil's shortcut.

Beyond the tin-roofed work shed and a scattering of vehicles that now included the Corolla, a row of small, concrete rooms ran along the partition to the rear of the mechanics yard, guest habitation for clients from out of town. Rasheed had tossed a tushak into the farthest for Jamil. In the back wall, a metal gate led into the rear quadrant of the compound. A large padlock kept the gate secure, but above the wall could be seen green, leafy crowns of trees, apples and apricots visible in the higher branches.

Unlocking a much smaller padlock he'd purchased at the bazaar, Jamil went inside. Not that there was anything worth stealing beyond his clothing, personal oddments, and the new prayer rug. There'd been a time when he'd have thought a beggar more fortunate. Now his scant possessions seemed riches.

Because he'd skipped the dinner hour, light still filtered through a small, barred window. Jamil stretched out on the tushak and pulled the camera manual from inside his vest. The diagrams and their terse English explanations entangled in his mind with the woman who'd commissioned him to decipher them, bringing back the twisting to his stomach. Dropping the manual, he turned over to bury his face in his arms. But cutting off the light was easier than cutting off his thoughts.

Ameera. Why did people like her have to come here? to shake up the convictions that had burned like acid into his soul? It was so easy to hate, to fuel the passion of his fury, when he saw what others were doing to his homeland. The foreigners with their extravagances and drunken revelries. Their convoys speeding with arrogant disregard through the streets. The endless conferences and surveys and programs that put money into their pockets but brought so little change to the people of Afghanistan.

And the leaders of his own people who were no better. Who restored to power the same brutal warlords who had ripped this country apart. Who posed in their Western suits for TV cameras or with the foreign dignitaries behind the high, guarded walls of their embassies. And who were now happily splitting up the foreign aid nest egg, as they'd squandered Soviet and American and Saudi billions in turn, building their own fortunes and futures instead of their homeland.

But then along came this Ameera, who did not fall into any of his equations. Who spoke to him, not as a woman to a man, but as two people who might even be friends, mind speaking honestly to mind, heart to heart as no other in his life had spoken. He hadn't even known a man and a woman could speak so to each other.

And her actions. The care—yes, and love—she gave to these women and children to whom she owed nothing. Jamil had seen the beggars on the streets, driven past the hovels of the poor and hungry, since his earliest recollection. But he'd never thought much about their plight until he'd come to share its desperation. Even then it had been his own that consumed him, not others'.

Nor would he soil his hands now for such women as shared these walls, quarrelsome and troublemakers, did he not need sanctuary and food enough to fuel his body. As would not Soraya without incentive of that generous foreign salary, Jamil had absolute certainty. He knew the arrogance of the aristocrat because it had once been his own.

As for Rasheed, Jamil knew the reason for the chowkidar's capitulation, if Ameera did not, because he'd overheard the man's complaint to Wajid. "The landlord will not permit me to evict these delinquents. He says foreigners grow angry at such things and complain to their press. And he is in need of the Americans at this time."

But this Ameera!

Jamil had seen on the TV screen the luxury in which Ameera's countrymen lived, so different from her present life. Yet she chose to live among his people, eat their food, learn their language, instead of remaining in the wealthy quarters of the foreigners. And the look on her face when she embraced a child. No, whatever reason Ameera had come to his country, Jamil could not accuse her nor convince himself that she did all he'd seen her do with any other thought than to help his people.

What made the difference? Ameera was an infidel. Yet she was nothing like the Christian world he'd seen on satellite TV, against which the mullahs railed with reason. She behaved like—

A better Muslim than I have ever been, he admitted into the tushak. *A Muslim such as the mullahs say women should be. Giving to the poor. Praying. Living a life of modesty and service.* More so, she was compassionate, kind, even to those who were not of her faith. And that the mullahs did not teach.

Rolling over to a sitting position, Jamil unearthed from a vest pocket the slim volume Ameera had given him. The olive green oblong roused in him both supreme distaste and curiosity. Was it the teachings said to be in these pages, teachings of the prophet Ameera professed to follow, that made her so different? What in those teachings differed from those of the Quran?

It was true that like Adam and Noah and Abraham and Moses, Isa Masih was lauded as a prophet by Muhammad himself. But Jamil had not been totally honest in his bold declaration to Ameera. If the Quran itself made frequent reference to the teachings and works of the prophet Isa, or Jesus in Ameera's language, it gave few details, and the book said to contain those details was so little favored by the mullahs, Jamil had never heard or seen its contents. The Taliban had banned the book completely as an instrument of the infidel West. But they'd banned so much else, and it had been reflexive protest against their autocratic dictates as much as the new ones these foreigners thrust on the Afghan people that prompted Jamil's impetuous pronouncement.

And yet why not? If the Quran did not forbid, was it not perhaps the duty of a Muslim to ascertain who this Jesus was, what he had taught? It would be useful practice for the translations Ameera had requested.

Or was this only a distraction, an excuse to please Ameera?

Jamil sat with the small volume in his hands, fingering its cover until a corner began to curl, as twilight cast a dappled pattern of light and dark onto the wall above his head. Soon it would be too dark to see its pages. With sudden decision, Jamil opened the book. Turning a page, he began to read.

"Hey, Steve, DynCorp just faxed over the final report on the MOI suicide vest."

Steve put aside Khalid's movement schedule to pick up the single sheet of paper Phil dropped onto his desk.

The medic saved him the bother of skimming through it. "Basic summary, no news. Jason had his trainees do a full workup, fingerprinting everything in sight and everyone in the building. Minus all the visiting police chiefs and their entourages, who'd long gone by then. Prints on the bomb components matched a couple good ones on the balcony railing but no matches to the fingerprint roundup. They're feeding their catch now into a computer database. Great training exercise, but without suspects for a match, it won't do us any good. The only interesting tidbit was the vest itself. Schematics right off the Internet, but the trigger mechanism was remote control. A cell phone. I thought these guys usually blew themselves up."

"I've heard of remote-control IEDs but not suicide bombs. Hmm." Steve swiveled his desk chair to stare out a picture window. The upstairs suite the CS team had co-opted as command center overlooked the same concrete slabbing as Khalid's reception salon but no longer offered a view of the massive Mi-8 helicopter. The minister had finally agreed to retire his monster to a well-guarded helipad on the PSD base where some out-of-bounds guest couldn't slap a magnetic explosive on its underbelly.

Steve ran a satisfied eye over an assortment of armored SUVs and Humvees with gun turrets that had taken its place. "So the perp wasn't the one who called off the mission. On the other hand, he had to make the choice to drop his vest behind. I wonder who had the remote and where. Or maybe we've got it all wrong, and the perp was just carrying the trigger separate from the bomb."

"Unless we catch the guy, we may never know," Phil said. "Nor is there any evidence of how the perp entered the building. Everything was locked up tight. No sign of break-in on doors and windows nor marks of grapple hooks coming over the perimeter wall. As to the apartments next door, no one admits to seeing anything beyond bazaar traffic and MOI's own security."

"According to Jason, those ANP K-9 trainees never went above the first floor with their demo C-4," Ian spoke up from across the suite where he and Phil had been calibrating computer screens and monitors for a network of security cameras. "But I was there. Those dogs were going nuts from the moment they were brought inside all the way up to the roof. Which suggests that suicide vest strolled through the first floor and upstairs."

"You don't suppose Khalid's capable of orchestrating the whole thing himself?" Phil gestured toward a flat-screen TV on the wall, its sound muted. Satellite feed was one perk Khalid supplied. The screen showed a live feed of the Afghan parliament, their principal currently addressing the assembly. "The whole thing's been a PR bonanza for him. Even the cable news back home's picked it up. The assassinated interior minister's brave successor standing up to death threats."

"Impossible," Ian responded. "Khalid's never out of our sight. What I'd like to know is does he really have the guts to clean up MOI the way he's been talking? You two worked with the guy, fought with him. What's your take?"

Steve eyed thoughtfully the minister resplendent behind the televised podium, McDuff and Rick visible in the background. "What Khalid's capable of orchestrating, I've never been able to read in that wily brain of his. But don't let the pop star facade fool you. Khalid doesn't go into combat without planning to win."

"One other bit of intel came in today. That ISAF attack outside MOI the day we arrived—they've managed to DNA-match the bomber. It was a woman, and no illiterate peasant either. A university student from Peshawar. Afghan refugee family."

So now they had to start suspecting every burqa drifting down the street. Not that IDing the perp solved that particular mystery. What could motivate an educated young woman—or any person—to enough passion they'd blow themselves up along with total strangers?

More urgently for the future of this region and maybe the world, what could motivate such passion to change its mind?

"Ameera-jan! Please tell us a story."

A mob of children clustered around Amy and Soraya as they stepped into the inner courtyard. The two women had spent the afternoon driving through dirt alleys in the impoverished neighborhood behind Wazir and Sherpur. With Jamil keeping wary vigil over the car, Amy and her companion knocked on doors to converse with suspicious veiled eyes or spoke to children playing in the muck. If all went well, New Hope would soon launch its first literacy and feeding outreach there.

The outing had taken longer than Amy expected, and the Welayat women were already clearing away the evening meal under the colonnade, washing dishes by the fountain. The women stopped their activity, falling immediately silent, as they caught sight of the new arrivals. Small bodies pressed against Amy, warm, sticky hands clutching hers. But around Soraya reigned a respectful amount of space.

The Afghan woman paused to fix the clamoring children with a stern eye. "Have you finished your schoolwork?"

Crestfallen faces gave the answer. The older children now spent weekday mornings in the large salon off the downstairs hallway, Rasheed having produced some secondhand blackboards, tables, and desks. Soraya had come up with the teacher, a young woman named Fatima, who showed up each morning accompanied by a teenage boy who returned at noon to escort her home.

"Then finish your studies and leave Miss Ameera to eat her meal in peace." Soraya cast a critical glance around the rest of the courtyard. Finding nothing amiss, she headed for the stairs.

Amy smiled at the disappointed faces. "Go on and do as Miss Soraya says, and when I'm done eating, I'll tell you a story."

As the children reluctantly scattered, Amy too headed for the stairs. With her leaving, the women below returned abruptly to life, a clatter of dishes and renewed conversation following Amy up the steps. Though she could comprehend their bashful reticence, it saddened Amy as she'd have liked to offer them friendship as well as survival.

I'm a woman like you, Amy wanted to cry.

But she knew she was not. Amy was a foreigner, an infidel, and their savior, and all three created a divide she could not cross. Conversation was still difficult except through Soraya, and since Amy didn't want to put a damper on the Welayat women's own developing group dynamics, she kept her distance from courtyard life unless there was need to intrude.

Soraya, who could speak their languages, didn't bother. Unless her authority was in demand, she spent her time at New Hope in the office or apartment. These illiterate peasant women, the flaring of her high-bridged nostrils made abundantly clear, might be her responsibility, but they didn't belong in her social circle.

Nor Amy either, it seemed.

Kabul's capricious power grid had been off-line when Amy and Soraya set out that afternoon. But by the local news blaring from the TV as Amy stepped into her apartment, the electricity was back on. Soraya didn't turn her head from images of the latest insurgent attack south of Kabul. Hamida had overheard the two women's arrival as she spread out their evening meal on the rug. Sinking cross-legged to the oilcloth, Amy stifled a sigh.

Soraya spoke Amy's language, was educated at least to her level, and Amy had looked forward to the other woman's companionship as much as her assistance. Especially since she felt a respect verging on awe for all Soraya had accomplished. But though her new assistant was quick to do anything Amy asked, to correct patiently, if tersely, Amy's Dari grammar or discuss the needs of their charges, she never chatted.

There was no companionable conversation over meals or any other time. Soraya spoke as much as was required to do her job and no more. When the two women were alone in their suite of an evening, Soraya turned on the TV or shut herself into her room.

And that too saddened Amy.

Not that she had a right to sadness. Soraya more than earned her salary, and that was all Amy had any right to demand.

Kebabs, rice, and fried eggplant in yogurt sauce were as good as all Hamida's cooking. Amy ate quickly, smiling her appreciation to Rasheed's wife, who lingered to wait on the two women with nervous gestures. Hamida hadn't joined the other women since the courtyard incident, but she appeared unharmed, physically at any rate.

Finishing first, Soraya headed back to the office, where Amy knew she'd be taking advantage of the returned electricity to type up the afternoon's reports.

Escaping to her own room, Amy picked up a suitcase-shaped box. The deluxe flannelgraph set had been a gift from her parents when Amy set out to her first refugee camp assignment and was one of the few extras she'd brought to Afghanistan.

That first evening the Welayat group arrived at New Hope had been chaos, children and mothers alike frightened and unsettled. Little Tamana and her brother Fahim, among New Hope's new residents, were the first to beg Amy for a repeat of the story she'd told at the prison. The flannelgraph set's brilliantly colored backdrops and vivid movable figures were sufficient improvement on Amy's amateur artwork to induce awed gasps—and immediate calm. Since then Amy's stories had become a ritual the children insisted on each evening.

And I enjoy it as much as they do, Amy admitted, heading back down the outdoor staircase. In the courtyard, a group was already settled beside the fountain, not just children, but some of the mothers, infants and toddlers nestled in their laps. A chair and low table were set out for Amy.

Farah stepped forward, a stack of Dari primers in her hands. "The children have all finished their work. I personally have checked that each was done correctly."

"Tashakor. That's wonderful," Amy thanked the girl with sincere delight.

The Welayat women had been offered the opportunity to attend classes, but only Farah and the youngest Hazara mother had chosen to do so. Farah devoured everything she was taught on the first hearing. Some of the older children were also leaping ahead.

We're going to need a second teacher soon. And another classroom. There's still that empty salon next to the schoolroom.

A breeze that had grown colder in the last hour tugged at Amy's loose tunic, tossed bright strands across her face, as she lifted the storyboard to the low table. She didn't cover her head in the privacy of the women's quarters, but for once Amy wished she'd brought a shawl, the bite in the air a reminder winter wasn't far off. Meals and community life would soon need to be moved indoors.

And that's more urgent than a second classroom. Or we can do both in there. Unless Amy could talk Rasheed out of those remaining locked salons across the hallway.

Meanwhile, her audience seemed inured to dropping temperatures and cold tiles beneath their thin clothing as Amy was not. The children squirmed with anticipation as she draped a backdrop over the storyboard. Inside the kitchen, a Hindi soap went abruptly silent, the evening cleanup crew emerging to join the group. Even Aryana, the accused murderer who still spent most of her time outside huddled silently on her tushak, had drifted to the edge of the veranda, her two-year-old clutched tight in her arms.

"Fahim. Enayat." Amy selected two older boys squeezed into the front row. "Would you like to see if Jamil is ready? You should find him finishing supper with Wajid in the guard shack."

Though under Soraya's tutelage and constant practice with the children Amy's Dari vocabulary had multiplied greatly, it was still nowhere up to narrating an entire story.

Jamil arrived before Amy had finished setting out the evening's illustrations, the women hurriedly pulling shawls across their faces as Fahim and Enayat tugged him across the courtyard.

Soraya would have been a more logical assistant—if nothing else, so that the women didn't feel the need to cover themselves. But the few times Jamil hadn't been available, the Afghan woman's frowning disdain discouraged Amy from repeating the experience, while the children always clamored for their original translator.

Crouching beside Amy, Jamil offered his small fans no encouragement, but the former medical student had by now tended enough of their scrapes and bruises that he'd earned an affectionate Jamil-jan, whether he liked it or not. As he obligingly shifted his back to the listeners, scarves dropped away from faces.

"Tonight I'm going to tell you about a boy who fought a great big giant with only a slingshot and five stones." Amy had wracked her brain for stories to satisfy her demanding audience. She had never realized how many dysfunctional family relations and frighteningly powerful villains the average fairy tale contained until she'd tried retelling them in this context.

So she'd returned to stories that seemed to make more sense to these children, perhaps because their own world and recent history were not so far removed from the tales of disaster and war and oppression and captivity that filled the pages of Amy's own holy book. If the paradise story was always in demand, the children loved such adventures as Joseph, Daniel and his three friends, the Syrian leper Naaman's captured slave girl, who'd all known just such injustice and imprisonment as this group.

The flat-roofed adobe dwellings, pastoral backdrops, and village life of Amy's flannelgraph set might have been Afghanistan as much as the biblical scenes they were meant to illustrate. Amy had deliberately stuck to the Old Testament, whose patriarchs were also claimed by Muslims.

If I'm telling the stories differently than the mullahs, no one's complained yet. I just wish I could tell them about Jesus. I wonder if Jamil has read that New Testament yet. He hasn't mentioned it.

"When the giant saw David was only a boy, he laughed at him. But David picked up his slingshot and faced the giant bravely." Amy placed the next figure on the storyboard. "'I am not afraid of you. You come against me with sword and spear and javelin, but I come against you in the name of the Lord Almighty.'"

David and Goliath was a new story by the enthralled faces of children and adults alike. Jamil looked as absorbed as his listeners, his hand gestures an exact mimic of Amy's. He didn't seem to have noticed the toddler who'd climbed into his lap. A small boy suddenly laid his head on Amy's knee, face turned to look up at her with rapt attention. On Amy's other side, seven-year-old Tamana sidled close to do the same.

As Amy brushed fingers across the nestled head, put an arm around the little girl's shoulders, something sweet and warm wrapped tendrils around her heart. She'd barely made a start here at New Hope and in Afghanistan. But on this night, these few children and their mothers at least would go to bed safe and warm, with stomachs that did not ache with hunger and no cause to be afraid.

Let them know too that like Joseph and Daniel and David, they're not alone in this great, big, scary world. You love them, Father God, and are watching over them. And maybe someday you'll open the door for me or someone else to tell them the rest of the story.

"'This day the Lord will hand you over to me. All those gathered here will know that it is not by sword or spear that the Lord saves; for the battle is the Lord's—'" Amy stopped at the sound of a quickly suppressed cough.

Rasheed came into view to lean against a pillar. How long had the chowkidar been listening from the open door under the stairs? Then Amy caught sight of another door standing open at the top of the stairs, a shrouded female shape at the railing. Soraya had stepped outside to listen from the balcony.

Not that it should matter, but even as Amy resumed her storytelling, something in Rasheed's expression, the watchful immobility of the listener above her, replaced Amy's former warm pleasure with a chill.

Jamil approved of the story Ameera had told tonight. To stand and fight the evil oppressor against overwhelming odds—more so, to emerge victorious through the strength and favor of Allah—were the daydreams brought home by every Muslim boy-child from his studies with the mullahs. Just such a warrior had been the prophet Muhammad himself, wielding a mighty sword in defense of the faith, conquering huge swaths of territory during his lifetime.

A very different personage from Ameera's Jesus.

Jamil dug Ameera's gift from his vest though twilight through the window bars was fading fast. He'd now read of Isa Masih's birth, the prophet's trial of temptation, his beginning as a miracle worker. It had taken several evenings, sounding out each word, refamiliarizing himself with the boxy script until night fell and Jamil could no longer make out the tiny letters. The reading was getting easier, the stories fascinating enough that he'd drifted to sleep for once with no thoughts that held fury or pain nor dreams that lingered when he awoke.

That this biographical account at least was true, there seemed no reason to doubt. The Quran spoke of Maryam, virgin mother of Isa. The prophet Muhammad also wrestled with evil jinn and received visits from angels. Every Muslim knew Isa was a miracle worker who healed the sick, cared for the poor, even raised the dead.

Still, Islamic lore was as filled with saints who did miracles as with heroes who fought great battles. The credulous still prayed at their shrines, pouring out treasure in hopes of miracles and healings, though Jamil's stricter instructors had been scathing toward those who turned to the dead in such pagan practices.

Impatiently, Jamil pushed on, leafing carefully through the thin, fragile pages. What of the prophet's teachings? There was nothing in these stories to explain why anyone would care to restrict the reading—or believing—of this book.

The answer was on the very next page. The prophet had climbed to a mountainside to get away from the crowds. Jamil could picture in his mind the surging, pressing multitudes like a New Year's pilgrimage to the shiny blue domes of Hazrat Ali's shrine in Mazar-i-Sharif. There on the mountain, Isa sat down to instruct his disciples. The teachings began with the rhythm of poetry:

Blessed are the poor in spirit, for theirs is the kingdom of heaven.
Blessed are those who mourn, for they will be comforted.
Blessed are the meek, for they will inherit the earth.
Blessed are those who hunger and thirst for righteousness, for they will be filled.

Hunger and thirst for righteousness. Night crept in, but Jamil could not put the book down until his eyes hurt struggling to decipher the small black marks. Taking the volume, he slipped outside. There were no streetlamps, but at the front of the property a security light powered by a generator next door cast a dim pool of illumination onto the mechanics shed's tin roof. Clambering from a pickup cab to the metal sheeting, Jamil pulled his patu tight around his shoulders and continued to read.

The Sermon on the Mount, a subheading called the prophet's instructions. This was what Jamil had sought. How did Isa's commands for his own followers compare to the many explicit instructions Allah's apostle had left behind?

And yet the words did not seem at first so different from the teachings of the mullahs, more so because they were in English that he understood and not in the Arabic he knew only by rote. A sternness in Isa's commands was like the preaching of Friday mosque. Good deeds were to be done, the law obeyed and not ignored. Lustful thoughts were as forbidden as adultery. Teachings on murder, anger, oath-taking, and giving alms differed in no significant degree from the hadiths Jamil had memorized.

Isa's strictures on divorce were more rigorous. But perhaps there needed to be strictness in such things. To throw out a woman who displayed no unfaithfulness on a husband's whim had troubled Jamil since in his childhood an aunt had returned home weeping.

The night chill seeped through the patu's thick wool, sapping Jamil's interest. His glance flickered down the page. Then it stopped, gripped by the words he read. *"You have heard that it was said, 'Love your neighbor and hate your enemy.'"*

Jamil nodded his approval. Here was a teaching that resonated the fierceness and strength of a warrior prophet, not the gentle and mild healer Isa had shown himself thus far in these pages, almost womanish, meritorious though his deeds might be, as humble and meek as the poor and downtrodden to whom he directed his blessings.

Jamil stiffened as his eyes reached the next line.

> But I tell you: Love your enemies and pray for those who persecute you, that you may be sons of your Father in heaven. . . . If

you love those who love you, what reward will you get? Are not
even the tax collectors doing that?

Love your enemies? That was not the way of Islam. It was not even
the way of manhood. An enemy was to be hated with the passion with
which one loved one's family. To be held accountable before Allah and the
ulema, the community of the faithful. To be remembered with unforgiv-
ing patience until Allah granted opportunity to redress wrong.

With swift fury, Jamil threw the volume from him into the night. He
heard the rustle and thud of its landing, but he did not go after it. No
wonder the mullahs called this book corrupt, refused to teach it.

Hastening back to his room, Jamil pulled the patu over his head and
fiercely shut himself into sleep.

That night the dreams were back in full measure.

Boredom was the killer.

Steve shifted from one foot to the other. Having your toes fall asleep while standing at your principal's back wasn't an item that made it into PSD how-to manuals. The meeting had gone on for hours, a dozen men around a conference table.

"There will be *no* aerial spraying!" The minister of agriculture's fist came down on the table. "That is no longer an item of discussion. The Afghan people will not stand for it."

"Aerial spraying could make a sizable reduction in a matter of weeks," an attaché from the U.S. embassy's Bureau of International Narcotics persisted patiently. "As we've explained, the spraying is very precise. And it won't harm your crops. With the time crunch we are currently facing—"

Khalid broke in smoothly. "Yes, the visit from your new—what do you call him?"

"Drug czar," DEA Chief Ramon Placido murmured. "Jim Waters."

"Ah yes, czar, as once ruled the infidel Russians. A strange name for a man who opposes these drugs. We look forward to showing your Jim Waters the hospitality of our country. And if we cannot yet offer him success, surely the new Colombian instructors you have provided will soon produce in our own forces such competence as they display against their own delinquents."

Was Khalid being serious or sarcastic? Across the table, DynCorp manager Jason Hamilton was listening to this exchange with a deadpan expression. The best that could be said for Colombia's own counternarcotics operation was that coca cultivation had somewhat stabilized under the U.S.–sponsored Plan Colombia while Afghanistan's opium production had exploded from two hundred tons at the height of Taliban rule in 2001 to over eight thousand tons in the most recent harvest. But Colombian hires were cheaper than American counterparts, and since U.S. tax dollars had paid for said instructors' training, offering America's south-of-the-border allies a piece of the action was a shrewd political gesture.

Still, it said much about how bad things were on the ground here when the mess in South America was held up as a yardstick to which the Afghans might someday hope to aspire.

Steve shifted his feet again, an annoying prickle signaling that blood was once more reaching his extremities. A secondary itch had started under the ceramic inserts of his tactical vest, but his mad urge to tear off boots and vest didn't register in a large wall mirror above the table. It reflected instead an impassive profile, stance straight and relaxed, M4 hanging loose but within instant grasp. Wraparound sunglasses offered anonymity for blinking and looking around, the comm wire curving from earpiece to Steve's mouth discreetly invisible.

"We will host a *loya jirga*," the minister of counternarcotics offered. "Ministers, governors, police, and counternarcotics commanders will all come to welcome your new leader. By then your Colombians will have finished their training. The new recruits can put on a demonstration."

"And my people can organize a tour of alternative development projects. The sugar factory won't be up and running again yet, but we've got some exciting new crop ventures." The USAID alternative development coordinator was one of several on the American side of the table who spoke no Dari, while Khalid alone of the Afghan ministers had learned English. At the end of the table, a translator murmured Dari and English alternatively for communication sets both sides wore.

"That isn't good enough," the BIN attaché answered sharply. "It isn't just Waters we'll need to impress but the congressional delegation coming with him, especially the chairman of the Senate Budget Committee.

You've got to understand the mood of the American people right now. They've invested billions into building up the Afghan security machine. And frankly, they're hard-pressed at the moment to see what they've got for their buck."

The embassy official's assessment drew no rebuttal from either side of the table. Following the Taliban's ouster, the biggest challenge facing Afghanistan had been restoring immediate security and rule of law. The new government and their Western allies had come up with an ingenious stopgap to fill the vacuum, deputizing in each district local muj commanders and their militias.

Rather like deputizing Bonnie and Clyde or Jesse James and their outlaw bands as the new sheriffs in town.

In the short term, it seemed a win-win situation, giving the task of preserving order to those already with the muscle to do so while providing a career opportunity for all those otherwise unemployed mujahedeen. Unfortunately, the losers proved to be Afghan civilians who'd trusted that establishment of law would liberate them from the rapaciousness and marauding of those same militias. With minimal funding attached to said deputizing, the new law in town simply squeezed their wages out of the local residents.

"My colleague has a point," U.S. Deputy Chief of Mission Carl Bolton interjected. "All this discussion hasn't yet resolved the reason we're here. We don't have a firm date for Waters and his team. But we can count on two months, three at most, since Waters plans to present his recommendations before Congress dismisses for year-end holidays. Welcome celebrations and tours are fine. But without some hard progress to present, we can kiss good-bye our current budget, much less the increased aid package we're counting on to turn this situation around."

If nothing else, the hours of monotony were proving educational about Afghan interior politics as well as Steve's own embassy. That American agencies represented at this table had as much reason to be concerned about the upcoming budget evaluation as the Afghans had never entered Steve's thinking. But then the same congressional committees threatening to cut Afghanistan's aid controlled their pocketbooks as well.

"Which brings us back to aerial spraying," the BIN attaché said. "There's simply no other tangible return we can offer at such short notice. I have a hard time understanding why anyone should object, since it's also the most equitable. Every poppy grower from the biggest landlord down to the peasant with a few plants gets hit the same. Any district not willing to cooperate can simply be assumed to be uninterested in other aid disbursements. We could wipe out the whole crop in weeks, case closed."

The logical argument was proof the counternarcotics official must be new in-country. With poppy cultivation all that stood between many Afghans and starvation, the Americans had been as pragmatic as other ISAF nations, eradication to date kept to a token 5 percent or less of this year's half-million-acre crop. That the highest bidder also determined which fields fell to police scythes was again no secret. It took only for the implications of the BIN attaché's statements to filter through the translator for protests to start.

Khalid's voice rose above the others. "We cannot penalize our farmers for trying to feed their families. And it is, after all, the opium merchants who profit most. If your Waters needs progress to report to your Congress, I myself will ensure he receives it. The regional commanders know who the delinquents are in their territory, though they do not always possess the strength to confront them. So I will prepare an order for each police district to cooperate, while my associate—" he nodded toward the new minister of counternarcotics—"mobilizes the counternarcotics task force I myself formerly trained. In two months, we can arrest a number of the worst offenders. Would this satisfy your Waters and Congress?"

"Sure it would, if you can pull it off," the BIN attaché answered sharply. "If it's that simple, why hasn't it been done before?"

"I was not minister of interior before," Khalid responded with an aplomb that left both sides of the table silenced even after translation was finished. After a moment he added as though an afterthought, "I will accompany the task force to oversee these arrests personally."

The bombshell left Steve struggling to restore his impassivity. *Khalid, you didn't just spring that on me.* In the mirror Steve eyed Khalid's deputy, at his side as always. Did that poker face suggest Ismail knew the minister's plans? Or was he just better at hiding surprise than Steve?

The U.S. joint task force commander gave voice to Steve's disbelief.

"Mr. Minister, is it prudent to expose yourself to such threat? Your country can't afford to lose another interior minister."

"Have I not already faced threat right here in Kabul?" Khalid answered placidly. "On the road it will not be so easy to find me. And I have my own excellent protection." He waved a magnanimous hand to the tall, silent figure at his back. "You will allow no harm to come to me; is that not so, Willie?"

No, he wouldn't, though at the moment an impulse to strangle his principal pulsed at Steve's temples. Unfortunately, while he might have some small sway in security measures, Steve could hardly dictate the movements and job performance of Afghanistan's top cabinet minister. And from the serene determination of the minister's reflection in that mirror, Khalid wasn't going to budge.

"Mr. Minister, if you're serious about this," Placido spoke up, "I'd sure like to have some of my boys ride along. We've been dealing with a lot of those same commanders—and those delinquents you mentioned."

"Of course," Khalid consented.

A fresh babble of discussion ended hopes of adjournment. Flexing his toes again in his boots, Steve blanked discomfort from his mind to settle himself to immobility.

At least he wouldn't have to worry about boredom for a while.

Thunder rattled the aerie where he crouched, slashes of lightning echoing the chaos of his thoughts, though no drop of rain had yet tamed the city's dust. Under his sandals, a chunk of concrete broke away, falling into the night's abyss, but he didn't retreat from the shattered edge. Was not the manner of his death already fixed around his neck at birth? And tonight, if Allah willed, he would record his declaration of shaheed, receive into his hands the replacement weapon.

Receive as well the confirmation that was his promised reward.

No, Allah's pleasure and mercy were the only rewards for which a man dared hope. Still, to know!

He turned from the opening to the darkness beyond which broken steps wound down flight after flight to the street. He'd been waiting for hours. Had there been a problem with the necessary materials to replace those tossed so senselessly away? The camera for taping? Or some more serious delay?

Feet sounded on the stairs, paused outside the ruined chamber. A narrow beam of light flickered across the cracked walls, then winked out before a shadow stepped into the room.

"Where have you been? I was on the point of leaving."

"There has been another change." Footsteps crossed the room. He'd never seen the newcomer in daylight, knew him only as a voice in the dark, on the phone. An irregular bulge above wide shoulders was a turban wrapped across the other man's face.

"Then you do not know."

"The time and place, no. But the season is now fixed."

"But that is so far distant. An eternity away." His body was shaking with the intensity of his distress, his hands clenched tight at his sides to contain it. "And what about the other?"

"Not yet. We are searching. It has not been so long. These matters take time. Inquiries must be made."

He twisted around angrily. "Perhaps I should go to search for myself if I am not needed here."

"No!" Hard fingers bit into his upper arm. "If you leave, do you think we would trust your word to return? We have the matter in hand. And resources beyond any you could summon. I have given my oath that it will be done. It is a holy matter. Do you doubt me?"

"No, of course not. It is just . . . I wish to see with my own eyes, to know before—" He bit off his words, got out with difficulty, "What am I to do then in all this time?"

The clap of thunder broke close enough the hand dropped from his arm with an involuntary gasp. He held his breath. For that single instant, a flash of lightning had reached through the broken walls, casting into sharp relief features no longer masked.

As night flowed back, he let his breath out quietly. It would be prudent to keep to himself that he'd recognize that stark profile anywhere, should he see it again. He heard the movements of the turban being yanked back into place, felt hidden eyes probing him in the darkness.

Then the voice answered with bored incredulity, "Do? What does any man do? Breathe, eat, sleep, work, live. I will contact you when the time and place are known. Until then do not seek me out. But do not deceive yourself. We will know of your every movement."

The first raindrops had begun to fall as he left the ruined building and hurried in the night. At this late hour, not even the generators of the wealthy offered scattered light, and he was grateful for continued flashes overhead to mark his way.

For the reprieve, he was not sure whether to be grateful or bitter. The time stretched out endlessly before him, yet so terrifyingly brief. What was he to do to fill the hours so that his thoughts did not spiral down into madness again?

Breathe. Eat. Sleep. Work.

Live!

In the end Jamil couldn't leave the book alone. What if someone found it there? So was the excuse he gave himself. By daylight, the memory of its words didn't ring with such effrontery. And anything was better than his present nights. On the third day he went discreetly looking. He found the book under an unpruned rose briar that climbed the wall beside the mechanics shed, the cover slightly damp because it had drizzled in the night but dry inside.

This time he stayed away from tales of Isa, leafing patiently through the pages until he found the words Ameera had first shown him: *"Husbands ought to love their wives as their own bodies."*

A good teaching. Though the Quran gave a man great power over his family, Jamil's father had not been a harsh man, raising his voice but rarely his hand. Still, Jamil knew the statistics from his medical training, had seen in Ameera's work injustices that could not be denied. Could it be true that unkindness could nullify prayers as easily as careless ablutions?

These epistles as they were called seemed to be to the hadith, a collection of Muhammad's teachings gathered by the apostle's most faithful followers, what the *injil*, the gospel stories of Isa's life and teaching, were to the Quran, Muhammad's direct revelations from Allah. Though he knew the individual English words, there were sections over which Jamil puzzled, especially those written by the disciple called Paul, his discussions of doctrine and teaching as intricate and circumambulating as the greatest Islamic scholars.

But his commands were brief, many, and unambiguous. Nor were these instructions for brushing one's teeth or arranging one's feet the proper way.

> Put off falsehood and speak truthfully. . . . He who has been stealing must steal no longer, but must work. . . . Get rid of all bitterness, rage and anger, brawling and slander, along with every form of malice.

To pray, refrain from immorality, obey government, help the poor, work hard, and avoid greed—all good teachings. But others were harder.

> Do not repay evil with evil or insult with insult, but with blessing.

> "It is mine to avenge; I will repay," says the Lord.

And over and over in many forms—live in peace with each other, be kind and compassionate to each other, love one another.

Then there it was again:

> Forgiving each other, just as in Christ God forgave you.

"Farah, have you seen Soraya at all today?"

The Tajik girl shook her head as she lifted the box in her arms to the back of the cargo truck.

"Then would you mind checking around to see if anyone else has heard anything? Maybe Soraya said something to them."

"Fatima will know. I will go find her."

"No, I already spoke with Fatima when she came in this morning. She has no idea why Soraya hasn't returned from the weekend. If I'd been thinking, I'd have asked her to check around for me when she gets home."

Amy wasn't sure just when she'd found out Fatima was a relative of Soraya's. Maybe when she'd stepped out the gate for a delivery of propane heaters just as the same youth who accompanied the teacher on school days escorted Soraya off a city bus down at the corner. Her cousin, Hasim, Soraya explained as the boy climbed aboard, and Fatima's brother, whose chores would seem to include escort duty for female family members.

Amy, who'd been wondering if it was appropriate to suggest Jamil's services, was relieved to learn Soraya wasn't crossing the city alone. The whiff of nepotism troubled her not in the least. If foreigners hired fixers, for ordinary Afghans, relationships were the grease that made society's wheels turn, someone inevitably having a "cousin" or "brother" or "uncle" who just happened to have or do exactly what you needed.

In fact, Amy was counting on Soraya to come up with at least a couple more teachers from among her acquaintances and possibly other personnel as well. Amy cast an impatient glance up and down the street. Morning classes were over, Fatima gone already with Hasim, the noon meal cleared away. A buzz of activity centered now around Rasheed's elderly cargo truck pulled up to the pedestrian gate.

More than a hundred children were registered for this afternoon's launch of their feeding and literacy outreach. Soraya had agreed to oversee the reading class until permanent teachers were hired. Jamil would drive and handle crowd control as well as documenting the event with the video camera.

The Welayat women too had pitched in. Roya and two others would go along to serve. But all had helped with food preparation and were now hoisting heavy pots, five-gallon water containers, and other supplies into the truck bed. Even Aryana had ventured out to deposit a load of drink mix cans, her toddler in one arm. In return each would earn their first small wage.

Only Soraya was missing. Several times now the Afghan woman's Thursday and Friday visits home had extended to an afternoon during the week as well. Amy hadn't objected since Soraya always requested leave first and worked long and hard, even into the evenings, when she was here. But now it was halfway through Sunday, well into the Afghan work week, and Soraya still wasn't back from her weekend. Nor was she answering her cell phone.

A screech of air brakes drew Amy's hopeful gaze. But a bus drawing up at the corner disgorged only a man in an Afghan security uniform.

Amy's attention moved on to a large jinga truck idling just up from the bus stop that hadn't been there a few minutes earlier. Wildly painted with intricate patterns and stylized scenes, Afghanistan's jinga or jingle trucks derived their name from chimes and bells and clanging tin strips strung along the vehicle's underbelly to frighten away jinn or just for decoration, depending on the piety of the owner. In a society where art and color and music held so many constraints, the jinga trucks seemed to Amy a delightful rebellion of Afghan creativity. A pride of peacocks spreading their tails on this one's wooden sides might have stepped down from an ancient Persian tapestry.

Unfortunately, it happened to be blocking her team's exit. Amy turned back to the cargo truck. "Jamil?"

But her driver had followed Amy's gaze and was already starting toward the truck. By the time he returned, the loading was finished, blue burqas that were Roya and her team sitting among the pots in the truck bed, the others drifting back inside the compound. Behind Jamil, the jinga truck was backing up around the corner where the street was wider.

"We'll just have to go without Soraya. We can at least do the feeding. I'd ask you to take Soraya's place, but you need to be free to run the video camera. And keep an eye out for trouble."

From the men, Amy didn't add aloud. New Hope's program, like so many others, was geared to the most needy and neglected of this society. But even during registration, there'd been trouble with neighborhood men who figured if there were to be handouts, they should be first in line. Another plus for the literacy class as the men were less likely to stand around through ABC's.

"I will teach."

Amy whirled around, surprised. Farah had been herding children back through the gate, her burqa flipped up over her head so Amy could see her young, eager face. Farah could have understood only Soraya's name in the other two's English conversation, but Amy didn't ask how the girl knew of their dilemma. Soraya's AWOL status was public knowledge.

"But you're not a teacher, Farah. You're just learning to read yourself."

"I can teach what I have already learned." The girl's eyes were pleading. "I will teach the first letters and tell your story of paradise. Please, I know I can do it."

"Well, I guess it can't hurt to try." Amy pulled out a key. "Why don't you get the story box. It's sitting just inside my room by the wall."

Jamil turned his back as Farah scurried up the cobblestone path.

Amy eyed him. "What is it? Do you think I shouldn't let her try?"

"That is not for me to say. I was only thinking—" as Jamil turned around, Amy saw that it was a half smile, not a frown, that curved his mouth—"this woman Farah is very like a sister of mine."

One more personal tidbit from Amy's companion. "You have a sister Farah's age?"

"No, she was small, in her first years of school, though she would now perhaps be this woman's age. But she too believed there was nothing she could not do, though she was female."

The half smile disappeared, and Amy probed no further. Whatever had happened to Jamil's family clearly held horrors he preferred to forget. Farah quickly returned with the story box as well as a portable blackboard she'd grabbed from the schoolroom. It was Farah's first outing since the move from prison, and she happily joined Amy in the truck cab, her face pressed eagerly to the window.

The selected neighborhood was not far from the New Hope compound. Their route led through a new housing development whose towers and cupolas and gabled peaks thrust up above high walls in the gaudiest colors Amy had ever seen.

Farah clutched Amy's arm with a squeal of excitement. "Are they the king's palaces?"

"No, they're just people's houses," Amy answered.

Farah didn't look convinced, and Amy didn't blame her. She felt none of the Afghan teenager's wide-eyed admiration. In a city filled with such desperate human need, the garish new structures seemed not only taste-less but borderline criminal. Amy studied one particularly ostentatious mustard yellow structure whose glass-and-chrome tower dominated the skyline where mansions gave way again to mud-brick hovels. Was Steve Wilson among the armed men patrolling any of these balconies and look-out towers? One of those colorful structures must belong to her landlord, since it was Steve who'd put Amy on to this particular neighborhood.

Amy had contracted with a local brickmaker to use his sizable court-yard two afternoons a week. While Roya and her team warmed up a protein-rich lentil stew, Farah set up her blackboard and story materials.

Soraya's absence was almost worth it, Amy decided on the way home, just to witness Farah's performance.

"I taught well, did I not?" the girl announced back at New Hope. The downstairs TV had been moved to the empty salon so Jamil could hook up the video footage he'd taken of the project inauguration as well as New Hope compound activities. Women and children alike buzzed with excitement to see themselves on the screen, and Farah justifiably preened herself on her own role.

"Yes, you did wonderfully well," Amy answered warmly. "I think Soraya has found herself a new assistant."

"Someday, *inshallah*, I will be a teacher, and I will start schools like you, Ameera-jan, for children who have none," Farah said with such determi-nation that Amy's eyes burned. In a just world, this beautiful sixteen-year-old would be thinking of prom and college applications, not hiding from forced marriage to a brutal old man.

Why do I have so much when they have so little? And so much of it has nothing to do with available resources but just plain human meanness. If I accomplish nothing else here, I'm determined to make sure Farah gets a chance at an education. That girl is a natural teacher.

Amy was feeling none of her charges' elation as she climbed the stairs to her own quarters. The afternoon's success hadn't solved the problem of Soraya's continued absence. Was it possible her assistant had simply quit?

What am I going to do if she doesn't come back? One way or another Amy needed something in place before the next neighborhood feeding. Would Fatima be willing to stay on two afternoons a week?

Amy couldn't even go looking for her assistant since she'd no idea where

Soraya lived. That Soraya herself had never invited Amy to meet her family puzzled Amy, even hurt her, as she'd come to know the Afghan reputation for hospitality. She'd only to walk the streets around their neighborhood program for women to urge Amy into their meager homes for a glass of chai.

Where Soraya went every weekend, Amy had determined never to ask nor to intrude unless by her assistant's own invitation. But now she'd have to confront the Afghan woman, one part of leadership Amy loathed.

I'll give Soraya till morning, see if Fatima's heard anything. Then if Soraya isn't back, I'll get Fatima to direct Jamil and me to her house.

Locking the suite door behind her, Amy dropped a metal security bar into place. The bar had been more Soraya's insistence than Amy's own security concerns. In truth, Amy hadn't expected to feel safe living as the only foreigner here. But she did feel safe, and not just because of that bar on the door. Afghans took hospitality more seriously than perhaps any other virtue. Whatever Rasheed's failings, Amy, Soraya, and the women and children were his charges, part of his household. The caretaker, along with Jamil and Wajid, were honor bound to protect their lives and this compound.

That Amy also felt lonely was harder to admit. Now that she could speak a child's level at least of Dari, the courtyard women were warming to Amy's persistence. They swarmed around her when she appeared, touched the sunshine of her hair, chatted about their children, and complained about each other.

But neither their conversation nor interest went beyond the compound. Since she'd gone to the airport to see off Alisha Chan and Debby Martini, Amy hadn't seen or talked to another Westerner, her only English conversation, beyond exchanges with Soraya, Rasheed, and Jamil, her Skype sessions with Miami or a sat-phone call from Bruce Evans or Nestor Korallis.

If I just had one other person to talk with at any real level. I'd have thought there'd be an international church, but it's not listed on any of the expat Web sites. I guess I can always check out the Thursday circuit. It was not an appealing thought.

"Ameera-jan. Miss Ameera!" The voice was Farah's and frantic.

Amy lifted the security bar. "What is it, Farah?"

"It is Aryana. I think she's gone——" Farah tapped her temple.

Amy didn't know the Dari term, but she understood Farah's gesture. Amy grabbed the first aid box. But once she'd followed Farah downstairs, there was nothing in it that was any help.

Amy hadn't noticed whether Aryana had been present at their home movie night. She was huddled now on her tushak, rocking steadily back and forth. Her eyes were shut, but tears streamed down her cheeks, and she was emitting the low, continuous mewl of some small, trapped animal. At her feet crouched her son, wide-eyed and frightened. The other women were gathered around, even the Hazaras, patting, murmuring helplessly. Quarrel though they might among themselves, for this moment they'd come together to share another woman's pain.

"What happened?" Amy asked.

Heads moved from side to side; hands waved as Amy strove to understand an excited babble.

"They say she's been like this all afternoon," Farah summed up, "and she will not stop. She has said only that she is afraid."

Amy hoped her panic didn't show on her face. Every one of these women had to be a prime candidate for post-traumatic stress disorder. That they maintained any sanity to function at all was a miracle and testimony to the resilience of the human spirit. Who knew what was going through Aryana's tortured mind? Unfortunately, here one couldn't call 911 or a trauma counselor.

Kneeling beside Aryana, Amy put her arms around the young woman and held her tight. "It'll be okay. I won't let anything happen to you."

It was just as well Aryana couldn't understand Amy's inane soothings. Not yet twenty years old, Aryana was wife of a murdered husband, mother of a two-year-old, and survivor of more horror than Amy could even picture. What possible remedies could Amy offer?

Soraya, where are you? I don't know what I'm doing here. And even if I had the Dari or she spoke English, I still wouldn't have the words to help her, to tell her how sorry I am—and angry too—that any human being should have to endure such pain.

Amy didn't realize tears were pouring down her own cheeks until a hand reached up to touch her wet face. The empathy of Amy's grief seemed to penetrate where she'd had no words to reach, because after a while Aryana relaxed and her head came down on Amy's shoulder.

It was late before Amy got back upstairs. She'd coaxed ibuprofen and an over-the-counter sleep aid into Aryana and left her curled up with her son. But though Amy had held it all together until the other women and children returned to their own tushaks, as soon as she closed the door of her room, Amy threw herself on the bed and burst into tears.

I can't do this, God. These people are hurt too badly. Who am I to even think I can help? Especially on my own. Steve Wilson and Bruce Evans were right—and Dad was wrong. This is just too big for me.

On impulse, Amy sat up and reached for the sat phone. It was still office hours in DC. "Mr. Korallis, I'd like to talk with you about additional personnel. I'm wondering what's happened as far as that permanent country project manager. Things are getting more than I—"

The New Hope executive interrupted. "We've just been discussing you. We got the first video clips you uploaded. They are truly inspirational. I've got to tell you the board is impressed—only one expat staff, and a woman at that; employment opportunities for any number of local professionals. A new project manager? Are you kidding? I've been talking to the board about making your promotion permanent, and they are thrilled. Congratulations, young woman."

Only a conference call coming in on another line allowed Amy to hang up. *I don't believe this. I've worked my own way out of assistance.*

Amy straightened suddenly. What was the noise she'd just heard? She sat still, straining to hear. Yes, it was the creak of the suite door being quietly opened. She'd forgotten to put the bar back down.

Noiselessly, Amy got up from the bed. She reached for the light switch, but the evening hours of electricity were over. Amy felt for the battery-powered lantern she kept by her bed, but she didn't turn it on. Was the intruder a thief after office equipment? Rasheed should be making the final rounds about now, locking the big entrance doors from the inside, and Wajid had been on guard all day. But the perimeter walls were still an easy hop, as Jamil had once proved.

Amy hoped it was no more than a thief. Thoughts of recent kidnappings, Taliban attacks, and suicide bombers were making it hard to keep her breathing quiet. The living room was as dark as her bedroom as she silently eased her door open. But Amy could hear quick breathing, the furtive movements of someone trying to move as stealthily as herself. *If I can just get by and out into the hall . . .*

Amy was feeling her way through cushions when the noise of a body bumping into a hard object was followed by a soft cry. Amy relaxed instantly. Switching on the lantern, she lifted it high. "Soraya!"

Soraya was pulling a burqa from her head. The two women stared at each other for a moment.

Then Amy set the lantern on the table against which Soraya had stumbled. "Where have you been? I've been worried sick that something might have happened to you."

Soraya's hands fluttered. "Please forgive me. There was a death in the family. It was necessary I remain for the funeral. There was no electricity to charge the phone, so I could not call. And tonight I could not find transport before curfew. It took long to find my way around the police. Wajid let me in the gate, but I did not wish to disturb you with my tardy arrival. I am so sorry that you should have worried. Fatima was to give you news of our emergency. Tomorrow she will ask forgiveness for her oversight."

Soraya looked unhappy and red-eyed enough for a funeral—were it not for that mention of Fatima. *And I'm sure you'll have her briefed by tomorrow. But this morning she had no idea where you were.*

"And your escort? Surely you didn't send him back out this late. Rasheed can certainly find a place for him to sleep downstairs."

"No, no, he did not wish to stay. He has work in the morning." Soraya stared at Amy's face highlighted in the lantern beam, and Amy suddenly remembered her own tear-streaked cheeks and reddened eyes.

"Has something happened?" Soraya demanded.

"No, of course not. I'm just tired." Amy lowered the lantern. "I'm glad you made it back safe. I'll see you in the morning."

Amy watched Soraya's door close before retreating to her own room. *She's lying to me, but why?*

As was I, Amy reminded herself ruefully.

From his perch atop the metal shed, Jamil had recorded Soraya's return. The camera manual spoke of night vision, ambient lighting, remote control, and other features he'd wanted to test. So when he'd stored away the video equipment after showing his footage to the children and their mothers, he'd slipped the camera into a vest pocket. That Ameera trusted him to lock up the equipment made Jamil shake his head. Though he wouldn't abuse that trust, his employer could not know that. Such innocent faith in other human beings was dangerous.

Though darker than useful, the zoomed-in image of a blue burqa stepping through the gate and hurrying up the cobblestone path was amazingly recognizable on the tiny screen. Less recognizable was Soraya's escort hurrying now back down the street. At first Jamil had thought the man to be the teenager he'd seen before delivering Soraya and Fatima. But this was a stockier build and taller, though he'd turned so quickly Jamil had caught only his back on film.

Jamil focused the camera instead on a kaleidoscope of peacocks spreading their tails on the side of a jinga truck parked across from the compound. He'd seen those peacocks before. Zooming in, Jamil made out human shapes in the cab. But they were too grainy for details. Out-of-town customers for the mechanics yard?

Satisfied he understood the features, Jamil slid the camera into his vest pocket and reached for Ameera's gift. Up the slope of the shed roof, music had begun playing next door, a foreign offbeat that was jarring and unpleasant to Jamil's ear. Though this was not a Thursday night, the neighbors were celebrating.

Perhaps he should expend enough of his next paycheck at the bazaar for a flashlight so he could read in his own room. Meanwhile Jamil inched up the roof to the pool of light the security lamp next door cast across the metal sheeting. Blanking his mind to the alien music, he flipped pages until he found where he'd left off reading: "Forgiving each other, just as in Christ God forgave you."

This time Jamil didn't allow his anger to fling the book aside but made himself read on. Forgiveness. Not just man's but God's. And there was the catch. How could there be not just the hope of forgiveness but assurance? "God forgave" spoke of something already finished. But no one knew how the scales would tip before the day of Allah's judgment. That was presumption. Perhaps even the presumption that had led Jamil to this place.

Maybe this forgiveness was for those who could obey all the commands in these pages. Or for Isa's personal disciples. But who could? To brush one's teeth, wash three times before prayer—these one could measure daily into Allah's scales. But kindness, compassion, love?

And to an enemy! Where was the call to fight the evil and apostate? to wage war against the unbeliever? to press forward with the faith until all the world lay prostrate as foretold in submission to Allah?

And yet . . .

Jamil rubbed a weary hand across his face. What kind of world might it be if instead of battle all people chose to follow the commands in these pages? "Children, obey your parents in the Lord" had been instilled in Jamil since he could walk. But that fathers should not embitter or discourage their children? That husbands should not be harsh with their wives? That servants should work hard and be honest and not accept bribes, masters be just and generous with their servants?

And the commands to love. Love God. Love one's brother in the faith. Love wives and children and servants and neighbors. Love the helpless, the widows, the downtrodden.

Most inconceivably, love enemies.

It would be a world of peace.

A paradise.

The noise next door was proving too distracting to continue reading. Jamil put away the New Testament. But it was a sound across the cinder-block partition from the New Hope compound that prodded him to sudden alertness. The metallic scrape of a dead bolt was followed by the rusty screech of the pedestrian gate. Ameera's assistant again?

Jamil reached for the camera to focus in on a dark shape rushing across the street. He relaxed as Rasheed's bearded features emerged from the shadows. As the New Hope chowkidar reached the jinga truck, a man climbed down from the cab. The camera screen displayed the two men's inaudible conversation. Then Rasheed strode back to the open gate while the other man returned to his cab. A customer, then, but one Rasheed didn't know well enough to invite to camp inside the gate.

The chowkidar's retreating shape blazed to white as oncoming headlights overwhelmed the camera's night vision setting. Jamil slid the camera back into his vest, but he didn't return to his reading. The commotion next door had grown suddenly louder. The sound of a vehicle stopping, a gate opening offered a reason. The combination of foreign music, loud voices, and laughter was so like that to which he'd once dropped off his employer that curiosity drew Jamil up the slope of the roof, though he lowered himself first to his belly. Security might be lax next door, but an intruder appearing suddenly on the perimeter wall was as likely to draw shots as questions.

Jamil scooted well outside the pool of light before raising his head cautiously above the edge of the metal roofing. The shed roof overlooked the back garden of the neighboring compound. He didn't need to worry about being spotted, Jamil saw immediately. A dozen large, pale foreigners sprawled out on lounge chairs were giving no attention to their perimeter security.

Their noisy high spirits were explained by what Jamil could see rounding the side of the house from their front gate. A food delivery from one of Kabul's growing number of Chinese restaurants. Not male attendants as an Afghan restaurant would have but female.

Jamil had been watching only a few minutes when curiosity became stunned disapproval, then horrified disgust. Sliding back from the roof's edge, he lowered himself silently to the ground and headed to his room. Removing his vest, Jamil laid the camera carefully in his clothing box. But Ameera's book he tossed recklessly to one side, the words he'd read earlier burned from his mind by his fury.

Besides, it had been only the illusion of dreams that such a world of which he'd fantasized, the commands he'd pondered, had any place in reality. What he'd just seen was a reminder of how great a deceit lay in any such offer of hope.

23

A perfect morning.

From the rise where Steve stood, the graying of dawn was sharpening into focus a pastoral landscape. A flat plain, the meandering curves of a river spreading out into cultivated fields and pastures. The fields held no crops this late in the fall, their earth freshly turned over. But green lingered in pasturelands, wind-twisted mulberry trees edging fields, almond and apple groves harvested of fruit but still grasping a few leaves.

Behind the plain, rocky, snow-tipped peaks blushed pink, though stars still glittered in bright patterns overhead. Down the hillside below Steve's boots, adobe houses and mud-brick compound walls slumbered like a Christmas frieze of Bethlehem. After Kabul's dust and smog, the air was as crisp and clean and sweet as fresh-pressed local cider.

And cold.

Steve's breath hung white in the air. These were times he didn't mind the inconvenience of body armor for the extra warmth it offered. Beside him, Khalid had shed his Italian suit for the camouflage fatigues of his muj days, a heavy Army parka matching Steve's own. Turning toward Steve, he grinned savage pleasure, dark eyes flashing with excitement. This wasn't the first time the two men had stood together on a mountain slope at the edge of dawn, and something in that remembered camaraderie, the tension and thrill of combat about to begin, curved Steve's mouth to exhilaration as he met his principal's glance.

It had taken two weeks and substantial negotiation before Khalid's task force lifted off from Bagram Air Force Base. The inclusion of DEA chief Ramon Placido's team greatly simplified Steve's arrangements. With American embassy personnel involved, the U.S. task force commander had volunteered not just a Black Hawk combat helicopter but a CH-47 Chinook transport helicopter capable of ferrying thirty Afghan counternarcotics police and their Colombian and DynCorp advisers. He'd also arranged hospitality at the nearest American-manned military outpost to each planned raid.

This was the ninth such raid in three weeks. The Black Hawk and Chinook had touched down after dark last night at a nearby PRT base currently home to a hundred Texas National Guard troops. Provincial Reconstruction Team outposts were part of ISAF's "hearts and minds" program, designed to offer a nucleus of military presence while winning over local support by sponsoring such projects as schools and clinics, wells and water pumps.

The PRT bases were too small to project any serious strength, their contingents vastly outnumbered by local militias, and as their orders were largely to hole up inside and not interfere with local government, they'd done little to stem Afghanistan's escalating lawlessness. But the Texans had proved hospitable, providing two troop transports to ferry the MOI force to this small market town, along with a Humvee bristling with gun turrets and troops in full body armor as escort.

The American soldiers were not, however, authorized to participate in the dawn raid, so the transport drivers lounged against their bumpers, watching the show with Steve and the others, while the Humvee contingent spread out in a perimeter watch. Steve approved of the guards' vigilance and discipline, though less of their adulation. To these young soldiers on their first combat rotation, private security contractors were the big guns, best of the best. Assumed was that all PSCs were former Special Ops who'd been there and done great and dangerous things.

Also assumed was that they were now doing still greater, secret, and more dangerous things while raking in as reward ten times the guardsmen's biweekly paycheck.

On Khalid's other side, DEA chief Ramon Placido straightened abruptly, a hand to his earpiece. He nodded to a cameraman behind a tripod beside him, a CNN reporter chronicling the MOI operation. A blinking red light signaled the camera had gone live. Down below, someone's perfect morning was about to be spoiled.

From this rise, Steve could make out only too plainly stealthy shapes fanning out silently and furtively through the dirt streets. The raid had been scheduled to strike just before dawn. But though the PRT transport had delivered their guests to the hilltop FOB—forward operating base—in ample time, the district police chief whose jurisdiction this was had been less punctual.

The target was a compound on the edge of town where fluted columns, domes, and arches of an elaborate poppy palace thrust themselves incongruously above high brick walls and the adobe hovels of its neighbors. The owner was an Uzbek opium merchant, Akbar Dilshod. By all accounts, Dilshod was a terror, famed for taking out local competition with his own private hit squad. His men were accused of everything from rape to torture.

The reputation of Dilshod's guards was the reason Khalid had insisted on waiting for those local police reinforcements. The town was still silent, but the gray of dawn was lightening. Any moment, someone staggering out a doorway to the vegetation that was their outhouse would raise the alarm.

The Afghan task force had now stopped their stealthy advance. Outside a tall, steel gate, MOI recruits slipped forward to slap explosive charges against the hinges. Did Dilshod have no sentries up on those walls? With Steve's next white exhalation, a loud blast shattered the dawn peace. As the gate blew off its hinges, troops rushed in.

Then without a single gunshot, it was over. An MOI recruit climbed the wall to wave a blanket as an all clear. The PRT contingent unearthed thermoses of coffee and were handing them around when a knot of camouflage fatigues trudged up the hill. Among them were the minister of counternarcotics and one of Placido's DEA subordinates, who'd both accompanied the MOI task force in the raid.

The DEA agent hurried ahead to address his superior. "Bad news: the compound's empty. Someone must have tipped them off we were coming. The good news . . . well, you're going to have to see this, sir, to believe it."

DynCorp held the embassy's security contract, and a quartet converged around the DEA agents as they hurried down the hill. As Khalid followed, Steve waved Ian, Mac, and Rick into a tight diamond around him.

Grabbing his camera from its tripod, the reporter hurried to join the protective bubble. The town was no longer sleeping as the group reached the first dirt street, eyes peering from cracked doorways and windows. But the MOI police were doing as they'd been trained, fanned out along streets and on corners, and the residents didn't venture to expose more than their eyes.

The district police chief, a burly, turbaned Tajik, welcomed the group into Dilshod's compound. Beaming satisfaction, the chief didn't lead the newcomers toward the villa but a sizable hole to one side of the courtyard. A large trapdoor had been removed to expose an underground passageway that had to extend far beyond the perimeter wall.

Steve preceded Khalid cautiously down the steps. Though he'd no real interest in this operation beyond his own principal's safety, he blinked in stunned appreciation. There had to be a thousand kilo bricks of opium down here, while burlap bags of hashish extended down the tunnel from floor to man-high ceiling as far as Steve could see.

"There's way too much to consider removing into evidence," DEA chief Placido said. "The value alone would draw Tallies like flies if we tried to convoy all this overland. My suggestion is that it be destroyed on the spot."

"Yes, yes," Khalid agreed. He turned to the CNN reporter. "And you will film it so that all the world will know it has indeed been destroyed and not removed to sell elsewhere."

It took some time for additional C-4 and explosives to be requisitioned from the PRT base. Back on the safe retreat of the rise, the cameraman made satisfied noises beside Steve as the blast ripped a trench in the ground at least a hundred feet long.

Before the dust settled, Khalid addressed the cameraman's mike. "The largest seizure Afghanistan has ever seen. . . . The MOI will set the example in ending the hold corruption and drug dealing has taken on this beautiful country. . . . The rich and powerful will not be spared. . . . The burning stench of this poison has reached the portals of Allah himself to cry out for justice."

Behind Khalid, the camera angle offered potential TV audiences a spectacular view of black billows from smoldering opium and hashish as well as the orange, green, and purple monstrosity of Dilshod's poppy palace.

The CNN reporter was nodding respectful approval of the minister's extravagant statements.

And why not? Steve demanded of himself. Despite Dilshod's escape, these last three weeks had been every bit the triumph Khalid had promised. In nine raids, a dozen major opium kingpins had been rounded up along with scores of minor arrests. Even without this last haul, opium seizures had stacked up to over two thousand kilos by Steve's running count.

Maybe Khalid really is the guy who can turn the MOI and this whole big mess around. In fact, with a few more like him, there just might be hope for this country.

All in all, Steve felt more approving of his former ally and client than he had in years.

24

"Did you give out any information?" Amy demanded anxiously.

Hitching his dusty AK-47 higher on his shoulder, Wajid scratched at his beard, expression baffled.

Amy realized she'd spoken in English and switched to simple Dari. "The man who spoke to you, did you tell him about the women who live here?"

The elderly guard shook his head. "I told the man what I know. Women live here as in any dwelling. They are respectable women who keep their faces covered in my presence. So I do not know their faces. Nor their names. Only the foreign woman Ameera."

Amy now had an idea of what had spooked Aryana. A man had knocked on the gate after Amy and the others left for the neighborhood outreach yesterday, Wajid was just now bothering to inform Amy. He'd asked for a woman he claimed to be a runaway female relative. Had Aryana spotted a face she knew loitering along the street while she'd been helping load the truck?

"And you don't remember a name? Or what the man said she looked like?"

Unlike Farah and some of the others, Aryana had kept her burqa firmly over her face when she'd stepped outside with a load, so Amy wasn't concerned the man could have actually identified the young woman. But the fact that anyone was making inquiries was worrisome. The Welayat bureaucracy wasn't supposed to release where their former prisoners had taken shelter, but Amy was under no illusions the information couldn't be bought at the right price.

"He gave no description, and I did not listen to names since I told him I knew nothing." Wajid looked agitated, so Amy desisted from further questions.

"Thank you. You did right. But next time please do not give them my name either." Ameera was not the name by which officialdom knew the New Hope country manager, so hopefully the guard's slip wouldn't be a problem. "And tell me right away if anyone asks about our people."

Turning to Rasheed, who'd brought her Wajid's report, Amy switched with relief from laborious Dari to English. "Unless he comes back, I guess we won't really know if this man was after Aryana or anyone else here. Either way I'm concerned about our security, especially if there's the slightest chance info is being leaked to family members. How long would it take to get some concertina wire on top of the perimeter wall? Maybe a second guard? Or even a guard dog?"

"A dog is an unclean animal," Rasheed said. "And marking the property with such defenses as the foreigners use announces to all who pass by that inside are rewards worth pursuing. It would draw thieves like flies. Would it not be simpler to talk with such men as came yesterday and find out what they seek? If there is a father or brother willing to take custody of this Aryana or any woman receiving shelter here, is it not their right and duty to do so?"

Amy had started walking back with Rasheed from the gate to the main house. Now she stopped to stare at him. "I couldn't allow that. The whole idea of New Hope is to give these women a sanctuary so they won't have to go back to family situations where they're mistreated. Certainly not against their will. Besides, Aryana is a widow, and it's her brothers-in-law she's afraid of, not blood relatives."

Rasheed looked down at Amy as though she'd materialized from another planet. "It is not for a woman to raise her will against the men of her family. Nor is it for outsiders to interfere with proper discipline within a family. If Aryana is a widow, the law is clear. She belongs to her husband's family, and one of her husband's brothers must take her as wife.

Islam does not permit that zakat, charity, be wasted on those not truly in need."

Amy breathed deeply to quell the anxiety beginning to squeeze at her stomach. As evenly as she could muster, she answered, "I certainly don't want to disrespect your country's law. But your MOI gave New Hope permission to run this shelter, and I've given my word to these women that they'll be safe here. So I hope you understand I must insist we get some security procedures into place. Not just to protect their physical well-being but their identities and whereabouts. If even one of these women comes under threat, none of them are going to feel safe living here. If I have to, I'll move our entire operation elsewhere before I let that happen." It wasn't a challenge Amy had any wish to carry through.

Rasheed was still staring at Amy, but she could no longer read his expression. Then he shrugged. "You concern yourself without reason. A runaway wife is a matter of honor, but these women have already received judgment and been punished for their crimes. What respectable family would wish for their return?"

A majority opinion in Afghanistan, no doubt. But Amy hadn't forgotten Debby's earlier warning about Aryana. It might not be the woman's return or a second marriage her in-laws were after.

"I am chowkidar, not owner," Rasheed continued. "I cannot make changes to the property without proper authorization."

An issue he'd never raised on any of Amy's past requests. "So I should contact the owner about the security?"

"Khalid is not in Kabul at this time," the chowkidar answered indifferently. "In any case, the minister is an important man and busy. He does not deal with such matters as properties and rent. It is his deputy Ismail through whom all arrangements have been made."

"Where can I find Ismail?"

Another shrug. "You do not need to concern yourself. If you insist on this, I will speak to Ismail myself as soon as there is opportunity."

And with that Amy had to content herself. But the tension didn't leave her stomach as she returned to the upstairs office. Soraya was at her computer, still looking exhausted and unhappy but clearly intent on making up for lost time.

When Fatima arrived this morning, she had hurried to find Amy. "Please forgive me. I forgot to inform you that a cousin died on Friday and my—yes, my cousin Soraya was needed to help with the funeral." Fatima had avoided Amy's eyes, and Amy chose not to press the matter.

At Amy's desk, Jamil was bent over her laptop, where the two of them had been picking through digital video clips. Always withdrawn, today he added agitated and restless.

What a gloom fest. In the wall mirror Amy caught her own tired face and puffed eyes. *Yeah, and I'm such a ray of sunshine.*

Picking up the week's chore list, Soraya headed downstairs.

Amy tapped the laptop screen with approval as a neighborhood project boy announced with the widest of gap-toothed grins, "I am learning to read so I can be a pilot someday and fly a plane."

"That's good. We'll need to put subtitles in English on the screen. Can you do that?"

Jamil nodded. His vest hung open as he bent over the keyboard. Tucked into an inside pocket, Amy spotted an olive cover. "I see you've been reading the book I gave you. So what do you think?"

Jamil's face darkened immediately. Snatching the slim volume from his pocket, he pushed it away from him along the desk. "Yes, I have been reading it, and you may have it back. It is not, as you say, the Christian holy book. It is lies!"

Amy was taken aback. "What do you mean?"

Jumping to his feet, Jamil paced around the office. "I have now read many teachings of your book. They are good teachings. Many the Quran teaches as well. But they are not what Christians follow. The Quran teaches Muslims the five pillars of Islam, and every Muslim obeys. But your teachings? Your book says to be holy and pure, to commit no adultery or fornication. But Christians have no respect for marriage. They do evil things, men with women, men with men, too. When I saw such things on your television and movies, I thought them only stories for men's imaginings. But now I have seen with my own eyes, and I know they are not imaginings but true."

Amy stared in astonishment as Jamil reached the window and spun around, clenching his fists. She wouldn't have believed the silent young man capable of such fervor. "You've seen with your own eyes? What are you talking about?"

"The foreigners next door. I saw them bring food from the Chinese restaurant. And more than food." Jamil flushed. "Please, I cannot even discuss such things. And there is the alcohol and opium. The Christians condemn my countrymen for growing poppy to keep their families from starving. But is it not Christians who buy and consume the opium? As it is Christians who make alcohol, which the Quran forbids above all other drugs. They use the power of their armies to bring it into my country against our laws even as they use their armies to destroy the poppy. Is that not hypocritical?

"Your book says to obey parents. But your children on your television and movies show no respect to parents or teachers, and no one dares rebuke them or discipline them to do right. No, if this book is true, then it is not the Christian holy book. If it is indeed your holy book, then it is a lie because Christians do not live according to its words."

Jamil's agitation was now making sense. Amy too had heard the Scandinavian firm partying last night, and even the expat guidebooks listed Kabul's growing network of Chinese restaurants as the latest front for brothels that serviced the foreign presence in the city.

"All the things you're saying, the things you've seen on TV—that's not Christianity," Amy said. How could she explain that the very freedoms Christianity's influence had originated could become the freedom to be very *un*christian? "Being American or European isn't the same as being Christian. Far from it. America is simply a country where Christians and others are free to practice their faith. Including Muslims. And free to live any way they choose."

"And this freedom is better than behaving in a way that respects Allah and religion and family? I have read that most people in your country claim to be Christian. Is this not true? And now that I have read your holy teachings, I see they are not so different from being a good Muslim. So why do your people not obey these teachings? Why does your law not require it?" Jamil stopped his pacing to add, "Though, please, I do not say these things of you. In truth, you live as a Muslim. A very good Muslim."

Amy was silent. She couldn't even imagine how much of what Hollywood represented as the American way of life must look to these people. It offended her, and she'd grown up in Miami. Could Amy honestly even make a case that the rampant sexuality, immorality, and materialism of the West were more pleasing to God than the puritanical and often brutal tyranny of the East? In reality, there were things she was finding admirable about Jamil's people. Not the warlords and corrupt officials but the ordinary people who worked hard to survive and took their faith as seriously as Amy did.

In fact, they could teach the Western churchgoer much in that regard. Their dedication to prayer. The way they lived consumed with pleasing the implacable, unknowable God the mullahs presented to them, while people back home obsessed over the latest clothing style, electronic gadget, or luxury vehicle. The warmth and hospitality that would give their last piece of bread to a stranger as a matter of course.

Then murder their daughter or sister for speaking to a man. And keep half the population from ever reaching its potential. *There* was the dichotomy.

"Part of freedom is making choices," Amy said slowly. "And that *is* a good quality of my country. People are free to choose to do right or wrong, whether to follow God or turn away. Many do turn away. But it isn't a real choice to serve God if it's not from your heart. Christians believe that real change must come from inside by personal choice, not be forced from the outside. That goes for countries as well. A friend of mine told me once that no country could really free another because freedom and the choice to change has to come from inside, from the people of a country."

"And you believe this will work? The Quran teaches that the world must be brought into submission to Allah. Only then can there be peace."

"Has there been peace where Islam has conquered? Did Islam bring peace to Afghanistan? Don't your Wahhabis and Shias and Sunnis fight each other? And the Pashtuns and Tajiks and Uzbeks and Hazaras?"

"That is because they are not good Muslims."

"Look," Amy said gently, "I can't condone everything done in my country as right before God, any more than you defend all the years of killing here or abuse those women downstairs have endured. I guess that's why our standards can't be how human beings choose to behave in any country but God's law. For a Christian, that standard of behavior is laid down in our holy book, the Bible. If you want to know what a Christian really is, don't look at TV or even politics. Read the Bible. A Christian is just someone who follows Jesus Christ and his teachings. If they don't, they're not a Christian, plain and simple."

Soraya reentered the office. Returning hastily to his seat, Jamil bent over the computer keyboard. But a moment later, his hand shot out and the New Testament disappeared within his vest. He was advancing to the next clip when Amy's cell phone rang. The voice on the other end was American and female.

"Amy Mallory? My name is Becky Frazer. I'm a nurse practitioner and trauma counselor. I've been working for about twenty years with an aid organization here in Kabul. Debby Martini thought you might appreciate an invitation to the weekly gatherings some of the expats take turns hosting."

Even over the phone Amy could hear a smile. "Maybe even a friend?"

Jamil went back to reading. This time he returned to the beginning and read without skipping. There'd been a time when Jamil devoured learning, relished pushing his sharp mind to its limits. Then an aeon when he'd schooled himself not to think at all. To maintain his mind assiduously blank and so survive horrors within and without.

But now curiosity and the old thirst for understanding were rekindling in him. If Ameera was a Christian, and a Christian was truly and simply no more than a follower of the prophet Isa Masih, Jesus the Christ, then to know what that meant, he had to know who this Jesus was.

That his predominant interest was to make sense of this very unusual woman, Ameera, who had entangled herself inextricably into his life, Jamil could admit. Yet as he read, the personage slowly emerging from shadows to sharp focus on these pages was fascinating, so that Jamil found he was no longer reading to wear himself into dreamless slumber nor thinking of Ameera at all.

Why Ameera had chosen this prophet to emulate was easy to understand. Isa's compassion for the sick and hungry never faltered. Yet the prophet was not always meek and mild as Jamil had first considered. He spoke up with uncompromising wrath against the Pharisees and teachers of the law, who seemed to be the Taliban and religious police of his day. Jamil approved when the prophet picked up a whip against those who enriched themselves from worshipers going up to pray. Were there not merchants even today who grew fat off credulous and desperate pilgrims swarming saints' tombs and holy places in search of miracles and answered prayers?

That the rulers did not kill him, unarmed though he stood before them, suggested the protection and favor of angels. Perhaps though he wielded no sword nor conquered territory for Allah, Isa had his own strength.

And his teachings! Some thundered with the power and fury of a mountain storm. Others were stories that one might tell to a child. And yet, like the one he'd read of treasure hidden in a field, the more Jamil pondered them, the more hidden meaning they seemed to contain.

Jamil pored over Isa's teachings on prayer. He'd wondered just what it was Ameera did while Jamil and the others were prostrate on their faces. True merit-earning prayer followed a strict pattern of posture and recited words, and at first the model Isa had given his disciples didn't seem a prayer at all.

Our Father in heaven, hallowed be your name,
your kingdom come, your will be done on earth as it is in heaven.
Give us today our daily bread.
Forgive us our debts, as we also have forgiven our debtors.

This time Jamil tamped down his anger to ponder the words. Did Allah truly count forgiveness as so meritorious an act it could in any way cancel out Jamil's own insurmountable debt?

"Your kingdom come, your will be done." That Jamil understood. But to pray to the Creator of the universe as to a father? It made no sense. Allah

was the all-knowing and yet unknowable. Though one might cry out for mercy and forgiveness, Allah was infinitely remote from his creation, demanding submission and obedience, not communication.

And yet that image of a child approaching a loving father with unquestioning confidence that his needs and hurts would be attended induced a pain in Jamil's chest.

The teaching that most gripped Jamil's imagination was a story. A simple one like those Ameera told the children. Two builders. A wise one who built a house on the rock. A foolish one who built a house on the sand. And when the storms came and the streams rose and the wind blew to gale strength, the house on the sand was destroyed, but the house on the rock stood firm. Here the analogy was not veiled. "Everyone who hears these words of mine and puts them into practice," the prophet Isa had said, "is like a wise man who built his house on the rock."

That night the story entered Jamil's dream. He was standing on a hilltop. Below him stretched Kabul, and though he couldn't see it, he knew that beyond his sight was all of his birth land. Afghanistan, land of his heart, his people. In the streets the people were rejoicing because the storms were over and they could rebuild their houses, their land. But as they built, the storm clouds rose, the sky grew dark, the wind began to howl until it was a gale driving the people before it in search of shelter.

But the new houses and tall buildings they'd erected did not offer shelter because, horribly, irreversibly, they were folding in on themselves, crushing those within. And as Jamil watched, helpless to intervene, he saw that all had been built upon sand. Floodwaters washed the sand away beneath the foundations, leaving the city and land once more in ruins as though by war.

Jamil sat up straight in the darkness, his heart pounding as though he'd run a hard race. Even as he recognized that it had been only a nightmare, his face was wet with tears.

25

"The fiber-optic fencing came in while you were gone. The new camera system should be here within the week. Totally noninvasive. They're so small Khalid's visitors won't even know they're under surveillance—" Phil broke off his status report as a blast rattled the CS command suite's picture window.

Steve beat his friend out onto the second-story terrace. A distant plume of smoke was already fraying out of shape under a brisk November wind.

"I'd say at least a kilometer," Phil commented, walking out between the two columns that held up the terrace roof to study the horizon. "That's number three in twenty-four hours."

As a wail of sirens started up, Steve frowned. This last month's travels embedded in the protection of military escort and constant movement had insulated Steve—and his principal—from Afghanistan's recent upsurge in violence. There'd been a spate of suicide bombings in Kabul and a dozen insurgent attacks around the country just in the few days since Khalid and his detail arrived back in the capital.

The plume of smoke was drifting away now, the same wind ruffling Steve's hair so that his teeth ached with cold, a reminder he hadn't grabbed up jacket, tactical vest, and helmet. Steve was retreating behind the shelter of a column when the shrilling of his cell phone rose above the sirens.

"You hear the blast?" It was Cougar. "Word just came in—a car bomb hit a local police precinct. Nowhere near the ministry building. Or you, of course."

That casualties didn't even come up was a sign of how commonplace large numbers of people dying had become. As Steve snapped the phone shut, he became aware of a fresh disturbance. And this one *was* close.

To Steve's right, a Guat patrolling one of the balcony walkways was peering over the perimeter wall, his M4 clutched nervously. Stepping over a flower bed, Steve joined him. The open balcony was even windier than the terrace as Steve leaned out beside the guard.

"Un alboroto." The Central American indicated the maze of flat roofs and mud walls that was the adjacent slum, then translated his Spanish to halting English. "A fight? It is coming this way."

The tumult audible above sirens could be a fight, a riot, or a sporting event. And it was definitely coming closer. Then the sirens went dead, and Steve relaxed at the shrill pitch of excited shouts.

"It's just children. And look!" Steve pointed at a blotch of yellow and blue taking to the sky among the rooftops below. A moment later, a red and green diamond rose to snap at the yellow and blue's tail. This was kite-flying weather in Kabul.

Children or not, prudence dictated checking out any large group coming this close to their primary. It wouldn't be a first for children to be used to cover an attack. Steve returned to the terrace. "Phil, would you mind driving for me? I'd like to see something."

"I'll meet you out front." Phil limped toward the stairs with alacrity. The medic's disability limited the active-duty roles Steve could offer, a reason he'd chosen his former comrade-in-arms for this little jaunt. Besides, there was no one Steve would trust more at his back if the chips were down.

Steve stopped in the command suite long enough to grab tactical vest, helmet, and coat. By the time he reached the front gate, Phil was backing out a dented Toyota Corolla, its rusty yellow proclaiming it had once been a taxi. At least for personal transport, Steve had attained the low profile he preferred. Taking shotgun position, Steve settled his M4 in his lap.

Steve kept an eye on fluttering blotches of color as he gestured to his companion to turn right or left. Deep ruts cut by truck and cart wheels scraped against their underbelly as Phil eased the hatchback through the dirt streets. Steve waved the vehicle to a stop short of their destination, the lane ahead too narrow to take the car.

"I'll be right back." The noise had not abated as Steve stepped out. But spurts of delighted laughter and the cheerfulness of voices were reassuring enough to push the M4 back up over his shoulder. Sheer joy was impossible to feign.

The alley ended in a dirt patch currently open because mud-brick walls were just going up around the perimeter. Above nearby roofs, Steve could see the mustard yellow of Khalid's mansion, a guard pacing a second-floor balcony. In the middle of the empty lot, several dozen ragged and unkempt children clustered around two kite strings. So did two taller figures, their shapes as well as heavy winter cloaks and headscarves female. All heads were craned skyward with such concentration that Steve's quiet strides carried him unnoticed to the edge of the group.

"Ms. Mallory, what in heaven's name are you doing here?"

The effect was electrifying. With startled screams, children whirled around or bolted away. Then mingled cries of triumph and dismay rose—along with the red and green kite. Most of the pack took off running after the drifting kite. Which allowed Steve to glimpse the other kite flyer winding his string.

One of the female shapes had scattered with the children, but the taller one first stiffened and then turned around. "*Mr.* Wilson, did you have to scare everyone half to death? And just when I'd finally talked Farah out of her burqa. Now look what you've done."

Steve felt apologetic as he took in frightened faces sheltering behind partly raised mud walls. The other female shape stood her ground staunchly at Amy's back, but her headscarf was snatched tightly over her face so Steve could catch no glimpse of her features. "Sorry. I didn't mean to startle you."

Amy's indignant look offered no forgiveness as she called to the children in soothing Dari, "Don't be afraid. He won't hurt you. He is one of the foreign soldiers here to protect people. You go on home now, and I will see you next time," she continued as timid heads, then bodies, emerged from behind the mud bricks.

Behind the two women, the children scattered. The other kite flyer with his blue and yellow structure in hand disappeared with it down the street.

Amy turned back to Steve. "What are *you* doing here? And how did you know it was me anyhow?"

"I'd know you anywhere, Amy Mallory."

Maliciously watching red rise to her cheeks, Steve pulled a hand radio from his belt. "Phil, Steve here. Everything's fine, just a bunch of kids playing. I'll be back shortly."

Returning the radio to his belt, Steve relented. "Actually, I can't claim clairvoyance. It was your boots. At least you're consistent."

Amy's glance dropped to the trim walking boots protruding under the dangling tassels of her long shawl. "They're the best shoes I've got for walking in all this dirt, unless I switch to plastic sandals like the local women."

"You want to tell me what you're doing here on foot and alone?" More sternly, Steve went on. "I thought we'd already had this conversation."

An impish smile offered no repentance. "Well, you did suggest we start a project in this neighborhood. Kind of hard for you to object when we take you up on it. Those were some of the project kids you scared away."

Amy briefly outlined the literacy and feeding outreach. "It's just down the alley in that big compound. We've finished for the afternoon, so some of the kids decided to show me how they fight kites. And I'm not alone. This is Farah, one of my helpers from another project."

The other female moved closer now that she'd seen Amy's ease with this foreign and armed stranger, but she still hadn't lowered her scarf for Steve to see if she was young or old.

Amy looked at Steve speculatively. "And if you're not clairvoyant, you must be here because we were making so much noise. So am I right in guessing one of those palaces over there belongs to my landlord?"

"That's right." Steve pointed out Khalid's mustard yellow monstrosity. "And don't think you're going to get off that easily. You did hear that blast not fifteen minutes back? It happened to be a suicide bomb, and not the first in the last day or so. Alone or not, you shouldn't be out on the streets like this."

"Yes, I heard the explosion," Amy said calmly. "But it was nowhere close. Whatever you think, I'm not careless of my own safety or Farah's. The bombings have all been downtown where there are valuable targets. No one's going to waste one on a dirt-poor neighborhood like this. I've seen plenty of other women, expat and Afghan, burqa or not, on the streets. I'm aware there's always some risk. But I'd rather focus on the fact that at any given moment, the odds are I'm safe enough."

Steve studied Amy with exasperation. He hadn't seen her since that abortive party that had ended for him on the MOI roof. Nor except in passing had she entered his thoughts.

She looks happy, he thought with irritation. The hazel eyes Steve had last seen shimmering with unshed tears still held some of the wide-eyed pleasure with which she'd been watching the kite battle, her expression a smiling serenity that made Steve want to shake some sense into her. *So Afghanistan hasn't wiped that look off your face yet.*

"And it's my job," he said grimly, "to focus on the fact that at any given moment you may not be."

At Amy's startled look, he amended, "Any generic person, I mean. You may not be a target here for a suicide bomber, but there are always sneak thieves or just a man with mischief on his mind who sees you as an easy mark. Where's your driver?"

"Jamil took our other personnel and equipment home. Farah and I are riding with Becky Frazer, an American nurse who helped us do a vaccination campaign this afternoon. She's giving a lift to some of the women with babies. Her van was full; hence the kite lesson." Amy smiled. "But Becky should be back pretty soon."

"Pretty soon isn't good enough," Steve said flatly. "Give her a call and let her know she doesn't need to pick you up. I'll run you home."

"That isn't necessary."

Reading rebellion in Amy's stiffening shoulders and glare, Steve said even more flatly, "That wasn't an offer; it's an order. I couldn't live with my own conscience if I left you here and something happened."

Amy looked at him thoughtfully, then wrinkled her nose in reluctant acquiescence. "Well, since you put it so nicely."

As she reached for her knapsack, Steve added, making some effort to modify his tone from command to request, "From the car, please." He glanced around the empty lot with its partially erected walls. There was nothing in the small faces still peeping from a safe distance to rouse alarm, but Steve didn't like the openness. He'd lingered in plain view too long. "Let's go."

Amy and her companion followed him through the alley and back to the car. Phil eyed the unexpected passengers with undisguised curiosity as Steve ushered them into the backseat but made none of the droll comments Steve could see rising to his lips.

"Phil, meet Amy Mallory." Steve climbed into the car as Phil started the engine. "Amy, may I introduce Phil Myers, part of Khalid's security detail. Amy's American, heads up an NGO called New Hope that's renting one of Khalid's properties over in the Wazir. You know the one," he added significantly. "Do you remember where it's at? We're going to give these two ladies a ride home."

26

Amy caught the significance in Steve's tone. Was there some history she was missing beyond their client's ownership of the New Hope rental? At least he hadn't brought up how they'd met. Phil Myers looked to be a few years older than Steve and less severe. Amy liked his smile, the lack of self-consciousness about his scars that must hold their own story.

As the older contractor reversed down the dirt street, Amy dug out her cell phone. "Becky?"

"I was just about to call you. Did you hear that blast? I'll be back to get you as soon as I can. Meanwhile, you need to get off the street and out of sight."

As she'd offered, Debby Martini's American acquaintance had stopped by last Friday to pick Amy up for the English-language "gathering," as the weekly worship service was euphemistically dubbed. Becky Frazer proved to be a small, thin woman with graying blonde hair and a brisk but kindly competence. She was also the first woman Amy had ever seen driving in Kabul, maneuvering a minivan through the congested streets with a practiced aggression that made Miami traffic look easy.

The gathering was larger than Amy expected, a multinational cross section of Kabul's aid and diplomatic community. That they met on the Muslim sabbath made sense since Sunday was a workday for expats as well as Afghans. That in this "fledgling democracy," even foreign Christians couldn't openly hold a church service would have shocked Amy a few weeks ago. Now it just saddened her.

The worship time and potluck afterward had banished Amy's feelings of isolation. Better yet, Becky had promptly volunteered a vaccination program, both at New Hope and the neighborhood outreach. Next on Amy's wish list was a clinic for the New Hope women. Maybe even that trauma counseling she talked about.

"You don't need to come back," Amy said now. "Someone stopped by and is giving Farah and me a ride."

"You shouldn't be picking up rides. Do you know how many kidnappings there's been?"

"Don't worry. He's an American, and I've met him before."

Before Amy could say more, Steve reached over and plucked the phone from her hand. "Hi, Becky Frazer. Steve Wilson here. I'm a contractor with Condor Securities. . . . Yes, I heard the blast. . . . I'll make sure Amy gets home; you just get yourself indoors and safe."

The man had hearing of a bat as well as memory banks that filed every data scrap he heard. Handing the phone back, Steve drawled caustically, "Your friend's got more sense than you do. She'll give you a call when she's safely off the street."

Resisting a sharp retort, Amy turned instead to Farah, huddled beside her, shawl-enveloped head pressed to the window where the mansions bordering their neighborhood project were rolling by. Was she frightened since she couldn't understand the English conversation?

But as Amy squeezed Farah's arm through the heavy winter cloak, her swaddled head swiveled from the window, and Amy saw that her blue green eyes peeping above the scarf held no fear but eager delight.

She's enjoying the adventure. Emotion tightened Amy's throat, admiration for the indomitable spirit of this Afghan girl. Would Amy have had the courage to run away from an arranged marriage at thirteen? to cross this country alone and without a penny in her pocket?

Gently, Amy tugged Farah's scarf down from her face, revealing the dimpled smile underneath. After a moment's resistance, the teenager let the scarf fall, lifting her tousled head proudly as she turned her gaze again to the world passing outside.

Soon Phil Myers pulled up to the New Hope compound. Steve climbed out to open the back door for his passengers. Farah scurried inside as soon as the gate opened but not without a shy smile and murmured "tashakor." The front courtyard was noisy with the shouts and laughter of playing children, and Farah was barely inside when a gaggle of small girls pounced on her, sweeping her away with them.

"Thank you for the ride." Amy hesitated on the threshold. "Would you like to see what we've done with our project? And your friend, of course." Her eye fell on the automatic weapon slung over Steve's shoulder. "That is, if you wouldn't mind losing the gun. We have a houseful of women and children now."

Basic courtesy necessitated the invitation, but Amy hadn't expected Steve to slide the M4 immediately from his shoulder. "Thank you. I will come in. I'd like to see what you've been up to.

Steve leaned into the Toyota to speak quietly to his colleague. When he straightened up, he was without weapon or helmet and he zipped his army green parka to conceal his tactical vest. The car pulled away as he stepped inside the compound.

"I sent Phil back to Khalid's," Steve answered Amy's questioning look. "He'd like to see your project, but policy doesn't permit leaving weapons unattended. Our team house is in this neighborhood, so I'll just walk over when I'm done here."

Uncertainty gripped Amy as Wajid fastened the gate behind the security contractor. Was Steve too remembering the acrimony of their last encounter? Not to mention his last stopover at New Hope.

But he seemed affable enough today as he surveyed the fresh paint inside and out, children climbing over a jungle gym Jamil and the older boys had cobbled together from scrap lumber, others kicking a ball around the dirt patch that had once held construction debris.

"You've been busy," he commented slowly, and his tone held nothing but approval. "I'd hardly recognize the place."

"Ameera-jan! Ameera-jan!"

A pack of preschoolers dashed around the jungle gym, an assault of small, warm bodies almost knocking Amy over before they took in her companion. Even without weapons, there was no denying the foreign visitor's tall, powerful frame was a formidable sight, and most scattered immediately. But two smaller girls clung to Amy's winter cloak, bursting into frightened tears. Amy understood their sobbing Dari only because David and Goliath had become a new story-time favorite.

"No, he isn't the giant," Amy said gently, peeling away their arms. "He's a brave warrior like David who fights bad people. Now go to your mothers. It is time for your bath and supper. Then I will tell you the story of the shepherd boy warrior and the giant again if you like."

Sidling past Steve, the preschoolers disappeared with more relief than reluctance up the marble steps.

Amy braced herself for Steve's derision. "Sorry about that—again." She managed a rueful smile. "Personally, I don't find you all that terrifying. But kids here don't see a lot of foreigners, and these especially aren't used to men."

But Amy could read no mockery in Steve's face nor any expression at all. As she became uncomfortable under his scrutiny, he said quickly, "Hey, I appreciate the character witness. But I was under the impression you didn't speak Dari."

Amy grimaced. "I'm not sure the children would define what I speak as Dari. But a five-year-old's vocabulary isn't hard to pick up in any language. Which is as far as I've progressed. Just don't ask me anything complicated." This time her smile was comic. "Anyway, it's been over two months since you pulled that crowd off me. I haven't been sitting around, whatever your opinion of NGO types."

"Has it been that long?" Steve seemed momentarily startled. He took another leisurely look around, his gaze sweeping across the jungle gym and ball field, where the children had now stopped their games to watch the strange intruder in wary stillness. "No, I'd say you haven't been sitting around. So tell me about these kids. Why aren't they used to men?"

Amy looked up at Steve doubtfully. His expression had gone unreadable again. Was he getting bored? "Are you sure you want to hear all this? I don't want to waste your time."

"I wouldn't have asked if I didn't." Steve's dry tone was more what Amy was used to from him. He shrugged. "My client owns this place after all. As head of his security, I'd be remiss if I didn't acquaint myself with the layout and your personnel while I'm here."

Amy kept her account deliberately brief as she led Steve on a tour, peeking first through the double doors into the inner courtyard before opening them for a quick view. An unnecessary concern. Now that cold weather had set in, the women remained mostly indoors. The extra downstairs salon next to the schoolroom had become the communal living area. A clatter from there indicated supper setup was in full swing, while the TV blaring in the background signaled the electricity was currently on.

"It's just as well we get power only a few hours a day or that thing would be on 24-7." Amy sighed. "I feel like I've unleashed a monster, but there's so little for the women to do once their chores are finished. My next agenda will be some long-term planning. Maybe some job training, cottage industry, some way to integrate these women back into society. Unfortunately, while for us they're victims, to most Afghans they're still considered criminals. At least some of them are helping now in our neighborhood program."

As Amy led the way upstairs, Steve nodded toward the locked doors on the other side of the entryway. "And what are these?"

Amy shook her head. "We don't rent that part of the property. Storage of some sort, I guess. Same goes upstairs. New Hope has this wing over here to the left."

From the entry porch steps, Amy had glimpsed Rasheed's cargo truck Jamil had used for transport that afternoon back in its usual parking spot over the cinder-block partition in the mechanics yard. But upstairs the New Hope wing was silent as Amy and Steve entered, all doors still locked as Amy had left them.

"Infirmary, office," Amy identified, unlocking them. She pushed open the door to her own suite. "And this is my apartment."

Steve frowned as he stepped past Amy into the living area. "You're living here full-time? I thought you were in an expat guesthouse."

"Sure, when I first arrived. I've been living here over a month."

Steve's frown deepened as he looked around, taking in the two bedroom doors, then walked over to a window that overlooked the front of the compound. "I'm assuming you've got more personnel than I'm seeing. Some expat roommates. This Becky Frazer?"

"Of course I've got more personnel. You met Jamil, my driver, and Wajid, our guard. Soraya, a translator and my assistant, shares this apartment with me. She and Jamil left the project before I did, so they must be somewhere around."

Crossing the room, Amy looked out the window to see what Steve was studying so intently. With their Ameera exhibiting no fear of the large invader, the children had returned to play. The older ones had started a soccer game, two pairs of cinder blocks marking the goals.

"There's a chowkidar too, Rasheed. And all the women and children, so I'm hardly alone. But if you mean other expats, no, there aren't any. And I haven't missed them either," Amy added resolutely, if not with complete accuracy.

She steered the conversation from herself, a gesture indicating the playing children. "As you can see, play equipment is still in short supply. In fact, it's hard to find even if I had the budget. Of course they don't have Christmas here. But Eid-e-Qorban, their holiday celebrating Abraham sacrificing his son, is just a couple weeks away, so I'd thought of getting something for the kids then instead. Unfortunately, they need winter clothing even more than they need playthings."

"What kind of playthings?" Steve said absently. "Your basic toys, balls, dolls? All the same or different for each kid?"

Amy shook her head. "Oh, nothing personal. These kids aren't used to a lot of individual possessions. What we really need are sports equipment and supplies they can all enjoy together. We're learning to improvise. We made play dough the other day with flour and salt and spices from the bazaar for coloring. A limited palette, but it sure smelled good."

But Steve's attention wasn't on the playing children. A 180-degree scrutiny of front courtyard, street, and neighboring compounds went on so long Amy wondered if he'd forgotten she was there. She was debating a discreet clearing of her throat when he nodded toward the cinder-block partition dividing the property. "And over there? What's that?"

"Oh, that's a mechanics yard belonging to the landlord. And parking. That big truck is what we use for the neighborhood project. And there're some rooms out-of-town drivers stay in sometimes while their trucks are getting fixed."

As Steve returned to his silent inspection, Amy ventured tentatively, "So what do you think?"

The contractor swung around abruptly from the window. "You may have a commendable project here, but your security is still lousy. A child could hop that wall or come over that roof."

The jerk of Steve's head indicated the concrete guest rooms built against the divider wall. "Your outer perimeter isn't much better, as I've told you before. I'm guessing your workers next door and any neighbor with a pair of eyes must be aware by now a foreign female lives here. That's an attractive target in the current political climate. Did it ever occur to you that your presence here with such inadequate safety measures could be dangerous to those women and children and to yourself?"

As much as she'd like to reject Steve's criticisms, they echoed Amy's own continuing disquiet. "I'm not disagreeing with you. I feel safe enough myself, but I've been worried about the women and children. After the incident we had last week—"

Amy explained briefly as they left the apartment and descended the stairs. "Maybe it was nothing. But sooner or later some prison bureaucrat may let slip what we're doing—or sell the information. It worries me that some male family member might show up demanding to take the women away. From what Rasheed tells me, I'm not even sure I'd have a legal right to say no. I asked Rasheed to see about getting some rolled wire or spikes or something up around the perimeter wall. He said he had to get permission from the landlord's deputy."

"You mean Ismail?" Steve asked. "Khalid's deputy minister?"

"Yes. But it's been over a week and still nothing. I hate to keep bugging Rasheed, but I'm not so sure he's really trying. He wasn't happy to start with about the Welayat refugees coming here, and he says putting up more defenses is basically hanging a billboard out for thieves. I would contact Ismail myself if I knew how."

"Well, I do," Steve said grimly, "and I will immediately."

They were now outside. The children had stopped their games again to watch Amy guide her visitor down the cobblestone path. Wajid emerged from his guard shack.

Amy stopped to eye Steve. "I didn't mean anything like that. The last thing I need is for Rasheed to think I'm going over his head with his landlord."

"You won't come into it, trust me. Like I said, Khalid's security is my province. I don't need Rasheed's permission. I'll be in touch as soon as I've talked to Ismail and rounded up some details. Meanwhile, let me see your phone." His outstretched hand and the inflexibility of his expression brooked no discussion.

Snapping her jaw shut, Amy meekly dug her cell phone from the shoulder bag she hadn't yet shed.

Steve showed no hesitation with its controls. "There, I've programmed number one on your speed dial as an emergency number. If you run into any serious trouble, hit it. That's a backup your agency should have arranged." Returning the phone, Steve dismissed himself as abruptly as he'd come upon Amy, striding rapidly toward the gate as Wajid hurried over to open it. On the threshold, Steve turned to look back.

Children had swarmed to Amy as soon as the contractor was beyond arm's reach. A preschooler was in Amy's arms, the rest clustered tight around her skirts. The child's tugging had freed Amy's hair, and so accustomed was she now to its cover, Amy refrained from pulling the scarf back into place only because it would have meant putting down the child.

A strange expression crossed Steve's face as his narrowed gaze rose from the children to touch the sunshine of Amy's uncovered head. Then Wajid snapped the bar into its lock behind him.

27

The prophet Isa Masih was a shaheed. A martyr.

It had been days after that terrible nightmare of the flood sweeping away his birth land before Jamil picked up Ameera's gift again. But his burning hunger to discover how this narrative played out overcame his terror of another dream-filled night.

He'd even forgotten his original skepticism over which stories were true and which were the corrupted pieces of which the mullahs spoke. The details were too precise and coherent to be anything but eyewitness accounts. And so Jamil had puzzled out page after page far into each night, reaching the prophet's final days with mounting apprehension, then horror so that he'd wanted to toss the small volume aside but found he could not.

Which was why Jamil had headed to the bazaar once he'd dropped the women and cooking utensils back off at the New Hope compound. Even with his patu wrapped close, the chill night winds sweeping across the shed roof were growing too cold for reading.

This morning Ameera had handed Jamil, Rasheed, and Soraya each an envelope filled with afghanis, their monthly salary. A flashlight and batteries would allow Jamil to read in his concrete cubicle. The truck Jamil had chauffeured was too big to maneuver through the bazaar, and Rasheed had taken the Toyota for some errand of his own, so Jamil had set out on foot. He'd been surprised to see a blue burqa gliding away from the New

Hope pedestrian gate just as he left the mechanics yard. The compound women didn't go out, much less alone.

But neither the doings nor safety of that lone burqa were any business of Jamil's. He'd followed only because he was heading the same direction. He'd turned the corner when the burqa did only because—well, because the open shop fronts along this street might have his flashlight, saving Jamil the long walk to the bazaar.

Or so he told himself as he loitered just out of sight around a fruit stand from where the burqa was picking over ripe melons. An action that piqued Jamil's interest. He'd delivered a load of fresh fruits and vegetables to the New Hope kitchens just this morning. Curiosity became disquiet when a man leaning against the fruit stand straightened up to accost the burqa. The two moved a few feet down the sidewalk, conversing in low, urgent voices.

As the man raised his head to glance around, Jamil stepped quickly into the shadows of a shop entrance. But not so far he didn't catch the burqa's swift pass from under her blue polyester. Jamil stiffened as he recognized what the man now held in his hand. An envelope identical to the one stuffed inside his own wool vest. The burqa must be Ameera's female assistant, Soraya.

This man was older than Jamil, though measurably younger than Soraya, and Pashtun by feature. Now that Jamil knew who was under the burqa, the stocky build and height could easily be the escort who'd returned the Afghan woman to the compound a week earlier. Jamil stepped all the way into the shop as the burqa flitted past him toward the New Hope compound. When he emerged again, her companion was nowhere in sight.

Did Ameera have any idea her housemate was meeting men clandestinely? Such a liaison was not only immoral but a crime under the penal code, punishable up to death during Taliban years. But to whom could Jamil report this? He had his own reasons not to entangle himself with local law enforcement. As for his employer, he'd no desire to explain why he'd lingered to spy on the Afghan woman.

Besides, from all Jamil had seen and heard, he did not think Ameera's people would consider what he'd seen the transgression it was in Muslim eyes. In any case, Soraya's sins were her own to account for in Allah's scales of justice. Jamil had enough to concern himself with his own.

Jamil went back into the shop, glancing around the single small room. Its inventory looked to have fallen off a supply truck for the foreign soldiers because dusty floor-to-ceiling shelves were stacked high with MRE rations, gallon-size cans with names like Del Monte, Kraft, and Heinz, bottled liquids called Gatorade and Starbucks Mocha, crates of non-alcoholic beer, strange sauces marked A1 and Tabasco.

On a top shelf, Jamil spotted the flashlight he wanted, olive green and sturdy in a package that read *Tactical Flashlight* and *Operation Enduring Freedom*. He hesitated over matching palm-size field binoculars before settling for a second pack of lithium batteries. By the time he returned to the compound, the burqa had disappeared. But as Jamil neared the mechanics yard, his steps slowed.

The man loitering behind a parked SUV across the street held Jamil's attention because he himself had just been skulking in precisely such an attitude. And if that full-bearded face had been blurred and dark in the screen of Ameera's camera, Jamil had seen it before in daylight when he'd requested the man to back out of his way. The jinga truck driver.

When the truck hadn't returned to the mechanics yard the next day, Jamil had thought little of it. Either he'd been mistaken in its reason for being there, or the driver had found another mechanic. Now the admonition Ameera had given her staff sprang sharply to mind. Could the jinga truck driver have been the man accused of frightening one of the Welayat women?

The Corolla had returned to its parking space, and Jamil spotted the chowkidar in conversation with one of the mechanics. Rasheed walked over as Jamil hovered near.

"It is perhaps nothing," Jamil explained in a hurried low voice, "but this is not the first time I have seen that man waiting and watching without seeming reason. After what Miss Ameera announced, I thought it best—"

"Ah yes," Rasheed interrupted. "The jinga truck driver. He will have been awaiting my return. I informed him last week there were no openings before today to bring in his truck for repairs. I will go make arrangements with him." He marched across the street.

Relieved, Jamil headed to his quarters. His jumpiness had exaggerated a business appointment to a mystery.

Pulling out Ameera's gift, Jamil leafed back to the page he'd been reading. It had grown dark enough to turn on the flashlight before he reached the final column of the Luke narrative. He shook his head with renewed incredulity.

Ameera's prophet a shaheed? It boggled the imagination. The mullahs taught that Isa Masih had never mounted the cross. Instead the prophet had sent Judas or Simeon of Cyprus or some other friend to take his place, living out his own life until he'd died at a peaceful old age. Unless, though none knew for sure, Allah had rewarded his prophet by transporting him in the manner of Elijah directly to paradise. From there tradition said Isa Masih would return one day to complete his interrupted ministry, battle the antichrist, and establish a thousand-year kingdom where the earth would finally in its totality bow in submission to Allah.

But the mullahs could not have read these injil. The prophet in these pages could no more have allowed a friend to sacrifice himself in his place than he could leave a blind man crying on the side of the road or a leper pleading for cleansing. No, the only conclusion was that Isa had indeed given his life in martyrdom. Possessing power to whistle up legions of angels, he'd laid down his life with the deliberation and free choice of any suicide bomber.

The resurrection part Jamil could dismiss. Perhaps this was where Muhammad had needed to correct the confused readers of the book. Or perhaps by some great miracle he had returned to his earthly life. After all, Elisha and Isa himself were said to have raised the dead. In that case the mullahs' teachings were easily reconciled with this account.

"Jamil-jan! Jamil-jan!"

The high, piping chorus drew Jamil out of the thin pages of the book. He'd missed supper, and the children were calling him for story time. Turning off the flashlight, Jamil tucked the volume away. But he was still deep in thought as he pulled himself up onto the divider wall and jumped down to the other side.

Why had Isa allowed himself to be martyred? It was not to strike down his enemies. It seemed, in fact, a final act of weakness. And yet, if there was anything that Jamil had gleaned from these pages, it was that there was nothing weak about the prophet Isa.

The image of that bright head and slim figure hemmed in by a crowd of children, the valiant smile paired with anxious eyes, stayed with Steve as he walked briskly to the CS team house. There a minor emergency awaited him. An entire container of weapons, body armor, and other gear intended to augment what he'd scrounged from Condor Security's in-country stock had been seized by airport customs. And since customs fell under the Ministry of Finance, dropping Khalid's name made little impact.

It was dark before Steve drove back to Sherpur in a commandeered Pajaro, but Phil was still at his desk. The medic tossed over a stapled pile of clippings and printouts as Steve walked in.

"Take a look at the coverage of your MOI surge. Every major newspaper's grabbing for some good news coming out of Afghanistan. And of course it's all over CNN. The MOI came out looking good. You and the rest made it into some background shots."

"Let's just hope it puts a smile on Waters's face. And that budget committee." Picking up the stapled file, Steve headed to his desk. "By the way, I've got an op I'd like you to put together. We've had some security issues develop at one of Khalid's properties."

"The one where we dropped Ms. Mallory?" Phil swiveled around in his chair with a knowing grin. "Cute kid but an NGO? I thought you'd sworn off the type."

Steve gave no indication he'd heard the jab. Pulling up Skype on his laptop, he settled the headpiece in place. The electronic ring of the Internet phone was replaced by a voice. "Hey, if you're not too busy, would you mind doing a couple things for me?"

"Here is the translation of the new ministry directives for your American employers," Soraya said. "I will fax it to them before I leave."

"Don't bother. I'll do it. It's Thursday, and I've held you up enough already. Jamil just took the permit papers for the second neighborhood outreach down to the ministry. With your two new teachers, we should have no problem expanding now. Which should make Mr. Korallis happy." Amy smiled across the desk at Soraya.

Her housemate had hurried in yesterday just as Hamida was laying out supper with good news of two available teachers. Even better, one was male, which should satisfy parental grumbling at their current project over a woman, Soraya, instructing their sons. *Never mind they're getting it all for free.*

"When you contact them, tell them to come see me first thing after the weekend Saturday morning. And Becky Frazer is going to give us a date for the women's checkups as soon as she works out her schedule."

Amy was still smiling, this time with gratification as she ran a pen down the agenda she was going over with Soraya. The Ministry of Economy oversaw foreign nonprofits, permits for each new project one more formality in the daunting red tape required to keep New Hope's presence in Afghanistan legal. But Soraya's years working for NGOs had made her an expert at navigating the shoals of Kabul's bureaucracy while Jamil never balked at long hours waiting on one government clerk after another.

I don't need a fixer. I've got my own in Jamil and Soraya and Becky and Rasheed.

Amy reached for her cell phone as it shrilled. It took a moment to place the deep drawl. "We're about thirty seconds out. You said your tenants get spooked around men, so I figured I'd better give you a heads-up."

"A heads-up?" Amy repeated blankly. "What for?"

"Why, putting up your perimeter defenses."

Despite Steve's pledge, Amy hadn't held her breath that she'd hear from the CS security contractor this soon. Getting to her feet, she met Soraya's questioning stare. "Before you leave, would you please let the women know some workmen are arriving? I don't want them alarmed. And Fatima, too. I know the children should be getting out of class soon, but if she could keep them indoors."

Before Amy reached the front gate, she could hear the screech of tires pulling up, the rumble of men's voices. Lots of them. Wajid hurried from the guard shack, fingering his rusted Kalashnikov.

"It's just some workmen arriving," Amy reassured. But she blinked as Wajid pulled back the bolt and opened the gate. This wasn't a few workmen but an army. Two pickups held at least a dozen men each, a mixture of Afghans and what looked like Gurkhas and other foreign security personnel. A market truck was piled high with sacks, wheelbarrows, buckets, tools, and giant metallic spools of barbed wire.

Steve was climbing out of a black SUV. With him were Phil Myers and another huge, bearded Caucasian with a long, tangled mane. If Steve Wilson was going for unobtrusive, he'd failed miserably. At least any weapons in the mix were being kept out of sight.

To Amy's left, the compound's vehicle gate stood open. A large jinga truck was turning into the mechanics yard, a process necessitating several men waving arms and shouting directions as the truck negotiated the tight fit. Amy glanced at peacocks parading along its side panel, then focused on Rasheed hurrying down the sidewalk.

The men started heaving out sacks and tools. Steve had to see Amy just inside the pedestrian gate, but wraparound sunglasses didn't shift her direction as he intercepted Rasheed. "Salaam aleykum. I'm looking for the caretaker of this property."

"Salaam. I am Rasheed, chowkidar here. What is all this?" Though Steve had spoken in Dari, Rasheed's answer was in his heavily accented English, at once boosting his own status and shutting out the mechanics and other bystanders avidly eavesdropping.

"Good, then you're just who I want." The security contractor shifted smoothly into English. "I'm Steve Wilson, head of security for Khalid Sayef, your landlord. We're in the process of upgrading security on a number of his properties. We'll be attending to this one today."

Rasheed showed no surprise. Everyone in Kabul knew of the minister of interior's foreign bodyguard. But he glanced at Amy suspiciously. "You were requested to come here?"

"Not at all. You will be aware of the many threats against the minister. It is our concern that his enemies, unable to reach Khalid himself, may turn to easier targets. That this property is rented to a foreign charity places it at greater risk. Which is why we are here."

Rasheed still looked suspicious. "I cannot allow you onto the property without proper authorization."

"Of course." Steve flipped open his cell phone. After a murmured exchange, he handed the phone to Rasheed. From the chowkidar's expression, Amy could guess the landlord's representative, Ismail, was on the other end.

Taking the phone back, Steve continued affably, "Now, if you'll come with me, I'll show you what Ismail considers appropriate for your situation. We certainly wouldn't want to call more attention than necessary."

Rasheed's reservations were visibly dissipating. His smile genial, Steve steered Rasheed toward the SUV where his expat associates were unloading some kind of electronic gear. He still hadn't so much as glanced at Amy. But her initial confusion, even resentment, at being ignored dissolved to reluctant admiration as she watched his performance.

Workers were now pushing by with loads of materials. Next door the jinga truck had finished making its way inside the mechanics yard. Retreating, Amy started back to the main residence. Children's faces and excited waves greeted her from the schoolroom windows. Entering, Amy found classes dismissed, and Soraya in conversation with the teacher.

"I have made an announcement all must stay inside until these workers are gone," Soraya informed Amy. "If you wish, Fatima can continue with the children's studies through the afternoon."

"That won't be necessary," Amy said. "Farah can help me organize some indoor activities. I'm sure some of the mothers will be happy to help."

Rasheed waylaid Amy as she emerged into the hallway. He'd resolved the problem of containing the New Hope tenants by closing the tall front doors that normally stood open during the day. Some of the suspicion was back as he frowned at Amy. "This foreigner—Wajid tells me he was here yesterday. You have known him long?"

"Yes, he was here yesterday. He wanted to see the project and was asking about our security."

Was it cowardice or prudence to follow Steve's own tack? Amy had to admit relief when the chowkidar nodded and walked away. And after all, like the CS contractor, she'd told only the truth.

Resisting the impulse to return Steve's earlier call, Amy applied herself to her office work. After lunch, the children helped push back the folding divider between schoolroom and communal salon. Roya and Najeeda pitched in with Farah in refereeing a succession of relays and games. But Amy found herself drifting to the windows as often as the children to check on the progress outside.

Workmen mixed water with bags of cement and sand in the wheelbarrows they'd brought in. Others slapped the concrete atop the perimeter wall, setting carefully into it shards of broken glass bottles. Above the broken glass workmen stretched ordinary barbed wire. The combination was an effective enough household defense and common in even the city's poorest neighborhoods. Again Amy had to admire Steve's astute handling of Rasheed's concerns.

Partway through the afternoon, Rasheed ushered workers into the inner courtyard to add barbed wire and broken glass to the plastic panels already shielding the back wall. By then the children were tired enough to settle down for Dari-dubbed Japanese cartoons. Despite the buzz of activity, when Amy answered her cell phone barely five hours after Steve's initial call, she wasn't expecting his abrupt, "We're done. You mind coming out?"

Workmen were trundling away wheelbarrows of tools and empty sacks as Amy slipped out the front entrance. Posts sunk into the brick wall supported three strands of barbed wire as far as Amy could see around the perimeter. Glass shards in still-moist concrete sparkled in the lengthened sunbeams of late afternoon.

Phil Myers and his long-haired associate were at the perimeter wall, inspecting their handiwork. Steve stood near the open gate in conversation with Rasheed, but as Amy came down the steps, the caretaker dodged a wheelbarrow to exit the gate.

Steve approached Amy. "I've just been explaining the system to your caretaker. And I'd like to line you out too. Don't let the low-tech facade fool you. Your caretaker's right that you don't want to scream high-value target. But we had some fiber-optic cable left over from our security setup at Khalid's principal residence. Mac and Phil have been stringing it along that barbed wire."

Steve indicated his two expat companions. "You can't even see it's there, but anyone tries climbing over that wire or even gets too close, and an alarm will go off. Not just here but over at our command center."

Amy shook her head. "I don't know about that. We have children playing out here. Something that could shock them or set off an alarm—"

"Fiber-optic fencing is proximity sensitive; it won't shock anyone." Steve brushed away the objection. "In fact, it doesn't use electricity at all, which makes it ideal for this kind of setup. It works on a radio frequency system, and you're close enough to tap it into our own central unit, so it's no extra trouble. But you're right about the kids playing. Which is why I got this for you."

Steve handed Amy what looked like a small remote control. "We keep our system up 24-7, but yours is rigged to turn on and off at will. The button there is a simple on-and-off switch. The green light means it's activated. If it's not activated by midnight, our system will do it automatically."

Amy took the remote from Steve. "This is incredible. The women are sure going to feel safer seeing all that up there. I really don't know how to thank you."

The literal truth. Regardless of how much Steve stressed his employer's interests, what he'd done here this afternoon was so far above the call of duty, Amy was at a complete—and rare—loss for words.

Steve looked embarrassed. "Hey, it was no big deal. Anyway, this should take care of your external defense. Internal is another matter. Which reminds me—"

The earsplitting wail of an alarm siren drowned out his next words. Simultaneously, just behind where Steve stood facing Amy, a torso pulled itself up above the cinder-block partition. As Steve spun around, a leg swung over. Its owner half dropped, half fell to the cobblestone path. Amy saw taut menace ease from Steve's muscled frame even before he reached to snatch the remote from her hand. An instant later, the siren went quiet.

Jamil scrambled to his feet, a file in his hand. Even as Steve handed the remote back to Amy, his eyes didn't leave the Afghan's face.

"You remember my driver, Jamil," Amy put in quickly.

"I certainly do. You were hopping a wall then as well. Sorry about that. I was about to add that we didn't have materials to run perimeter defenses down your interior partitions. But with strangers in and out of that mechanics yard, we did run a fiber-optic cable along the top of the wall there."

Jamil responded neither to the contractor's slight smile nor proffered handshake. With dismay, Amy saw that shock had drained his olive complexion to such a sickly gray she was worried he was going to faint. Then Jamil put a hand to the wall to steady himself. Holding out the file to Amy, he said, "I brought the permits you requested."

"I am so sorry to spring this on you," Amy said remorsefully. "Why don't you take that up to the office? I'll be there shortly."

Steve's hard gaze followed her assistant as he disappeared up the steps. "Is it your driver's regular habit not to bother with gates?"

Amy looked at him reproachfully. "He has a room on the other side. And since the gates are kept shut, it's easier to hop the wall than wait for someone to open them every time he needs to go back and forth. If you'd asked first, I'd have said to leave your cable off there."

"Well, don't expect an apology," Steve said. "As I was about to say, you can put up all the external defenses in the world, but you've still got to consider the possibilities of internal threat. These people you're living with—what kind of background checks have you done? What if one of them turns out to have a beef against expats? For that matter, what's to keep one of them from selling these women's whereabouts? Does your staff have access to personal records?"

As Amy's face gave away the answer, Steve went on. "And what if one of those prison women snaps and gets violent? Who'd ever know for backup? It's clear you like it here, but does your HQ understand the security implications of an American woman living alone in what's essentially hostile territory? At least with a guesthouse, someone'll come checking if you don't come home."

"Don't do this to me," Amy cried out vehemently. She had to bite her lip to stop her voice from trembling. "Look, I know you're trying to be helpful. I appreciate everything you've done today. And okay, so it's your job to be suspicious. But your own boss trusts Rasheed to run this place. And Soraya has done incredible things considering all the roadblocks she's faced.

"As for Jamil, I do know he's some distant relative of Rasheed's. And he's one of the nicest and hardest-working people I've ever met. I-I can't live with these people or do what I have to do if I'm going to start distrusting them or their motives, especially when they've never given me reason. I *won't* live that way."

"Hey, believe me I'm the first to hope you're right." Running a hand through dark, clipped curls, Steve let out a sigh. "And you're right that I suspect anything and everyone. An occupational hazard. Just—well, like I said before, watch your back. And if things ever do blow up, don't forget you've got that speed dial."

Rasheed was coming back through the gate now, so Amy excused herself quickly. Strange how awkward it suddenly seemed to be found speaking to an unattached male. Was this how Afghan women felt?

The project permits were on Amy's desk, but she didn't see Jamil until she stepped farther into the office. He was hunkered down against the wall in that chairless Eastern sitting position, head resting against the plaster, eyes closed, hands clenched at his side. Amy again felt remorse. The loudness of the alarm had startled her, and she'd known what it was. Had the explosion of sound flashed him back to some past trauma?

But as Jamil raised his head, Amy saw it wasn't fear or distress that tightened his jaw muscles and blazed from his dark eyes but anger. His low, fierce demand made no reference to the alarm. "Why is that American soldier here again?"

His challenge took Amy aback. Steve had with patent calculation presented himself and his associates to Rasheed in official safari-style contractor uniform. But neither body armor nor weapons had been in sight. Then Amy remembered her first encounter—and Jamil's—with the PSD contractor, an M4 over his shoulder, the pistol he'd fired in the air.

Then too Jamil had seemed pale and shaken. Amy had put it down to exertion and his wound, even reaction to the bombing. After her early abortive probings, she'd respected Jamil's clear desire to leave his past *in* the past. But somehow—perhaps because it was easier, because Jamil had opted to work for Amy, a foreigner and American—she'd chosen to assume her driver's family were victims of that endless Taliban-muj conflict.

Had they instead been casualties of the American liberation campaign? Was that the horror Steve seemed to provoke in Jamil? However unavoidable the collateral damage, those on the losing end of this war didn't see the patriotic defenders of freedom that lifted Amy's heart every time she saw red, white, and blue on a uniform lapel, but killers of their sons and daughters and husbands and wives and parents and friends.

"Mr. Wilson isn't a soldier. He's head of security for our landlord. Part of his job is making sure the minister's properties have adequate perimeter defenses. I'm sorry he disturbed you, but he shouldn't need to come again unless we have a problem."

The hand Amy laid on Jamil's shoulder was an instinctive comforting gesture, but it was the first time she'd touched her assistant in any way except bandaging that cut foot, and she knew it was a mistake before his hand came up to cover hers.

Jamil's fingers were ice-cold against hers, and it was with utmost gentleness that Amy said as she withdrew her hand, "We'll take down the wire on the partition wall. I won't let him block you from getting back and forth."

"No, in that the American is right. I have been thinking the same. Anyone from the trucks that stop here could come across as I do. That you and the children should be secure is of greater urgency than my convenience."

"Then maybe I can ask Rasheed to give you your own gate keys so you can get in and out once the mechanics go home."

Jamil shook his head. "I do not wish a key. If a vehicle or other valuables should go missing, I do not wish a finger to be pointed at me." He produced a faint smile as he tapped a vest pocket. "If there is ever such an emergency that I must get out after the gates are locked, I can call."

Jamil seemed calmer now, so Amy retreated to her desk. Opening the file to official-looking stamps and curlicue script that meant nothing to her, Amy said dismissively, "Thank you. This looks good."

Taking the hint, Jamil pushed himself to his feet and headed toward the door. But he'd taken only two steps when he turned around. "I do have one other matter I have wished to ask about."

Amy looked up from the file. "Yes, Jamil?"

"Your prophet—Isa Masih. Why was he martyred? With his power to stop storms and raise the dead, could he not have prevented the soldiers from putting him on a cross?"

Amy was startled at the abrupt change of subject, at the intensity with which Jamil seemed to be waiting for the answer. She considered her words before she said carefully, "Because he loves us. Because God loves us. Like it says in the book I gave you, in the Gospel called John—'For God so loved the world that he gave his one and only Son, that whoever believes in him shall not perish but have eternal life.'"

Jamil's black brows drew together. "But how does dying show love? Would not living be more profitable?"

"Boy, you sure don't ask easy questions." Amy pushed away the file with a rueful sigh. "I'm no theological scholar, but let me see if I can explain. Jesus is God come in the flesh to walk among us in our world. That's the meaning of another name the Bible calls Jesus. Immanuel—'God with us.'"

"Yes, I read that. But God is one. Jesus cannot be God." Jamil looked more shocked than confused. "That is blasphemy."

"God is one," Amy agreed. "Christians believe that too. And yet the Bible also says Jesus is God. And the Son of God. I can't explain how that works. Some things about God are just too big a mystery for our brains to figure out. Except, well, if God wanted to reach out to the people he created, how would he do it, how could we possibly hear him? Unless he came down to earth to live with men and tell them himself how much he loves them and how they should live. If God became only a man with the limitations of a man's body, what would hold the universe together? Somehow God remains up there."

Amy's upward gesture encompassed the universe. "God chose to become human, to be born of a virgin as a man, Jesus Christ, so we might know God's love and love him in return. Being born as a baby, Jesus became God's Son, and the one and only God his heavenly Father. And when he allowed himself to be killed on the cross, it was to offer himself in our place to take our sins on himself. It's like—"

Amy's mind flashed to the upcoming holiday she'd been researching, Eid-e-Qorban, celebrating Abraham's offering of his only son Isaac, or Ishmael in the Muslim retelling, and God's provision of a lamb as a substitutionary sacrifice.

"Well, it's like God providing a sacrifice for Abraham in place of his son. I know with all my heart there's no sacrifice I can make, not even my own life, that could ever make up for all the sins I've committed before God. Jesus gave himself as sacrifice in my place. And in so doing, he demonstrated just how wonderfully and immeasurably the very Creator of the universe loves me—and you and every other human being."

Amy smiled wryly. "And if you find that hard to understand, you're sure not alone, even among theologians. And yet the more you get to know Jesus, the more it makes sense because he's so much more than just another human being—or even a prophet. He is God's gift of love to us. And like that verse says in John, if we accept that gift and put our trust in him, he offers us eternal life and freedom from sin and the fear of death."

There'd been no sound of footsteps in the hall, so the clearing of a man's throat was the first warning they were no longer alone. Amy jerked around in her chair. Rasheed stood in the doorway, his glance darting back and forth between Amy and Jamil, his disapproval patent. Amy was only glad he'd come upon her at her desk, not with a hand on her driver's shoulder. How much had the caretaker heard of Amy's final statement?

"If you are satisfied with the permits," Jamil murmured, "then I will take my leave." Eyes lowered deferentially, he slid past Rasheed into the hallway.

Amy discovered her hands were trembling and buried them in her lap. It disturbed her just how alarming she'd found Rasheed's sudden appearance, how rapidly her heart was racing. It was a warning just how comfortable she'd become—in some ways even more so than stateside, personal faith in God so taken for granted here, her Bible story times even a freedom this job wouldn't permit back home—that Amy had stopped considering any danger to herself . . . or others.

Had she been wise in giving Jamil that New Testament? Did she have a right to put him in possible harm's way by encouraging him to question the dictates of his own faith? to explore forbidden truths?

And yet Jamil knew the risks as well as Amy. More so. And he was not only a grown man but an intelligent one. Didn't he have a right to weigh the risks and rewards for himself? When did prudence become cowardice?

The gaze Amy raised was clear and uncompromising, her voice composed. "Is there something I can do for you, Rasheed?"

"No, I came only to inform you I will be traveling out of Kabul this weekend. With the bombings in the city and the man who frightened your women, I did not feel it wise to go before. But now your protection no longer requires my presence, so I am able to go. Hamida will travel with me to attend to my needs. We will return Saturday."

The chowkidar's flat tone held only statement of fact, but a cold scrutiny still roamed from Amy's face to stare down the hall. She could almost hope his displeasure stemmed from the new perimeter defenses. Amy watched Rasheed leave with dismay. After all her earlier brave words to Steve, had she just made an enemy where she desperately needed an ally?

Ameera's recoil at Rasheed's sudden appearance told Jamil his employer was not as unaware of the perils their discussions could occasion as he'd assumed. His question had been burning on Jamil's lips all day, but he was so rarely alone with Ameera, and he hadn't ventured to ask with Soraya or others present. Ameera's gift was a treasure most safely kept secret.

The furious pounding of his heart, the involuntary clenching of his fists had eased so that Jamil could stride with equanimity through workers loading the last cement-encrusted wheelbarrows and buckets into a truck outside. As Jamil hurried head down toward the mechanics yard, the three foreigners climbed into their vehicle without a perceptible glance in his direction.

The alarm had startled Jamil even as his fingers encountered the unfamiliar wire duct-taped along the top of the cinder-block partition. But it was the shock of finding himself face-to-face with the American soldier that had driven every question from Jamil's mind. Worse, there'd been instant recognition in the gray eyes, though their past encounter was so fleeting.

Jamil gave a quick shake of his head as he stepped into the mechanics yard. Was it truly the foreigner's invasion of his sanctuary that had so enflamed his emotions? Or seeing Ameera speaking so easily with her countryman?

Jamil could still feel the warm comfort of her fingers under his, see the sympathy in her face that said she truly cared he was upset, the frankness of her gaze as she carefully thought out her answers. Honesty could admit he'd come to count such personal discussions as uniquely his privilege. And yet in her own country, Ameera was surely allowed such interaction with any number of men.

Well, the American warrior with the narrowed stare so penetrating Jamil had feared it could read his thoughts was gone now. The man's association with his own landlord could be a danger—or a bonus.

And with Ameera? Little though he liked to see his employer beholden to the foreigners, Jamil couldn't disapprove of the compound's new fortifications. At least fretting over a decrepit Wajid's ineffectual watch would no longer be such a distraction to his own purpose here.

"Tu! Jamil!"

Jamil turned around as Rasheed's rapid steps overtook him. To his relief, the chowkidar made no reference to his earlier eavesdropping but pushed past to head toward the Russian jeep, barking over his shoulder as he did so a succession of directives. He would be back within two days. Wajid would be responsible for securing the premises at night. The clients parked inside the mechanics yard had an engine part on order and would be tendered the customary hospitality and protection from the city's lawless nighttime streets until after the holiday. Rasheed's departure was unexpected news. But then the caretaker wasn't in the habit of sharing personal affairs with underlings.

Jamil closed the gate behind the jeep, then headed across the mechanics yard. He'd noted the jinga truck with its now-familiar peacocks when he'd detoured earlier to avoid the work party crowding the pedestrian gate next door. Its crew had started a campfire behind the massive rear tires. There were three in all, passing a water pipe around the crackling flames, a Pashto music station blaring from a radio perched on the back fender. If the truck carried cargo, it wasn't perishable from their lack of concern over the delay.

At Jamil's approach, the driver he'd already encountered, a large-framed, well-nourished Pashtun, raised the water pipe, a grin of invitation splitting his long beard.

"Salaam aleykum," Jamil greeted courteously as he waved away the offer. The warmth of the fire he left behind less easily. As November advanced, the temperature in the high mountain valley was plunging ever more sharply each time the sun dropped behind the western ranges so that Jamil's concrete cubicle now offered little more protection than the shed roof.

Jamil had appropriated two of the blankets he'd purchased in bulk at Ameera's request from the bazaar. Wrapping both along with his patu around him until he was as swaddled as a baby, he maneuvered loose a now well-worn small volume and leafed to find the John injil Ameera had mentioned.

John was a close companion of Isa Masih, Jamil already knew from the other narratives of the prophet's life and death, and though this injil proved more difficult to comprehend, Jamil liked the music of its words. "In the beginning was the Word, and the Word was with God, and the Word was God." Whatever they meant, the phrases sang with the mystic and lyrical ambiguity of a Persian court poet.

Jamil read until he came to Ameera's earlier quotation. "For God so loved the world that he gave his one and only Son, that whoever believes in him shall not perish but have eternal life."

He broke off at the children's call to story time and to retrieve from Wajid the cold plate of food Rasheed's wife had left behind for them. He remained with the old man to lift heavy bars into place across the double doors at each end of the main hallway and lock exterior doors upstairs and down. Wajid accompanied Jamil to the mechanics yard to lock that gate behind him with shaky hands, then retreated to his guardhouse. Jamil waited to hear the lock click on the other side of the wall before heading back to his own quarters.

The campfire was now out, the jinga truck party retired to their assigned guest quarters. The city power had gone off again as well, and night's darkness would have been profound except that a brief shower earlier in the afternoon had settled the worst of Kabul's dust, allowing the stars and a full moon to penetrate the usual haze of smoke and pollution.

Digging out his flashlight, Jamil returned to his cocoon and his reading, trying this time to place the narrative against Ameera's disturbing statements. The freedom of which she spoke was the desire of every man. The yearning for so many long years of Jamil's own country.

But to be free of sin's guilt and shame? of the all-consuming fear of death? of standing deficient before Allah's judgment seat? That would be a greater freedom than any army could secure. Ameera had spoken with conviction. But how could such freedom be more than a wish, a man's hopeless desire?

As Jamil flipped the page with an impatience that wrinkled thin paper, words jumped out at him. "Then you will know the truth, and the truth will set you free."

Jamil slapped the volume shut. *The truth will set you free?* But what was truth? A powerful political leader had asked that same question during Isa Masih's own trial and had received no answer.

And which truth? Love or hate? Forgiveness or vengeance? Isa Masih's or Muhammad's?

The impossibility of decision pressed on Jamil's mind so heavily he felt paralyzed with its vacillation. A soft shuffle of sandals on gravel, the murmur of men's voices was a welcome distraction. The jinga truck drivers tending to final bedtime needs. Leaning his head against the cinder blocks, Jamil allowed his fatigue to carry him into lassitude until new sounds jolted him to full wakefulness. The jingle of padlock and chain. The creak of a gate needing oil.

Sliding out of his cocoon, Jamil slipped noiselessly to the window. There was no real reason, but with natural wariness he shut off the flashlight before cracking open shutters closed against the night chill. Outside the full moon was not strong enough to show more than dark shapes slipping past his quarters through the gate that now stood open in the rear partition wall of the mechanics yard.

"Men loved darkness instead of light because their deeds were evil."

Jamil had come across that in his reading tonight, the words branding themselves into his mind because they resonated so with his own cynicism. If it was legitimate business these men conducted, why skulk around in the night like thieves or assassins? And there were no longer just three of them. There must be at least a dozen.

Jamil's heart was racing far more than it had earlier, so fast it seemed those dark shadows had to hear its pounding. He stilled even his breathing as he watched, bracing himself for one of those furtive shapes to turn its head. But the roof's overhang came down far enough to cast his window in black shadow, and Jamil's noiseless immobility these last hours had simulated slumber because not one shape paused to focus awareness his direction.

Jamil waited until he could no longer hear the stealthy footsteps before slipping outside. His bare feet made no sound on the gravel, and he darted across moonlit open ground to the concealment offered behind the open gate. The padlock with its chain still hung from the dead bolt. Jamil's fingers felt out that it was not broken but opened as though by a key.

Or a burglar's tools. Because any lingering hope that this was some legitimate activity dissipated as Jamil took in the back of the jinga truck, its wildly colored rear panels no longer reflecting the moon's dim glow, but standing open to reveal a black maw that was its cavernous interior. Jamil could now put together the sounds he'd heard, those too-many dark shapes. Not cargo but men had sat patiently and silently inside that painted frame while the foreign soldiers and their subordinates completed their task, night fell, and sleep overtook the inhabitants of the compound.

But why? This place held no treasure worth such planning and effort. Unless—

The threads wove together with a surety Jamil knew was truth even as his cautious steps carried him through the open gate. The jinga truck driver was no client as he'd presented himself to Rasheed, but what Jamil had first feared, a male family member who'd come searching for Ameera's charge and her child.

And who had not, as they'd hoped, so easily given up.

As he'd seen above the wall, the other side held an orchard, and Jamil stepped quickly into the cover of a tree. Its branches hung low enough for Jamil to relax, its burden of unpicked apricots sweet in his nostrils. Under his feet, the grass was frigid with condensation and squelchy with rotting fruit so that he regretted not taking time to grab his sandals.

French doors and windows opening onto this orchard from that downstairs locked salon were protected by sturdy wrought-iron grilles. But one set of French doors stood open, and though the jinga truck party was nowhere in sight, a bobbing flashlight beam, low cursing, and the muffled bangs and thuds of men stumbling in the dark told Jamil where they'd disappeared. If they'd so easily breached the first two barriers, they'd be inside the main hallway within minutes.

Jamil slid his cell phone from his vest before he remembered Rasheed was no longer in his quarters to be summoned for help. Should he call Ameera? But that would only draw her from a locked and barred suite to rush downstairs into the intruders' arms. Jamil cast his mind back over the shape of those hurrying shadows. Had they been carrying weapons? He had to assume so. No trucker would traverse Afghanistan's dangerous roadways without armed protection.

Maybe the most prudent course would be to let them take what they were after, this runaway woman and her child. Jamil had not come to this city to get involved in the affairs of others. And if this was a matter of family and honor, it was no business for outsiders. If it were not for Ameera, would he even contemplate risking his own aspirations on behalf of those faceless, shrouded shapes that scurried away like ghosts at his appearance?

And yet there were the children, who were not faceless but vivid in Jamil's mind, crying with heart-wrenching anguish or stoic with mute bravery as he tended to their hurts, eager and smiling as they tugged him to story time, their small, warm hands and piping "Jamil-jan" carrying him unwillingly to a past he'd striven to forget. They would be terrified at strange men bursting into their sanctuary.

And even the women. What if it were his own sister or mother hidden behind those face veils, whose pitiful story was spelled out in those personnel files he'd translated for Ameera? In young Farah, had he not glimpsed courage and hope and dreams not so unlike those he'd once known? Was it possible she was not unique?

What would Isa Masih do?

The prophet in the pages he'd read tonight could never just turn his back and walk away. But what could Jamil, unarmed as he was, do against so many invaders? Without Rasheed, there was no aid to be summoned, the elderly Wajid more liability than help. Had the intruders known in plotting this raid that the compound would lie helpless? Perhaps Rasheed had let slip his plans when the jinga truck driver approached pretending to be a client.

But, wait, help did remain for the summoning. The foreigners and their subordinates who'd erected the compound's new fortifications even while danger had already crept inside its walls. The jinga truck driver had been watching and listening enough to know how to avoid the perimeter defenses. But if the alarm should be triggered, the foreigners would come running.

And yet to bring the American soldier with his too-seeing gaze back onto this property, into Ameera's orbit, his own sanctuary? The agitation and loathing that rose in Jamil at the thought choked him with its intensity, paralyzing him again with vacillation.

It was shame that freed him. What manner of man could place his own antipathy ahead of the well-being of Ameera, the children, the women Rasheed had left to his care?

What would Isa Masih do?

His mental debate had been furious and painful, but only seconds had been expended. Through the open French doors, the bobbing light beam had reached the other side of the salon. Above shuffles, suppressed coughs, whispers of men trying to be silent, Jamil heard the clink of metal against a keyhole.

Without making any further effort to avoid noise or detection, Jamil raced back through the orchard gate. Springing to pull himself up on the cinder-block partition, he vaulted over. The blast of sound exploding the night's tranquility was all he could have hoped.

Steve's first reaction to the alarm was annoyance. He'd only arrived back to the team house and his own bed—he checked the phosphorescent glow of his alarm clock—less than an hour ago.

That Steve could hear the alarm two streets and more blocks away was a reminder he'd had Mac turn it to the highest setting. Two alarms in the first eight hours wasn't the kind of record designed to improve relations with the neighbors. This was Thursday—actually, Friday now. Had some Thursday circuit party carousing its way back to their own compound done something to trip the alarm? Or maybe that wall-hopping assistant of Amy's?

False alarm or not, Steve was already tugging on his boots when his cell phone rang. He could barely make out the frantic whisper on the other end, but a far louder rendering in the background of the alarm disrupting the night outside left no doubt as to the speaker.

"Steve! The alarm went off. I can hear men inside the house."

Steve was no longer annoyed. Now it was his M4 and tactical vest he was scooping up. Tucking his Glock into the small of his back, he started down the hall, rapping on doors, even as he demanded, "Rasheed?"

The panic in Amy's voice made that a futile suggestion. "No, he's gone for the weekend. And so is Soraya. I-I think they must be the ones after Aryana. I can hear them downstairs in the hall. I'm looking for the remote control to turn off the alarm—" The anxious whisper broke off suddenly.

Steve recognized with grim incredulity the firecracker spat punctuating the wail of the alarm.

"They're shooting! I have to get downstairs to the women and children."

"No! Stay locked in your room. Your tenants will know to do the same. They'll have been through this kind of thing before. We'll be there in less than five. And don't turn off the alarm. You want to keep them off-balance."

Men were already boiling out of bunk beds into the hall. Mac and Phil were among the first. Rick, Ian, and McDuff of his primary team were all on night shift, but when Steve spotted Bones emerging from a dormitory, he tossed the lanky cowboy a set of car keys.

"We've got a situation, so let's move. Bones, you're my wheels. Mac, you take the Humvee. Phil, there were shots fired so plan for casualties."

Steve didn't need to give instructions as they divided themselves between the CS Suburban and a Humvee whose wheel Mac had taken. Phil hefted his medic pack into the Suburban. Bones had the accelerator floored before the Guatemalan guards had the gate open.

The streets were empty, and Bones continued accelerating, slamming the brakes only as they reached the checkpoint. Steve leaned out the window to shout to the Gurkha sentry as he hurried to lift the boom. By now the alarm was having its effect. All up and down the streets, compounds that had their own generators were turning on lights, armed guards swarming to walls and rooftops. The Suburban's tires screeched around the corner onto the street containing the New Hope compound.

Steve punched Redial on Amy's number. To his relief, he could hear no more gunfire on the line or through the open window. "They're retreating? That's great—it's what we want. Just stay put. We're only a few blocks out."

The headlights picked up blue green walls with their new trim of barbed wire and broken glass at the next corner. And just beyond—

They were still half a block away when the double gates of the mechanics yard burst open, followed so immediately by a truck's massive boxy frame, its driver had clearly not bothered with a key.

Phil spoke up from the backseat. "Steve, wasn't that truck parked in the compound this afternoon?"

The SUV's headlight beams picked up a peacock motif. After lecturing Amy on internal threats, had he driven off leaving a hostile force already in place behind her defenses?

Despite their haste, the jinga truck crew couldn't back out too quickly without doing to its paneled sides what they'd done to the gates. The truck cab was still inside the gates, and with that alarm siren, maybe they hadn't yet heard the approaching vehicles.

Steve looked over at Bones. "Can you get around and cut them off?" Grabbing a Motorola hand unit from the dashboard, he radioed the Humvee. "Guys, this is our target. Don't let them get by."

Bones had the accelerator to the floor again. For one breath-snatching moment, Steve could have sworn the truck's massive rear was going to ram the SUV like a squashed bug into the opposite compound wall. Then Bones somehow had the vehicle up on a sidewalk and jouncing back down on the other side just as the jinga truck's air brakes seized the tires to slow for the tight turn into the street. Steve could hear shouting as the occupants of the truck cab caught sight of the Humvee in a mutual glare of headlights. This time the air brakes squealed loud as the jinga truck's getaway slammed to a complete halt.

Bones skidded the SUV around to block the other side. Steve jumped out of the vehicle, marching toward the truck cab, the other contractors piling out behind him.

"Get the back!" Phil called.

As half his group peeled off, Steve swung to the running board, the butt of his M4 knocking out the window so that he had the muzzle against a bearded face before the man could reach for an AK-47 on the seat beside him. On the far side of the cab, Mac reached in to yank out the driver. From the rear, Steve heard Phil call, "Clear! We've got a bunch back here."

"Clear! Clear!" echoed around the outside of the truck.

That quickly it was over. There were three men in the cab, ten more inside the cargo compartment. Along with the Kalashnikov in the cab, two more turned up in back along with an assortment of cudgels and sticks. These men definitely hadn't planned on a convivial discussion.

Steve turned to Bones, indicating the jinga truck. "Can you get this out of the street?"

Bones climbed into the truck cab. As its engine rumbled to life, Steve turned his attention to the prisoners. An assortment of bearded Pashtuns ranging from late teens to forties and with enough similitude to stem from the same gene pool, they had looked both frightened and stunned as they'd stumbled out of the truck. But defiance was returning as they realized the M4 barrels ringing them in were not about to be precipitously unleashed.

"We are not thieves!" the leader shouted over the racket. "We were told a runaway woman we've been searching for is in that house. We sought only to retrieve her. You have no right to detain us."

Another was trying to calm the leader down. "I do not think she is here. Can you not see this place is a business of foreigners? We must have been given the wrong information."

Unfortunately, it was the first man who was right. Whatever their security role, PSDs had no legal jurisdiction in Afghanistan, and the locals had shown themselves prickly about foreign civilians holding their citizens prisoner. So what to do with these men?

But first things first. Punching Redial on his cell phone, Steve announced matter-of-factly, "You can turn off that alarm now. The neighbors might appreciate getting back to bed."

The night went mercifully silent. Then Amy's voice, breathless with relief, returned. "You got them?"

"Yes, and they were definitely after your women."

"It was the jinga truck, wasn't it? I watched it crash the gate. I am so sorry. I saw that truck here the same day Aryana was so frightened. But there're always trucks and cars coming and going next door. I didn't even think to put two and two together."

"You, me, and your caretaker too," Steve dismissed firmly. "There's no point in anyone beating themselves up over this. The question is what to do with them now."

"Do you want me to come down and talk to them? Or Aryana to see if she recognizes them?"

"Not a good idea," Steve interdicted. "Right now with all these men around, they're thinking maybe they were mistaken. We want to encourage that thought. Why don't you get your people back to bed, and we'll handle it from here. Though you might have your guard open the gate, so we can get this bunch off the street."

"I'm surprised he's not out there already. That noise was enough to wake the dead. I'll see if I can get him or Jamil on the phone. If not, I'll come down myself."

That didn't prove necessary, because when Steve walked over to the pedestrian gate, it swung open under the touch of his hand. The city electricity was still off, and the compound was dark except for a single fluorescent lamp shining from a second-story window. Steve raised a hand in acknowledgment even as he spoke into the phone. "We're in."

"Good, then I'm going to check on my people."

The light disappeared from the window. Stepping farther inside, Steve dug a pencil flashlight from a pocket of his parka and shone it around the guard shack. Unbelievably, the elderly guard hadn't moved from his tushak, a gentle snore reassurance the sprawled figure was even alive.

The flashlight beam touched a pipe dropped to the concrete floor by the sleeping mat, then a small brown lump that caught Steve's nostrils with a strong pungent smell as he stooped for a closer look. Opium. An entire army could invade this compound, and the old man wouldn't awake. What Steve didn't see was the ancient AK-47 the guard had carried on other occasions. And where was Amy's driver?

All questions to be answered. But first to deal with the prisoners. The correct protocol would be for the chowkidar as the landlord's representative—or failing that, some other male household member—to call in the police and file a complaint. As for the property's expat manager, the last thing Amy needed was to find herself embroiled in legal proceedings involving family conflicts.

So who was next up the chain? Khalid was the owner, but Steve couldn't see him bestirring himself over a trespassing incident, especially at this hour of the night. That was what subordinates were for.

As the mental lightbulb went off, Steve punched in the number. "Ismail?"

In the background Steve heard men's voices and the live entertainment of *tabla* drums and *rabab*, Afghanistan's traditional stringed instrument. The minister had been making up for a month on the road by nonstop entertaining since he was home. In fact, tonight's guests included the chief of police responsible for that spectacular Dilshod bust.

"You're still at the party?"

"It is the weekend, as your people say. The guests will spend the night and attend mosque tomorrow with Khalid in honor of their victory and Allah's blessing."

Steve said, "Would you mind popping over to the Wazir property for a few minutes? I've got some prisoners I don't know what to do with."

"I'll be there."

Leaving Phil in charge of herding the prisoners into the yard, Steve went over to the mechanics yard. Bones was pulling the jinga truck back through the broken gates. Steve shone his flashlight inside the guest quarters, noting only piled-up tushaks and cushions until he reached the final concrete cubicle. Here personal items set neatly along the windowsill, some clothing folded in a cardboard box, indicated a more permanent resident.

Amy's assistant, presumably. Unlike Wajid, he hadn't slept through the commotion. But where was he? Steve walked over to examine the open gate, then strode through into the orchard. As he moved his flashlight over the French doors, he called Amy again.

"No, I haven't seen Jamil. And if you're suggesting he had anything to do with this," Amy added defensively, "he has no more access to keys over there than the jinga truck crew—or me."

"It wasn't even in my mind," Steve returned mildly. "These locks look like they've been picked anyway. Quite expertly, I might add. Either way, the local authorities are on their way to take these boys in. Oh, and you might want to be aware as far as your guard, Wajid . . ."

By the time Steve rang off again and walked out to the front, headlights were pulling up outside, not just Ismail and an entourage of Khalid's personal militia in one of the Sherpur residence SUVs but a green Afghanistan National Police pickup full of blue gray uniforms.

Ismail was wearing the fine silk chapan and turban Steve had seen earlier, a heavy army parka adding an incongruous note. He marched over to Steve, militia at his heels, while the police squad headed for the prisoners. "I radioed the Wazir precinct to send over an arrest party. They will take custody of the prisoners. Now let us see what these men have to say for themselves."

31

Yes, where was Jamil? Amy hurried across the courtyard to where doors that had been locked and barred when she'd gone to bed now stood open onto New Hope's inner sanctuary. She'd rushed downstairs as soon as Steve gave the all clear to find the Welayat group retreated into the kitchen salon, its heavy shutters closed and barred, sturdy door blockaded with furniture.

Steve was right—these people were more experienced in crisis management than Amy. They'd opened first a shutter, then the door only after the alarm went off and a cautious inspection assured them Amy was alone.

Farah had been first to throw her arms around Amy. "We heard the men and guns. We were afraid they had you. We could not get inside to bring you safely here."

Their patent relief, their pats and hugs, brought tears to Amy's eyes. They'd been worried about her. With the alarm now off, the sounds of men's voices and engines could be heard from the front yard, and though Amy passed on Steve's reassurance, the women and children were too unsettled to return to bed. Roya, always the organizer, directed preparations for making tea while others pushed furnishings back into place.

So Amy had availed herself of their preoccupation to check out the intruders' entry point. The front entrance was still barred, the heavy metal crossbar that had been across the inner doors dropped just inside the hallway as though hastily abandoned. Though the men had managed to access the inner courtyard, they'd evidently been scared into retreat before taking advantage of that breach.

Amy lifted her lantern high to shine its beam through doors standing open to her left. She now knew what at least one of those locked salons contained. Why it wasn't rented out now made sense. Every extra item this compound had ever contained or former renters abandoned must be stored in here. Dusty, well-used furniture was piled to the ceiling. The lantern beam picked out blackboards and tables and desks, even some Western-style bedsteads and mattresses. So this was how Rasheed had so quickly furnished the New Hope quarters.

There was scrap lumber and other construction debris. Barrels and buckets stacked against another wall looked to be everything from paint and cleaning solutions to engine oil. The mechanics yard used this place too, because there were engine parts, tools, a pile of fenders, even detached car doors. The locked hallway doors made sense now too. Rasheed could open this side for the mechanics without granting access to the New Hope rental.

Amy picked cautiously through to the other side where doors stood open to a chill wind. This was a compound quadrant Amy had never seen, though she'd glimpsed treetops above the cinder-block partition. The headlights of the jinga truck that someone had driven back into the yard shone through an open gate to outline grass, rose trellises climbing walls, fruit trees packed close enough together to seem a small wood.

This late in the season, the leaves were mostly blown off, and what looked to be apricots, apples, maybe almonds too, lay thick on the ground. Though not so thick someone hadn't collected a rudimentary harvest. Did some of the fruit Hamida served come from here?

Still, after the dust and dirt that was all Amy had seen in Kabul outside that expat guesthouse, the garden looked beautiful even by night. And here the windows and doors held real glass. A door beyond the salon matched the one under the stairs that led from the inner courtyard into Rasheed's quarters. Amy had seen it from the other side but never open.

If the mechanics used this place as their depot, Amy understood why Rasheed kept it out of bounds. But surely there must be some time slot when the men could forgo access for a few hours. It would be wonderful for the women and children to have access to a real garden.

The headlights cut off just then along with the engine. Amy lifted her lantern high. Her stomach jumped into her throat as the beam impaled a ghostly flutter among the trees. She snatched back her startled yelp as the pale movement she'd seen became white shalwar kameez emerging from the woods.

Amy lowered the lantern in relief. "There you are. I thought you might have left. In fact, I was hoping you had and that it wasn't something those men had done to you."

Jamil stepped hastily out of the lantern beam into the concealment of the storage depot.

But not before Amy caught sight of the weapon hanging over his shoulder. Her eyes opened wide as the happenings of the last quarter hour clicked into place in her mind. "You set the alarm off, didn't you? And that shooting, that was you, wasn't it?"

"Yes, but I shot only into the air. I did not know how else to frighten the intruders away, and I was afraid the foreign soldiers would not arrive before those men reached you or the others."

That he was carrying Wajid's AK-47 suddenly seemed to occur to him as needing explanation, and he added quickly, "Wajid—he is old, and at times he has great pain in his arms and legs and back. When he does, he smokes some of the opium to help him sleep. So I took his weapon and opened the gate to let the foreign soldiers in."

Amy didn't need further explication. Reality was, with so little access to medical care, much of Afghanistan used opium—readily available and cheap as its processed cousin morphine was not—as a painkiller and home remedy for any number of ailments. Understandable, if an added complication to the global counternarcotics war. When she got a chance, she'd have to ask Becky Frazer what she should do about Wajid.

Meanwhile, she said fervently, "Well, you certainly saved the compound, because they had the doors to the courtyard open. If it wasn't for you, they'd have been inside long before Steve and the others arrived. But why are you hiding out here? The men are all caught, and the police are coming. Don't you want to tell them what happened? let them know what you did?"

Jamil stepped farther back into the storage depot, and his voice turned harsh. "No, I do not wish to see the foreign soldiers or for them to see me. Nor do I wish them to know I was here tonight. I wished only to be sure you were well. Now I will go."

"No, wait, please." As she shifted the lantern, Amy suddenly realized Jamil was barefoot and without coat or patu, his features pinched and blue with cold. Was her assistant so worried Steve or the local authorities would accuse him of being involved in the break-in, he'd endure exposure to this freezing winter night?

And is that so far-fetched? Putting out a hand, this time without touching him, Amy infused firmness into her tone. "I understand if you don't want to see them, though I'd be proud to explain how much you've done to help. But there's no reason to go back out in that cold, at least until they're gone."

An idea jumped to Amy's mind. "I was thinking it might be good to get some pictures of the men who broke in to show Aryana so we could ID if they really are her relatives. You said the camera has night vision capacity. Since you're here, do you think you could take some pictures of all those men out there in the yard? You should get a good angle from the infirmary." *And some blankets to keep warm.*

"Here are my keys. You know which is for the office and infirmary." Amy could think of no better way to reassure the Afghan of her trust and gratitude. "I'd like to get back to the women and children until the strangers are all gone. Wait, the electricity's off. You'll need a flashlight."

"That I already have." In her lantern beam, Amy saw a rare half-smile lighten Jamil's expression as he tugged a small flashlight from the vest he wore over his tunic. "It is what I use to read your book at night. And it will be my pleasure to take your pictures."

Turning on the pencil-thin beam, he made his way sure-footedly through the room's congestion. By the time Amy followed more slowly, he'd disappeared up the stairwell. Amy detoured to look out the school-room window onto the front yard.

As earlier in the day, it swarmed with men. Not just the expat contractors or the bearded jinga truck prisoners but any number of uniformed Afghans. All of which Amy could see well because of portable lanterns that had been set up to fence the prisoners into a grid of light. Jamil should have no problem taking his pictures.

Despite the press of people, Amy spotted Steve Wilson standing with a police officer and an Afghan civilian. The security contractor seemed to have the situation under his usual competent control.

Amy headed back through the hallway to where the kitchen shutters were cracked open so fresh air could leaven propane fumes from cookstove and heaters. The warm, yellow glow of a Coleman lamp spilled out through the cracks. So did a clink of enamel cups, the scent of cardamom Roya added to the tea on special occasions, and a babble of voices that sounded no longer worried but cheerful.

Amy quickened her pace in sudden eagerness to join them.

Wrapping closer a blanket he'd snatched up from an infirmary cot, Jamil ignored the wind whistling through a half meter of opened window to focus the video camera's night setting on the jinga truck driver. He'd tried it first with the plastic pane shut, but dust coating the outside blurred the images. Counting slowly to five, Jamil moved on to the next captive and repeated the count.

Rewinding, he checked the results. They were worth the chill shaking his thin frame despite the blanket. The portable lights set out around the courtyard offered enough ambient light that the faces were sharp and clear. Jamil shifted the camera screen slowly from one prisoner to another. Some had their backs to the camera, but Jamil waited patiently until one by one shifted position enough to catch a profile at least.

Satisfied he'd fulfilled Ameera's request, Jamil wrapped up with a slow pan across the rest of the assembly, the zoom catching policemen, foreign mercenaries, an Afghan official in civilian dress, a cluster of bodyguards at the official's heels. It was truly amazing how even in such gloom, this tiny machine could pick up the men's very expressions.

But it wasn't just the camera's selling points that filled Jamil with satisfaction. Though he'd brushed away Ameera's gratitude, he knew as well as she that he had indeed saved this sanctuary from violation, perhaps even bodily harm. He'd have saved it even if the foreigners never showed.

His grabbing of Wajid's Kalashnikov had been a gesture of desperation when he found the old man unconscious. But as he'd hoped and silently prayed, the bursts he'd fired into the air until the weapon was empty had convinced the intruders their target was not so undefended as they'd assumed. Lying prone on the flat roof of his quarters, Jamil had watched them retreat until the arrival of the foreign mercenaries sent him to conceal himself in the orchard.

Yes, he'd done a righteous deed tonight. A deed that must surely weigh favorably in Allah's judgment scale. A deed such as Isa Masih might approve.

But it was no thought of his own righteousness that warmed Jamil in some inner place the frigid air pouring through the window frame couldn't touch. His thoughts were of this house and its vulnerable residents, who because of his decision to act were returning to disrupted slumber warm and safe and unafraid behind these strong walls. Was this what Ameera felt when she helped the Welayat tenants and the children in those hillside hovels and the refugees from other disasters of which she'd spoken?

It was a good feeling, one he could wish to feel again.

Jamil had run out of faces and was panning back when he stiffened. He waited for a head to turn, zooming in until the screen became a blur of colored pixels. The men were leaving, the police herding prisoners ahead of them, the others drifting through the gate to their vehicles. Across the cinder-block partition, Jamil could see that a blue gray unit of police uniforms had stationed themselves to guard the broken gate. The sight of them didn't trouble Jamil. They were but local precinct recruits, hired not for inquisitiveness but unquestioning obedience.

With his targets out of range, Jamil replayed the footage, studying each frame with unblinking concentration. No, he hadn't been mistaken.

The battery gave out just as he ran his taping to the end. Jamil stored the camera meditatively, placing its case on Ameera's desk for her use in the morning, leaving her keys beside it. What use this information might prove, he did not yet know. But one thing this night had taught him.

Truth was not only freedom.

Truth was power.

32

"Thank you for meeting at such short notice. Khalid, thank you for your hospitality. Now, as you're all aware, the most important item on the agenda is the arrival of Jim Waters and his delegation. They'll be flying out of DC this evening—" Deputy Chief of Mission Carl Bolton glanced at his BlackBerry—"and landing here sometime tomorrow afternoon."

The assembled group was virtually the same as had gathered around a conference table over a month ago now. But this time Steve was seated with Cougar and DynCorp manager Jason Hamilton among the American embassy personnel and Afghan ministers scattered around the plush sofas of Khalid's reception suite. Behind the minister stood a Russian operative who, along with Roald, a retired German commando, was Steve's most recent tier one hire. Neither spoke fluent English nor any Dari at all, but they'd become Khalid's favorites for agent-in-charge duties.

"But why have we not been told this before?" The minister of agriculture looked aggrieved. "Were we not informed he would be coming during your American Christmas festival? This allows little time to prepare a welcome that will properly honor such distinguished guests."

"Moving things forward was a last-minute decision," Carl Bolton answered smoothly. "Congress just recessed for the holidays but not before approving the full expanded aid package we've requested for Afghanistan. Jim Waters felt it would be appropriate to offer his congratulations in person as well as look over the good work you're doing here."

Unspoken was the reality that the State Department didn't offer travel plans for their high-ranking personnel any further ahead than necessary. The less advance notice, the less likelihood of someone seizing opportunity for a potshot at the U.S. government's top counternarcotics spokesman. Which was the reason Steve and Jason Hamilton were included in this VIP assembly. Between DynCorp's embassy contract and Steve's position as head of Khalid's detail, security for this shindig would be their headache.

"Yes, the new budget appropriations were better than we'd hoped for, not just for counternarcotics but across the board." DEA station chief Ramon Placido looked over at the U.S. task force commander. "Our government wasn't happy that satellite surveys show poppy planting up again. But drug arrests are up even more so, which tipped the scale in our favor. For that we can express our appreciation to the Ministry of Interior."

From his armchair, Khalid beamed. Beyond that spectacular destruction of Dilshod's hoard, the Black Hawk and Chinook had ferried back to Kabul an accumulated ton of seized opium bricks and close to two tons of hashish. The MOI "surge" had continued after Khalid's return to Kabul with the new counternarcotics police force racking up more arrests and even more seizures all around the country. Which made up for the freshly planted fields Steve had noted everywhere. Opium poppy was seeded in late fall to be harvested in the spring.

"Though it is short notice," Khalid said, "we will be honored to offer our hospitality to this czar Jim Waters and his associates. But not tomorrow. It is Eid-e-Qorban. All will be occupied with the feast day."

"And we understand that," Carl Bolton put in quickly. "Our staff will welcome Jim Waters and his team, and they'll spend the day with embassy personnel. But maybe Saturday we could start with that loya jirga, then a troop review and a look at your overall operation. We've only got three days. He flies on to Iraq Monday."

Both Ramon Placido and the minister of counternarcotics shook their heads. As the translator murmured into his headset, Ramon Placido explained, "The trainees will be heading home to spend the festival with their families. We'll be lucky if half of them are back by Saturday, much less ready to show off."

"I can arrange a Black Hawk for an air tour Saturday," the U.S. task force commander offered.

Khalid looked less than pleased at the proposal, and Steve knew those few hundred thousand acres of recently seeded poppy fields were going through his mind. But the tailored shoulders of his Italian suit rose and fell. "That will be satisfactory. On Sunday then I will offer hospitality for the loya jirga. My people can quickly make things ready. This will also permit time for the ministers and governors and commanders we have invited to arrange their schedules."

"Pardon my frankness, Minister," Ramon Placido replied, "but the MOI's perimeter defense is as leaky as a sieve, as I'm sure your head of security would agree." Steve kept his face expressionless. "If the participants have time to make travel plans, so do the bad guys."

"What about our embassy complex?" The U.S. task force commander spoke up. "There's tons of room, and it would avoid exposing Waters and his people."

Bolton frowned. "May I suggest the new Justice Center? I know it's not quite finished, but at least that means no occupants to screen. The U.S. embassy is always happy to cooperate, but they don't feel they can handle so many outsiders at short notice."

With the recent upsurge in bombings, Steve didn't blame the embassy for a reluctance to throw their doors open wide. And he approved the alternative. Another multimillion-dollar donation of the American people, Kabul's new Counternarcotics Justice Center boasted courtrooms, offices, interrogation chambers, and jail cells where drug suspects could be held, investigated, prosecuted, and sentenced all in one stop. That it wasn't yet occupied would make it easier to cordon off for such a high-security event.

Khalid pondered, then nodded. "An excellent idea. In fact, we will make this loya jirga the center's inauguration. Who better than your drug czar to cut the ribbon? And after the inauguration, we will arrange a parade of our new forces and a ceremony to burn the drugs we have seized."

"Then it's settled." Bolton straightened up. "That is, if our DynCorp and Condor Security colleagues feel they can secure the place. We don't want to take any risks with our personnel."

"We won't let a flea by," Steve agreed gravely, an amused glance going to Jason Hamilton.

The meeting wound up quickly. Khalid's retreat to the warmth of his own home meant Steve had only a quick walk down the hall to reach his desk.

Cougar intercepted Steve halfway there. "Khalid's initial three-month contract comes up for renewal in just a couple more weeks. Our contract comes out of the overall MOI aid packet, and it's going to be one major budget line the Waters team will take a crack at. They're sure to want your assessment of the ongoing threat level, so you might be thinking about that."

There'd been no incidents directly targeting Khalid since that rooftop suicide vest. Could Steve and his men claim credit, or was there no personal vendetta out there against the current minister of interior after all?

Regardless, Steve could count these last few weeks as a victory—and not just for keeping his principal alive. They'd put real bad guys behind bars or at least run them out of town. Maybe his own role had been a minor one, but standing beside Khalid and Ramon Placido on those dawn raids, Steve had felt for the first time in years he was back in a battle worth fighting—and winning it!

Was he still astonished this could be Khalid's doing? In these last months Steve had learned far more about his former muj comrade than when they'd hiked Afghanistan's mountain trails together. The man's penchant for luxury and adulation. His harshness with subordinates and lavish generosity with guests. His strict fundamentalism when it came to the women he kept corralled at his Baghlan provincial compound, minus a favorite tucked so tightly into his living quarters Steve had never glimpsed her face. Meanwhile, prayer times, dietary rules, and other religious observances were reserved only for public.

But those were all external observations. Steve could admit he'd no more idea what lay behind Khalid's beaming features and extravagant speech, what was actually going on in that wily brain, than when he'd first returned here. As for Ismail, had the tall, hard-eyed deputy always been just a mouthpiece for his master, with no more opinions or personality of his own than a shadow, back when he'd been Khalid's voice to the Special Forces team and vice versa?

Not that the man hadn't proved useful this last week at New Hope.

Another victory. And if much smaller, this one was personal. Steve didn't like men who ganged up on defenseless women.

Through the command suite picture window, Steve could see Jamie McDuff and Ian Grant readying a convoy to head out to the helipad. Khalid would be spending the holiday in his home province. Phil and Roald were at the security monitors, while Cougar, Mac, Rick, and Bones were on their way out of the suite.

Mac paused to inform Steve, "We're off to the DynCorp team house. They've brought in a seventy-two-inch screen for the game, real American Bud, all the fixings. Nothing like partying with the big dogs. Sure you don't want to join us?"

"No thanks. I've got an old friend in town."

"Your loss." Mac nodded toward Steve's desk. "By the way, you've got mail."

As the four Americans disappeared out the door, Steve walked over to pick up a small, padded mailer. Tearing it open, he studied its contents, reading through the letter tucked inside before reaching for his cell phone. There was a smile in his voice as it rang through. "Hello to you too. And happy Thanksgiving."

"Okay, that's our last, and another reasonably clean bill of health." Becky Frazer jotted notes on a clipboard as the woman she'd been examining slid down from the table Amy had set up as a makeshift examining couch.

"Except for Najeeda's cough, they're all healthier than they've got reason to be considering the lives they've led. And the cough is only bronchial. We'll need to add TB vaccinations to the rest, but you can cross off worrying about an epidemic. We'll get Najeeda on antibiotics and steam therapy, and she needs to stay out of the dust as much as one can in Kabul."

A discreetly cleared throat from the doorway interrupted the American nurse practitioner. "Excuse me, Miss Ameera, but another patient has arrived."

Soraya handed Amy the medical questionnaire she'd been filling out as another draped female shape scurried into the infirmary. In celebration of the upcoming Eid-e-Qorban holiday, Amy had suspended today's classes and extended her housemate's weekend leave through Saturday. But this morning was the first Becky had been able to squeeze from her own busy schedule, and since Amy could hardly solicit Jamil's assistance with the women, she'd asked Soraya to postpone departure until after the clinic.

Becky's Dari and Pashto had proved excellent, leaving to Amy tasks requiring minimal language skills like helping women in and out of their voluminous clothing and ferrying water from her own shower for a wash-basin.

While Amy gathered up a black chador, Becky glanced over the final patient's questionnaire. "Mortality rate here's so high, if they do survive to adulthood, it's because they've got the constitution of a mule. The aches and pains your women complain of are real enough, but a fair part's emotional. Unfortunately, there just aren't resources to treat the amount of trauma they've endured. Ibuprofen and keeping them busy are as effective as any other prescription I can hand out. Though your idea on that orchard is a good one. Some trees and flowers and real grass might do even more than ibuprofen. At least your tenants don't have to deal with the biggest health risk women face in Afghanistan—pregnancy."

Their final patient might not consider that such a blessing. Amy had informed Hamida of the visiting doctor, as Becky was categorized here. But she was as surprised as pleased Rasheed's wife had taken advantage of the offer, even if only after the Welayat women were out of her path. Then, as Hamida raised her head, Amy sucked in her breath sharply. Covering one whole cheek was a fiery red welt shaped like a large human palm.

"Hamida, what happened?"

The Afghan woman quickly covered her cheek with her hand.

Becky translated her distressed murmur. "She says it was her fault. She's now been married six years and is still not pregnant. She's hoping I might have a cure."

"Her fault," Amy said indignantly. She hadn't forgotten Rasheed's disdainful dismissal of Hamida as barren. "How does not getting pregnant give anyone the right to treat you as a punching bag?"

Hamida couldn't understand Amy's words, but she looked more distressed at her tone.

With no more patients waiting in the hall, Soraya had joined the other two women inside the infirmary, and she cut off Amy's fuming. "There is no point in speaking of this matter. It is a husband's right. When I did not bear a son, my husband—"

Amy glanced at her curiously. Though she'd chosen to respect her housemate's reticence, she'd wondered that a woman of Soraya's age and social value would remain single and childless in this society. "Then you've been married?"

"He died when the mujahedeen battled over Kabul." Soraya hesitated; then as she met Amy's inquiring gaze, she shrugged. "Many rockets were fired by the mujahedeen into our neighborhood. One hit our apartment. He died. I lived."

Amy waited for more, but Soraya walked over to the door. "If there are no more patients, do I have your leave to go? My family will be expecting my help with feast preparations."

"Of course," Amy said warmly. So like everyone at New Hope, her housemate too had a story of tragedy in her past. "I hope you have a wonderful feast time with your family. Oh, and just one more thing." Hurrying to the office, Amy returned with a package she handed to Soraya. *"Eid mubarak."*

The latter was the Muslim equivalent of merry Christmas, meaning literally "A blessed Eid."

Carefully removing wrapping paper from a dictionary-size book, Soraya looked more puzzled than pleased as she turned it over.

"It's an anthology of English poetry," Amy explained. "You mentioned you'd always wanted to find some of the pieces you memorized in the university." One of the rare times Soraya had discussed anything beyond work. "I think you'll find a lot of them in there."

Though Amy's guidebook mentioned small gifts to children as an Eid tradition, she'd wanted to do something special for her New Hope adults as well. Hand creams and makeup items from the bazaar would be appreciated by the Welayat women, but she'd looked for something more personal for Soraya. The poetry collection had been among Persian and Arabic titles in a downtown bookstore.

Soraya's expression cleared as she turned pages. "Yes, I see. Thank you for thinking of me. Eid mubarak."

As Soraya left, Amy returned to the infirmary.

Becky was scribbling final notes on Hamida's chart as she explained briskly, "You are in good health. There is no physical reason I can see that you shouldn't be able to bear children. If you have not yet become pregnant, it isn't your fault or anything you're doing wrong. Do you understand? But because there is nothing wrong with you, neither is there anything I can do or give to you to help you get pregnant. You just need to be patient. If God wills, he will give you children in his time."

"Inshallah. If Allah wills." Hamida looked disappointed, but she also seemed more cheerful. After all, no matter how hard one strove, there was no bucking Allah's inscrutable and sovereign choices.

Becky shook her head as Hamida left, her chador turning her back into a black ghost. "I sure wish a woman's worth in this society wasn't so tied to having children, because unless a miracle intervenes, her chances aren't good."

"But I thought you said she was healthy." Pushing the table against a wall, Amy gathered up disposable gloves, tongue depressors, and other debris to restore the infirmary to order. "That you could find no physical reason she couldn't have children."

"That's right, at least not without more sophisticated tests than I can offer. I wish I could say the same for her husband."

Amy straightened up. "Rasheed?"

"That's right. From what Soraya wrote down of Hamida's family medical history, Rasheed's first wife was a widow with a son who died like so many here before age five. But she never got pregnant again during her marriage to Rasheed."

"You mean—?"

"I'm saying the difficulty in conceiving is likely Rasheed's doing, not Hamida's. Though just what the problem is would need medical testing I'm not qualified to give."

"Then shouldn't we tell her that? And Rasheed? At least so he can stop hitting Hamida for not getting pregnant."

"He won't believe it," Becky said decisively. "Certainly not from female medical personnel. If your chowkidar was a professional with some science education, maybe. As it is, he not only wouldn't believe it, he'd consider it an insult. No, what matters is that Hamida knows it's not her fault. And in the end, it is in God's hands. Miracles do happen."

Amy tried to imagine herself presenting the tall, burly caretaker with this new tidbit and quailed at the image. She hadn't even mustered the courage to broach the use of the orchard. Since Rasheed had returned to New Hope after the break-in, he had been in the darkest of moods. *The way he stomped around that broken gate, you'd have thought we did it.*

Amy's diffident explanation had been brushed irately aside. "If we were not harboring criminals, we would not have to concern ourselves about such assaults."

Maybe looking for a new location for New Hope wouldn't be such a bad idea.

The sky overhead was gray and pregnant with moisture as Amy saw Becky out to her battered van. Was rain going to spoil the afternoon's plans? Or from the nippiness burning at her nostrils, maybe even the first winter snow Soraya had been warning her to expect? For Miami-bred Amy, the intensifying cold was one of the worst aspects of Kabul life. The propane heaters she'd scattered liberally through New Hope's salons barely touched the chill except to make the place smell like rush-hour traffic, and Amy had reluctantly shelved play equipment for Eid to purchase winter clothing in bulk.

Wajid ambled over from the guardshack to open the gate. Amy had asked Becky about the elderly guard's opium smoking, and the nurse had shaken her head. "At his age, if he's functioning, I'd leave him alone. You'd have to find a substitute for the pain anyway, and likely as not, it'd still be morphine-based. Just don't count on him as part of your security."

"Tashakor, Wajid." The lightest of drizzles was quickening Amy's steps back up the cobblestone path when her phone rang. Caller ID told her who it was before she heard Steve's amused drawl.

"Thanksgiving!" Amy gasped. "Oh, my goodness, you're right, it *is* the fourth Thursday of November. I've been thinking so much about this Eid holiday, I totally lost track. And I had Becky run a clinic this morning. Whatever is she going to think? I hadn't heard anything about it at the expat worship gathering."

"That's because it's one holiday that's exclusively American. For the rest of the planet, it's the middle of the work week. Except this year it also happens to fall the day before Eid-e-Qorban."

"Well, thanks for that intel," Amy said tartly. "At least now I can remember to Skype home tonight. Is a little cultural update why you're calling?"

Steve chuckled. "No, that was a freebie. I wanted to pass along an update from Ismail on your perps from the other night. It seems they're all one family. Four brothers-in-law of Aryana, along with cousins, uncles, etc. One of them just happens to be a locksmith."

All of which Amy already knew, Aryana having unhesitatingly picked out her husband's relatives from the footage Jamil had shot. After the young woman's earlier collapse, Amy had been worried this new scare would trigger even greater trauma. But seeing her in-laws cowering under all those weapons proved to have the opposite effect. If still quiet, Aryana was venturing out to join the other women as she never had before.

"They've also admitted they paid one of the Welayat wardens for intel. I figured you'd be pleased to know that as deputy minister Ismail stepped in to sack the guy. The other good news is that your intruders are steaming mad they paid for bad intel. As long as they don't learn otherwise, we can hope you've seen the end of this."

"At least for these ones." Amy sighed. "I've been wondering if I should try to find a new location the Welayat doesn't know about."

"As long as it's rented to a foreign entity, there'll be records out there. On the flip side, you won't find many places as large and solidly built as the one you've got. You've tested your security now and know it works. And at least you know your perps were disgruntled amateurs, not Tallies targeting an expat aid worker."

"Amateurs!" Maybe that was all that frightening mob had been to former Special Forces Steve Wilson. Still, his words echoed Amy's own misgivings. She didn't *want* to start over again elsewhere. She could end up jumping from the frying pan into the fire, and after all, an amiable relationship with the caretaker was hardly part of a rental contract.

Besides, Rasheed had offered no protest to Amy's latest request. Along with repairs to the smashed vehicle gate, metal security bars like those protecting the main entrance and Amy's suite had now been added to every door with outside access. There'd be no repeat of last week.

And Steve's report reassured Amy on one niggling concern. She hadn't wanted to believe one of her staff was capable of betraying her charges. But *someone* had passed on Aryana's whereabouts. Jamil's intervention was his own best alibi. But Soraya had been less than truthful at least once, while Rasheed made no bones of his disdain for Amy's tenants. Steve's confirmation that it was none of the above was a relief that tinged Amy's tone with gratitude. "Well, thank you for letting me know. I'll pass on the good news to Aryana. If there's anything else—"

"Actually, there is one more thing. I'm heading over to a Thanksgiving service this afternoon, and I wondered if you'd be interested in riding along."

"You're inviting me to a Thanksgiving service?" Amy couldn't keep surprise from her voice. She was not unacquainted with the signs of a man intrigued with her, and Steve Wilson had shown none of them.

"You sound so suspicious, I'm not sure I shouldn't feel insulted." Steve's voice still held amusement but now exasperation as well. "Is it because I'm inviting you specifically or that we're talking church service here?"

"Neither," Amy countered. "It's just—well, like I said, I hadn't heard anything about Thanksgiving services here in Kabul."

"It's not in Kabul. It's at Camp Phoenix, the American base out toward the airport. An old friend of mine, a chaplain from Fort Bragg, is in-country with a singing group to do some special holiday services with the troops."

"Well, I certainly appreciate the invitation," Amy said cautiously, "but I'm just heading out to our neighborhood project. We're doing kind of a movie-and-a-meal thing with the kids for Eid-e-Qorban, since we're celebrating the real thing tomorrow here at New Hope. Besides, if you've got a friend visiting, surely you can't want some outsider tagging along."

"I wouldn't have asked you if I didn't," Steve said evenly. "Look, there's no big catch here. Today's Thanksgiving, you're an American away from your family, and I can certainly use some company. Besides, you'd like Garwood; he's nothing like me." The addition was dry. "And the service isn't until four. Unless like so many humanitarian types, you've got some beef with the military. I can assure you they won't bite."

Now Amy could hear definite sarcasm. "Of course I've no problem with the military. I've had family in the armed forces."

As Steve's challenge hung on the line, Amy considered. She'd no real reason to say no. Once this afternoon's program was under way, Jamil and the others were perfectly capable of finishing up and getting everyone back to New Hope. And why not? It was Thanksgiving, and if Amy couldn't be with family, then to be with fellow countrymen for a few hours without having to wrap her tongue around alien sounds, to be able to speak without weighing every word was suddenly an irresistible proposition.

Amy paused on the marble entry steps to wipe dampness from her face, then inspected her sleeve in surprise. Yes, that dusting of white was snow. She hurried indoors. It was drier but no warmer. "Is the building where you're meeting heated?"

Steve's laugh was the delightful one that made the security contractor a disturbingly attractive man. "Not just the building but my car."

"Done then," Amy said. "You can pick me up at the project."

"Three thirty. Bring your passport. And by the way, that's military time, not local."

33

"I can read a watch," Amy said indignantly. Locals had little regard for punctuality, calling it American time or European time, and long-term expats tended to have a more easygoing attitude toward promptness. "I'll be waiting on the dot."

"See you then." With another laugh, Steve rang off. Down below outside the picture glass window, Khalid was climbing into the BMW limo for the convoy run to his Mi-8.

As soon as Steve slapped his phone shut, Phil limped over. "I wasn't trying to eavesdrop, but about what you just told Ms. Mallory, there's something you should know."

Phil's switch to quiet Dari was mystifying until Steve caught Roald's uncomprehending glance from the security monitors. A soberness in Phil's expression roused him to instant alert, and in the same language, he asked quietly, "What's wrong?"

"I'll let you be the judge." Phil angled his body to block Roald's curious stare. "For starters, that report Ismail gave you earlier just happened to leave one thing out. I talked to the Welayat myself this morning like you asked, and the perps we rounded up the other night are out walking free. In fact, it seems they were in custody only a few hours. No charges were filed against them. After all, they did no real harm, and since every man can understand their very honorable compulsion to retrieve a wayward woman—I'm quoting here—one wouldn't wish to keep them from their families and employment."

"But Ismail—" Steve stopped himself. Quoting or not, Phil had it right that the deputy minister—or Khalid himself, for that matter—would likely see last week's escapade differently than an American did. Nor, despite the displeasure tightening his jaw, was there a thing Steve could do about it. Only Khalid had more authority over local law enforcement than the deputy minister, while Condor Securities had none at all.

"Well, they were bound to buy themselves out eventually." Steve shrugged. "At least they seem to have lost interest in New Hope."

"Anyway, that's not why I've been sticking around for you." Phil jerked his head toward the security monitors. "You know the new surveillance cameras."

The CS team's new spy-cam network had been inside that seized container Steve had negotiated out of customs, and like the fiber-optic fencing, was part of a strategy to keep Khalid's defenses as unobtrusive as they were thorough. With the tiny cameras CS command could keep tabs on every inch of the property outside Khalid's living quarters without the minister's touchy guests ever knowing. Though Phil monitored the surveillance network, McDuff and one of the newer operatives were the team's electronics specialists, and they'd installed the system the same day fiber-optic fencing had gone up at the New Hope compound.

"The protocol I gave was video only, but McDuff must have missed that memo, because by the time I checked out the system, it had been recording audio for twenty-four hours. That was the night the police commander from Dilshod's district was here."

Also the night they'd been rather occupied over at New Hope, excuse enough for Phil's oversight.

"I was running through the footage to see if there's any reason not to erase it. There was nothing we couldn't do without until I ran through the footage from Khalid's reception suite. I've left my screen cued to the relevant section. You might want to take a listen before heading out."

Phil waved away Steve's interjection before the words got past his teeth. "No, I'm not going to say more. I want you to make up your own mind. Maybe I'm all wrong. Either way, you're the boss, so it's your call. I'll catch you later."

Phil had left a headset plugged into his laptop so that when Steve settled it into place, the Dari filtering through the earpiece was as clear as though Steve were sitting among those small, gesturing figures lounging Eastern-style on cushions.

The segment was a continuation of the festivities that had been going strong when Steve left the night of the break-in. All but a few trays of honey pastries and tea were cleared away, and only half a dozen men remained, among them several police commanders Steve remembered from the raids, including the regional leader of the Dilshod op. The screen showed Roald standing at agent-in-charge duty behind Khalid. By Ismail's absence, he'd already been called away to meet Steve at the New Hope compound.

At first Steve listened with impatience, tempted to fast-forward through seemingly aimless conversation. But before long, he was no longer giving any thought to the passage of time, the displeasure that had tightened his jaw mounting into a fury he tamped down forcibly lest he put his fist through those smug faces on the monitor as he'd like to do to their real-life counterparts. Outside, overcast skies had given way to a flurry of white that looked as ice-cold as the heaviness squeezing at Steve's chest.

I can't believe I fell for it, fell for him *again.*

No wonder Phil hadn't wanted to share this tape with the rest of the team. Its content was pure C-4. And no wonder Khalid was so gung ho about the CS team's latest two additions. Their lack of Dari skills permitted the minister and his associates to speak as openly as though the two bodyguards were deaf-mutes.

Did Khalid even realize there was a spy-cam trained on him? Or hardly conversant with high-tech toys, had he assumed the new system entailed the same hall and perimeter cameras as the old one? Steve certainly hadn't taken it upon himself to outline the difference.

In any case, it would seem the surge Steve had so fervently applauded—and his principal's role in it—hadn't been quite the valiant battle against internal corruption and external villains the media had been playing up for weeks.

More like the godfather and cronies taking out turf rivals.

Dilshod was a prime example. Steve could still taste the exhilaration of that dawn raid, smell the acrid sweetness of burning opium and hashish, hear the shouts of triumph even if the perps had gotten away. Now from what he was hearing, it appeared Dilshod had been chosen less for his brutal notoriety than that as an Uzbekistan transplant he'd no local tribal alliances to spawn reprisals. The raid had been a sham, an amicable negotiation surrendering the Uzbek's stockpiles for destruction in return for an unhindered retirement to his native land and Swiss bank accounts.

Nor could Dilshod be dismissed as aberration. One high-level tribal leader whose arrest Steve had witnessed was, according to conversation, the chief political rival of a guest deferentially pouring Khalid a cup of tea. Other detainees were behind on police protection fees—i.e., bribes. Even those substantial drug seizures could be seen in a different light by their discussion, increased production leaving such a stockpiled glut that sacrificing a few tons was more tactical maneuver than serious loss. It might even push prices back up.

Why am I so surprised? Steve asked himself savagely. Wasn't this the Khalid he'd known before? No champion of law and reform as the international media had jumped to proclaim but a wily fighter bent on building his own personal power base, by negotiation where possible, but never shrinking from battle, as long as it was a winning hand.

That Steve wasn't the only one played for a fool was no consolation. How was it he'd broken his own cardinal rule? You didn't have to like your principal or even approve, just keep him alive. Don't get involved. Don't take it personal.

Because I wanted to believe this time was different. That Khalid—and I—were actually doing something to make a difference. That maybe I was wrong before, and there really was hope that this place and a man like Khalid could change.

It was just as well Khalid was on his way out of town so Steve couldn't storm in to face him before he got his temper under control. Need he remind himself he was little more than a glorified security guard? While his former muj ally was the most powerful politician in this country next to the president himself—and with comparable armed force at his command beyond the foreign weaponry to which the president could appeal. No, bracing Khalid over this would be just plain stupid. Maybe the reason

Phil, who knew his one-time teammate so well, had waited until liftoff to bring it to Steve's attention.

Still, there were others who would and should find this intel of interest. It was the State Department that signed Steve's paychecks. And they should know what kind of pig in a poke they'd bought in the new minister of interior.

Powering down Phil's computer, Steve reached for his phone. With DynCorp holding the embassy security contract, Jason Hamilton would know who best to approach.

A Gurkha sentry stepped into the room, startling Steve back to his current surroundings. "Excuse me for interrupting, sir, but there is an unusual disturbance outside. Though it may sound foolish, I am sure it was the sound of wild animals I heard. Lions, perhaps, or tigers."

The DynCorp manager—and Khalid—would have to wait. Grabbing his parka and the mailer he'd opened earlier, Steve followed the anxious guard onto the terrace and listened briefly. Yes, that was a lion's roar all right above the music and loud voices of a celebration. He clapped the guard on the shoulder. "It's nothing to worry about. I'll go check it out."

The flurry of white Steve had noted through the picture window was now a steady snowfall, making the dirt streets slippery enough to keep the elderly Corolla at a crawl as he negotiated the alleys behind Khalid's mansion. The noise of celebration grew louder ahead. So did the snarling of wild beasts.

Then, as the car slid around a tight corner, Steve braked to a stop. Just ahead was a mud-brick compound wall, its top lined with bodies perched as tightly as a flock of birds on a telephone wire. Others crowded the bed, hood, even cab top of a two-ton truck pulled up tight to the compound gate.

Only one person was paying no attention to the commotion inside the compound. A female, tall for an Afghan and slim even under a voluminous winter cloak, stood with her back to Steve in the middle of the street. At a fresh crescendo of animal growls, Steve punched a speed dial on his phone. As he did so, he slid out the contents of the mailer and studied them again.

Steve waited until that slim female figure raised a hand to her ear to demand with incredulous irony, "*Lion King?*"

"*White as snow.*"

For all Steve Wilson's talk of military time, the security contractor was more than a little late. But Amy found her irritation fading as she tilted a face alight with wonder to the softly falling snow. It had been growing steadily thicker since the opening scene of the DVD Jamil was projecting onto a whitewashed wall in the brickmaker's courtyard. Though Amy's suggestion they cut the festivities short had been greeted with perplexed opposition.

"It will be just as cold in their own homes," Farah had pointed out. "They do not have stoves like we do."

Amy couldn't remember when she'd last been warm, her hands and feet presently so chilled she couldn't feel them. But the enchantment of this gentle, white cascade had driven the cold from her mind. Since the New Hope team's arrival, it had accumulated enough to drift across flat roofs and wall tops, transmuting heaped rubble and muddy ruts to sparkling white mounds, settling as well dust and smog so that the delighted breath Amy drew into her lungs tasted clean and fresh.

Amy had seen snow before—in holiday movies and one childhood winter visit to some Chicago relatives. There'd been sledding then, a snowman. But that snow was packed down and dirty with the churned-up slush of snowplows and car tires. She'd never seen it drifting fresh and new from the sky. Never imagined just how glisteningly clean and pure and very, very white it could be.

"*Though your sins are like scarlet, they shall be white as snow.*"

Amy had never thought of Kabul as anything but ugly and dirty, a place of overwhelming devastation and human suffering. But at this moment under its carpet of white, the adobe hovels and winding dirt alleys climbing barren hillsides were as beautiful as a Christmas card.

Jesus walked streets that must have looked just like this one. The manger where he was born could have been behind just such humble mud walls.

Cheers and applause greeting what must be a battle scene by the movie's Dari-dubbed soundtrack had drowned out any sound of an approaching car engine, so it wasn't until Steve called that Amy spun around to see the Corolla pulled up behind the two-ton. Slapping her phone shut, Amy picked her way through the snow.

As Steve rolled down the driver's window, she bent to peer in, an impish smile belying her indignant demand. "Do you know how hard it is to find a movie around here no one can object to? The princesses don't have enough clothes or are too independent. Aladdin thinks it's okay to steal if you're poor. At least *The Lion King* is only cute animals and the good guy winning. As you can see, even the parents have all turned out. Fortunately, we cooked extra. And by the way, what happened to military time? You're late."

She'd caught Steve stuffing mail back inside a small envelope, and despite his levity on the phone, something in his expression drove the smile from Amy's face. Glancing at the mailer in his hand, she asked quietly, "Is something wrong?"

Steve's face went blank as a quick toss landed the envelope on the dashboard. "Not at all. Just a last-minute glitch at the office. Sorry I'm late. If you're ready now . . ."

Maybe she'd imagined that earlier bleakness. As Steve leaned over to open the passenger door, Amy said hastily, "Sure, just let me find Jamil and tell him I'm leaving. He's showing the movie and will get everything back to New Hope when it's done."

Snow was certainly less messy on a Christmas card, Amy decided ruefully, trying to hurry and keep cloak and skirts out of the wet at the same time. But she didn't have to go far, because just as she reached the two-ton, Jamil stepped out around its hood.

"I'm glad to catch you out here. As you can see, my ride's arrived. If you can make sure everything gets packed up after the movie and back to New Hope, I'll be there in a few hours."

Jamil made no response to her instructions. He was staring past her toward the car. "It is with the American soldier you are going today? This is what you call a date then?"

"No, of course not," Amy answered, then stopped. "Well, I suppose in the strictest definition you could call it that. Today is a holiday in my country, like Eid here, and Steve—Mr. Wilson—has kindly invited me to accompany him to a celebration of it."

"To have fun? To get to know each other better?"

"I can't talk right now. We're already late. I'll see you all later this evening at New Hope."

Amy stomped snow from boots and clothes before sliding into the front seat.

Steve nodded toward the two-ton as he backed up, tires spinning against the snow and mud. "Your driver doesn't look too happy."

Amy turned her head to see that Jamil had still not moved but was watching their departure. Steve was right. Even through the falling snow, there was no mistaking the fury blazing from Jamil's dark eyes.

Jamil wasn't sure which was churning the bile of his stomach to acid. Fury that the American soldier had intruded again into his personal universe. Or Ameera's smile as she'd bent to the car's open window. A smile that had been missing when she crossed over to speak to Jamil.

Jamil withdrew his hostile glare from the retreating vehicle as an impatient vibration brought him back to the reason he'd emerged from the compound. Not Ameera's own exit but because it was too loud inside for a phone conversation. Pulling his cell phone free from a vest pocket, he strode away from the music and cheers. "Yes, who is this?"

"Has it been so long you've actually forgotten my voice?"

The light amusement of the question turned acid to ice in Jamil's stomach. As he listened, the chill of melting snow seeping through thin sandals and wool socks traveled up to squeeze air from his chest. When his caller finished speaking, Jamil turned back to the Eid celebration without so much as a glance toward where the car had vanished into a flurry of white. Time would deal with the American soldier.

As for Ameera, how had he so easily permitted himself to live in a world where the smile of a woman, the cool challenge in a rival's eyes, the doings of any other human being could matter enough to breach the careful shell he'd erected against thought and emotion?

Neither fury nor hate played now across Jamil's face but an expression as glacial as the packed snow beneath his sandals as he headed back into the compound to begin carrying out the instructions left to him by his employer.

Both of them.

Amy let out a sigh as the car fishtailed around a corner, leaving Jamil out of sight. "Sorry about that. Please don't take it personally. Jamil's got a thing about soldiers, especially American. I think maybe something happened to his family during the war. And I'm afraid he's got the wrong idea we're on some kind of a date, something he probably disapproves on Muslim moral grounds."

Steve made no response, perhaps because it was taking all his concentration to keep the vehicle from skidding out of the slippery ruts. Or from his tightened jaw, could he be regretting his invitation?

At least Amy was warming up, the blast of the car heater thawing her face and hands delightfully. Pushing her head covering back to shake out her damp hair, Amy offered a lighter topic along with a tentative smile. "I'm just glad you reminded me it was Thanksgiving. My sister was supposed to fly in from Peru for Thanksgiving. I'd have hated to miss her. If I Skype this evening, they'll still be cooking the turkey back home in Miami."

Amy squealed as the vehicle skidded across melting slush. The steering wheel spun rapidly in Steve's hands. Then the road straightened out, and the front tires touched pavement.

Turning right onto a congested boulevard, Steve glanced over as though nothing had happened. "Sounds like your family's scattered pretty far. You out here. A sister south of the equator. And you mentioned a brother in the military."

"Marines. Reconnaissance Force, specifically. That's their Special Ops." Amy made no effort to tone down the pride in her voice.

Steve's lips twitched as he murmured, "Yes, I'm aware of that."

"Though he's been out a couple of years. He's working for World Vision out of Seattle. I guess we're kind of scattered, but we do try to be together for the holidays. My younger siblings will have driven down from Florida State last night for our church Thanksgiving dinner. If I can get away for Christmas, we're hoping it'll be all of us."

The twitch of Steve's mouth had become a genuine smile.

Amy looked at him suspiciously as he slowed for a checkpoint, then turned onto a main boulevard. "Did I say something funny?"

Steve shook his head, a half grin still crooking his mouth. "It just sounds so *Leave It to Beaver*. Parents still married to each other. Brothers and sisters who get along. College students rushing home for a church Thanksgiving celebration. Let me guess—you were all straight-A students, maybe valedictorian?"

Amy turned pink. "Actually, only two of us. And believe me, it's not like we're some kind of angels. As for church Thanksgiving, Miami-style— well, who wouldn't rush home for American turkey with Cuban beans and rice, Brazilian samba, and a mariachi band?"

"Hey, hey!" Steve braked to avoid a motorcycle carrying an entire family that was cutting across their path. "Don't apologize for having a family that sticks together and loves each other. It's nice to know there's a few of those still around."

"I think you'd be surprised at how many are still around." Amy eyed Steve. "And what about you? What's your family like?"

A deft turn of the steering wheel jockeyed the Corolla between a horse cart and an ancient bus. Then Steve shrugged. "I can think of few topics less interesting than my family tree."

"Oh no, you don't. You've grilled me about my bio and job every time you see me. Now it's your turn. Or we can just sit here the rest of the trip, because I'm done talking until you tell me something about yourself."

Steve's eyes met Amy's. "Are you always this pushy?"

Amy grinned unrepentantly. "I've got three brothers. Are you always this evasive?"

"Probably." Steve let several blocks go by before he finally spoke up. "Fine. I'm an Army brat both sides, Dad a medic, Mom a survival instructor. Which meant a lot of moving around. Let's just say I wasn't a planned career choice. At least they were smart enough to stop at one."

Steve shrugged again. "Anyway, that lifestyle's hard on relationships. My parents were divorced when I was six, which meant bouncing around even more, depending on who had family quarters. I saw Germany, Korea, and Japan before I was nine. That's when both my parents were mobilized for the first Gulf War. My mom came back, my dad didn't—a routine evac mission that went wrong. Chopper crashed, no survivors."

"That's terrible. I am so sorry." Amy was wishing now she hadn't pushed so hard. No wonder the security contractor avoided his bio.

"It didn't turn out so bad. My mom was still deployed, so I ended up with my grandparents. My father's side. My mom was raised in foster care and has no family I know of. Small-town Indiana may be a culture shock after Army bases, but it's not a bad place to raise a hyperactive teenager. If I spent more time playing basketball and football than studying, my grandparents managed to keep me out of trouble. At least till Gran died when I was seventeen. By then school seemed pretty pointless, so instead of prom, I joined the Army. Been traveling ever since."

His brisk summary didn't succeed in banishing compassion from Amy's gaze. "I didn't mean to bring up painful memories. Or to sound like—well, like I take the privileges I've had for granted. I've only to hear stories like yours or the women at New Hope or my mom's own childhood in Cuba to know how lucky I am in my family and home or even things like getting to finish high school."

Steve's eyebrow shot up. "Who says I didn't finish high school? I joined the Army, not a street gang. I passed my GED before I was out of boot camp. Finished my bachelor's doing foreign language training for Special Ops. Added a master's in international relations during my last deployment in Iraq."

Amy gritted her teeth. Why was it every time she mustered up kindly thoughts toward this man, he managed to make her feel like an idiot? She was clearly wasting her sympathy. Steve was as tough as he looked, which happened to lie somewhere between steel nails and a bear trap.

"As to family, my grandfather's still alive and kicking. And my mom remarried when I was in my teens. Not armed forces, a pediatrician. He's been good to her, and they've got a couple kids of their own, a boy and a girl just hitting their teens. I don't see much of them—been overseas since they were out of diapers—but they're decent kids. Blame them I can recognize a *Lion King* soundtrack when I hear it. Now, you did remember your passport?"

They had just pulled up to a security checkpoint. A gate beyond marked the entrance to Camp Phoenix. While an Afghan guard used a mirror on the end of a steel pole to check their undercarriage, an expat soldier with a red, white, and blue flag on his lapel emerged from a concrete guard box with a clipboard. Taking Amy's passport as she dug it from her shoulder bag, Steve passed it out with his own. "Steve Wilson, Condor Security, and party for the Thanksgiving service."

The soldier ran a pen down the clipboard, then rifled through the passports. "Your outfit's on the list. Go on through."

Handing back her passport, Steve grinned at Amy as he drove through the gate. "You're not strictly CS, but I was crossing my fingers an American passport would get you through. Now, are you ready for some toe-tapping holiday fun? Because you can count on that from Garwood and crew."

No man with such capacity for aggravation should have access to that irresistible smile. Amy grinned despite herself. Outside, the snow had stopped falling, and she felt warmed through. Whatever had earlier troubled her companion, he'd evidently pushed it aside to enjoy the day, and Amy made up her mind to do the same. "I'm more salsa than toe-tapping, but lead on."

On the outskirts of Kabul, Camp Phoenix was as sprawled out as a small town. Dirt alleys between prefabricated huts and shipping containers converted to living quarters were so slick with melting snow that Amy was thankful for her walking boots as well as Steve's firm grip at her elbow. The holiday service was being held in the recreation center, a huge Quonset hut where sports equipment had been pushed back for folding chairs now filled with winter fatigues. Among the uniforms was a scattering of civilian dress, including Steve's contractor friend, Phil Myers. Amy's cheeks grew hot as she intercepted Phil's knowing glance and the sudden ironic line of her companion's mouth.

The uniformed jazz chorus on a makeshift platform was as toe-tapping as promised, and by the time a lively Christmas medley had the audience clapping and stamping along, Amy was enjoying herself. Perhaps one reason she'd pushed Thanksgiving from her mind was the depressing recognition that she'd be with neither family nor friends, the date just another workday. But among these servicemen and women, the snow falling softly in her mind if no longer in sight, it felt like the holidays for the first time.

Maybe they weren't family, but they were her countrymen, and Amy was surprised at a fierce surge of patriotic pride as she looked around. Every soldier here was a volunteer, most so young they could be her college-age siblings, all away from home for the holidays to serve their country. And regardless of political wrangling, no one could deny these men and women as a body had served with dignity and honor and decency unmatched.

"'I'll be home for Christmas . . .'"

As the audience joined in fervently, Amy found herself swallowing hard. She stole a glance at Steve, whose strong baritone rose without self-consciousness above her soprano. This had once been Steve's world, and despite civilian dress, he still fit into this group as though he belonged in fatigues.

Then as a tall, powerfully built African American man in Army chaplain uniform began to speak, Amy straightened up to listen. This must be Steve's friend. The chaplain might have been anywhere from forty to sixty, his fitness making it hard to estimate age, head and face shaved clean so there was no hint of gray.

"'Though your sins are like scarlet, they shall be as white as snow.' Maybe that doesn't sound like a Thanksgiving theme to you. Me, I'm a Louisiana boy, and I had no idea what that meant until I flew in over the Hindu Kush a few years back in the dead of winter. We were fighting a little group called al-Qaeda who'd just hit our homeland and killed a few thousand of our people. I was edgy and nervous, a feeling you all know, and I couldn't help wondering if our Chinook helicopter was in the crosshairs of some Stinger missile as we dropped into the most desolate country I'd ever seen.

Then I saw the snow, mountains of it, so sparkling white it didn't make sense anymore to apply that color to human beings who were tan and beige and pink, but certainly not what I was looking at."

A ripple of chuckles.

"And I understood for the first time that God's promise meant every bit of ugliness in my life could be scrubbed as clean and white as that snow. Isn't that what the Christmas season that starts today is all about? In the darkest, deadest winter of human desolation, God stepped into our world in the person of Jesus Christ, blanketing the ugliness of our sin and despair with the pure, clean beauty of God's love and mercy and redemption. As Isaiah tells us in chapter 1, verse 18, 'Though your sins are like scarlet, they shall be as white as snow.' That's the true promise of Christmas."

The fatigues poured out of the rec hall after the final song. Steve's hand again cupped Amy's elbow as they waded forward against the stream. Phil had made his way forward too and was speaking to the chaplain when Steve and Amy reached the platform.

The chaplain's face lit up as he saw Steve. "Wilson! Glad you could make it." A powerful grip almost crushed Amy's hand. "Nice to meet you, Amy Mallory. I'm Robert Garwood, though the troops call me Rev. And I'm glad you've pulled yourselves away from your other Thanksgiving celebrations to drop by."

The chaplain's wide grin was contagious. Amy smiled at him. "Actually, I hadn't expected to celebrate Thanksgiving, so this is a wonderful treat. And I loved your sermon. I was just thinking of that same passage when it started snowing today. I'm from Miami."

"Then you know just what I mean." Rev Garwood beamed at Amy. "I've still got a half hour before liftoff, and I hear they're saving us turkey in the mess hall. You got time to join us?"

Steve's cocked eyebrow her way gave Amy no direction, so she made up her own mind. She liked the chaplain as she'd liked Steve's other acquaintance Phil. Why were the security contractor's friends so much easier to get along with than Steve himself? "I'd love to. Oh, and your singing group was incredible. Are they all armed forces too?"

"You bet—the best Fort Bragg has to offer," the chaplain agreed. "My first chaplain posting was at Fort Bragg just when Wilson and Myers were coming through. They were both in my congregation till they shipped overseas. Myers here can't sing a note, but Wilson was my lead baritone when he wasn't disappearing on some op or other."

Steve interjected dryly, "What he isn't telling you is that before he switched sides to a backward collar, he was the toughest, meanest survival instructor in Special Ops, and we were terrified to say no when he ordered us to be in the front row Sunday morning—or sing in his choir. Or that when 9/11 came along, though he was well past recall age, he was first in line to volunteer for Afghanistan with us. There are guys who'll never forget who was with them in the back of an evac chopper, Phil here being one of them."

The chaplain's chuckle at Amy's disbelieving look was rich and deep. But at the last statement, he sobered and gripped Steve's forearm. "You know all the rocket launchers in the Taliban's arsenal couldn't have kept me home."

"I know. That's why we're here instead of at DynCorp's beer bash. Just wish you had more time."

The chaplain's other huge grip was around Phil's forearm. Amy swallowed again as the three men exchanged looks. There was a brotherhood forged under the heat and sweat and adrenaline and fear of battle neither she nor any other civilian could fully understand. But she couldn't miss the almost-palpable bond between these very different men, and it was giving Amy a whole new image of the skeptic with abrupt manners and caustic tongue who'd so unexpectedly invited her here today.

Rev Garwood released his grip. "So who's joining Ms. Mallory and me for turkey?"

Phil shook his head. "I've got a date with my kids on Skype." He nodded at Amy. "A pleasure to see you again. Steve, about that other, will I catch you later?"

"Count on it." Something in the two men's exchanged glance carried Amy back to that grim look she'd noticed when Steve picked her up. But the security contractor was smiling as he and Amy walked with the chaplain to the mess hall.

As promised, the chef was keeping hot a food bar of turkey and all the traditional Thanksgiving trimmings.

Rev Garwood led Steve and Amy to a quiet corner. "I sure was tickled it worked out to cross paths with you here, Will. How long has it been since you rotated out? Five years? More? Too long!" The chaplain murmured a short grace, then turned to Amy. "Wilson was one of the most dedicated soldiers I've ever known. We've sure been sorry to lose him from Special Ops."

As Amy stole a glance at Steve's wooden expression, Rev Garwood turned back to her companion. "Which is why I sure wish you'd come back inside."

When Steve didn't answer, the chaplain added forcibly, "Come on. You've got to be bored doing guard duty by now. Don't you know we've been bleeding out Special Ops personnel these last years like a slit jugular? We need you."

Steve's silence dragged out uncomfortably until he lifted his head to meet Rev Garwood's fierce gaze directly. "You know why I got out. I still believe in the team, but I can't support the mission. Not after what I've seen over here. What I'm still seeing. I fought once to put these people in power. I won't lift a finger to keep them there. And if I had my way, we wouldn't spend another drop of American blood doing so. I'd have thought you of all people would understand."

The force with which Steve put down a fork rattled his tray. "We've talked about this before. We call these people moderates, welcome them as our allies, if they promise not to cross the ocean and blow us up. And yet we're propping up regimes that make it a capital crime for their own citizens to worship God as they choose. You want to call that building a democracy? I don't."

"You think I don't recognize that?" The chaplain looked troubled, a hand running across his shaved scalp. "There are people in prison and dying in this part of the world for their faith in the name I serve. Believe me, I don't take that lightly. But what's the alternative? The consensus back home is if we can just stay engaged in the zone, things *will* get better as the locals learn by our example what human rights and freedom are all about."

"It'll never happen," Steve said. "Not while sharia's the law of the land. Oh, sure, if we throw around enough money and blood, we might eventually bring some lessening of violence, even stability. But freedom?"

Again, Amy caught that harsh bleakness in his tone. "Right here in Kabul this year, we've had journalists sentenced to death. Religious converts arrested for apostasy. And those are just the government-sponsored acts. Forget little things like corruption or drug dealing. Meanwhile, they haven't so much as seen their aid packages skip a beat.

"As long as we keep pumping aid and military support into Islamic fundamentalist regimes without any serious accountability, why should they believe we're serious about optional little items like human rights and freedom? or anything else but catching terrorists in their backyard instead of ours?"

"And letting the region disintegrate into civil war is a better option?" Rev Garwood shook his head. "You know what a bloodbath there'd be if we walked out of here tomorrow."

"If our presence is the only thing keeping this country from reverting to savagery, what does that say about its people?" Steve asked. "If they want to fight it out among themselves, let them. If they attack us, slap them down hard. But if we don't quit making deals with the enemy, we're going to compromise ourselves literally to death, at least as far as freedom of conscience goes. Because unlike us, they have no intention of compromising. Why should they when we're happy to do that for them? And that's what I can't forgive."

Steve's mouth twisted wryly. "Which is another reason you wouldn't want me in uniform anymore. I'd never be able to keep my mouth shut about how I feel. Not all superior officers are as forgiving as you."

"Yeah, well, forgiving is also part of my business. And I can hardly order you to drop and give me forty these days."

Amy might have thought the two men had forgotten her presence, but as Rev Garwood let out a deep sigh, he turned to her. "As you can see, we'll have to agree to disagree. Forgive us for getting carried away. Now I need to get my crew on the road if we're to catch that chopper back to Bagram."

As the chaplain rose, so did his entourage across the mess hall. His large hand enfolded Amy's again. "It really was a pleasure to meet you, ma'am. Wilson, it's always good to see you. I'd have liked to get into Kabul to check out what you and Myers are up to these days. In Iraq at least I was allowed off-base to visit some historic churches. Not that you'll find those in Afghanistan. And if there are any Christians, they're smart enough to keep themselves hidden well away, especially since that convert you mentioned was arrested."

"And there you are," Steve put in forcefully. "Our new allies are happy to have you hold the line against the Taliban and rebuild their wells and schools. But you can't visit an Afghan Christian without worrying about one or both of you being killed. Now why did you say we're staying?"

The chaplain laughed and patted Steve on the back. "No, you're not going to draw me into that again. Fact is, we need men like you. But uniform or not, I haven't the slightest doubt if the time comes that you're really needed, you'll be boots on the ground and running—in the right direction."

Rev Garwood was heading away when he turned around. "Oh, I almost forgot. We collected some gifts for that children's project of yours as per your guidelines. They're up at Bagram. How can we get them to you?"

Amy's incredulous glance saw red rising up Steve's neck as he answered, "I'll take care of it. I'll be up there myself tomorrow."

"Good. I'll leave the stuff with the chaplain's office."

35

"You were right," Amy said as she stretched her legs to keep up with Steve's long strides back to the car. "I like your friend."

"Yeah, Rev's quite a guy. One of the original Green Berets and a POW back in Vietnam before he became a chaplain. Which is why he can fill up a chapel on Sunday morning. The recruits know he's got credibility because he's been where they're at. No one before or since has ever talked me into singing in public."

The lightness of Steve's tone did nothing to downplay his affection and respect for his former superior officer, and Amy looked up curiously as he opened the passenger door for her. "But you've really never considered what he said? joining back up?"

"Never." Steve's answer was immediate and flat. "Well, never say never. Like the Rev said, if my country came under attack again, I doubt there's a PSC still weapons-qualified who wouldn't have their gear packed and be first on the bus. But under the present circumstances—you heard what I had to say. It isn't just that I don't buy the mission anymore. I could no longer blindly follow orders, at least not in the kind of missions I'd be handed. I've seen too much, and I know more than I should."

Steve rounded the hood to slide into the driver's seat before grinning at Amy. "Enough of that. Rev's right; we got kind of carried away there. Blame me. You may have noticed I've a talent for starting arguments I hadn't planned."

"I noticed," Amy said dryly. But her return smile was wholehearted.

She was starting to get this guy—or thought she was. He wasn't being deliberately provocative. He just said what he thought, as though the life experiences he'd passed through had stripped away the usual social shield of prevarication and diplomacy. It could be exasperating. But there was also something reassuring in a person who said exactly what he meant and meant what he said.

"Actually, I enjoyed myself. And the Thanksgiving service. Thank you for inviting me." Amy waited until the car was moving before asking, "And this children's project Rev Garwood mentioned?"

Red deepened up Steve's neck and ears as the guard waved them through the gate. "It's no big deal. I just happened to mention your project when I heard Rev Garwood was heading this way. Didn't know he'd take it seriously. My granddad sent some stuff too. They were thinking Christmas, of course. But with this Eid thing, I'll make sure the stuff gets to you tomorrow. Our team house guys got a few things for the kids too."

Amy stared at him, stunned. "It's a very big deal—to the kids and me. Especially when you've already done so much for New Hope." Slowly, she added, "*I* should be apologizing. I don't think I've had a very . . . well, shall we say, accurate picture of you."

"Is that so? And just what kind of picture did you have?"

Amy hesitated. But under his quizzical glance, she gathered her breath. After all, the guy believed in straight talk. "To be honest, since I met you, I've thought you were kind of . . ." *Daunting? Bossy? Disapproving? Tough as nails?* Amy wrinkled her nose. "Intimidating comes to mind. And I guess I had the idea you'd no use for things like faith. Or humanitarian projects like New Hope. That you thought what I was doing was somewhere between stupid and hopeless."

"I hadn't noticed you're so easily intimidated," Steve answered as he eased the car back into traffic. "Make no mistake, I've got faith enough in God. It's people I have no faith in. So don't give me too many kudos. I hope I'd never be so rude—" another quick grin—"to use words like *stupid* or *hopeless* for what you're doing. I'm just not convinced it makes any difference in the long run. Or even that you're doing these people any favors when you keep stepping in to save them from what are also consequences of their own choices. Maybe not individually but certainly as a society."

Amy abruptly lost her smile. "I'm not sure I understand what you're saying. It bothers me too that we—the West—should cooperate with ideologies that put people to death for their faith. But you can't be suggesting we withdraw humanitarian aid from countries that don't share our ideas of human rights and freedom. Why, there'd be millions starving this winter right here in Afghanistan if we weren't here to offer food and shelter. I can't believe you'd want that on your conscience."

"It's not a matter of conscience. You think I don't feel sorry for starving kids on a street corner?" Steve took a hand from the steering wheel to run through his hair. "But let's be honest. For years I've heard people in your line of work blaming poverty for corruption and violence. And always with some bighearted idea that with enough food and cash, the world's problems would disappear. Yet for all the decades organizations like yours have been handing out aid, do you see any fewer starving children, abused women, corrupt dictators?"

Steve took in Amy's mutinous expression. "Exactly. Because in my rather extensive experience, corruption and violence breed poverty, not the other way around. This planet has plenty of resources. I'm not talking natural disasters. Pitching in there's understandable. But how much aid goes to bail out countries that have created most of their own problems? And forgive me if it sounds hard-hearted, but more often than not, the very aid that saves a few lives also enables bad governments to keep their grip.

"All I'm saying is maybe it's time to stop interfering and let the natural consequences of bad human behavior play themselves out. If there're no more bailouts, maybe the locals will get desperate enough to lay their own lives on the line against tyranny. Or not. But let it be their decision—and consequences—not ours."

"Which all sounds good and logical." Amy found that her voice was shaking and steadied it. How had she let herself consider this man worth liking? "Except what about all the children and women at New Hope? Maybe you can dismiss them as easily as natural consequences. But to me they're people I care about, not statistics. How can you be so unfeeling?"

"And how can you be so naive? You speak of faith in God. Well, isn't free will one of the things God gave man? And didn't God almost wipe out humanity once before because of our choices? So what makes you think human beings are any more salvageable now? And I'm not just talking about this part of the world. Believe me, I'm under no illusion our free West has any corner on human decency. All you can really do in this crazy world is take care of yourself, survive the best you can, and be as decent a person as possible while you're at it. What you *can't* do is save people who don't want or deserve to be saved."

"Yet you're here in Afghanistan." Amy's annoyance was evaporating as she studied her companion. "And you've rounded up presents for needy children and put up perimeter defenses to keep us safe."

Steve's grin held no humor. "Well, now, that's the advantage of being a civilian. I don't have to practice what I preach. Like you, I'm hired to do a job that can take me anywhere in the world there's a trouble spot. The difference is, I make no pretence to try to change or save the world. But if the Christmas season brings out the warm and fuzzy even in a hard case like me, I've got no problem putting a temporary smile on a few kids' faces even while I'm well aware my drop in the 'do-good' bucket doesn't make a bit of difference to this planet's big picture."

"Maybe not," Amy said slowly, "but to these particular kids, it sure does."

The traffic was no less chaotic at this late afternoon hour, the earlier snowfall already churned to slush and mud. But Steve drove as though there were no slickness under the tires, and with his next turn, Amy recognized the quiet paved side street and a familiar blue wall coming up fast on the next corner.

She broke the silence. "In any case, I can't agree with you. I let you convince me once I had no hope of making a difference here. But New Hope is proof you're wrong. Maybe not about all the political stuff. I'll admit I don't know the answers for Afghanistan or the world. What I do know is that the kids at New Hope, my women who've gone through so much, the staff I'm working with—they're incredible people. Resilient and hardworking, and they've survived things I can't imagine putting up with. And I have faith that working together with them, I can make a serious impact to change this country."

"Faith." Steve braked hard in front of the black pedestrian gate before turning to Amy, his eyes hard, disbelieving. "You have got to be kidding. You have faith in people who all benefit from you, who all have something at stake in playing nice with you. I'm guessing you've never had your heart broken, have you?"

Amy shook her head, confused. Why was he changing the subject? "You mean, falling in love?"

"I mean betrayal. Breaking your heart over someone else, someone you've trusted, their lies, the pain and suffering they've caused to people you care about." His tone was harsh. "Even your other missions, all those floods and earthquakes where you've handed out MREs and blankets. You've never had to be personally, emotionally invested in those people. If one lets you down, there's always a dozen more waiting in line."

Amy looked at him contemplatively before she answered. "I suppose that's a fair enough assessment."

"Then it's easy for you to have faith. Naive and unfounded but easy. Keep your faith in God, but if you're going to have such unjustified faith in man, you're just setting yourself up for heartbreak. Believe me, I've made that mistake."

The small security panel in the pedestrian gate slid open and shut again. Then the gate creaked open to let out Wajid. But Amy made no move to get out of the car. She was watching Steve. His long fingers were tight on the steering wheel, his head turned to watch the guard's approach so Amy could see the rigid line of his jaw.

Wajid ambled over to peer through the windshield. At his eyes on her uncovered head, Amy reached for the scarf she'd discarded when she'd first climbed into the vehicle. As she shook it into place, it brushed across the dashboard. Steve grabbed for the yellow mailer as the tassels knocked it off, but not before its contents slid out the open end and fluttered to the floor.

"Oh, I'm sorry." Amy stooped to scoop up a handwritten note and a four-by-six snapshot. The floorboard under her boots was damp from melting snow and mud, and she brushed a mud fleck from a scrawled *Granddad* on the notepaper. "I hope I didn't ruin these."

Amy turned the snapshot over. Despite a few wet streaks, the picture was as vivid as the day it had been taken. A girl, still in her teens, with shoulder-length flaxen hair and an anxious expression. A group of small children were pressed around her, smiling at the camera.

With astonishment, Amy demanded, "How did you get my picture?" She turned the snapshot over again, this time reading a familiar scrawl across the back: *We're praying for you.* "Wait! You can't be—!"

A flicker of annoyance crossed Steve's face as he plucked the photo and note from Amy's fingers and shoved both with the mailer into a coat pocket. "If you mean the lucky soldier you and your Sunday school class picked out of the hat, I'm afraid so."

"I can't believe it! So that's why—" *That's why you acted so interested in me, when I knew I wasn't your type. It wasn't because you were really interested in me or New Hope or even because you felt somehow responsible after rescuing me that day. You were just trying to figure out who I was.* "How long have you known it was me?"

"Not until it came in the mail today. You don't think I've been carrying it around all these years. But there was something familiar about you, and when I saw you last week with all those kids crowded around—" Steve leaned back in his seat as he looked over Amy's face—"well, you hardly look a day older. I remembered you saying something about coming to Afghanistan someday. Being me, I like to check things out. So I asked my grandfather to dig that out of my old junk."

"I just can't believe you kept it," Amy said dazedly. "I'd forgotten all about it. I never even knew who the soldier was who got that letter. He never wrote back, so I thought maybe it had gotten lost."

"Don't take it personally. I only kept it to remind myself what a fool I was."

"What do you mean?" Amy demanded.

"What do I mean?" Steve turned toward the windshield, a muscle bunching along his jaw. "Do you even remember what you wrote with that picture?"

"Not really. Something about how my class and I were praying for you, that you'd be safe and that you and the other soldiers would be successful in the fight to free Afghanistan."

"Yeah, well, what you had to say stuck in my mind. You said you were praying all our fighting would make Afghanistan 'land of the free and home of the brave.' Nice-sounding words. Funny thing is, I was going to write you back and tell you how we'd freed Kabul. That you could tell your kids their prayers were answered. Except I found out right about then what an empty victory we'd won. That we hadn't helped the Northern Alliance bring freedom to this place. We'd just helped a bunch of robber barons stake out their booty."

Steve shrugged. "I didn't figure that was the kind of news you wanted for your precious Sunday school class, so I decided I'd do your kids a favor and not answer."

Amy looked at that rigid profile. "I get it now. That's what you meant about breaking your heart over betrayal and—and everything. It was Afghanistan you were talking about." She shook her head slowly, compassionately. "I've always thought about how hard the war was for the Afghan people. I never really thought what it was like for you, for our soldiers. I can't even begin to guess what all you might have gone through, how you might feel about the way it's turned out. I am so sorry."

"I don't know why." Steve kept his gaze on the windshield. "It was a much-needed lesson in reality. One of which I'd been needing a reminder. Now, if you don't mind, I think your chaperones are here to collect you."

The security contractor was right. Wajid hovered at Amy's door, trying to catch her eye. Behind him, the open gate was crowded with children peering out to see why Ameera hadn't emerged from the foreigner's vehicle. As Amy reached for the door handle, the elderly guard was already opening it. Stifling a sigh, she swung her feet to the pavement.

"Thanks again for this afternoon. And I do appreciate what you've had to say. It's been—" Amy reached for any word that could be appropriate— "educational."

"I'd say you're welcome if I thought you'd learned anything from it." Steve turned at last from the windshield, and any friendliness Amy had glimpsed there during the afternoon was swallowed up in that aloof gray gaze, his unreadable expression. "You do what you have to. Just don't come running my way when these people you've put so much faith in break your heart—or worse."

"In other words, take your advice or the consequences." Now Amy's tone was hard. "Like you've been saying since we met, you don't do bail-outs."

"Now you've got it."

36

Why am I letting her get under my skin?

Steve stalked across the courtyard from the parking shed into the CS team house. Picking up the phone after pulling that photo from this morning's mail had been a matter of impulse. As Phil had been quick to point out, blonde aid workers with candid hazel eyes that could shimmer in a heartbeat from held-back tears to fire to irritating compassion were hardly his type.

So why was Steve wasting time and words and an interference that was against every life principle he'd developed on some collateral citizen who'd dropped into a war zone and fell nowhere within his sphere of responsibility, no matter what excuses he'd offered her?

But Steve knew why. He paused to pull free the contents of his coat pocket. Yellow mailer and crumpled note dropped into the trash can. But the photo didn't immediately follow. He hadn't been totally honest with Amy. In actuality, this image had remained tacked up by his bedroll for all the remaining months of fighting. And not just as a reminder of what a credulous fool he'd been. The girl's wide-eyed innocence, her protective stance over her students, their own small, joyous faces had been reassurance to a heartsick, young soldier that despite lies and betrayal and too much death all around him, there still remained better reasons for fighting this war.

Not until he'd left Special Ops for his first PSD contract had Steve thrust that photo along with other extraneous belongings into an action packer he'd shipped for storage to his grandfather. It must be those sleepless night hours staring at a reminder of life that even years later had tugged at Steve's memory from the moment he'd glimpsed Amy Mallory on the Ariana flight into Kabul.

"Hey, that you, Steve? Come on in. Denise wants to say hi."

Steve shoved the photo back into his pocket as he followed Phil's voice. The CS team house was virtually empty, its American contingent down at the DynCorp compound, the others at their various duties. Steve's former Special Forces teammate was in the lounge. His laptop was hooked up to the HD flat-screen to allow him to enjoy a full thirty-two-inch image of crackling fireplace, hung stockings, Christmas tree, and three towheaded preschoolers rowdying in front of their own TV set.

"Happy Thanksgiving, Steve. You're looking good." Phil's wife, Denise, held up a plate of cinnamon buns. "Wish we could share these with you. Maybe next year."

As she turned to rescue a tree ornament from her youngest, a crawling infant, Phil turned his back to the Skype cam to say in a low voice, "I didn't want to ask in front of the Rev and your guest, but what did you think of that footage?"

The question ended any pretense of holiday Steve had dredged up when he'd rushed to keep that appointment with Amy Mallory and Rev Garwood. "Someone on our side should have this intel before Jim Waters lands tomorrow to hand out accolades and all that American cash."

At the grimness in his tone, Denise looked up quickly on the TV screen. Steve stepped out of camera view.

Phil followed. "And . . . ?"

"I'm thinking Jason Hamilton. He hobnobs with all the embassy brass." Steve nodded toward the laptop. "Can you take a breather to run a few clips if I get him over here?"

"No problem; I've got all day."

"Daddy, look. It's SpongeBob flying."

As Phil hurried back to the televised parade, Steve called the DynCorp manager.

"Good timing, Wilson, I was just about to buzz you. We've got forty-eight hours to get security in place. And less than twenty-four before Waters and team touch down."

Steve was having a hard time hearing. From the noises in the background, the DynCorp crowd had managed to supply their Thanksgiving celebration with female company along with football, beer, and turkey.

"So I trust your people weren't planning on celebrating tomorrow. Can you walk through the Justice Center first thing in the morning? Then we get all the players together to coordinate who's doing what. We need to be ready to roll as soon as Eid's over."

"Will 8 a.m. do it?" Steve said. So much for that Bagram run tomorrow. Rev Garwood would understand the mission came first. Though Steve had a feeling Ms. Amy Mallory might consider promises were made to be kept regardless of excuse. At least to children. "And one more thing. If you've finished your turkey, would you mind popping down to our team house? There's something I'd appreciate your opinion on."

"Any reason it can't wait till morning?" Jason sounded impatient. "Or just give it to me over the phone."

"That won't do," Steve answered inflexibly.

There was a pause. "Does this affect our current mission or Jim Waters's arrival?"

"That's what I'm hoping you might be able to tell me."

"I'll be right there."

The DynCorp compound was on the next block, and Jason Hamilton was not only there within five minutes but had DEA station chief Ramon Placido with him. "His bunch crashed our party, so I dragged him along. If it touches Waters, it touches DEA."

But neither man was as affable by the time Steve finished explaining and Phil had broken off his Internet connection to play a video clip.

"You tapped the minister of interior's private business sessions?" Jason demanded. "Are you crazy? I don't want to hear any more. I'd like to maintain deniability if I'm ever grilled on this."

"It wasn't planned," Steve defended. "But how we came by the intel should be irrelevant to its content, shouldn't it?"

Jason shook his head as though addressing the town idiot. "You don't think anyone can use this. Can you imagine the repercussions if it *ever* gets out that a civilian security company used a State Department contract to wiretap a foreign ally? DynCorp would be first in line to throw you to the wolves before we're all run out of town on a rail. Tell 'em, Placido, how many regs they've just broken."

"The misapprehension here," the DEA chief intervened, "is that what you've just given us is any big surprise. How else did you think Khalid managed to do in two months what we haven't been able to in years? What counts are results. We've confiscated real drugs, arrested genuine bad guys, more than in years. If we don't particularly care for their methods, it's a start. In time, hopefully, we can instill a more ethical culture of law enforcement. But you've got to take things slow around here. Khalid's immediate predecessor is a good example of what happens in this culture when you push too hard or move too fast. We don't expect miracles. But these last months have shown our new MOI is willing to work with us. The rest will come in time."

"And you don't think letting him get away with pawning off this kind of setup on Jim Waters and his team might just encourage further corruption instead of change?"

But Steve could see he'd already lost even before Placido said firmly, "No one pawns anything off on Jim Waters. He's been handling Khalid types since you were in diapers—and utilizing them in the best interests of our national security. Our new MOI may be no saint, but compared to a lot of these warlords, he's a reliable leader, a strong one, and more importantly, he's pro-West. The general consensus at State is that he can be forgiven a lot as long as he keeps up the strong hand he's been demonstrating."

Except who's utilizing whom?

The last straw was when Jason Hamilton turned back in the doorway to suggest kindly, "You might want to erase those tapings before your principal or anyone else finds out what you've been up to. Your HQ hears about this, and you'll be lucky to be guarding ammo dumps."

Steve wasn't sure whether he was more furious at the sucker he himself had once again been or Placido and Hamilton's pragmatic acceptance of Khalid's con. Another thought struck him as the visitors left. "You know, Phil, if the whole thing was a con, what about our PSD contract?

We never did find evidence that suicide vest was anything more than an inside setup."

"Except the sugar factory bombing was real," Phil pointed out, "and that came first."

Steve swung suddenly around on Phil, who'd followed to the door. "What are we doing here? Would you ever believe back at Fort Bragg when we were getting set to save the world that ten years later would find us watching some lowlife's back for a big check?"

Phil looked at Steve thoughtfully before he answered. "I know why I'm here, and you've been saying hi to them. That big check and a few holidays on the far end of a TV screen to me mean funds for the credits I need to upgrade from medic to physician's assistant so I can support Denise and the kids the way they deserve."

Phil shook his head as he limped toward the lounge. "But you? You may be footloose with no strings holding you back. But you're the one who needs to get out of this business. There're guys in our business who'll never want to do anything else. They live the travel and adrenaline and guns and chicks and no strings. But you're not one of them. Your heart isn't really in it."

"Is that so?" Steve's tone turned harder than he'd intended. "I didn't realize I was so easy to read."

"Not everyone knows you like I do." Phil turned to the flat screen and his family's living room.

"And you've got an alternative suggestion? Back to the barracks? DEA like Placido? Street cop? Maybe security guard at the local mall? It's not like there's much of a peacetime list for my particular set of life skills."

"That's not for me to say. But I've never yet seen you go after anything you couldn't pull off. Find something you believe in and give it all you've got. I say that as a friend. You're too good a man to waste your life watching the backs of Khalid and his like."

Steve headed for his room. If he was to do that walk-through in the morning, there were some blueprints he needed to hunt down. But something hot burned in his chest as unfamiliar sounds of family and home followed him up the stairs.

"Find something you believe in and give it all you've got."

And if there was nothing you could find in which to believe?

37

"Miss Ameera, the foreign invaders are at the gate requesting to speak with you."

The description was how Wajid referred to Steve Wilson and the other contractors who'd come to install the fiber-optic fencing. Amy's breath left her with a whoosh that gave away just how much she'd been anticipating the call.

Or hoping, at least. And not just for those promised Eid gifts. Amy had already distributed sweatshirts, woolen leggings and socks, winter cloaks, and other items she'd collected at the bazaar, and the delighted New Hope residents wouldn't be expecting anything else. But however infuriating Steve's rudeness, Amy had come away from yesterday's Thanksgiving celebration with a new respect for the security contractor, and she'd regretted parting on such an unhappy note.

The fragrance of roasting meat made Amy's mouth water as she descended the marble steps. Two yearling sheep were revolving slowly over a wood fire in the front courtyard, several older boys turning the spits under Jamil's supervision. One was for the men from Rasheed's quadrant, the other to accompany the dishes New Hope women and older girls were cooking for their own Eid feast. Amy hurried toward a tall, lean form in Army parka and cap carrying a large cardboard box through the gate.

It still seemed unbelievable Steve Wilson should turn out to be the same American soldier she'd written in the wake of 9/11 so many years ago. He couldn't have been many years out of his teens himself when he'd dropped into these mountains to fight the Taliban. One of the most dedicated soldiers he'd known, Rev Garwood had called him. But though he'd walked away with no overt injuries, the former Special Forces sergeant's faith—if not in God, then in any difference human beings could make in this world God had created for them—would seem as much a battle casualty as Soraya's husband or Jamil's family.

Amy stopped short as the newcomer deposited the cardboard box on the ground so that she caught sight of his face—and limp. It wasn't Steve but Phil. "What a nice surprise. Wajid told me there were expats at the gate. I didn't realize it was you."

Phil straightened up with a grin. "We're in a bit of crisis mode, so Steve couldn't come himself. But he wanted to make sure these got to you this morning. Something about your Eid celebration."

Had Steve really been unable to break away himself, or had he just chosen to avoid further contact with Amy? She swallowed back disappointment.

A pair of men in security uniforms finished ferrying in other boxes and bags as fast as they could move back and forth from the SUV outside the gate.

Phil turned to Amy. "I guess that's it. Do you need help to handle all this? Some of those boxes will require assembling."

Despite the courtesy of his offer, Amy could see from the haste of his speech and glance at his watch that he was tamping down impatience. "No, I wouldn't want to delay you any further. My assistant and the kids can help me. But I sure appreciate you taking time for all this. I can't tell you how much this means to the children. Thank you."

The children abandoned their running to swarm over boxes and bags.

Despite his hurry, Phil took time for another smile and a handshake. "My pleasure, really. I couldn't be home for the holidays. Doing something for these kids makes my own seem not quite so far away." He slapped an open palm against his forehead. "Oh, just a minute. There is something I'm forgetting."

Hurrying out the gate, Phil returned with another box, this one open. High-pitched yips told Amy what to expect even before he set it down. Scrabbling to climb out was a fluffy, roly-poly German shepherd puppy.

"That's from Steve. One of the K-9s had a litter, and he snagged the last one, a female. Figured your kids would enjoy her. And she'll be a better guard than any barbed wire."

"Oh, she's adorable." Amy lifted the squirming animal beyond the children's excited clutches. "But I don't think we'd be able keep her. Dogs are unclean animals, our caretaker told me."

"Oh, but this isn't a dog," Phil responded, deadpan but with a twinkle in his eye. "It's a *gorg,* a wolf. That's a clean animal here."

Amy looked at him doubtfully, but just then Wajid ambled over to scratch the puppy behind an ear. "A gorg. I have long wished for one of these. I am told they are excellent guard animals. I will prepare a bed near mine to keep watch over it at night."

For the children at least, the puppy was all that was needed to complete a perfect feast day. Once the visitors were gone, Jamil helped with the packages. He hadn't been available for story time the night before, leaving Amy to her own halting narration. So she'd braced herself this morning for explanations, though she wasn't sure how to erase that anger she'd glimpsed earlier.

It hadn't proved necessary. Jamil displayed no lingering animosity as he returned with Rasheed from Eid services at the mosque to help distribute clothing, pile wood, and lift sheep onto spits. But neither remained any of the companionable partnership Amy had thought they'd developed these past weeks. It was as though Jamil had reverted to that silent shadow he'd been when Amy first hired him, offering no word or glance except those necessary to carry out his duties.

Which didn't keep him from making short work of instructions and diagrams as the children gleefully unpacked their treasures. Two portable goals were quickly assembled and dragged onto the playing field while Jamil turned his mechanical skills to an assortment of push trikes. One box held field hockey sticks, another Frisbees and deflated balls. There were crayons, markers, tubs of finger paints, and Play-Doh. Another box held kite makings. Safe, gentle children's kites, not the lethal battle weapons Afghan kites could be with their metal- or glass-studded strings.

Nothing personal that could be stolen or fought over, I told him. Amy hadn't even thought Steve was listening, but Rev Garwood had said he'd followed Steve's guidelines. How had a man without children of his own, who didn't even believe in Amy's mission here, read so exactly what she'd have chosen herself? And the "wolf," which Rasheed had already looked over approvingly—Amy hadn't needed Phil to tell her that was Steve's astute thinking.

No, she wasn't going to let Steve's contradictions, any more than Jamil's continued aloofness, dampen the pleasure of this feast day. By the time Rasheed pronounced the sheep ready to lift from their spits, Amy had demonstrated how to throw a Frisbee and proved that even in long tunic and headscarf she could outscore the older boys in field hockey.

Though the snow had melted, it was too cold to unroll the vinyl eating cloth outdoors, so the paneling between schoolroom and its neighboring salon was folded back to lay out a sumptuous feast. There were platters of saffron-hued pilau speckled with orange rind, grated carrots, and raisins. Others piled high with *mantu* and *ashak*, pierogi-style pastries stuffed with spiced meat and vegetable fillings. There was fried eggplant with yogurt sauce and potato-stuffed *boulani* pastries. Plastic basins overflowing with sticky puddings, melon slices, figs, and nuts. And of course, the roasted sheep.

Amy had retained Becky's DVD projector from yesterday, and when the feast was cleared away, the children worn-out from playing with their new treasures, she set up *The Lion King* on the schoolroom wall. Exhausted from being bounced from child to child, the puppy fell asleep in Farah's arms.

As Simba roared, Amy searched out her remaining staff with their own Eid gifts. For Rasheed, Amy had chosen a solar-powered radio too large for carrying around so Hamida might have opportunity to listen when the caretaker was off working. Maybe she'd even come across Christian broadcasts, beamed over the border through satellite feed. *Nothing is impossible for you, God.*

Amy set aside a collection of Persian poetry for when Fatima returned to classes. Jamil and Wajid had received smaller solar-powered radios. For Jamil, Amy had added a full pocket Bible like the one she kept in her shoulder bag for daily prayer times. For just a moment as Jamil looked over the gifts, his aloofness slipped, and as once before, Amy caught a swift play of confusion and grief and longing across his face before he thanked her colorlessly and walked away.

But he wasn't allowed to escape so easily. Despite the treat of a movie, the children clamored for their customary story time. "The Eid story. Abraham and Ishmael."

Amy shook her head. "I don't know that story as you tell it."

Though based on the Genesis account of Abraham obeying God's command to sacrifice his son Isaac, the Quranic version replaced Isaac with Abraham's illegitimate son Ishmael. To Christians, God's supplying of a ram to take Isaac's place was an image of the Son of God's substitutionary sacrifice on the cross for their sins. In Islam, the emphasis was on every good Muslim's willingness to sacrifice themselves to please Allah. Her Eid preparations had prompted Amy to do some digging on the Internet. She'd come away with more questions than answers.

Why did the Quran change this particular biblical account so drastically? Had Muhammad, an Arab and descendant of Ishmael, been so desperate to be counted one of God's chosen, he'd rewritten history itself to make his ancestor, his people, and not Israel, the original people of God? How had he missed so completely the truth that God's grace and mercy, Jesus' atoning sacrifice, cared not for ancestry or color or gender, but a yearning, seeking, repentant heart? Still, a feast day celebrating the local version was hardly the time or place to challenge it.

"Paradise, then!" the children clamored. "Paradise!"

"Paradise," Amy agreed. This one she could tell herself. Retrieving the bright story boards, Amy began the now familiar phrases. "In the beginning God created the heavens and the earth."

But when she finished, the children weren't satisfied. It was Tamana who stood up to demand, "You promised to tell us what happened next. Why do we no longer live in the garden and play with the beautiful animals?"

"I did promise, didn't I?" Amy admitted. "But that story is a little sad. You don't want to hear it tonight on Eid."

Yes, they did. Maybe it hadn't been such a good idea to gorge this bunch on so many unaccustomed goodies. The circle of bright eyes and small, eager faces were wide-awake and determined.

Roya spoke up for the mothers. "If you do not mind, Miss Ameera, they will not sleep tonight until they have had their way."

"Fine. But I will need Jamil because I do not know the Dari well."

Jamil emerged from the shadows before Amy had to send a child for him, hunkering down beside her chair.

"Okay, then, I told you how God made Adam and Eve. But I haven't told you yet about Satan, the enemy of God. One day he took the form of a beautiful serpent and came to talk to Eve as she was walking near the Tree of the Knowledge of Good and Evil. Do you remember what God told Adam and Eve about that tree?"

The sadness of this narrative of human disobedience and paradise lost gripped Amy more than she read in the absorbed faces around her. This group was acquainted enough with human wrongdoing to accept it unquestioningly. It was Amy's own distress that hastened to add, "But even though Adam and Eve had lost paradise and would no longer live forever, they or their descendants, God still loved them and forgave them. He made a sacrifice of an animal just like the Eid celebration today as a promise that someday a Savior would come from the seed of Adam and Eve who would bring forgiveness and restore paradise and eternal life to the human beings he had created. Best of all, because of this Savior, one day mankind would walk and talk with God again."

"Muhammad," Tamana spoke up.

The other children raised her statement in a chant. "Muhammad! Muhammad!"

"No, not Muhammad," Amy said as she felt unfriendly eyes on her. Sometime during her story, Rasheed had stepped unnoticed through the double doors from the main hallway into the schoolroom, and he was unsmiling, dark gaze hooded and watchful.

Then Amy realized Rasheed wasn't the only newcomer.

"But that is another story for another day," she finished firmly. Closing the story boards against an outbreak of protests, Amy hurried across the salon. "Eid mubarak, Soraya. But what are you doing here? I thought you were celebrating with your family today."

"Eid mubarak," Soraya murmured, but she too was unsmiling, and Amy wondered fleetingly if her latest story had crossed some line until she saw that Soraya's eyes were rimmed with red as well as the usual black kohl.

As her housemate edged away from the released children into the hall, Amy followed to say quietly, "I wasn't expecting you until Sunday. Is something wrong at home?"

"I—yes. There has been a medical emergency. My family—they were hoping—I had hoped—they need to pay the hospital—I thought perhaps an advance on my salary—"

The awkward jerkiness of Soraya's speech was so uncharacteristic Amy stared at her, bewildered. "I'm sure we can—"

But just then Soraya drew herself up to her full, stately height, a mixture of shame and defiance on her proud features. "No, it is not my family who requests. It is I. The bonus that is customary for Eid, I did not remember to pick it up before I traveled home, and because of the great need there, I felt it best to come for it immediately."

"Sure, of course, just one moment." Amy was completely bewildered. As she sprinted up the staircase, she pulled her cell phone from her ever-present shoulder bag. Thankfully, Becky Frazer answered immediately.

"Becky, I don't know if I'm being conned, but was I supposed to give a salary bonus for Eid? Soraya's here hinting for one."

"Oh, honey, are you saying you didn't pay it? Yes, definitely. It's what they call the thirteenth month salary, so they can all shop for Eid. Unless you paid the extra month for the Ramadan feast, in which case you can get by with less. But a lot of NGOs give both. After all, they can afford it."

The nurse's dismay gave away the enormity of Amy's mistake. "I did get them a gift, but what must they be thinking of me?"

"Well, it's still Eid, so it's not too late," Becky consoled. "They may be too polite to ask, but they'll sure be expecting it."

Amy still had afghanis on hand from her New Hope Eid shopping. Quickly filling four envelopes, she slipped back downstairs. Reticent as Soraya was, only a serious crisis could have propelled her across town to accost her employer, and Amy felt absolutely terrible.

"Forgive me for forgetting this yesterday with your other gift," Amy said quietly, handing Soraya an envelope. "I am so sorry I made you come all the way back here."

Soraya's expression lightened as she slid the envelope inside her tunic. "It is of no importance. Forgive me. If it were not for my family's need, I would not consider disturbing your feast celebration."

Amy grabbed a fluorescent lantern to light Soraya's way back to the gate. It was still two hours until curfew, but with the shortening days, night had already fallen, and Amy looked doubtfully down the dark street. The sounds of partying could be heard behind compound walls, but Amy spotted only a single man loitering among parked vehicles across the streets. Lifting the lantern high, she made out a silhouette of average height and stocky build.

The man straightened up under her suspicious stare, and as he headed down the street and around the corner, Amy asked uneasily, "Are you sure you shouldn't spend the night? It's pretty dark out."

Soraya had not yet dropped her burqa into place, so Amy could see her shake her head. "No, no, my family is in need of my return."

"Then at least let Jamil take you home in the car."

Jamil had followed the two women to the gate, and Wajid was in the process of letting him into his sleeping quarters in the mechanics yard.

"No, my family would never permit it. It is not so late. And look, the bus is coming now."

Sure enough, the sound of air brakes signaled an approaching city bus at the corner. Dropping her burqa into place, Soraya hurried to catch it. Jamil had turned to stare down the street where the loiterer had disappeared.

As she watched to see Soraya safely aboard the bus, Amy called, "Jamil, that man who was over there, could you see if he was one of the men from the other night? I wonder if they've been released."

When Jamil shook his head, Amy dug into her shoulder bag. Jamil and Wajid had eaten the Eid feast with the men on Rasheed's side, so Amy had been filming the New Hope feast herself. She pulled out the camera and handed it to Jamil.

"Then would you mind taking this and keeping a bit of a lookout, just in case that man comes back? Maybe see if you can film him if he does? Then we can check if any of the women recognize him."

Jamil nodded as the camera disappeared into his vest.

Then Amy handed him an envelope. "Oh, and here's your Eid bonus."

Without waiting for a reply, Amy rushed back inside the gate. She still had two more envelopes to deliver. But she paused for a final stare after the bus, now departing with Soraya aboard. The fluorescent lantern had been full on her housemate's face, and Amy had seen Soraya's smile evaporate, a glance flicker to Amy as she'd dropped her burqa into place. Something in those dark eyes had been disturbingly similar to what Amy had glimpsed in Rasheed's hooded glare.

Was it dislike she'd seen there?

Or guilt?

Paradise lost.

Jamil had lingered only briefly to carry out his employer's directive. He too had watched the loiterer's retreat and had seen what Ameera missed, a stocky shape boarding the bus as Soraya hurried over. Should he have told Ameera the man was no spy but her housemate's lover?

But no, he'd finished with such interference. Jamil walked through the vehicle gate. If only it were as easy to leave behind the tale Ameera had told tonight. But translating her words had burned them too firmly into his mind to dislodge. Her story of paradise given and lost was not in the book he'd now read so many times he'd lost count. But it differed little from the versions mullahs recounted in schools and mosque. The Garden of Delight, which foolish mankind had tossed away, accessible now only to those successful in earning Allah's favor and forgiveness.

The mechanics yard was empty of travelers on this feast day. The snow was now gone underfoot, but the moon floated bright and high. Stars glittered against the night's freshly washed backdrop. Their silver touched the swaying crowns of the orchard across the back wall so that they might have been a blurred mirage of a garden where men played with wild beasts and God walked with his creation.

Paradise. Jamil longed for it so deeply it haunted his dreams. What was in those dreams, he could never be sure when he awoke. Greenness. Beauty. Lush vegetation like Ameera's pictures, so different from the barren rock of much of his country. The dreams always evaporated with his waking like mist when sunlight hit the fields.

Still, what he'd seen in his dreams didn't matter. It was the assurance of paradise for which Jamil longed. The fear that in Allah's absolute sovereignty and stern justice paradise was already lost to him haunted the nightmares that came with his dreams. For it was so much easier to attain hell than paradise. At least for such as he. The smallest fraction, an infinitesimal tipping of Allah's scales toward death rather than life, condemnation rather than mercy, guaranteed his doom.

To fail in carrying out the five pillars of Islam, in following the exact lifestyle of the prophet, in protecting the Quran from defilement—these were only a beginning. There were other worse things. Things that weighed the scales so far down in debt that no hope was left of tipping them back to Allah's favor, if one prayed and fasted and offered every earning for the rest of one's days.

Ameera spoke so glibly of freedom in serving her prophet. Only it wasn't freedom that offered paradise but truth. So assured the mullahs. With enough unswerving, submissive devotion to truth, there was, if never a certainty, at least the hope that in the divine will of Allah, who wrote a man's destiny and tied it around his neck before he was ever born, paradise might be attained and hell's fires averted.

This was what the West did not understand in their sneering censure of Muslim mobs rioting for the purity of Islam. The fear and the urgency involved because a person slack in their defense of the faith might find himself on the wrong side of those scales. The fear that lived in Jamil right now, consuming him with each passing, fleeting day.

And this was what else the West did not understand, what Ameera would never comprehend should he try to explain—fear, more than hate, prompted followers of the faith to take the ultimate step that alone assured Allah's favor. Because only in taking it could one lay down the burden of fear that had become so all-consuming Jamil could no longer live with it. Was not hate all too often the reaction to fear? How to explain that for one as soiled as Jamil, there was only one way to make up for past infractions. One hope that Allah might still open to him the doors of paradise.

And yet he was so weary of both fear and hate.

Jamil shut his eyes to squeeze back the images. Children's innocent, unspoiled laughter. Softness in a woman's face.

And the words. A Savior who would come. Jamil knew of whom Ameera had meant to speak. A man—a prophet—walking streets like his own. Not with a sword or a soldier's gun but on sandaled feet with a healing touch and kind words for poor and rich alike. Such a man as Jamil could have wished to follow even without the prophet's own assurances of paradise and eternal life.

If only such a thing could be.

"You will know the truth, and the truth will set you free." Those had been Isa Masih's words.

But it was too late now for freedom. Only truth remained.

Jamil had reached the cold, concrete box of his quarters. The closing of his door shut out that fleeting mirage of paradise. He took time only to set Ameera's gift carefully into the purloined crate that held his possessions before throwing himself on his tushak. Then the tears came. Jamil wept for what could not be. He wept as he had wept in his dream. As he had not in all the long, dead years.

If only.

He'd arrived before the dawn call to prayer to make his own preparations. A fresh feathering of snow drifted through openings in the broken walls, but he'd swept the blast-shattered floor and spread a patu as a work space. A heavily swaddled figure was spreading out on the blanket an assortment of computer-printed digital images. Faces. A location from various angles.

It was the first time he'd glimpsed his mentor by light of day, if the sullen gray dawn filtering into the ruined building could be deemed such. The heavy winter swathing, a wool scarf wrapped over turban across the lower face, were intended for disguise as much as warmth. But there was no concealing height nor breadth, the hooded eyes and arch of a nose—or the voice.

"As you see, we have the place now as well as the day and hour. And this time it is no test. The only question, are you ready for shaheed? to make your confession to the world?" A hand waved toward the reason for this deviation from operational protocol, a tripod and video camera. "To strike such a blow for Allah that will leave your name praised forever among the ulema of the faithful? to achieve at last the justice for which your own dead cry out?" His companion's formal, flowery words were the pep talk of a commander sending a subordinate into battle. An incongruity in this ruined environs with winter's breath whistling through every crack.

And if he said no? that his faith and commitment, even his hate, had waned? His gaze rose from photo array to hard eyes, dropped to an automatic weapon balanced across squatting thighs. He would not leave this place alive.

He looked at the instrument of shaheed lying beside the photo array with no indication of the ugliness and death it held. "I have long been ready. But I do not see how this can be done. There will be many guards. They will surely not let me pass with this so easily."

"Trust my competence. All you need is here." His companion handed over a market bag.

Immediate understanding came as he looked inside. He picked up a plastic ID card. The picture was not his own, but it would be close enough with what this bag held. No impediment remained now but one. "And your own promise? You said you had confirmation. I will not take this step until I have your vow they will be safe and cared for."

The voice hardened, a hand tightening on the weapon lying across his companion's lap. But his rebuke was peaceable. "Did I not say it is done? that I will give you the confirmation? May Allah himself strike me if I do not keep my word. Your sacrifice will ensure their well-being for the rest of their days. But first let us finish. I have appointments to keep."

It was well his statement was written out and memorized so that impatience did not taint it. He positioned himself against a remnant of wall as backdrop but not with the instrument of shaheed. Such an ingenious scheme might be used again by others. Instead his companion handed him an automatic rifle, though without its magazine, and a Quran. It took every effort not to shiver, the finery he wore chosen to look good on film but not for warmth.

"Allahu Akbar . . ."

From his companion's approving nod, his face was conveying the resolution, his voice the defiance for which he strove. It did not take long, the parameters of a shaheed statement dictated by no mullah but YouTube. No sooner had he tightened a blanket back around his thin clothing than he demanded, "Now, your vow."

The envelope held two sheets of paper. The handwriting on the first was not familiar, but then it wouldn't be. Its words held authenticity—names, places, biographical details. But that could be counterfeited, however great the difficulty.

The second sheet was a computer printed photo like those still spread out at his feet. Two females. He walked over to a jagged opening that had been a window to take advantage of the strengthening dawn. The tallest wore full chador, only eyes, nose, and forehead visible, one arm around the other female.

He studied the exposed features, doubt warring with hope. The eyes were right, like his own in the mirror. And the nose. But his gaze had already moved on to the other female. A girl not far into her teens, slight, the scarf draped across hair and around shoulders allowing a glimpse of dark, curly hair, dark eyes enormous and wide-set in slim, olive-skinned features.

His breath drew in sharply. There was no mistake. What greeted his stunned scrutiny was a female version of himself.

Only a cleared throat brought him back to how long he'd been standing there motionless. "It is satisfactory?"

There was no longer doubt or hesitation as he turned to face those watchful eyes. "You have fulfilled your vow. I may keep this?"

"Of course. I will tell them myself of your courage and faithfulness in the service of Allah."

He waited until the cloaked figure emerged into softly falling snow far below before gathering together his own load. Last of all, he tucked the envelope against his heart with the care given to a priceless treasure. There was no longer confusion nor anguish nor rage nor even resignation in his thoughts as he made his way down the broken stairwell. Rather, peace.

The peace surprised him. There was a certain serenity to having fate and future removed from his own grasp. His decision had been made. There would be no going back now.

"Miss Ameera, may I have speech with you?"

Amy looked up as Jamil's shadow fell across her laptop, her smile uncertain. The Afghan had been as silent and remote all day as he'd been since Thanksgiving, and these were the first words he'd addressed directly to her. "Of course. I'm just logging off here."

Closing her laptop, Amy folded her hands on the lid as Jamil crossed from the doorway to her desk. Something had been hurting in her chest ever since she'd glimpsed Soraya's hostility last night. She'd come to Afghanistan determined to love these people, had succeeded more than she'd anticipated. Somehow it had never occurred to her to question whether those she'd worked so hard to serve might not reciprocate her affection.

First I get Rasheed mad at me, now Jamil and Soraya. Is Steve right, and they've only been friendly because I'm feeding them?

Then Amy's gaze fell on what Jamil was setting down on her desk. The Bible she'd given him as an Eid gift along with the now-tattered New Testament. Had he come to return them? The hard knot tightened in her chest.

Amy had enjoyed the occasional discussions Jamil initiated when Soraya and other New Hope tenants weren't within earshot. But had she overlooked that what to Amy was a pleasurable dialogue about faith might be to Jamil a threat, not just to his peace of mind but his survival? Was it possible his icy withdrawal these last days hadn't just been anger at Steve Wilson's intrusion into New Hope's small world?

If he gives back the Bible, I won't mention it again unless he does first. God, I really thought I was doing something good here.

But it wasn't the volumes he'd laid down that Jamil was pushing her direction. It was the tiny camcorder in his other hand. He said diffidently, "I am sorry that I was not able to obtain good pictures of the man you inquired about last night. He has not returned. But I have taken pictures of all the men who broke in and others too who have been along the street. Perhaps this man was among them. It was my thought that if I looked through the film we have taken, I could find all such men and put them together on one of your disks as we have done for your patrons."

The disks he referred to were recordable DVDs Amy had purchased to make copies of the videos Jamil had been putting together for New Hope headquarters. Jamil set next to the camcorder what looked like a miniature laptop. A portable DVD player.

"I purchased this with my Eid bonus today. It will play the disk so that

Wajid and Rasheed and the workers in the mechanics yard will know what these men look like. If you do not require the equipment, I have time to do this now."

"Jamil, that's a wonderful idea. I should have thought of that myself. Our own ten most wanted."

Jamil looked puzzled before he went on. "I had thought to print some pictures too. For Wajid so he will remember who to watch for. And perhaps to show some of the guards along the street. Only a few."

"Do however many you need. It's just paper and ink." Amy was so relieved his request involved nothing more alarming, she'd have happily authorized a hundred printouts. "I can't tell you how much I appreciate this. You're always going the extra mile."

That too was an idiom that drew a puzzled look. Pushing back her chair, Amy gathered her shoulder bag and other personal belongings. "Just let me know when you're done so I can lock up the office. I'll be in my apartment or downstairs with the children."

Jamil set to work at the laptop, expertly connecting the camera to upload digital footage. He'd set the small volumes he'd brought with him next to the computer, and catching Amy's eye, he said, "There is another question I have wanted to ask. I read the story of paradise in the new holy book you gave me for Eid. I understand now what the Paul disciple was speaking of when he wrote of Adam and Eve and sin coming into the world. And why he calls Isa Masih the new Adam. He is the savior you spoke of to the children. The one who would show a new way to paradise, is he not?"

"That's right." Amy couldn't believe her ears or eyes. The chill of these last days might never have been there in Jamil's earnest speech, his probing gaze.

"Then perhaps this book will explain other things I have not understood in this one." He touched the small leather-bound Bible, then the New Testament before he straightened up to look at Amy squarely. "You said these holy books could be read in Dari and Pashto as I have done now in English. I looked on the Internet and found this is true. But I did not see where they might be purchased here in Kabul. Rasheed has requested I go early to the bazaar in the morning. I thought I might search for these books."

Amy had to swallow to find voice to answer. "I don't think you'll find them in the bazaar. Let me ask around. I think I know someone who might be able to get them."

"Thank you." The briefest of smiles touched his lips.

Amy lingered in the office doorway. "You do understand why I haven't told the children the rest of that story as it is in the Bible."

His expression turned grave. "But of course. You are a guest in this country. The mullahs do not tell the story so. If you teach the children to question the mullahs, it would be considered a great insult to my country, to Islam. The mullahs might be angry enough to demand you be sent back to your own country. Perhaps even enough to punish the women for allowing their children to listen."

Footsteps sounded in the hall, and Amy saw Jamil sweep her gifts into his lap. The footsteps belonged to Hamida, carrying Amy's supper down the hall. Amy started toward her but turned back in the doorway as Jamil spoke up quietly.

"I understand why you would not wish to tell these stories to the children. But in your holy book, did not the mullahs of Isa Masih's time become angry with the truths he told? And when they told his followers to be silent, did they not reply to the mullahs that they must obey God and not the commands of men? Were they not even beaten and put in prison and killed with stones because they would not be silent?"

"Miss Ameera, where do you wish me to serve your meal?"

It was well Rasheed's wife had interrupted, because for these questions of Jamil's, Amy had no answer to give.

Jamil slid the shiny disc of a newly copied DVD and its accompanying stack of printed photos into an envelope, which he left with Ameera's camera and laptop neatly arranged on her desk. But a second DVD along with three printed images he slid against his heart, the folded paper crackling inside his vest, as he left the office. The second video was much shorter than the one he'd left for Ameera, shorter than the YouTube clips that had come to fascinate Jamil since he'd discovered them. But its contents held the explosive force of that martyr's blast he'd witnessed with Ameera the day he'd arrived back in Kabul.

Jamil had expected to need subterfuge to keep Ameera from observing just what footage he wished to duplicate. Her trust once again dismayed as much as it surprised him. Did his employer not know how many there were who would be pleased to exploit such faith?

As I once thought to do.

Jamil made one last stop before heading to his quarters. To keep the children from rummaging through them, Jamil had helped Ameera stack the boxes of Eid bonanza in the infirmary until other storage could be arranged. Jamil quickly found what he needed, then added some items from the first aid supplies. These he regretted taking, because he could not be sure of replacing them. But his alternatives were even less palatable.

Wajid was already sleeping when Jamil reached the front gate. This had been one of the old man's painful days, and his opium pipe had fallen from an outflung hand onto the guardhouse floor. Jamil didn't try to wake him, lifting the gate key instead from the guard's belt. He'd have it back before Wajid awoke, since Rasheed had assigned him a meat run in the morning. The fattest and healthiest animals were snapped up before the sun cleared the mountain peaks, and Jamil would be expected to be at the bazaar before Rasheed rolled from his tushak.

Inside his room, Jamil slid his handiwork from his vest. Folding the printouts once to hold the DVD disc in their fold, he slipped the oblong into a plastic bag and sealed it with first aid tape. He repeated the process with a second plastic bag, then slid the whole package out of sight into a gap between cinder-block wall and tin roof. He would retrieve it if all went well. And if it did not . . .

If it did not, his efforts would no longer matter.

The camera images stored, Jamil went to work with his other acquisitions. It was painstaking labor, and the night was far gone before he'd finished. But though he turned off the flashlight, it was not to sleep. He sat crosslegged on his tushak, face tight with concentration, nails digging into his palms. He was setting out a train of thought.

Jamil had been an ardent pupil of his mullah professors since he'd first sat on a classroom bench, legs too short to touch the floor. Even then his aspiration had been to please not just those impressive robed figures with their tall turbans and long beards but the god they served. Allah. The Beneficent and Merciful One, as the rakats proclaimed. Creator of a universe that to Jamil's youthful eyes and ears had been as beautiful as it was exciting.

Muhammad, those instructors had taught Jamil, was the apostle of Allah, final and greatest of a long procession of prophets Allah had sent to call mankind to submission. To please the Almighty One, to gain merit in the scales of Allah, the faithful were called to emulate the prophet's life to the smallest detail. And of course, the ultimate emulation was to wield the sword in jihad. Even better, to lay down one's life in the glorious fight to extend Allah's kingdom on earth, thereby securing the only absolute hope of paradise the Quran and all the other teachings of the faith had to offer.

But Isa Masih too was a prophet. A great one, next only to Allah's apostle, according to Muhammad's own words. And here was where Jamil was laying forth each step in turn with the meticulous deliberation of solving a difficult mathematical equation. An equation on which his life and future—yes, and his very breath—hung in those same scales.

If to emulate the prophet Muhammad was meritorious, was it possible that emulating the life of another great prophet was also meritorious before Allah? that walking in the footsteps of Isa could also balance the scales of divine justice? Healing the sick and feeding the hungry did not advance Allah's kingdom on this earth. But Isa Masih had said that he called people to a different kingdom. A kingdom not of this earth but within a person.

Was it possible that in not teaching of this other kingdom, the mullahs who'd brought the faith to Jamil's homeland at the point of a sword had left out something vital? that without the expression of this other kingdom that was not of this world, as Isa Masih had stated again and again, the conquest of earthly kingdoms under the banner of Allah was not enough, even if that conquest should reach the ends of the earth? Perhaps this lack was why, for all its long subjugation under the rule of Islam, Jamil's homeland still lay battered and gasping for deliverance from violence and cruelty and corruption and oppression.

The dream he'd had of this city, this country, being swept on its sifting foundation of sand toward the cliff was as vivid in Jamil's mind as though he were again in the grip of sleep.

"Everyone who hears these words of mine and puts them into practice is like a wise man who built his house on the rock. The rain came down, the streams rose, and the winds blew and beat against that house; yet it did not fall, because it had its foundation on the rock. But everyone who hears these words of mine and does not put them into practice is like a foolish man who built his house on sand. The rain came down, the streams rose, and the winds blew and beat against that house, and it fell with a great crash."

The equation Jamil had been laying out step by step now came together in an unassailable conclusion. His country, his people, prostrate, bound, and helpless, were still sliding inexorably into floodwaters that even the blind could not help but see amassing on the horizon. And not all the rakats and ablutions and right postures and foods and clothing could free Afghanistan from the chains that held it in bondage.

An inexhaustible flow of handouts, advice, weapons, and foreign guardians could not safeguard his people from each other, much less from outside threat. Above all, the sword of jihad would never transform his homeland. How many more generations would it take his people to learn that lesson?

Only the wise words of the prophet Isa Masih, taught to his people and, more urgently, put into practice, could break those chains, offer the freedom Jamil's people, his own heart, had yearned to see for so long. A freedom that came from peace and righteousness and justice and truth, not power. Isa Masih's kingdom that was not of this world where men fought, hated, betrayed, and killed but built on a bedrock no storms of war and oppression and greed could sweep away.

The kingdom of heaven.

Paradise.

Stiff from immobility, Jamil shifted position. As he did so, a foot nudged his handiwork spread out beside his tushak. A shudder of unease swept over Jamil's body, caught at his quiet breathing.

And Isa's martyrdom?

39

America's new drug czar was as tough and unyielding as Ramon Placido had described. An iron gray crew cut still held streaks of sandy brown, his grip as hard as his pale blue eyes. There was military training as well as law enforcement in Jim Waters's background, Steve would stake his 401(k).

"So you're running Khalid's security detail," Waters said as he released Steve's hand. "How essential do you consider your services?"

Steve looked over to meet Ramon Placido's impassive gaze. The DEA chief was well aware how much he resented being pushed into this call. But Steve couldn't offer less than his best and honest evaluation.

"Sir, all I can really confirm is my own experience in this current mission. The overall threat level in Afghanistan is as high as it's ever been. Is there a specific threat leveled against our own principal? That's a harder call. There have been any number of public bombings since the sugar factory, bigger and more deadly—and not involving our principal. We've had no solid evidence of any personal vendetta against the minister of interior."

"And this suicide vest I'm told your people found? That isn't evidence enough?"

Steve was silent, thinking, before he answered cautiously. "There are some questions about that. The biggest that it was designed for remote detonation—like an IED rather than a suicide bomb. And of course it was never detonated, which makes us wonder if it wasn't intended as a statement rather than a serious attack. There have been no attempts since. Undoubtedly Khalid could duplicate our current procedures without us, assuming he can trust his own inner team. Which is where all this started."

Jim Waters nodded. "That's fair enough. We'll see what else this trip brings to light. But one way or another, Condor Securities can expect my decision within the week."

Steve caught the slight easing of Placido's shoulders, and both men looked satisfied as they walked away. But the exchange left a sour taste in Steve's mouth. What would they have said if Steve spilled out what he was really thinking? Not that any evidence remained to back it up. At Steve's direction, Phil had deleted the audio recordings. Jason Hamilton was unfortunately accurate that their existence would land the CS team in more hot water than Khalid.

A dozen agents closed in protectively as Waters and Placido joined the congressional delegation, Khalid, a handful of other Afghan ministers, and an array of news crews waiting to greet the arriving guests just inside the Justice Center's massive front gates. Whatever Steve's personal frustrations, this was one day paranoia was justified. Add to that welcoming committee the delegations of governors and provincial commanders beginning to collect outside the gate, and you had a high-profile target.

A concern that had occupied Steve's every waking movement for the last two days. A skift of snow yesterday had almost moved the ribbon-cutting indoors. But this morning was dry, if cold, so the courtyard between the front gate and main building held rows of folding chairs fronting a podium. Behind this, steps led up to a ribbon taped across closed double doors.

Steve raised binoculars to complete a surveillance sweep. Every security precaution Steve and Jason Hamilton had hammered out looked to be in place. All entrances but the front were sealed under armed guard. Just outside the front gate, a pavilion shielded an airport-style security checkpoint. Security had been simplified further by restricting guard patrols to MOI's own well-vetted new counternarcotics force.

A group of these were even now passing through the metal detectors. Once through the metal detector, Ismail and the counternarcotics police commander supervised a pat down of their heavy Army-issue parkas and visual check of knapsacks before a uniform with a clipboard directed them to their posts. Whether in honor of his American guests or for his dignity as deputy minister, Ismail displayed under his own thick parka the first Western suit Steve had ever seen him wear.

Steve focused the binoculars on individual faces as the arriving guard shift dispersed. He'd come to recognize a good part of this group after several weeks on the road. But an outraged bellow shifted his attention to a commotion erupting at the gate. The first delegation was now entering, among them a white-bearded Pashtun who refused to unwrap a thick, ornamented patu for pat down.

"I have surrendered my weapons in the name of peace. But you will not put your hands on me!"

Dropping the binoculars, Steve caught Phil's eye a few meters away, who joined him in hurrying over to the checkpoint. Security details were already closing in front of Waters, Khalid, and the other guests, M4s coming up.

Ismail reached the fracas first. Stepping forward, he kissed the white beard soundly on both sides as he offered a warm embrace. "Hassan, my brother, welcome!"

A snap of the deputy minister's fingers brought over one of the newly arrived guards. "The esteemed governor of Kawgar does not need to be delayed further. You will show the governor personally to his seat."

The governor made no objection to his entourage undergoing the manual double check. Phil's quick grin told Steve he'd seen the same thing. Ismail handily frisking the old man in the process of that embrace. *Good show.*

Steve raised a hand to Ismail in salute. The deputy minister nodded gravely. Steve turned away. *This is going to work.*

Leading the white-bearded dignitary to a seat of honor in the front row, he looked around to match his surroundings to the map he'd memorized as he waited for the old man's entourage. As the first straggled over, he strode along the side of the main building.

He'd arrived too early outside the gate. But he'd loitered out of sight until others wearing the same uniform he'd been supplied were lining up to pass security. To be one prompted dangerous scrutiny. To blend in like a desert chameleon was anonymity, safety.

He'd felt panic when he'd noted ahead that manual search, more as he'd spotted those probing binoculars. By then it was too late to bolt. But the pat down proved cursory, and as he'd showed his ID, he'd recognized with relief an indifferent gaze above unfamiliar clothing.

It took effort to walk unconcernedly. The Army-issue parka he wore was far heavier than its appearance, the thick layer between the coat's exterior and lining no longer soft down but at once solid and flexible. Panic rose again as heads turned in that huddle of dignitaries and cameras and sharp-eyed foreign mercenaries. Among them was the face he'd been seeking, and despite the cold he could feel perspiration dotting forehead and upper lip.

But there was no flicker of recognition or interest in the watchful glances sliding over him. Turning a corner, he paused to wipe a sleeve across his face. The back entrance was where the map had indicated. Two sentries in the same uniform he wore scanned his ID as he announced tersely, "Guard duty for the loya jirga."

The building was like any other, a maze of corridors and doors. To his left, doors opened into a council room. Unlike the ribbon-cutting ceremony, this had been arranged for the comfort of the loya jirga participants with rugs and tushaks and cushions. A row of chairs across the front provided for the foreign guests. Scattered uniforms were already in place against the walls and in the hallway. Though they were out of the wind, there was no heating indoors, and those standing guard had their Army parkas zipped up tight, caps pulled down low against the chill.

As planned.

He headed past them to the end of the corridor. To the left was the hallway down which the loya jirga guests would come through the front entrance. He turned instead to the right. The toilet facilities were as new and clean and expensive as everything else. There was also a basin with running water, a mirror above it. He drank deeply to relieve the dryness of his mouth, then lifted his gaze to the mirror.

What he saw explained any lack of recognition. Hair several shades lighter than his own. He peered closely at his eyes. He'd heard of contacts. They were now available even in Kabul to the wealthy. But that they could change his eyes to the green of summer pasture seemed somehow an intrusion on a province that belonged to Allah, not man. If not his own, the image in the mirror was that on his ID card.

Satisfied, he locked himself in the farthest stall. His wait stretched long enough he began to wonder if he'd mistaken his directions. Then he heard quiet footsteps, a metal latch sliding shut across the toilet facility's outer door. A soft tap came on the stall door. As he unlocked it, the man who stepped into view was dressed as he'd seen him outdoors. But the now-familiar turban and scarf hid his features. At this stage, the precaution seemed almost ludicrous. But he said only, "I was afraid I would not be able to pass the guards."

"Did I not tell you to trust me? You've seen where to go? where to stand?" The man did not ask if there'd been a change of mind. "To destroy all would take a miracle. Allah will choose who will live and who will die today. But if you position yourself as we have spoken, among them will be your enemy and ours."

"I understand my mission. I do not need further instructions." He pulled a cell phone from a pocket of his parka. It was the same this man had dropped into his hands in a dark alley so many weeks ago. "All except the code. You said you would give it to me here."

But to his consternation, the man made a gesture of refusal. "That will not be necessary."

He stared in astonishment. "What do you mean? A shaheed chooses his moment of martyrdom. Last time you said this would not happen again. Do you no longer trust that I will complete the mission?"

"It is not a matter of trust but timing. It must be exact, and so my employer and yours considers it best this remain in his own hands."

"Then he is here. Why can I not see him then? I will appeal to him myself."

"No, no, do not press for what I cannot grant. Be satisfied that your family will find blessing through your sacrifice. And that this day you will indeed meet Allah in paradise. Enough!" His companion produced a Quran from a breast pocket. "You have performed the ablutions and fasted? Then let us pray."

The ritual was one he'd never seen, but he knew it because it was part of childhood hero worship, stories told and retold by elders to a wide-eyed next generation. The prayers were those of a warrior going into battle and for absolution of sins. He could understand now why so many chose this route, because there was indeed a euphoria, an adrenaline rush and sweet release of knowing oneself completely clean inside and out, forgiven, all worries of past and future, all ties to this earth, relinquished. Ahead, only one quick step into eternity.

The very potency of that euphoria became the strength of the doubt that shook him. *Forgive me if I have chosen wrong. Let me not waver now from my pledge.*

Then they were rising to their feet again, his companion embracing him gingerly. "The guests are in place now. The ceremony will start shortly. Then the delegates will proceed to the loya jirga. You must be in place before them, or questions will be asked. It would be most prudent if you remain in here—" a gesture indicated the stall—"until I signal you. Keep your phone on vibrate. I will call you when it is time. Now, may Allah be with you. May Allah give you success so that you achieve paradise."

He gave the ritual response. "Inshallah, we will meet in paradise."

A moment later he was alone. But for once he did not obey his orders. Instead he retraced his steps to the back entrance and walked to the corner where he could witness the opening ceremonies gearing up to start. As his visitor had stated, the folding seats were now full. Though these were all strangers to him, images of their bodies broken and bloodied aroused no pity. If any single group in Afghanistan could be singled out as responsible for the state in which his country now languished, it was these men, and every morality he'd ever been taught said they were all deserving of death. But his eyes were drawn inexorably to a single face.

He'd wondered what it would be like to come face-to-face with his target, his enemy. He'd dreamed of this moment. Its hate and rage and triumph. First as fantasy. Then as a mission. And yet now that triumph was in his grasp, it was not rage and hate that added to his cold sweat a hot prickle behind his eyelids but grief and longing.

Longing for a world no retribution would ever return to him.

He closed his eyes, breathed quick and shallow to retrieve that serene resolve with which he'd risen from his prayers.

Do not think. Do not feel. Only do what I have determined in my heart.

Shrugging his heavy burden more comfortably into place, he turned and headed back inside the building.

40

The ostensible reason Becky Frazer had showed up this morning was a follow-up clinic. Already a group was camped out in the hall outside the infirmary. Najeeda was among them, her cough still worrisome. So was Najeeda's son, his quiet hacking a replica of his mother's, which was even more worrisome.

The other reason lay in the two volumes Becky was digging from her medical bag. Both used Arabic script. Amy would have to take Becky's word that one was a Dari and the other a Pashto New Testament.

"I tried to get full Bibles, but those are hard to find these days."

"That's okay. The person who requested them will be happy enough for these." Amy hadn't told the American nurse for whom the New Testaments were intended, and Becky hadn't asked.

"Your contact is aware of the need for discretion?" Becky added as Amy tucked the volumes out of sight between her shawl and tunic. "It isn't technically illegal for us to hand these out to a local who asks for them, not like Taliban times. The receiving end is a little more iffy. And unlike an English version, which few of the mullahs would recognize, much less read, they can all read these."

"He's aware of the risks," Amy said more sharply than she intended. "Excuse me. I'll get these stored away."

She had to step over feet and laps to reach her apartment. The patients were spilling out of the hallway into the stairwell. Beyond them were the padlocked doors leading into the second floor of that unused wing.

That would make a perfect infirmary over there. We need more room.

Only yesterday the women's prison had called to ask if New Hope could take a dozen more tenants. Amy was hesitating, not because she couldn't find room for a few more tushaks, but because all other services were being stretched to breaking.

I want the whole building, maybe even the whole property, including that mechanics yard. I'm going to talk to Mr. Korallis about it tonight. If we come up with a big enough rent offer . . .

Part of that conference call was the pending issue of a permanent country manager. Amy still wasn't sure if she wanted the job. And even if she agreed to extend her interim commitment, Amy had already made it clear to Mr. Korallis that among her conditions would be adding on a deputy country manager.

I can't keep doing it all myself. I can't remember when I last had a day off other than those few hours at Camp Phoenix. With Eid and the break-in, I haven't even been to the expat worship gathering in weeks.

Amy stored away Becky's delivery by sliding the volumes under her mattress, then headed downstairs. She and Becky needed additional hands before they opened the clinic. Soraya was to have been back from her extended weekend by now. But Amy hadn't yet seen her housemate, and when she'd asked Fatima, she'd just received an uncomprehending look as though the teacher couldn't understand her Dari.

No, Amy refused to think about Soraya now. Farah would be pleased to help, though Amy hated to pull her from classes, especially since she'd become Fatima's de facto assistant with the younger children. But at least for Najeeda's son, Amy would have to call on Jamil. For male patients beyond the six-year-old milestone when boys typically left their mothers for the men's quarters, it would be inappropriate for a female to do the physical examination.

But Jamil's phone number went straight to voice mail, and when Amy walked out to the guard shack, Wajid ambled out to say with a yawn, "He went to the bazaar, but he returned long ago. Perhaps he has returned to his quarters to sleep. He left very early."

"Well, if you can take a minute to check, please let him know we need his help in the clinic."

Jamil's phone might be dead. With no power in his quarters, he could only charge it when there was electricity to do so in the office. Looking around, Amy noted another absence. "Where's Gorg?"

The German shepherd puppy had been immediately and unanimously designated Wolf by the New Hope residents. Keeping the puppy from being loved to death had been the biggest challenge, and since she wasn't housebroken, there'd been a certain amount of cleanup. But seeing even Aryana's somber expression break into delight at Gorg's antics was worth any mess. Had Steve any idea how therapeutic the cuddly animal might prove to these women and children? Or was perimeter defense the only thought on the security contractor's mind?

And speaking of perimeter defense, Amy had forgotten to turn off the fiber-optic fencing in the rush of setting up the clinic. Not that there was any real urgency until the children finished morning classes. Digging Frisbees out of the barbed wire and off the roof tiles had become a sport in itself.

Amy thrust away an unwelcome pang as she glanced around the yard. She hadn't seen or heard from Steve since Thanksgiving. Had she irretrievably offended him? Or now that he'd satisfied his curiosity that Amy was indeed the teenager in that old photo, had he decided Amy—and New Hope—held no further interest for him?

Did Amy even want to see Steve again? *I can't change who I am nor can he, so what's the point?*

"The child took the gorg." Wajid yawned again. By his listlessness, last night had involved opium again. Amy was going to have to talk to Rasheed about an assistant, if not a replacement. *We need a night guard who's actually awake.*

"What child?" But even as Amy made the sharp demand, her survey landed on a slight figure stepping out from behind the jungle gym, a wriggly bundle clutched close to a thin chest. Tamana's older brother.

"Fahim, what are you doing here? Why aren't you in classes? And why aren't you wearing your sweatshirt?" The blue material identified a winter pullover all the children had received for Eid.

Then Amy took in fever-bright eyes and flushed cheeks. Fahim bent to cough into his squirming burden before he explained. "The teacher said I was making too much noise. Farah said I should go upstairs to see the doctor. I just wanted to see the gorg first."

"Well, you're going up right now." Unraveling the puppy, Amy sent her scampering into the guard shack as Fahim tugged the sweatshirt over his head. "Now come."

Fahim obeyed, sliding a hot, small hand into Amy's as they walked back up the cobblestone path. He doubled over to cough when they reached the marble steps. But as they stepped into the hall, his fever-bright eyes held joy as he lifted them to Amy. "The gorg—she is so beautiful! And though her teeth are sharp, she does not bite. Is this how the first man and woman played in the garden with the animals? Do you think when the savior comes, we will truly be able to play so with the snow leopards and tigers and lions like Simba?"

"There *is* no savior!"

Amy's heart jumped as a door slammed shut behind Rasheed's burly frame. The chowkidar had walked out of the storage depot in time to hear Fahim. A large hand came down on the boy's shoulder as he said sternly, "Such stories are infidel teaching, not Muslim. Miss Ameera will not tell such a story again. *Illaha illa Allah. Muhammad rasul Allah.* There is no God but Allah, and Muhammad is his prophet."

As Fahim obediently repeated the shahada, Rasheed stared at Amy with a coldness that sent a chill through her. "Now go back to class!"

As the boy turned toward the schoolroom doors, Amy roused herself to interfere. "No, he's sick. He needs to see the doctor. Go on up, Fahim. I'll be right there."

Rasheed slammed the door behind him, then explained curtly, "As you requested, I have looked for more shelves to hold the supplies the foreigners brought. But there are no more. We will have to purchase new from the bazaar." Turning a key in the lock behind him, he strode away.

Amy looked after him with dismay. Despite the chowkidar's recent sullenness, this was the first time he or anyone else had directly challenged one of the stories Amy had told the children, and she didn't know whether to be more worried or angry at his blanket interdiction.

He may manage the property, but he has no authority over my project. What does he think he can do—call the cops on me?

That this was not, in fact, out of the realm of possibility fanned Amy's anger higher. She'd thought little about Islam before coming to this place.

Like Buddhism or Hinduism or atheistic Communism, it was simply one of many belief systems that happened not to be her own, all jostling for human hearts and power and position.

But Amy was fast coming to hate this one with a passion that dismayed her. Not as she'd seen it operate in her own homeland, where its followers were at least free to choose its tenets. *Free because Christian values guarantee their right to worship as they choose.*

Ironically such fundamentalist regimes that would never even allow someone like her to operate on their soil inflamed Amy less than her current circumstances. But this was a country inundated with an international community giving time and funds to help at every level, much of it coming from those Christian nations Rasheed dismissed as infidel. The very government of this place was propped precariously in place only because of the efforts and weapons and money of those same infidels.

Steve is so right.

How much so was suddenly clear. All that Amy had come to admire about these people's resilience, hospitality, and deep spirituality could not weigh against the grim reality that any Afghan could be condemned to prison or death if they followed their own conscience in matters of faith or even their own reading material. That women could still be possessed and dispossessed as chattel. That dress, food, learning, and even the smallest actions within the privacy of one's own living space had to conform to some rigid code. And all because Islam and the sharia law that gave it teeth dominated every waking and sleeping breath its subjects took.

It seemed so vastly unfair Amy wanted to scream out in rebellion, rail her fists in frustration against that solid wall behind which a billion of the planet's population were locked away in the greatest totalitarian regime humanity had ever known. The more so as Amy had come to know and love individuals bound beneath its powerful grip and blinded by its mockery of the truth. To share, however vicariously, in their suffering and their despair.

When Amy went up the stairs, she found Fahim beside Najeeda's son, the two boys' heads together in whispered conversation and a duet of coughing.

There is a Savior, Fahim. There is hope and beauty and love. A God who is not distant and angry but who loves you enough to come himself to walk this earth. If only I could tell you about him.

Reentering the infirmary, Amy demanded stormily, "How can you stand it?"

Becky looked up in surprise. She'd finished laying out the contents of her medical bag and was shrugging on the white jacket that turned her from guest into physician. "Stand what?"

"All of this. You've been here years now helping these people. And the local authorities are happy to let you do their responsibility for them. They take and take and take. Yet you can't share with your patients what matters most—how much God loves them, that Jesus died for their sins, that there's hope for their lives."

Amy caught interested eyes from the hallway and closed the door to a crack. It was just as well none of them spoke English. "How can you keep it in? I just want to shout out to them what I feel and believe."

"It isn't easy." Becky looked at Amy serenely. "But it's a choice we've all had to make before coming over here. Maybe you're having such a hard time because this was something sprung on you and not something you had time to weigh for yourself. Those of us allowed into this country in a humanitarian capacity are required to come to an agreement we won't use that concession to proselytize. That doesn't mean we can't answer questions about our personal faith when people ask, but we can't openly encourage people to become followers of Jesus Christ. Especially children, which would be so easy because we're working directly with so many and have built relationships of authority as well as affection."

"But isn't that—" *Cowardly?* Amy didn't finish aloud. Jamil's challenge was still burning in her ears. "I mean, Peter and Paul and the other disciples and early Christians didn't wait until they had the blessing of the local authorities, or they'd never have talked about Jesus."

"Do you think that isn't a question we all grapple with? Countless followers of Jesus Christ have taken their lives in their hands to carry that good news into hostile territory. And they continue to do so. But they go in openly with their faith. The difference here is that as Western foreigners, we've only been allowed into Afghanistan through a specific contract with their government. The choice isn't whether to speak or not to speak but whether to come here under certain restrictions—or not to come at all."

Becky finished buttoning her white coat, but she showed no impatience as she went on mildly, "We come here believing that showing God's love through meeting these people's survival needs—as Jesus did so often—is better than nothing. And obeying the conditions we agreed to before coming isn't just a matter of honesty and integrity. Breaking those conditions puts every other Christian expat here in a humanitarian or any other capacity in jeopardy. Meanwhile we keep praying that one day conditions will change and the doors will swing completely open."

And if for these women, these precious children, that comes too late? Aloud, Amy said bitterly, "You mean, like we all thought was happening when the Taliban were overthrown."

"That was a hope that never materialized," Becky admitted. "God's ways aren't always ours. Or his timing. I believe that God can work even through restrictions to show his love. But if you aren't willing to do your work here under the conditions we all face, you may want to consider whether you should be here at all. Or whether maybe you need to turn this project over to someone else before you place yourself and others around you at risk."

It was an admonition Amy might have expected from Steve. But from the American nurse who'd become her friend, it stung even as Amy recognized its justice. Amy might not have asked for this situation. But she'd accepted the conditions even if she hadn't been completely aware of what it would entail.

"I know the issues. I know what's required of me. It's just—never mind, we need to get started." Amy took a step toward the door. "We'll have to wait for Jamil to examine the boys. But I'd like to take Najeeda first. She's been getting worse. And now some of the others are showing the same symptoms. Do you think we need to set up a quarantine?"

The handle was still under Amy's fingers when the shock wave blew the door open. The thunderclap of sound bursting against her eardrums followed so close Amy could not have told which it was that picked her up and threw her across the room.

41

So far, so good.

The opening ceremony had ended earlier than Steve anticipated, the cold dampening any inclination for speakers to ramble. Jim Waters and his congressional delegation had listened with deadpan courtesy to passionate pledges to turn the new Counternarcotics Justice Center into an all-out weapon on opium production. The Afghans had listened with equally straight faces to Waters's ambitious strategy of eradication, alternative economy, security, and brotherly love.

Now a solid phalanx of counternarcotics police and a Gurkha unit steered a much smaller group to the council room where Afghan leadership and the Waters deputation would dialogue directly. Another security team channeled the entourages to the center's new cafeteria, where they'd be corralled until the loya jirga was over. The news crews thrust microphones and cameras at anyone in their path as they were herded out the gate.

Meanwhile, the DynCorp PSD had whisked their principals through the cut ribbon as soon as the last speech was over. Only the CS detail remained on alert in the front courtyard. Though the event had been shifted from the MOI compound, Khalid was technically still the host, and he embraced and kissed every VIP before they moved indoors. A display for lingering news crews, Steve wondered sourly, or buttering up potential collaborators?

The reception line was dwindling, so Steve headed down the hall for a final check of the loya jirga setup. At least two-thirds of the Afghan VIPs were already seated on the cushions and tushaks. Waters, with his embassy handlers, DCM Carl Bolton and DEA chief Ramon Placido, was chatting with the ministers of agriculture and counternarcotics. A translator stood behind a lectern. Scattered around the rugs were trays of honey pastries and bazaar-bought Oreos and other imported cookies and crackers, offered to honor their American guests. Servants were handing around cups of red chai.

Police uniforms along the walls eyed the refreshments covetously. Steve's glance was caught by one uniform directly across from the door. Light hair and eyes of a Tajik or Uzbek northerner under a jammed-down cap rang no bells. But something in that slight frame hunched against the cold in a too-big parka tugged at Steve in vague recognition.

Then he placed that nagging familiarity, and tension eased. The uniform who'd jumped to the snap of Ismail's fingers during that fracas at the gate earlier. Satisfied, Steve went back down the hall. When he stepped outside, the front gate was shut. Only Khalid still stood between the marble columns of the entrance portico, his CS detail hovering watchfully close.

Khalid looked pleased, and his broad smile held neither guile nor any consciousness of guilt as he turned to Steve. "It goes well, does it not? Why do you frown so?"

"Forgive me, Minister," Steve said even as he thought, *I don't get this guy.* He was itching to propel his principal after Waters and team. Too many rooftops and windows had line of sight on the marble-columned entrance portico, and Steve had no intention of offering anyone even the smallest odds of completing what that sugar factory bomber had failed to achieve. "Your guests have been served tea," he hinted delicately. "Would you care for something?"

Just then Ismail hurried out of the entrance behind them. "Minister, all is ready. They wait only for their host."

"Then let us go." But Khalid didn't move immediately. He turned to survey his surroundings, his broad smile even more complacent as a satisfied gaze ran across freshly painted buildings, tiled courtyards, walkways, and high walls. And with reason. The multimillion-dollar facility was one more massive jewel in the Ministry of Interior crown.

One eye on his watch, the other on the skyline, Steve let another sixty seconds tick off before he debated a suggestive clearing of the throat.

Ismail saved him the trouble. "Minister—"

The shrilling of a cell phone inside his parka interrupted Ismail. Steve discreetly edged his principal inside the cover of the entryway as Khalid's deputy answered. Steve's antenna sprang to high alert at Ismail's expression. "What is it?" Steve asked.

Slowly, even shakily, Ismail lowered the phone. "There has been a bombing."

"A bombing? Here at the summit?" Surely, even with the size of the Justice Center, they'd have heard the blast if there'd been an explosion anywhere.

"Not here. On the minister's own property."

If Steve had suspected Khalid's wily maneuverings in that remote-control suicide bomb, he did so no longer. There was no faking the shock and fury that were shaking Khalid, the draining of blood under the skin that left his lips chalk white.

"My property! Sherpur? Baghlan? But why would anyone try to kill me there?"

"No, no, not your personal residence. Only a rental property," Ismail reassured.

"Which means you probably weren't the target," Steve consoled automatically. Then as his brain continued to process, he demanded, "Which property?"

Before Ismail could answer, Steve's phone rang. "Yes?"

The incoming call was the same Aussie operative who'd installed the spy-cam system, on monitor duty this morning at the Sherpur command center. "Wilson, that fiber-optic extension over in Wazir just went haywire for a second. It's back online now. I'd guess a power surge except there's no electricity involved. Maybe a malfunction?"

"No, not a malfunction." Steve no longer had any doubt to which property Ismail was referring. Licking dryness from his lips, he hung up and turned to Khalid. "Our command center confirms a situation at your Wazir property."

"Then it was not after all an attempt on my life." The minister had brought himself under control because the fury and shock on his face were now tight-lipped annoyance as he threw Ismail an irritated glance. "Perhaps not even a bomb. Accidental explosions are common enough in winter when people are careless with their heaters. Come, we waste time. Our guests are waiting."

"But there may be casualties."

"The chowkidar will report any damages to my aide." Khalid indicated Ismail. "In any case it is not of great concern. I am informed the current tenants are only female criminals an American charity has chosen to shelter." The minister spoke over his shoulder as he walked, his detail and Ismail hurrying to close up. "Perhaps this is Allah's judgment for their sins."

At that moment Steve hated Khalid. He swung around to his shift leader, Jamie McDuff, bringing up the rear behind Khalid's diamond. "He's all yours. Let Hamilton know I've got an off-site emergency. I'll be in touch."

Steve had taken two steps when his strides became a trot. *I told you your security was lousy! That a female expat living alone in unsecured quarters was begging to be made a target! But would you listen to me?* Steve brought his Aussie shift supervisor back on the line. "I need you to rustle up an emergency response team and get them over to Wazir. Call the team house. They're closer."

Steve wasn't surprised when Phil caught up just as he slid into the driver's seat of the Suburban.

"You may need a medic. DynCorp can handle things here."

"Then hurry up and get in," Steve said between gritted teeth. "I've got a neck to wring."

42

The screams propelled Amy to her feet. Nothing felt broken, though her left temple throbbed as though someone had struck her a sharp blow. She sucked air back into her lungs, choked at its acridity, then gasped for another breath even worse than the first as she groped through smoke and fumes for her companion. A hand closed on her arm, and together Amy and Becky stumbled toward the open door.

Black, foul-smelling smoke boiled from the main stairwell. The women and children gathered for the clinic were moving down the hall, a hysterical bottleneck jostling at the door that led onto the balcony and outdoor stairs. Coughing and choking, Amy stooped to swing Najeeda's son into her arms while Becky helped support Najeeda. Fahim buried his face against Amy's tunic while they inched forward.

Then they were out onto the balcony. Amy hadn't even had time to consider the source of the explosion or that acrid stench billowing down the hall. Now she could hear that shrieks of terror and pain weren't all from the hysterical mob around her. "The children!"

Amy couldn't push through the traffic jam on the balcony staircase. Disentangling herself from the boys, Amy climbed over the balcony railing, dropping with a hard thud onto the tiles below. The air out here was little more breathable, and Amy could see that the entrance hall doors were blown from their hinges, smoke thickening in the inner courtyard to become a dark, oily cloud. Women had emerged from their living quarters, smaller children in arms and at their skirts. Some were pounding on the heavy, wooden door leading to Rasheed's quadrant. Why was no one responding?

And now the first school-age children were stumbling, crying and choking, from the main wing's rear salon. Why they sought refuge in the courtyard was immediately evident as Amy waded against the flow. Someone had lifted down the metal bar securing the French doors, but these were locked, and window grilles prevented any escape that way. Amy pounded frantically on the French doors. Surely someone out there had to hear.

Then she spotted Fatima staggering through the small door in the paneling that divided the rear salon from the schoolroom. Above the bedlam, Amy yelled, "Are there any more children inside?"

Fatima looked dazed, blood spilling down her face and one arm. When she didn't answer, Amy stepped past her through the opening. She immediately regretted it. To this point, the paneling had shielded her from whatever was responsible for those burning, choking fumes. Now Amy could neither breathe nor hardly see. Just enough to take in doors not only blown open but lying flat on the floor.

The smoke was too thick to see into the hall as Amy shuffled across carpets and cushions, scarf tight over her face. She could be thankful now for that shortage of glass. Though plastic panes bulged against metal bars, they hadn't shattered. Fatima's desk and blackboard were tipped over, workbooks, pencils, and crayons scattered widely. But Amy's fumbling hands felt no small, limp forms as she'd dreaded.

Two propane heaters were overturned, their flames blown out, but intact. And from the smell, still pumping out deadly fumes. By the time Amy managed to turn them off, she was growing woozy. Groping back to the paneling, she was in despair of finding the opening when an arm grabbed hers. It was Farah. Half lifting Amy over the sill, the girl slammed the door on that thick, black smoke.

But this side offered little improvement. And to Amy's horror, children were pouring back into the salon, screaming, crying, and choking. Stumbling back to the French doors, Amy saw that the gate from Rasheed's quadrant now stood open. Could the caretaker and his wife have just abandoned them? Here those plastic panes were a disadvantage because she couldn't even break them to let in fresh air.

Oh, God, please have mercy on these women and children. Don't let them die before they ever have a chance to know your love.

Two people dashing through the open gate didn't look like angels, but they had to be. A black chador holding a key ring. Soraya running on her high heels. The French doors flung open, a stampede of small bodies pouring out. Amy gulped in a wonderful taste of diesel-laden smog as she hurried toward Fatima, still slumped onto a rug.

But Soraya was ahead of her, face white, eyes wild with horror. Soraya lifted Fatima to her feet and supported her toward the French doors. "Fatima-jan, I feared you were dead. I could not reach you until Hamida opened the gate. And then all was locked, and we had to find Rasheed with the keys."

Farah had gone to Fatima's other side to help, so Amy headed to the courtyard. Smoke still poured from the main doors. But Hamida had unlocked the side door, and here too women and children flooded into Rasheed's garden. Becky Frazer had lingered to help some of the women. Amy grabbed a toddler in each arm while Hamida lifted another.

The New Hope tenants retreated through the gate to cluster as far from the fire as possible. Carrying her burden over to their mothers, Amy saw the front entry doors lying smashed into the fountain, the same black, acrid smoke pouring through the opening. As she reached the others, she could also see there were more injuries than she'd thought. Contusions already turning purple. A limp arm that looked dislocated. Bloodied faces and scraped limbs. Becky had thought to grab her medical bag and was helping Soraya settle Fatima to a sitting position.

I should go help her, find out who's hurt worst.

But a dazed lassitude gripped Amy, the throbbing at her temple spreading through her head, so that she swayed. For one weak moment, she wished fervently that instead of acting the leader, she could throw this mess on some stronger, wider pair of shoulders. Just a week ago, Steve's speed dial would have been her first reaction. But the security contractor had made it clear any further appeal from Amy would earn only a biting, "I told you so."

Then Amy's eye fell on Rasheed striding toward the fountain, a coil of hose over his shoulder. Behind him, other men rushed through the front gate with pails and shovels. A stocky frame of medium height was among them. Had that loiterer the other night simply been a mechanic from next door?

Amy bestirred herself to move toward Rasheed. "What happened? And what do we do? Is there a fire department to call?"

"I have already informed the landlord." Rasheed lifted aside a smashed door. "As to a fire department, I have heard of such things. But who would wait if they wish their home to survive? We will put out the fire. Then we can enter to discover what has happened." He threw a disapproving look over his shoulder as he began attaching the hose to a water fixture. "Your women are indecent. They must cover for the firefighters."

He was right. None of the women had taken time to grab a burqa, and some had even been caught without headscarves.

"Does that matter right now?" Amy said indignantly. "We almost suffocated in there. We could have died if Hamida hadn't let us out."

Rasheed now had the hose connected. Pulling a scarf over mouth and nose, he turned it on. "That was not intended."

It was hardly an apology. Amy suddenly realized that among the men arriving, she hadn't yet seen her assistant. Wajid had thought he might have returned from his dawn shopping to sleep. A horrible thought caught at Amy. Her one relief had been that there were no apparent serious injuries. Had she been wrong? Jamil's quarters were very close to where that blast had gone off.

I have to find someone to send over. No, there's no time. I'll go myself.

Amy turned away. But just as a stream of water penetrated the smoke, a fresh explosion sent a noxious cloud through the broken doorway to catch Amy full in the face. Coughing and choking, she groped for her scarf to follow Rasheed's example. This was now soaked a sticky scarlet, and that terrible lassitude had settled over her again so that she couldn't lift a limb. Nor could she breathe, her whole world reduced to a throbbing fire that seized chest and throat.

"No, turn off that water! You—bring the fire extinguishers!"

Had the command been Dari or English—or both? Hard arms closed around Amy. She must have lost consciousness because when she swam up out of darkness, there was air in her lungs, a grim voice saying, "Breathe, will you? Didn't I tell you something like this was bound to happen? Just too stubborn to take anyone's advice. No, don't you dare give up on me. Breathe!"

A shuddering gasp eased pressure on Amy's rib cage. She lifted heavy lashes to gray eyes blazing with anger, a mouth compressed so tightly it was bloodless. But Amy didn't mind the anger because she'd heard raw fear in Steve's tirade, the relief that greeted her first labored breath.

"You came!" Then Amy's last conscious thought flooded urgently back. "Jamil?"

Steve's expression went blank; then he got to his feet.

Struggling to a sitting position, Amy took in a thick, down coat beneath her. Becky Frazer was hurrying her way, concern on her face. Men swarmed around the house.

But all that was driven from Amy's mind by a new movement bursting through the open gate. Eyes wide with emotion were black instead of brown, features thinner, a taut frame slighter. But the anger and fear were the same. So was the relief as that dark gaze fell on Amy's sitting shape.

This time Amy's exclamation held its own delight and relief. "Jamil!"

43

Now that Amy was sitting up, Steve stepped back, his face turning to granite as the aid worker's assistant dropped down beside her. "Miss Ameera, you have been hurt! And the children? I saw the smoke at a distance and was so afraid."

Jamil wore only shalwar kameez with a vest, and he was shivering. But he didn't seem to notice the chill breeze as his hand went toward the gash at Amy's temple, the joyous relief lighting his face as revealing as his earlier distraught expression. Did Ms. Amy Mallory know her Afghan assistant had fallen in love with her? The man's unreasonable antipathy now made a world of sense.

And mine?

Jamil snatched his hand away as Amy pushed herself to her feet, her fingers probing her hair. "It's nothing, just a cut. And everyone got out okay. Wajid said you were already back from the bazaar, so when we couldn't find you . . ." Her voice shook. She stared at bloodstained fingers, then wiped them on her scarf. "Where have you been?"

"I—" Jamil glanced at Steve as he got to his feet. "I had to return for another errand. Forgive me if I caused any inconvenience."

"Now that you're here, maybe you can give Becky and me a hand. Do you still have that first aid kit in the truck? We've got a lot of cuts and bruises, and the infirmary's cut off by the fire. I'll meet you over there."

Amy gestured toward the huddle of women and children. From a black bag and the cut arm she was tending, Steve guessed an older expat woman who'd turned back when she saw Amy sit up was the aid worker's American nurse friend. Despite a lingering pallor and harsh breathing, Amy appeared in control again. As her driver hurried toward the gate, she reached for the parka she'd been lying on and handed it to Steve.

"This is yours, isn't it? I'm not sure what happened, but I have a feeling I have you to thank again. I just hope I didn't get it too dirty."

"That's the last thing that matters right now," Steve said roughly as he shrugged the coat on. "And we'd better deal with that cut on your head before you start in on anyone else."

"That I can handle." Phil came up beside them, carrying a field hospital kit.

"Phil, what are you doing here?" Amy said with pleasure. She glanced around to take in the dozen or more CS personnel. "What are you *all* doing here?"

The Special Forces medic threw Steve a wry glance as he opened his kit. "Let's just say Wilson was pretty worried about you. Now let's get you patched up."

Amy's eyes went wide, but Steve turned away to see Ian approaching. Behind him, the shattered entrance and black billows now reduced to negligible wisps screamed this was no heater accident.

"Boss, we've got the fire pretty well out. Good thing we brought those foam extinguishers because the blast zone had enough toxic chemicals to turn this whole block into a poison cloud with the water they were pumping in. That last explosion was a couple barrels of acetone going off."

He didn't get any further because Amy spun around from the pressure pad Phil was applying to her temple. "Toxic chemicals? You mean—that explosion was something poisonous? What about the children and others who've breathed it in?"

"Hey, no worries," Ian said quickly. "From what I can tell, we're talking industrial chems here. Turpentine, paint thinner, engine oil—workshop stuff. Of course those are hazardous enough, especially when mixed with water, which can turn any and all of them from highly flammable to toxic gas."

Glancing at Amy's pale face, Phil intervened. "The good news is most of that stuff is also explosive enough to burn off in the initial blast. If your people are all breathing and walking, you're likely looking at smoke inhalation, nothing worse. Why don't we go take a look?"

By now Jamil was back with a red and white box. As the three moved away, Steve ignored something cold settling into his chest to swing around on Ian. "Nice going."

"Sorry. Forgot there were civvies present." Ian watched Amy head toward the huddled group. "Your lady friend's really something. Thinks of her troops before herself. I'd take that one at my back in a combat zone any day."

Steve didn't bother disabusing the other contractor of any personal connection between himself and Amy. "So what weren't you saying back there? Or are you telling me this whole thing is some little industrial accident?"

"I wish." Ian's admiring stare sobered instantly. "You'd better take a look for yourself."

The two contractors strode toward the shattered front door. The Afghan men who'd been tackling the fire when the CS team arrived were clustered around the fountain, the chowkidar Rasheed among them. Hostile glances could be explained by two armed Guats standing guard among the blackened columns of the entry portico.

"I ordered everyone out to protect the scene," Ian elucidated as they entered the hallway. "The primary blast was through there."

Lingering smoke and chemical fumes, along with the reek of extinguisher foam, were strong enough for Steve to reach for a bandanna to tie over his mouth and nose. He saw immediately why Ian was so sure where the explosion originated. The heavy entrance doors at either end of the hall were blown from hinges, and those leading into a salon that had been locked when Amy gave Steve a tour had been ripped away with enough force to smash through the doors into the schoolroom beyond. A chill went over Steve at the thought of children sitting among those cushions at the time of the blast.

Ian stooped to work something out of a fractured door panel. He held it out to Steve. It was a sliver of stone as sharp as a carving knife. The slab was studded with such. Steve tugged loose another that proved to be a shard of glass. Others looked to be bone fragments.

"Shrapnel. Designed to make it through a metal detector." Ian's comment was muffled by his bandanna as he glanced around the schoolroom. "Talk about luck. If those first doors hadn't absorbed most of the blast and the second set caught the rest, or if those windows were glass instead of plastic, we'd be looking at shredded bodies instead of cuts and bruises."

"Then this *was* a bomb," Steve said slowly.

"There's not a lot of fragments that I saw. But that's my take, yes. Do you know someone who'd want to do this kind of damage to your lady friend out there?"

"I certainly do," Steve said furiously. "And I told her not to worry, that they were just amateurs. But why a storage room? Unless the idea was to frighten more than kill."

Steve stepped over debris into the actual blast zone. The polished mosaic floors, high ceiling, tall windows, and French doors might in another world have been intended as a ballroom. Here they looked to have held stored goods from household furnishings to construction and automotive materials to the barrels and plastic containers of workplace chemicals.

Now only firewood remained of any furniture. Plastic containers were melted puddles. Burned-out barrels had flown around the salon, one even across the hall into the schoolroom. Their contents accounted for more damage than any actual bomb blast, shrapnel piercing aluminum and plastic to set off the fireball responsible for all that black, oily smoke.

The black of char contrasted everywhere with the dissolving white of chemical foam. But from the direction of tossed debris and fire damage, Steve judged the explosion to originate just inside those French doors. He threaded carefully across to look out onto a fruit orchard. Here there'd been no plastic panes. Nor, any longer, glass. Doors and windows were blown out, showering the grass beyond with broken glass and twisted ironwork, even nuts and bolts and other wreckage that had ripped into tree bark with the lethal force of gunfire.

Glass crunched under Steve's boots as he stepped outside. A gate separating the orchard from the mechanics yard was standing open, and by scattered shovels, pails, and another hose, an attempt had been made to fight the fire from this side as well. But here too Ian had taken charge, the orchard cleared of personnel and two more third country nationals standing guard at the gate. Steve's fury deepened as he inspected a screw-driver buried to half its length in the trunk of an almond tree. This was no break-in to haul off a wayward sister-in-law. This was a vicious assault that only by chance had destroyed property rather than lives.

Then Steve spotted a cloth fragment caught on the tree bark above the screwdriver. The initial explosion must have thrown it far enough the sub-sequent flash fire hadn't caught it because a camouflage pattern was still distinguishable. A sharp exclamation drew Ian over as Steve's pocketknife maneuvered loose the cloth fragment. A sniff confirmed suspicion.

"That looks like one of our parkas."

"Not quite." Steve compared the fragment to his own sleeve. The dif-ference in brown and green and olive pattern was notable only on close inspection. "It's U.S. Army surplus, same as we handed out to all those new police troops. And it's got C-4 trace on it."

"Then we're talking suicide bomber?" Ian said blankly. "I thought the local Tallies stuck to dynamite and duct tape like that vest we found on the helicopter pad. No, wait—I know what this is. I saw something similar in Iraq with a suitcase. You roll out C-4 nice and thin inside the lining."

The military grade plastic explosive was not only as malleable as Play-Doh but had unfortunately become as available on Afghanistan's black market.

"Work as much shrapnel as you can into the explosive, add a detonator, and sew the lining back in place. If it's done well, you'd never know that piece of luggage sliding through security is a ticking bomb. With the right shrapnel, it won't even set off a metal detector."

"Which means Ms. Mallory wasn't the intended target," Steve said flatly. "Or even this compound. It's got to be the loya jirga. Half of Afghanistan's top leadership in one room, including the owner of this compound. This thing was designed to come through security on one of those counternarcotics police."

"So why is it here? Or are you're thinking the bomber couldn't get through, so hitting one of Khalid's properties was fallback?" Ian searched the ground. "And if we're talking suicide bomb, where are the body parts? Unless—"

Both men came to the same thought together. "Remote control detonation."

Ian straightened to look at Steve. "You think this might be the same guy who dropped that other vest on the roof? It's hardly the same signature."

"That means zip. If the first was a statement rather than a serious threat, it makes sense they wouldn't use the same design. They wouldn't want to give us a heads-up to be checking out every surplus Army coat coming near Khalid."

"Any chance this wasn't the only one?"

"I'm about to find out." Steve hit speed dial. "Meanwhile, seal off this property. No one goes in or out."

Jamie McDuff answered on the first ring. "I was just about to call you. The loya jirga finished without a wrinkle. Everything okay on your end?"

"No, it isn't." Swiftly, Steve explained. "Don't trouble Khalid or Ismail until their event finishes, but I want complete body checks of anyone within a hundred feet. I'm calling Hamilton now."

By the angry shouts and running feet, Ian was carrying out his orders. The two Condor operatives at the orchard gate now had their M4s up.

"Jason? Those forensic trainees you had sweeping the MOI roof—I need a team here now. Yes, I've every reason to believe it's connected to Khalid, maybe even Waters. That's right, the whole works. I want this guy found before he tries it again."

"Steve, why are your men sealing off the gates and keeping people inside?" Amy called out. "And the house. I need to get everyone out of this cold, and your guards won't even let me in for supplies. I had to have Phil make the guards bring me over here." Stepping through the orchard gate, she picked through glass to the veranda. A neat bandage now showed white under her headscarf. Her eyes went wide with horror as she peered past Steve into the blackened wreckage of the storage depot.

"Sorry about that." Steve lowered the phone. "I'll give orders to safety check enough space to get you all out of the weather. But I'm afraid this is just the beginning. You might warn your people that everyone and his dog are about to descend on this place."

Amy shook her head dazedly. "But I thought your friend said this was just an accidental explosion triggered by the chemicals and stuff stored in there."

"Sure, except a bomb triggered the chemicals. And since your security system is functioning properly, whoever planted that bomb either had access to this facility or was let in by someone who did."

Steve hardened himself against a sudden stricken look in her eyes, his tone impersonal. "Which makes this property a crime scene and every person on it a suspect."

44

By afternoon, it seemed to Amy all the peace and sanctuary she'd worked so hard to establish at New Hope had been blown apart in the same explosion that blasted those doors. Within the hour of Steve's horrifying announcement, the compound was swarming with armed and uniformed men. And dogs, Steve's comment having proved literal. K-9 units, Amy gathered, watching animals and handlers sniffing around the orchard quadrant. Maybe even Gorg's parents.

By then Steve had kept his word. Amy was still explaining to Becky and the others when the contractor named Ian came by to say the kitchen salon and its neighboring dormitory had passed inspection and could be put back to use. What they'd been looking for, Amy couldn't imagine. She was just grateful to get everyone back inside.

The dormitory became a sickbay, and Amy was soon even more grateful for Steve's medic friend. From somewhere, Phil requisitioned additional first aid supplies when New Hope's own scant stock ran out. With Jamil's help, he expertly tugged that dislocated shoulder into place. And between him and Becky and Jamil, they made short shrift of swabbing, stitching, and bandaging, along with doling out cough drops and sedatives with a liberal hand.

Now that Amy had seen that burned-out storage depot, she was even more grateful it hadn't been worse. That shattered glass and wood and metal could so easily have been the flesh and blood of precious small bodies. *Thank you, heavenly Father. Thank you for your mercy! Thank you for watching over these precious human beings you've entrusted to me.*

All in all, it astonished Amy how quickly and matter-of-factly all the children and mothers settled back to routine with a resilience of people so accustomed to their world falling apart; a bomb blast was just one more inconvenient interruption. By the time the last patient was resting and Steve's men had vacated the inner courtyard, a warming lentil stew had been dished up. Scavenged plywood offered a temporary barricade over the broken hallway doors. And though an odor of smoke still clung to everything, air quality had improved to Kabul's usual smog.

Amy wished she could muster as much resilience. Perhaps because she'd breathed more fumes than the others, her throat and face hurt so she could hardly speak, every movement an effort as she walked Becky to the gate.

Amy's hug was fervent. "I can't thank you enough. I don't know what I'd have done if you weren't here."

"You'd have managed. If I didn't have that TB clinic this afternoon, I'd stay. I don't like abandoning you like this."

"Of course you have to go. And I'm hardly alone, as you can see." Amy gestured to the swarm of CS personnel and police uniforms.

"You know what I mean. You look like you should be in bed yourself. Just be sure to take that ibuprofen as soon as you can get off your feet."

As Becky's minivan pulled away, Amy turned back toward the house. The burned-out front entrance was still a beehive of uniforms and guns. Missing were the volunteer firemen, who'd been herded over to the other side. Rasheed had opened the guest rooms to shelter the detainees, among them that stocky loiterer from two nights ago.

I forgot to ask Rasheed if he's one of the mechanics.

No, Amy didn't even want to think about Rasheed. If he had seemed appreciative of the CS team's help in putting out the fire, he'd been infuriated at the arrival of police uniforms, even more so at the quarantine. He'd ranted and raved so furiously at the security personnel who'd taken over gate duty Amy could be glad they'd confiscated Wajid's Kalashnikov. He'd yelled even more angrily at Hamida when he caught his wife helping the women to their quarters.

Amy had tried not to think of Steve's assertion that someone on her property was responsible for placing a bomb in that storage depot. After all, why would any of her personnel risk possible injury to themselves?

Except that none of Amy's resident staff had been in the building when the bomb went off.

A coincidence, surely. And as in that earlier invasion, Amy could rule out Jamil at least. She'd seen horrified shock when he'd rushed in, witnessed the distress and compassion with which he'd tended the injured children. *I've got to change his mind about going back to medical school; he'd make such a wonderful doctor.*

But Amy hadn't forgotten how Aryana's in-laws had paid their way to this compound. Soraya had been troubled over some financial emergency. Certainly she'd shown distress over Fatima's injuries, but had she even realized the teacher had returned ahead of her from the holidays?

And Rasheed. Surely he wouldn't destroy so much property, some undoubtedly his own. Unless he was paid enough to compensate. Hamida had evacuated the New Hope residents, not Rasheed. Did he really not realize the danger they'd all been in? And those past comments about wanting the Welayat women off this property. Had he perhaps thought only to add a further scare that would drive them away? Or been paid to allow someone else that privilege? Maybe he hadn't known how much damage those stored chemicals could cause.

No, please let it be a stranger. Even one of the mechanics.

Walking through Rasheed's quadrant, Amy stepped through the French doors. The plastic window panels had been pulled down to air out lingering smoke and fumes, and a cold wind whistled across the salon. From the other side of the paneling, she could hear male voices, Steve and Phil among them. What were they doing? What had they discovered?

Amy considered opening that small wooden door in the paneling to demand a report. But she felt too weary, her throat too raw to carry through on the thought, so she headed instead toward the door leading to the inner courtyard. Now that things were settling down, maybe it wouldn't hurt to retire to her own suite. It must be breathable because she'd seen Soraya helping Fatima upstairs to her quarters as soon as the all clear was given.

A quick tap of sandals signaled Jamil before he appeared through the door. "Miss Ameera, I was just coming to find you."

"What is it?" Amy's sore face managed a perplexed smile as she looked her assistant over. He wore a patu for warmth over his shalwar kameez, and a bundle was tossed over his shoulder. "You look like you're hitting the road. Are you going somewhere?"

An answering smile flickered in the dark eyes as Jamil set his pack down. "The police broke the lock to my quarters in their searching, and since there are strangers present, I thought it best to retrieve my belongings. But I wished to speak to you because—" he glanced at the wooden barrier beyond which drifted those voices—"well, I was thinking it would be good to go to the bazaar. I have cleaned the infirmary, but there are no more bandages left or cleansing solution. And some injuries must be dressed again tonight."

"Good idea. Let me give you some cash for that. And we'll have to ask Phil to get you past the guard."

"Not so fast!"

The dry command spun Amy around.

Steve was ducking through the door in the paneling. His scrutiny going from Amy to her assistant showed none of the concern she'd seen when she recovered consciousness.

As Jamil stiffened, Amy stepped between the two men. "Is there a problem, Steve? Phil let Becky leave. Or is it just expats who can break quarantine?"

"Not at all. Your assistant is welcome to go to the bazaar—with an escort—just as soon as we get his fingerprints. Since he's been helping out, we left him till last. But Phil tells me you're all done now."

The tension left Amy's muscles. "Well, sure, I was kind of expecting that. Do you want to fingerprint women and children too? I can promise you none of them have access to that storage unit. So if it isn't essential, I'd sure hate to get them all upset again."

"No, just the men."

When Steve didn't explain further, Amy turned to Jamil. Guessing the reason for that frozen immobility, she said gently, "It's okay. It doesn't mean they're accusing anyone. They just have to take everyone's prints so they can eliminate them against any strange ones, right?"

"Something like that," Steve murmured, but he was watching Jamil with narrow-eyed intensity. "Do you have a problem having your prints taken? You do understand what fingerprints are."

Jamil came back to life, something unreadable flaring in his eyes as he said bitingly, "I am not ignorant. I know about fingerprints. And I have no objection. Why should I?" He stalked toward the door in the paneling. "Come, let us be done with this. I have nothing more to hide."

Amy would have followed, but Steve put out an arm. "He's a big boy. He doesn't need you to hold his hand." His expression softened fractionally as he looked Amy over. "You look all in. Not to mention, that's quite a black eye you're developing. Ask Phil for an ice pack, and go get some rest. I'll call you if you're needed."

"No, call me when you're done," Amy answered tightly. "If Jamil has to have an armed guard just to go to the bazaar, I'm going too."

"Afraid we'll hurt your pal?" Steve jeered softly. Before Amy could reply, he shut the paneling in her face.

Amy picked up Jamil's pack and went upstairs. She didn't trust all those policemen and mercenaries any more than the strangers detained next door. The pack was disturbingly light to hold a man's entire possessions, so its burden wasn't the reason Amy found herself dragging each foot to set it on the next step the way a toddler climbed stairs. Her only thought now was to reach bottled water so she could take Becky's ibuprofen and lie down.

Steve's right; Jamil doesn't need me to hold his hand going to the bazaar.

She had stepped into the upstairs hall when she heard voices. Not unexpected since Soraya had retreated to their suite with Fatima. Except that one of these voices was male and angry. It wasn't Rasheed's, and Amy's first thought was that a policeman had drummed up some pretext to harass her female residents. Then as she hastened down the hall, she made out Soraya's raised cry.

"Nay! I cannot ask for more. I will lose my position. I have already given you my—. It is still two weeks until my next—"

If Amy had missed some Dari terms, she could guess they referred to

JEANETTE WINDLE

salary by the harsh reply. "The infidels have money to throw away. They can spare some to you. If you do not succeed, then do not bother to come home. Or ask again to see Fariq."

So the man was no stranger to Soraya. It was a measure of how completely Amy had been immersed in Afghan life that she found herself profoundly shocked Soraya would permit a man inside the shelter of their suite. She was hardly less shocked that her proud, even arrogant, housemate could sound so pleading.

"Nay! Please do not say such things!"

The sob in Soraya's denial shot Amy's hand to the doorknob. It was unlocked. Stepping inside, she froze in disbelief as she recognized the man who whirled in her direction.

It was the stocky Afghan she'd first glimpsed two nights ago, then among the detainees below. Up close, Amy could see he was younger than Soraya and good-looking. Curly hair and beard. Olive-skinned, aquiline features. A high-bridged, strong nose. Though his good looks were spoiled by the disdainful glare that took in Amy's intrusion, the angry compression of lips. He looked in fact enough like Soraya to be a family member. Which hardly excused his presence in Amy's sanctuary.

Turning his back to Amy, he said sharply, "You will do what I say. I will wait for you below." Spinning around again, he strode past Amy so close she had to scramble out of his way.

Across the room, Soraya stood tall and motionless, her proud, beautiful features as stony and blank as though Amy had never heard her pleading. And now through a crack in Soraya's bedroom door, Amy could see Fatima's frightened eyes peering out.

Stepping into the room, Amy set Jamil's bundle on the floor. "Who is that man? What is he doing in our quarters?"

How he'd slipped up here, Amy didn't have to ask because she'd glimpsed ink-stained fingers. The man must have stolen up the stairwell after he'd gone through the fingerprinting process. Soraya groped for a chair. Only as she sank into it did Amy realize she'd done so to keep from trembling. Looking down at her hands, Soraya didn't speak.

Amy sighed. "Soraya, I don't want to lose you, but it's clear something has been going on you aren't telling me. Either I get the truth, or I'm

376

going to have to let you go. Who is that man, and what does he have to do with you?"

Slowly, Soraya raised her head. Then the impassivity of her perfect features crumpled. "His name is Ibrahim. And he is my husband."

45

Nothing more to hide.

Jamil's final statement nagged at Steve as the Afghan man rolled inked fingers across white paper with a competence that said he'd done this before. That very personal hostility in his glance as he obeyed Steve's order was one reason his inclusion was little more than procedure. The man would do nothing to hurt his employer, and he'd been as shocked as Steve when he rushed in. But did he have other reasons to avoid police inquiry?

Steve had set up a command center in the schoolroom at the far end from its windows. Technically part of the crime scene, it was also the least damaged area, and Steve was reluctant to intrude further on the compound's residents by annexing more of their living area. The finger-printing zone was the teacher's desk, where a pair of police trainees were taking down personal data as well as fingerprints.

Phil strolled over as a pair of uniforms escorted Jamil to a knot of inky-fingered Afghans who'd been the last of that crowd next door. "Anything new?"

Jason Hamilton held up a bag containing a chunk of duct tape and plastic. "Here's why we're running fingerprints. It's definitely part of the detonator. And it looks identical to the one in that suicide vest. Even if assembly's different, I'm betting the same bomb maker."

The difficulty with bomb-scene evidence was that the blast itself left little behind. Even fingerprints that might have been inside that storage depot had burned off in the explosion and ensuing flash fire. But a bomb was a funny thing. Its primary effect wasn't fire (those stored chemicals had been a bonus), rather to propel its pieces outward at unbelievable velocity. Which was why the shrapnel embedded in a suicide vest did far more damage than the explosive itself.

And if a piece was thrown hard and fast enough to escape incineration—well, more than one bomb maker had been identified by a print surviving on some bit of debris its creator presumed destroyed in the blast. In this instance, a shard of cell phone casing had been sniffed out by a K-9 unit in a low-lying fork of an apricot tree. Neatly preserved under the duct tape holding the device together had been a single, perfect thumbprint. A man's print by the size. Hence their current undertaking.

Steve had become well acquainted with such devices in Iraq, where cell phones were favorite triggers for IEDs. Connect a detonator to a phone's internal alarm clock, and you had a time bomb. Connect one instead to the phone's ringer, and it could be set off by a single tap on the speed dial. If you knew what you were doing, it took less than five minutes with screwdriver and duct tape to take a phone apart, wire it to a bomb, and put it back together.

Steve's blood ran cold at the thought of someone with murder on his mind slipping in so easily to leave that deadly offering. Someone who had to be part of New Hope's regular routine, Amy's daily life. What if the bomber had chosen the schoolroom or inner courtyard or even those upstairs offices instead of an uninhabited room?

Because there again was the hole in the best defense strategy. Security systems were designed to protect against outside assault. There simply was no foolproof defense against an insider with free access to the innermost circle of trust. Which was why a traitor from within was always the most deadly and effective of enemies.

The police were now shepherding the final detainee group back to the mechanics yard. Steve frowned as his gaze settled on a stocky man in his thirties two uniforms were restraining by the arms. Hadn't that guy been part of the last batch?

"My money's on one of the mechanics," Ian spoke up. "They come and go. And they have access only to the storage area and only during work hours—which would explain why they didn't go for a more lethal target. Or maybe some guy slipped past when they were working on his car."

"I guess that's possible," Phil said. "But how could the perp count on carelessness?"

"Which brings it back to the mechanics—or chowkidar," Ian insisted. "What makes no sense to me, if the bomber couldn't get through this morning's security, why choose here as backup? Granted, it's easier than Khalid's primary residence. But why not the ministry or some regular part of Khalid's routine? If it's the same guy, he didn't have any difficulty getting inside the MOI last time."

"I can't even hypothesize—this thing makes so little sense." Steve turned back to Jason Hamilton. "You're the expert. Hasn't your team squeezed anything out of the locals we rounded up?"

"Hey, you were there. Name. Address. What are they going to say about the bomb but no? The Afghan commander wants to take the entire lot down to Pul-e-Charki, even the neighbors who just stepped in as volunteer firefighters."

Pul-e-Charki was the local maximum security prison made notorious under the Soviets and, later, the mujahedeen and Taliban. Its rep hadn't improved as much as it should have in the years since liberation.

"I've convinced him to wait for fingerprint results. This is the last batch, so if we don't get a hit, we're out of luck. But I don't want to be responsible for turning some local Good Samaritan over to the interrogation methods I hear they're still practicing up at Pul-e-Charki. A single match, and we can let everyone else go." Hamilton snatched up a folder a policeman laid in front of him. "And here we go."

Steve turned to his two subordinates. "I'm heading over with Jason. It won't make the system work any faster, but at least I can be looking over a shoulder and get right back over here if anything comes up."

"So what do you want us to do in the meantime?"

"Nothing much left *to* do now but wait."

"Your husband?" Amy had braced herself for family tragedy, even a clandestine relationship. This was the last answer she'd expected. Amy pulled the other chair over and sat down. "But you said your husband was killed in the mujahedeen bombing."

"Yes, my first husband, Kareem. Ibrahim is—was—his cousin and mine. His wife, my younger sister, was killed too in the bombing. To marry was a logical solution for the family and our children—my daughter and his son."

A conclusion leaped to Amy's mind. "Fatima." How had she missed the resemblance?

"Yes, she is my daughter. But she is also a teacher, a good teacher." At the sound of her name, the girl emerged from Soraya's bedroom to curl up at her mother's feet. Soraya touched the bandage on her head lovingly. No wonder Amy's housemate had been so frantic.

"And the young man who usually picks you up? He is Ibrahim's son?"

"No, Hamid is Kareem's youngest brother. Fariq is Ibrahim's son and my nephew." A flicker of anguish crossed Soraya's face. "But though he is my sister's son by birth, he is the son of my heart. He was still an infant when Ibrahim took me as wife. He is now ten years old and knows no other mother."

Amy wasn't sure if she was more disturbed by Soraya's falsehoods or that she'd felt any need to make them. "Why didn't you just tell me you had a family? Did you think I wouldn't have offered you the job if I'd known you were married? Because it wouldn't have made any difference."

"Would you have asked me to live with you?" Soraya's expression was more defiant than penitent, but she was wringing her hands in her lap.

"Well, probably not," Amy admitted. "I was looking for a single roommate like myself, and I wouldn't have wanted to take you away from your family. As it seems I've done. But you could have lived at home and commuted. I meant what I told you at the time—that living in was not a condition of the position."

"And that is why I did not tell. We had lost our home—again. Our new rooms are too far to come every day. At least two hours in public transport. But Ibrahim does not understand."

"He doesn't want you working here?"

"No, no, I have his permission to work. More, I have his command. Ibrahim does not speak English. He is an engineer with the city water system, but the pay is small, and there is little opportunity for baksheesh."

Baksheesh. Tips, handouts, or to the American mind, just plain bribes, and the only way any government employee in Afghanistan could afford to eat on their miniscule salary.

"So it is necessary that I work for the foreigners because you pay much better salaries. But I must also attend my husband and his home. And now that we have moved far from where the foreigners live and work, this is difficult. I travel to attend his needs as much as I can, but sometimes it is not enough, and he becomes angry and does not wish me to return here."

So instead of extended weekends, Soraya had simply been heading to another job. Amy's sympathy was quickly moderating her exasperation. *And I thought you were so privileged compared to Farah and all the others.*

"Your husband sounded very angry," Amy agreed cautiously. "Your son—I mean, stepson—would he really . . . ?" She broke off at a sight she'd never expected to see from the proud aristocrat who was her assistant. Though her head was held high, tears were running down her cheeks.

Soraya unknotted her hands to make a sweeping-away gesture. "He does not mean it, I am sure. Ibrahim is a good man who does not hit me or my daughter. He is only desperate. You must understand it is hard for him. I am some years older than Ibrahim. My father was an engineer. My first husband was an engineer too. He helped to build many of the streets of Kabul. He was a modern man and wished his daughter to study and know the world beyond Afghanistan."

The words spilled out of Soraya as though she wanted Amy to understand what had brought her to this place and point in time. "But Ibrahim, you must understand that for him it has been different. The mujahedeen destroyed the university before he could finish. Then came the Taliban. Ibrahim had to leave his studies to work. He was not able to earn the title of engineer though he has learned to do the work."

A title which here carried all the prestige of a PhD back home, an indicator of how highly their social scale rated the technological skills necessary to propel this country into the twenty-first century.

"And now Ibrahim is angry that even with my work here and Fatima's, we must again lose our place of residence."

"Again?" Amy was missing something in this account. "But why? Has something happened?"

"Happened?" Soraya stared at Amy as though her employer were the one not making sense. Then anger flashed in her magnificent eyes, burning away tears. Her hand flung wide to encompass the suite and beyond its walls. "*This* is what happened. The foreigners came here—and we of Kabul lost to you our homes."

"I'm not following you." Amy shook her head. "New Hope didn't take this place from anyone. We rented it."

"Yes, you rented it. And for how much?" Soraya didn't wait for an answer but went on impatiently. "My family was not wealthy, but they were educated, professional people. We lived in an apartment building where many professionals lived. The wealthiest then could rent a home in the Wazir for a few hundred dollars in your currency. Our apartment was perhaps fifty.

"Even under the Taliban we kept our homes. Then the foreigners came and began paying thousands of your dollars for any home with electricity and high walls and running water. So those who had rented here moved instead to our building. Our rent became five hundred dollars. We had to move to a few brick rooms with no electricity or sewer. Then those rents became three hundred dollars. We moved again to a mud house such as peasants inhabit far from the city center.

"And now there too the owner wishes to raise the rent to more than two hundred dollars. A teacher earns only fifty dollars. My husband earns little more. We have his mother and a widowed aunt to feed. Ibrahim wishes me to request an advance on my salary to pay the rent. He came with me today to ensure I obeyed. He doesn't understand that next month it will be the same. But where cheaper rents remain, there is not even running water or buses to come to work. My husband will no longer be able to reach his job. So you see why I must stay here even if I cannot see Fariq."

Soraya was wringing her hands again. "Please do not ask me to leave. I will work longer hours. If necessary, I will remain here Fridays."

The inadvertent consequences of even the best of intentions. If Amy had been frustrated at New Hope's ridiculous rental costs—many times what a similar facility would rent for in Kashmir or India—what had the expat real estate boom done to ordinary Kabulis? *Like a game of musical chairs until the bottom rung ends up on those dirt terraces up the mountain.*

"I am so sorry" was all Amy could say. "But how does Fatima get here every morning then? And your nephew Hamid?"

"A cousin lives not far. Fatima pays their board with her teaching, and Hamid attends school. At least for now."

Soraya's foreign-earned income paid for school bills and books and uniforms as well as food and rent and all the rest of the family's needs. And that was the flip side. The expat economy that skyrocketed rental values also pumped in much-needed income, at least to Kabulis with skills of value to Western employers. How did you explain the trickle-down economics of international aid to those on the bottom of the trickle-down? Amy could now forgive even Ibrahim's arrogant hostility. It had to be galling to watch his wife earn far more than he only because she could speak to the foreigners overrunning his country.

If Amy couldn't fix all the broken pieces of the international aid system, at least she could do something for this single piece dropped into her path. "I don't want to lose you or Fatima either. To be honest, I can't afford to lose either of you. And I think I have a solution for all of us. Why don't you bring your whole family here? The suite next to the office is still empty, and Fatima could have your current room. Call it a salary bonus for the two of you."

Amy's offer was a generous one even if she did need Soraya as much as Soraya needed the job. So she was taken aback when Soraya demanded, "For how long? My husband will not be pleased if he must move again soon."

"Well, I hadn't actually been thinking of a time limit." Amy studied her housemate. The cool glance, no longer tearful, that dropped quickly under Amy's gaze to her hands. The sullen droop of the full mouth and rigidity of posture.

Slowly, even reluctantly, Amy asked, "Why do I feel you are still angry with me? My offer was only a suggestion. You certainly don't need to feel obligated to say yes. But I need you to be honest with me. Have I offended you in some way?"

Soraya didn't look up immediately, the submission life had instilled warring with the strength of her emotions and personality. Then she raised her head proudly to look at Amy, and there was no mistaking the defiance. "I am not angry with you. You are a woman hired as I am to do a job in my country. You do the job well and are kinder to these women than required. But your superiors in America, how long will they wish to pay lodging and food for these women and their offspring? If I bring my family here, how do I know tomorrow you will not be gone and we will be again in the street? Is that not the way of your people?"

Soraya's shoulders hunched. "I think the Russians were better for us in Afghanistan than the Americans. At least they made no promises. They came in with their guns and helicopters and tanks, and they told us how it would be. If one did not protest their rule, at least there were books, schools for girls, jobs, no burqas. But the Americans—you gave us hope. You made promises, and we believed them. If the Russians could bring so much, how much more the Americans? There was to be a new world. Democracy. Freedom."

Soraya's lips twisted with contempt. "But it is always the same. I was translator for one of your literacy programs. The women were excited to read the Quran, to see if it truly says what their husbands and the mullahs say it does. But in three months the instructor took her pay and went back to America, though the women had not yet learned to read. Then I worked for a sewing institute. The women learned to make clothing and so feed their families. But after six months the sewing machines were carried away. The program was over, they said. So I have seen over and over. And all the money promised to our country to help—where has it gone? We see your houses and new cars and restaurants. What is left for us?"

The worst was that Soraya had hit the nail dead-on. There was no denying most aid projects were limited commitments, personnel even more so. Few aid workers were like Becky Frazer, staying long enough to learn the language and culture. A typical stint ran from a few weeks to a year at most, with Amy's current three-month contract at the top of the bell curve.

"I'm sorry, Soraya. I can sure understand how it would seem that way. And I know projects aren't always coordinated well. But it's better than nothing, isn't it?"

"Better than nothing? When we had nothing, we endured! To give hope and then snatch it away is not better than nothing. It is cruel. As to freedom, the mullahs and the warlords are still in charge. Women must still wear the burqa and be treated as property. And when the money runs out, will you not all leave to some other country where your services will again be paid? These women and their children—where will they go then? Or do you promise you at least will stay?" Soraya looked challengingly at Amy.

Amy felt weary. Somewhere in someone's wiser brain than hers was the perfect answer. But she had no idea what that might be. *Soraya is older, smarter, and better educated than I. She knows good and well that in a just world she'd be the one in charge here, not me. But even if maybe it shouldn't be, New Hope is my responsibility.*

"No, I can't promise that," Amy said quietly. "I certainly hope to be here awhile and that if I go, someone will take my place. But I can't promise that tomorrow a suicide bomb won't go off at our gate. Or that all foreigners won't be ordered out of your country. Only God knows what tomorrow holds, as your faith and mine teaches.

"What I can promise is that you and your family can use that suite as a refuge so you have time to look around for something better. And if something does happen to New Hope, I will do everything in my power to make sure you and your family are taken care of and the other women and children as well. That is my personal commitment—not New Hope's or my country's but mine."

Amy wasn't sure she even wanted to look at Soraya to see her reaction. But when she did, her housemate's expression had softened. Getting up from her chair, she came over and hugged Amy in the first expression of affection Amy had experienced from Soraya.

"You are a good person, Miss Ameera," she said, smiling. "I will go down now to inform my husband we have a wonderful new place to live."

46

"Don't be too optimistic," Jason Hamilton told Steve as they watched a blue gray uniform at a computer screen. "We've got a match between this bomb and those earlier fingerprints from that suicide vest. But unless the perp's in the system, that's not much. Those other prints never got a hit. And unless this guy was dumb enough to hang around his crime scene, he's not going to be in today's bunch."

The DynCorp manager had barely spoken when the Afghan police officer threw up his hands with voluble excitement. A printer spit out paper.

Jason shook his head as he handed it to Steve. "Unbelievable! Someone really is dumb."

Steve was staring at the readout, stunned. This was impossible. And yet the evidence was as incontrovertible as it was damning.

At least one mystery's solved.

Amy emerged from her bedroom to an empty apartment. Fatima must have accompanied Soraya down to look for Ibrahim. That her house-mate's deception involved nothing more than trying to protect family and husband was one good thing that had come out of this day. Maybe even a new understanding between Amy and the Afghan woman.

Now if the remaining mystery could be resolved, so that invasion force would leave and New Hope be restored to its tranquility. *I've still got to call Mr. Korallis to let him know what's happened. He's going to freak out. Especially since we'll end up paying repairs.*

Which, like the injuries, could be worse. In the office, Amy had found her laptop case knocked over under her desk, Soraya's keyboard dangling from its cord. But farther from the blast, Amy's quarters had been hardly touched, a few books off their shelf, pictures on the living room wall now crooked.

Amy stepped over cushions to straighten a framed photo of her family. Her parents' two-dimensional faces smiled at her, and Amy found herself fiercely envying Fatima, who could retreat to lay an aching head on her mother's shoulder, surrender herself to loving arms soothing and fussing away this day's grief and fear. A wave of homesickness swept over Amy such as she hadn't felt since blithely setting off on her first overseas adventure.

I'll go home for Christmas. Even if it's just for a few days. Even if New Hope hasn't found me a deputy yet. I need to go home.

Then Amy caught her reflection in the mirror above the TV. Electricity had been down since the explosion, so she'd done her best with a cold sponge bath and changed into fresh clothing. But the black eye Steve had pointed out was in full bloom, her forehead mottled purple and green above it. Amy's grimace hurt as she rubbed at a lingering rust streak along her jaw. *But not until that's improved or they'll never let me come back.*

"The mirror does not tell the truth, Ameera-jan."

Amy's spin was so hasty she knocked into the TV. She grabbed to keep it from falling to the floor. "Jamil, what are you doing here?"

Amy would never expect her assistant, like Soraya's husband, to step into her private quarters, and she found herself taking a step backward, snatching her scarf over her head with a haste that snagged at her bandage. She took another step back as Jamil closed the door behind him, not latching it but leaving no more than a slit to maintain propriety.

"Please. I did not mean to startle you." Something in his voice halted Amy in her tracks as Jamil crossed the living room. Setting a large sack on the table, he pulled out an antiseptic wipe and tore open the packaging.

Then he'd been to the bazaar. Amy had been so preoccupied with Soraya, she'd forgotten his earlier request. Her eye fell on the bundle she'd left just inside the door. Of course, he'd come to retrieve his belongings.

Amy stood stock-still as deft fingers dabbed the dried blood from her jaw. "There. Does it hurt? Did Miss Becky leave you medication for the pain?"

"I took ibuprofen." Amy's voice was shaky as he dropped his hand. "But I'm not sure it's kicked in because I feel like I've been run over by a truck." Her mouth crooked ruefully. "And despite your kind words, I'm afraid I look like it too."

"What you look is hurt. Here—please sit." Pulling a chair out for Amy, Jamil crouched on sandaled heels so that his head was tilted up to hers.

Amy suddenly realized what was missing in him. The diffidence and quiet aloofness of a subordinate. And her assistant hadn't called her by his usual punctilious Miss Ameera, but the familiar and affectionate Ameera-jan by which the children and women of New Hope addressed Amy.

"But hurts will heal, and you will never be less than beautiful, Ameera-jan, because your beauty is inside. A gentle and quiet spirit—is that not what your holy book calls beautiful? That is what I see when I look at you."

"I—thank you." Amy looked down at Jamil's uptilted face. He had bathed today, his beard freshly trimmed, dark curls under a cap shining with a health that hadn't been there when they'd first met. His hunkered-down posture held coiled tension, but the wide-spaced dark gaze was free of shadow as Amy had never seen it in these weeks, a tenderness that had been there when Jamil swabbed her cheek still curving his mouth. Had he any idea, Amy wondered with confusion, how much he looked like so many artists' renditions of the Isa Masih who interested him so?

She made a sudden movement to get up. "Let me get your pack. I brought it up because I was afraid someone might carry it off. And I owe you money for those supplies."

Jamil's hand went out to stop her. "No, please, don't move. I knew you would have brought my things here. But that is not why I came. I-I did not wish to leave without saying good-bye and thanking you for all you have done."

"Leave?" Amy repeated blankly. "To the bazaar again?"

"No, I am leaving New Hope—and Kabul. I . . . I should have gone before. But when I saw what had happened, I could not leave without being certain that you and the children and others would be well. Only now I must go quickly. I sought to speak with you before, to tell you this. But it has been difficult to encounter you alone."

Because Steve Wilson had turned up. And at the sound of his voice through the paneling, Amy remembered now, Jamil had turned the conversation to his bazaar trip. "But I don't understand. Why would you leave? If it's Steve, the American soldiers, the fingerprints—no, wait, you said you were planning to leave even before the explosion. Haven't you been happy working here?"

"I have been happier these weeks here than for as long as my memory can reach." The flat statement held reassuring conviction. "Than I ever thought to be again."

"Then why are you leaving?"

It had to be exhaustion that brought tears springing to Amy's eyes. Only now was Amy recognizing just how much she'd come to lean on Jamil's steady, quiet, uncomplaining support. No, not just his support. Somewhere in these last weeks of working companionably side by side, Amy had come to think of the man before her not as a hireling unexpectedly competent to help her make a success of her project but as a friend.

A friend such as Amy had once envisioned—perhaps because she'd been so lonely, and they shared a citizenship and culture, and the security contractor had been kind in his own brusque fashion—that Steve Wilson might be. Amy's hand across her eyes was not only to press away the weariness. "I . . . I don't want to see you go. I don't know what I'd do without you, especially after today. This job is too big for me. If it isn't the fingerprints, is it finances? Would a raise help? You've earned it a hundred times over. Just tell me what it would take to make you stay."

"Oh, Ameera-jan." Jamil's rare smile lit thin features to sweetness. "Do you not think I would stay if I could? that my heart cries out to say yes? But you do not truly need me anymore. You have Rasheed and Wajid and Soraya and Fatima and little Farah. And you no longer need my voice to speak for you to my people."

Amy could hear his determination as clearly as the regret. "And it is for your well-being and the others too that I must go. There are things I have not been free to tell you. Things that may perhaps cause you to think ill of me. I pray only when I am gone that you will believe, whatever others may say, I would do nothing to cause harm to you nor anyone under your charge."

"Going somewhere?"

There'd been no warning of Steve entering the living room, the apartment door hitting the wall behind it with enough force to send a chip of plaster flying. A hard gaze swept the apartment, and Amy took in with disbelief the pistol in the security contractor's hand. Only this time it was not aimed toward the sky.

Behind him, blue gray uniforms poured into the room, weapons unslung and aimed.

Jamil had not so much as straightened up from his stooped position, but Amy was on her feet, taking an indignant step past her assistant. "Steve Wilson, what do you think you're doing?"

Instead of lowering his weapon, Steve snaked out a free arm and yanked Amy to his side. "On your feet, Jamil!"

The soft, hard command was as deadly as the Glock in the security contractor's hand, his other arm a barrier of steel holding Amy back. Jamil straightened slowly, hands in the air.

"Now lose the blanket."

The patu slid to the floor. Ian moved forward to run his hands over the prisoner.

"I am not armed," Jamil told him quietly.

"Excuse me if I don't take your word for it." Ian gingerly nudged Jamil's pack out of reach with his boot, then looked over at Steve. "All clear."

Amy found voice again. "Why are you doing this? How dare you come barging into my apartment!"

Steve didn't look at Amy. The narrowed eyes he'd fastened on Jamil were two chips of gray steel. "Your pal here knows why. Oh yes, we've already processed those fingerprints. Maybe you've never heard of a database scanner, or I'm betting you'd have hit the road by now. Downstairs with the others!"

A police uniform yanked Jamil's hands behind his back and twisted nylon flexicuffs around them. Amy stepped out of the way as gun barrels prodded him to the door. But now Steve had turned those steel-gray chips on Amy, his hard mouth twisting. "Oh no, this time you're coming too."

Ian straightened up from Jamil's pack. "Nothing here, boss, but personal items and a few books."

"Leave it." Steve's grip on Amy's elbow was no longer supportive but a shackle as he propelled her down the stairwell.

When Amy entered the schoolroom, she could see it had now become a tribunal. Like judges, an older, blond expat contractor and an Afghan police officer sat behind Fatima's desk near the rear wall. The blond contractor was one who'd arrived with the Afghan police force. Jason, Steve had called the man. Around the room, expat contractors and police uniforms held unslung weapons. Amy was relieved to see Steve's friend Phil among them, but the medic didn't return her uncertain smile, his expression holding cold disbelief as he stared at the man he'd worked beside all afternoon.

As Steve forcibly propelled Amy to an empty chair, she saw more uniforms ushering in Rasheed and Soraya's husband, Ibrahim. Amy noticed her housemate out in the hallway, proud features frantic. The two men were also bound with flexicuffs, and unlike Jamil, who'd withdrawn to that invisibility with which Amy had become so familiar, they both appeared furious. This time Amy took one look at Steve's unyielding face and made no protest.

After Steve took his place with the other two "judges," the Afghan officer turned to Ibrahim. "You were arrested in a forbidden place, and other residents testify that your tale of visiting family is a lie. You will tell the truth here or at Pul-e-Charki."

Catching the tears pouring down Soraya's cheeks, Amy jumped to her feet. "He was not in a forbidden place. He is the husband of my assistant, and their living quarters are upstairs."

The Afghan officer looked surprised at the intrusion of a foreign woman.

Steve turned a cool gaze on Amy. "For real, or is this another of your rescue bids?"

"No, Ibrahim is just moving in. That's why Rasheed and the others don't know him yet."

Steve murmured into the Afghan officer's ear, and the police uniforms cut Ibrahim loose.

As he hurried out to Soraya, Jason picked up a sheet of notes and turned to Rasheed. Amy's hands twisted in her lap. Had her earlier fears about the chowkidar turned into reality? "A week ago you offered certain delinquents hospitality. An employee working on their truck overheard you agreeing to absent yourself for the night, giving them opportunity to break in. He also says money changed hands. Is there any reason we shouldn't hold you responsible as well for today's assault?"

To Amy's astonishment, Rasheed's defiant expression immediately crumpled. "It is true. I am responsible for the bombing. I am deeply ashamed. Allah will judge me."

Steve leaned forward to demand in sharp Dari, "Wait, are you saying you put the bomb in the storeroom? Or took money to let someone else in?"

"Nay! Nay!" Rasheed shook his head. "But I allowed my brothers in the faith to retrieve their wayward woman. They swore an oath to Allah none would be harmed, that they wished only their lawful rights in which the foreigner had interfered. I never thought they could do such evil as this—hurting children and women under my protection. Nor, as Allah is my witness, do I know how they gained entrance this time. Perhaps they paid another. But the guilt is mine for ever permitting these evil men into this place."

Rasheed's fierce gaze was actually pleading as he looked at Amy. She found herself believing him. The same strict code of a devout Muslim that had forced Amy into a burqa and found merit in handing over a runaway female had left Rasheed devastated over betraying his duty as host and protector to Amy and her charges. It hadn't been anger eating at Rasheed all day but shame and remorse.

"He's telling the truth," Steve said. "He may be a jerk, but he's no killer." That last had switched to English as he looked at Rasheed sternly. "And you weren't responsible for the bomb getting in, which doesn't let you off the hook. We'll deal with you later."

Rasheed looked more reprieved than worried as he hurried out. Now only Jamil's straight, bound figure was left in the center of the room, a resigned expression giving away none of the discomfort those flexicuffs digging into his wrists must be causing. Like Jesus standing before his accusers was an inevitable parallel.

Which made Steve Wilson a furious, stony-faced Pilate or Herod. Amy's mind was still reeling at the security contractor's unbelievable actions. Had Jamil been right in his apprehension about the former American soldier? Should she tell Steve how Jamil had earlier saved the compound, that his behavior toward her assistant was as intolerable and unwarranted as toward the other two men just released?

But Steve had already turned to their final captive, and his hard tone became glacial. "You see, we already know who planted that bomb, don't we, Jamil? If that's really your name."

Amy was on her feet again, and the pain throbbing at her temples and catching in her chest no longer physical. "What are you saying?"

"What I'm saying is that your pal here is our bomber." Amy could not tell whether Steve's biting contempt was for her or Jamil.

"No, it isn't true." Amy's denial came in a whisper even as a horrible realization gripped her stomach as she took in Jamil's expression. Defiance, sadness, even relief were there.

"He is telling the truth, Ameera-jan. I am the bomber you seek."

47

What tip-off did I miss?

The disgust knotting Steve's stomach was as much at himself as the man standing across the room, a calm resignation on his face Steve itched to wipe off. From the beginning, he'd had misgivings about this man, even as honesty compelled him to recognize they were founded on no more than Jamil's own antipathy toward himself. If nothing else, Steve could have sworn the man's emotional attachment would never permit him to bring Amy harm.

That the bomber he'd been pursuing all these weeks had been living and working with Amy and her charges, that he'd narrowly missed killing or maiming any number of them, a flashback of Amy pallid and not breathing on the ground, sent a wave of cold fury over Steve that burned away the self-disgust.

Or was it the softness in Amy's face when Steve had burst into the living room, the frantic horror there now, that was responsible for both his fury and disgust?

"I have nothing more to hide."

Brave words. Except if Jamil knew his fingerprints might come up in the system, he was less acquainted with how quickly American technology could process them, or he'd have skipped that bazaar run Steve had considerately arranged with two Guats before leaving with Jason. Though how he hoped to get past Steve's guards if he'd planned to skip town as he'd told Amy was hard to fathom.

Which just showed Steve was losing his touch. What else had he missed? Well, that he was about to find out.

"We've got you cold with fingerprints on two bombs. So just tell us who you really are and who you are working for. Al-Qaeda? Taliban?" Steve could have made his demand in Dari, but he did so in English, in part because those uniformed grunts crowding around didn't need to hear this interrogation but mostly to put the prisoner on Steve's turf and not his own. "And where were you earlier this morning? Trying to get through security at the new Counternarcotics Justice Center, maybe?"

"Boss." A flurry in the hallway was Ian. He walked in with a bundle. "You said to check the perp's quarters and any vehicles he's been driving. The quarters were clean—nothing but a tushak, not even personal gear. But one of the mechanics was happy to point out a Corolla. These were stuffed inside the lining of the backseat."

Ian held out an Afghan counternarcotics police uniform, a light brown wig, and an ID badge.

"Wait a minute." Jason leaned forward, his gaze shifting from wig and uniform to Jamil's face. "I've seen this guy. He didn't try to get through security. He was inside. Right near Waters and Khalid in the loya jirga."

But Steve too had now put the pieces together. This was what he'd missed. The nagging familiarity of that guard, that uneasy disquiet he'd dismissed, the light hair and green eyes under that deliberately tilted cap were all wrong. Disposable contacts, he'd hazard now.

Steve had glimpsed Jamil only a handful of times before today, always fleeting or at a distance. Which Steve knew now was not because of Jamil's distaste for a former American soldier—or even any perceived relationship between Steve and his employer. Amy's assistant had known whom Steve protected, and he'd feared recognition.

And that too must be how he'd planned to slip out of this compound. In the uniform of the very police trainees now on guard, he'd receive no more than a second thought.

"There's more. A second bomb. Or another Army surplus parka we're assuming is a bomb. I've sealed off the vehicle and called for the K-9s."

"You don't need to worry. The dogs didn't even whimper." Roald had also formed part of the emergency response team. Steve stiffened as he walked in with a thick camouflage coat. But as the German held it up, he could see the lining slit open. Inside was not C-4 but Play-Doh.

The wounded look in Amy's eyes told him she too had recognized what must have been part of those Eid gifts.

"Take it away and process it." Steve leaned across the table, his body language growing menacing. "So why the toy? And why here and not the loya jirga? You couldn't get the bomb through, so you figured you'd just blow up a few innocent civilians who've been kind enough to offer you a roof and employment? You'd have succeeded too if you hadn't left us a nice forensic trail. A little careless, wouldn't you say?"

"Perhaps. But you see, I did not expect to live so that I should care."

A fresh commotion in the hallway drowned out further speech. The loud demand was in Dari and only too recognizable. "I do not care about your orders! I am minister of interior, and this is my property. If you do not remove yourself from my path, my bodyguards will shoot. Willie!"

Steve stood just as Khalid burst into the schoolroom, Ismail at his heels and CS detail tight around him. "What is the meaning of all this, Willie? I was told you have grave news for me, that you have found the man who has been trying to kill me."

The minister's agent-in-charge responded to Steve's glance. "McDuff passed on the good news. We made a beeline here right after the bon-fire."

Khalid stared at the silent, immobile figure standing alone in the center of the room. Steve couldn't quite make out the expression that flitted across the minister's bearded face. Fury? Triumph?

"Do you know this man, Minister?"

"He is not familiar, but my enemies have access to many hirelings." Khalid moved majestically farther into the room. "What I wish to know is what he is doing on these grounds and why he has destroyed my property."

"That we're about to find out," Steve said grimly. "Minister, would you like to take over the interrogation?"

"No, I wish to hear what he has to say to your questions. But this is not discreet. If this is the man, as Ismail informs me, who has been trying to kill me these many months, I wish to hear what he has to say without so many listening ears." Khalid gestured to the uniforms around the walls. "How can we know if one of these is not a spy who will carry tales back to his employers?"

Which explained why Khalid was speaking laborious English instead of Dari. Ismail murmured to the Afghan force commander. At his curt order, the uniforms around the wall followed the officer out of the room. As Ismail dragged the vacated chair to a less cramped viewing angle for Khalid, Steve's own orders left only Phil and Ian at the prisoner's back, Rick on agent-in-charge duty behind his principal, Ismail glaring at the prisoner from the broken doorway.

And Amy.

As Steve's frown moved pointedly to her, Amy raised her chin. "I'm not leaving. This is my property—at least I pay the rent for this—and Jamil is my employee. You're going to have to pick me up and carry me out of here if you want me to leave."

Khalid raised a hand. "So this is the American woman who has abused my charity to bring such distasteful residents onto my property. No, no, the Americans have different ways, and I owe them much."

Under the minister's knowing glance, Steve gritted his teeth.

"I am understanding now, Willie, why Ismail tells me you have interested yourself in the defense of this property. Let the woman stay. If it is true she employs this delinquent, he may be more cooperative in her presence. Let us find out who this man is and how he is so incompetent I remain alive." There was raw contempt in Khalid's tone.

Steve picked up where he'd left off, throwing the questions hard and fast like hammer blows. "So you did come to Kabul to target Khalid. Who paid you? How did you get ID to get on the grounds? And the bomb? It was remote control. Were you carrying the detonator or someone else? And why, when you couldn't get the bomb past security, did you come here instead?"

But his prisoner did not so much as glance at Steve, and when he took a step forward that raised every weapon in the room, it was toward Khalid. "Incompetent! Do you think you are alive because I could not kill you, Khalid Sayef? Do you not know who I am? Jamil, son of Asad. If you do not recognize me now, you knew me well the day you killed my father and brothers on these very grounds. The day you stole my family's home from under my feet. The day you lied to the Americans that I was a terrorist so that they shut me away in their prison."

Jamil shifted to the two American contractors behind the desk. "Yes, I did come here to kill Khalid. As was my right and my blood duty. And if he is not dead, it is not that I was incapable of my mission. I was indeed inside your defenses today—as I was once before.

"Oh yes," he added as Jason Hamilton straightened suddenly. "I saw you on the rooftop that night—all of you." A hand indicated the CS contractors, Khalid's deputy by the door, the dark eyes moving to Steve for the first time. "As I saw you this morning and feared you might know me."

No wonder he'd been fooled. Steve would not have recognized that passionate, defiant, confident voice as belonging to Amy's sullen assistant or even the silent, immobile captive his men had ushered into this room. As he'd have never recognized in this man the angry adolescent with grief twisting his face and murder in his eyes Steve and Phil had walked away from that long-ago day the Northern Alliance and American forces had rolled triumphantly into Kabul.

Phil's disbelieving glance told Steve he too held memory of that day. Did Jamil recognize his two American captors? He'd given no indication, and they had looked very different in muj clothing and long hair and beard, that entire encounter a matter of minutes. Had perhaps some subconscious recall contributed to the Afghan's immediate antipathy toward Steve?

And Khalid? Had he ever believed Jamil was a Taliban insurgent—or had he just wanted this house? And the note Steve had written in an impulse of compassion, by ironic coincidence in a New Testament Ms. Mallory had mailed him, designed to avert precisely what Jamil accused—where had that gone? Though Steve had avoided looking directly at Amy, he was conscious of every movement in that slight frame, the hands twisting in her lap, the stunned horror in her eyes.

"Do you know what this man's talking about, Minister?" Jason Hamilton addressed Khalid. "Do you recognize him now?"

The minister's narrowed gaze hadn't left Jamil's face. "There was war. Many people died. But if the name he shouts is truly his own, then he is an insurgent we captured on these very grounds. You remember, Willie. And if he is of the family who once occupied this place, they were collaborators of the Taliban, whom all know dwelled here when we freed this city. Which is why this property like others was taken from such traitors and given to those who fought the enemy."

"That is a lie!" An M4 barred Jamil's way as he took another step forward. "My father was a doctor, a surgeon. He treated all who required his services without distinction. This man, Khalid Sayef—" the name spat out like a curse—"was then a supplier of foreign goods to my father. Above all, the morphine and other medicines that could not be obtained in the city. I remember well his visits to this house when I was a child."

In other words, Khalid had been a smuggler. Steve had no doubt now Jamil had the right guy. He could personally testify the muj commander knew every contraband trail in the Hindu Kush like the back of his hand. Though that was less a crime in these parts than honorable business tradition.

"When the mujahedeen turned against this city, my father took our family to find refuge in Pakistan. But our chowkidar remained to safeguard our home. Yes, the mujahedeen seized it and the Taliban after them. By then I was a medical student in Islamabad. But when the chowkidar sent word that the Americans were bringing freedom at last, my father declared we would return to Kabul. So I obeyed my father and left my studies to join them here. Only when I arrived, it was not freedom I found but death. My father and brothers killed by the mujahedeen who claimed to be our liberators. And standing over their bodies in my home to claim it as his own, the man who once served my father, Khalid Sayef."

Jason Hamilton sneered. "That's quite a story. And right out of the al-Qaeda manual. Blame your captors. Blame the Americans. Except if you were arrested as an enemy combatant, why aren't you in Gitmo? And why wait all these years to go after Khalid?"

Jamil drew himself to his full height. "If I did not kill him before, it was because I was a prisoner. First by you Americans at Bagram. Like you, they believed Khalid and said al-Qaeda taught their warriors to lie so. And since my possessions had been taken away, I had no papers to prove otherwise. They would not even listen when I begged them to find out if my mother and sister had survived that day. They only laughed and told me I was a good liar."

Then that note hadn't reached its destination. Steve made no effort to take the reins of the interrogation back from Hamilton. He was having a hard enough time keeping emotion from his face. Khalid, on the other hand, was surprisingly quiet for someone accused of murder and worse, a bored interest the only expression Steve could read.

"When the Americans grew tired of receiving the same answers to the same questions, I thought I would be freed like so many others. Instead I was taken to another prison. I did not know it was near Khalid's home in Baghlan until I was released. But I soon came to consider the American prison a paradise. Until in time I no longer wished to live long enough to obtain vengeance but to die."

Jamil hadn't looked at Khalid since that first accusation, and he didn't do so now, but his tone had thickened with bitterness and revulsion. "Then one day not many months ago, I saw Khalid walk through the prison. I called out his name. I pleaded with him to tell me what had happened to my mother and sister. I screamed after him that he was a liar and murderer and thief. That he would not escape Allah's avenging justice if I had to come back from death itself to exact it. But he only walked away, and I saw that he had truly forgotten me. That while his face had consumed my every waking thought, I was so little to him, he did not care enough to know whether I had lived or died."

Ameera believed him, Jamil could see in her face. Though he was addressing the American mercenaries, to make Ameera understand, to wipe away the horror and disbelief that had greeted his arrest, was what mattered most to him.

But now to his dismay, Jamil saw Ameera was crying, silent tears he knew to be not for herself but for him. So he thrust down the terrible details he'd allowed to surface to his voice. Details too horror-laden and shameful to be relived. The beatings and brutality of the prison guards.

The metal transport containers where a dozen or more prisoners were squeezed to freeze in winter and bake in summer. The food, vile and unclean and never enough. The lack of water to make ablutions or even for basic hygiene so that it was no wonder the guards chose not to enter the stench of the prison quarters. The two years Jamil had spent in shackles until at last he was considered too broken to cause further trouble.

And worse things. The punishment for being young and good of appearance and undiseased in that hell, so that he'd wanted to die, even as he dreaded death because he'd known beyond any shadow of hope that he was irredeemably soiled now in the eyes of Allah. That not all the rakats and ablutions and meritorious deeds of a lifetime would suffice to balance again the scales of divine justice.

But though so many others had died of the guards' beatings or violence at the hands of their peers or lack of medical care, perhaps also because he'd been young and strong and healthy, Jamil had survived. And in so doing, he'd passed beyond despair to endurance and determination. And above all, hate.

Then had come the miracle.

Conscious of watchful eyes, Amy wiped her scarf across her eyes, then wound it as Farah or Roya might over her face. No wonder Jamil hadn't wanted to speak of his family, had closed up at any mention of his mother or the young sister of whom Farah had reminded him.

Amy couldn't tell if Steve and Phil believed his story. But the older blond contractor's skepticism was patent. "A heart-wringer story and nicely rehearsed. Minister, does this prison incident ring a bell?"

"There was a madman when I went to interrogate an opium merchant," Khalid said calmly. "He knew my name and began screaming curses down on me. I paid little heed. It is possible this is the prisoner involved. What I wish to know is why he is no longer in chains and how he found his way to my presence."

"Yes, let's cut to the chase," Jason said. "We're not here for your excuses.

Just how you managed to plant two bombs under our noses. And don't think you can lie to us."

"I am telling the truth. *I* have nothing more to hide." Jamil glanced at the two Afghans in the room. "That very night I saw Khalid, a man came to me. He asked if I meant it that I would give my life to destroy Khalid. He told me if my commitment was true, he could help me achieve a martyrdom that would not only destroy my enemy but strike such a blow for Allah that paradise would be assured. He swore his people would find my mother and sister and grant to them the allowance given to the families of martyrs."

"And who was this man? Who was behind this mission?"

Jamil glanced again at the two Afghans before he shrugged. "The man came at night and kept his face covered so I would not see it. But I was given money to travel and papers for the chowkidar of this property that said I was the son of distant relatives who died in the fighting. Its truth was not questioned."

Amy let out a breath in relief. So at least Rasheed had not been in on this deception.

"I was given instructions to a meeting place high in a ruined building where I found all I needed. A cell phone to receive orders. Materials and instructions to make a suicide vest."

"The one we found at the ministry building." Steve broke his silence. "But how did you get in? We checked every entrance."

"I wore the uniform of the police. I was told a side door would be open, a truck making deliveries. As instructed, I lifted boxes from the truck to carry them in. No one asked questions."

Amy saw the disbelief in the glance that Steve and his companion exchanged before Jason said, "But you never carried out that mission. You could have blown up Khalid's chopper, wiped out his entire party. So what went wrong? Someone else yanking your chain, or did you just chicken out?" He was deliberately trying to provoke his prisoner, his tone thick with contempt.

But Jamil's shake of the head showed bewilderment. "Yes, I . . . I should have achieved shaheed that night. I was prepared to make the sacrifice. I built the bomb as I was told. I pressed the detonator. I thought I would be then in paradise. But I did not die. Then I was told to leave the bomb behind as a warning. That the mission had been changed to a new target, a bigger one."

"The loya jirga," the blond contractor said. "And that's what makes you a liar. If we buy your story, you might try to justify going after the guy you blame for taking out your family. But how do you justify going after an entire assembly of innocent people who've never done a thing against you?"

"Innocent!" Jamil's eyes blazed. "Those I saw this day in your loya jirga, the men who now call themselves governors and ministers and commanders—you call them innocent? Are they not the very muj commanders who laid waste to my country? They are worse than infidels because they claim to speak for Allah even as they break his laws. The Quran itself teaches that such deserve to die. No, I felt no pity for them when I received new instructions and built the new bomb."

"And Waters and his team? Are you trying to tell me the arrival of the American drug czar had nothing to do with this? After all, if your mission was to take out crooked Afghan politicians, there've been plenty of other opportunities—and with a whole lot less security restrictions."

Jamil looked surprised. "But of course the American visit was necessary to the mission. How else could martyrdom's reward be assured if there was not the death of infidels?"

"Wait, are you telling me you targeted American citizens just to make sure you had an in to paradise?" Jason shot out of his chair. "In case Allah didn't quite consider assassinating your own government leaders meritorious enough to earn seventy virgins and all the rest?"

Steve's hand on his companion's arm brought him back into his seat, a sharp gesture waving down weapons that had come up. But his demand was no less harsh. "You still haven't explained why, if you were actually in place at the loya jirga, you're standing here breathing, and there's a hole in this house. Why go after this place? Did you think because your employer was also an American and an infidel, you'd get points for taking her out? And if you had the bomb there, what went off here?"

"That was a mistake." For the first time Jamil's gaze met Amy's directly, and in them she saw deep sadness and regret. "I—the bomb I carried into the loya jirga was not the real one but that." He pointed to the sliced-open parka lying across a chair, its Play-Doh lining visible. "I had to carry out my instructions lest those who sent me make new plans. So I made a duplicate that looked and felt the same. I had Wajid's keys, so I hid the bomb where it would not be found, that I might find a way later to dispose of it.

"Even when I learned that I was not to be given the code to detonate the instrument of shaheed myself, I did not think there was danger because the bomb was many miles away. But while I waited in the loya jirga, my phone received a message from Rasheed that there had been an explosion. I knew then what must have happened. So though Khalid was not yet in place, I left my post to rush here, praying that none had been killed. And my prayers were answered. But—" Jamil glanced at Amy again—"I am so sorry for the trouble it has caused, the injuries. I did not intend that any should be hurt."

"I don't know what's harder to believe. That you waltzed a bomb through our security—a fake one at that—or that you didn't realize a detonator connected to a cell phone could be set off anywhere phone service could reach," Jason said. "And yet you had no problem building the thing."

"I am good at following instructions," Jamil said simply. "That was not included."

"Which brings us to the big question." The blond contractor's tone was even more sarcastic. "Why the charade? Why the change of heart? The target wasn't big enough? You decided dying just wasn't worth it? Or you had some epiphany that Khalid and his pals weren't such bad guys after all?"

Jamil didn't answer immediately. Every eye was on him, every breath, so it seemed to Amy, held like her own in anticipation.

Then with absolute simplicity and conviction, Jamil said, "It is none of those things. Only that it was not in my heart any longer to kill."

48

Steve was silent. Everything he'd just heard, even those parts he himself could testify to be true, gave motive for killing, not a change of heart. And yet he found himself believing Jamil. He could even make a good stab at just what would bring about such a drastic reversal. Not that it was any excuse or mitigation.

As Jason beside him was making his business to point out. "You think that's good enough? That you can somehow wash your hands of this because you chickened out of your mission—and didn't mean all the damage you've caused to this place? Sure, no one died here today. But what about other attempts? What about that sugar factory bombing? We know that was an attack on the minister and his predecessor too. And unlike today and that little roof episode, a lot of people died."

Jamil looked more confused than guilty. "I do not know of what you speak. Every week this country endures bombings. But I was in prison until the day I traveled to Kabul. As Khalid can testify, should he choose. The fingerprints you have taken are enough to confirm I was released no more than two days before I arrived here."

"In this at least he tells the truth." The minister of interior spread his hands. "I remember the day I saw this man in the prison. It was just before you yourself arrived, Willie."

But Jason wasn't letting up. "Then you know who pushed the button, because I'm betting it was the same people who put you up to this. Who were they? Are they still planning on going on without you?"

Jamil shook his head in silent confusion.

Jason slapped his hands down hard on the desk. "Fine, I think we're about done here, don't you, Steve? I'm sure they'll get more out of him at Pul-e-Charki than we are. Minister, what authorities need to be notified here?"

Khalid's intent gaze didn't leave the prisoner's face. "None. Let him go."

Even Jamil looked stunned at the pronouncement.

"Let him go? Minister, you can't possibly be thinking—"

Khalid's majestic gesture cut off Jason's protest. "As the man said, he did not kill anyone. He has already paid for earlier crimes. And this house is my own. If I do not hold the damages against him, who should? Shall we not celebrate a shaheed who chooses life over death? It was against me he did this, and I will forgive—so long as he leaves this city immediately and does not return."

At the snap of Khalid's fingers, Ismail pulled out a knife and sliced the flexicuffs from Jamil's wrists.

Jason muttered to Steve, "This guy tried to take out Waters and an entire congressional delegation. Who cares about some last-minute conscience attack? The embassy's going to have a fit if we let him walk."

Steve's own emotions were conflicted as he murmured back, "I don't know what we can do. Khalid's the only government authority in this room. You talk about causing an international incident, try telling the Afghan minister of interior who he should or shouldn't arrest in his own country."

Now that they'd disposed of the prisoner's future, Khalid and his deputy showed no further interest but were whispering, heads close together.

With a resigned shrug, Steve nodded to his men. "You heard the minister. Let the perp go. Ian, Phil, if you'd walk him past the guards."

As Jamil took an uncertain step, Steve got suddenly to his feet. "No, never mind, I'm going to make sure this one gets off the property without doing any more damage."

"Wait!" Amy stepped quickly into their path as Steve's M4 motioned Jamil toward the broken doors into the hall. "Aren't you going to let Jamil get his belongings? They're upstairs. You can't just throw him out without clothes or money for food."

She'd let her scarf drop so Steve could see signs of tears, eyes stormy as they looked pointedly at the weapon covering her assistant.

Steve's jaw tightened. "Personally, it's against my better judgment he's walking off this property at all. But since I want him out of this city, sure, he can take any belongings and money that will hurry things along."

A glance detached Ian and Phil from the background to fall in behind the prisoner as Steve pointed Amy ahead of him up the stairwell. A police uniform still guarded the apartment door. Steve held Amy back as he opened the door. Stepping into the living room, he looked into both bedrooms before nodding an all clear.

Amy hadn't yet so much as glanced at Jamil. Now as she stepped ahead of Ian and Phil and their prisoner into her quarters, she turned to Steve. "Please, I need to speak to Jamil for a few minutes. To say good-bye."

Steve's mouth twisted sardonically. "Who's stopping you?"

"Alone, please!"

At first Amy was sure Steve was going to deny her request. The line of his mouth was hard and bitter, his eyes as cold as ice. Then his head lifted, that cold survey panning the apartment again as though looking for anything that could be turned into a weapon.

"Fine, you've got fifteen minutes." His gaze rested on Jamil. "And no locking the door, or I'll kick it in."

The door closed behind the three contractors, leaving Amy alone with Jamil. She immediately scooped his scattered belongings back into the patu. "Here are your things, and I'll give you your next salary so you'll have afghanis for the road. And here, you should take some of these first aid supplies you brought." To Amy's dismay, her eyes filled up again with tears.

Jamil was at her side. "Please do not cry. You cannot believe I would hurt you."

"Hurt me!" The chair Jamil had pulled out for her earlier was still on the rug by his bundle, and suddenly dizzy with grief and confusion, Amy groped for it and sat down. "Jamil, you don't have to explain anymore. I know with all my heart you were telling the truth, that you'd never do anything to deliberately hurt the children or me. It was an accident, and everyone's going to be okay. And I understand now why you felt you had to leave before Steve—anyone—found out who you were. But you!"

She made a helpless gesture, the tears she'd striven to hold back spilling down her cheeks. "You're the one who has been hurt so badly. Your family and home, your mother and little sister, all those terrible years stolen from you. Like Farah and Aryana and Najeeda and so many others. There's just so much pain, and I am so angry this world should have to hold such terrible things for all of you. I-I even understand why you'd want to repay Khalid and others who are responsible, though I'm so glad you chose not to."

Amy mopped her face with a sleeve. "I just wish there was something, anything, I could do to change it all, to make things different. But it's just too big and—and too broken."

"Oh, Ameera-jan!" Jamil knelt in front of Amy, his expression alive. "Do you not know how much you have done? I was trying to tell you before. I came here with such hate in my heart. And you . . . you taught me to love." Jamil raised a hand at Amy's sudden movement. "Please, I must say before I go what has been building in my heart for so long."

But despite his words, Jamil was silent for a moment. Then slowly, as though explaining to himself as well as Amy, he said, "You must understand. Since my earliest memory, I have been taught what I must do— what my people must do—to please Allah. The five pillars of my faith. The practices of the prophet. The fasts and holy days. And I have never understood why, no matter how closely my people followed such commands, were made to follow them by the Taliban and mullahs, my country remained filled with violence and corruption and cruelty, one man to another.

"Then after the Soviets, we could not even point the finger of blame to others. Because it was no longer foreigners raining down evil and violence on Afghanistan but ourselves. I have never wanted anything more than to bring freedom and peace and righteousness to my people. It was not just for my mother, my sister, nor even to take vengeance for the death of my father and brothers that I consented to this mission. I believed it when I was told that the mission of shaheed—of martyrdom—that I was given would destroy many powerful and evil rulers and so give my people a chance to obtain more righteous leaders and with them freedom.

"So when I came here to New Hope, I came already dead, so focused on the mission I could not see life around me. I did not want to see. And then the mission was changed, so that I still lived. And I came to know you."

His eyes were alight again with that blaze of emotion Steve had interrupted what seemed a lifetime ago. They were also uncomfortably close, but Amy did not draw away, could not even breathe.

"I know that for such as I to love you—as a man loves a woman like in the Hindi movies—that is not possible for more reasons than there are stars in the sky. I have not let myself ever dwell on such a thing. But I did not know there could be other love. Love that will not allow hate to endure. I did not know, because my people's ways do not permit it, that friendship could be between a man and woman that is a meeting of two hearts, two souls."

He was blinking rapidly now. "And I did not know a foreigner, an infidel such as the mullahs have always told us to fear and hate, could show such love to those not of her family, her tribe, her people, even her own faith. Love as I have watched you bestow on these children, these women. I did not understand it until I read your book."

Suddenly busy in his pack, Jamil held up the well-worn, olive-hued volume that was the first Amy had given him. "I . . . I must tell you I was at first very angry that you gave me this book."

"Because it was Christian?"

"No, because it was not the first like it I had seen. A foreign fighter with the mujahedeen who destroyed my home carried such a book. He promised I would not be hurt, and he wrote in the book a message he said would ensure my story was heard and believed. Khalid took it away, so that I could not give it to my captors."

Jamil hesitated before going on. "I did not then hate the Americans. My father had always told me good things of them. When I learned of the lies Khalid had told my captors, I had hope the American would return and keep his promise to tell them I was not a Taliban. But he never returned.

And so I knew my father's dreams and hopes held no merit. I came to believe the Americans were no more to be trusted in their promises to bring freedom to my people than the mujahedeen or the Taliban."

"You're saying someone gave you an Army-edition New Testament? There were thousands mailed out to troops during the war. I mailed some myself." Amy straightened up, her eyes wide, at his story. "Did you ever find out who the American was? Would you recognize him if you saw him again?"

Jamil shrugged. "He looked like a mujahedeen. I knew him to be foreign only when he spoke. And my heart and my eyes were on Khalid alone. It does not matter now. Except that I was angry at first you would give me such a book. And then I was angry because of what the book said.

"But as I continued to read, I grew confused. To forgive one's enemies instead of hating. To love all men, not just your family and tribe. To treat others as you would be treated. To work hard and share instead of stealing. To help the poor and widowed and orphans, not to earn merit with Allah but out of love. To return good for evil. These teachings of Isa Masih seemed good teachings. Teachings that could change my people, my country, as not all the fighting nor the mullahs' traditions nor even the shaheeds have ever done."

Jamil shook his head as he went on. "But then I was even more confused because I had witnessed the foreigners who are called Christian indulging in the alcohol and undress and other immorality your television and movies show us. So I believed either you or your book lied. Then you told me it was those alone who followed Isa Masih's teachings who were his disciples and that only by reading the prophet's words could I know what truly is Christian.

"So I began to read again. And I saw that the way you lived, the way you loved the children and women of New Hope—this was what Isa Masih spoke of, what it meant to be his disciple. And my heart cried out to know this love and forgiveness for myself, even as my head instructed me to remain focused on my mission and the hate and vengeance that would give me strength to carry it out."

Jamil's expression darkened fleetingly. "Then I read the words of your Isa Masih: 'You will know the truth, and the truth will set you free.' But the very night I taped my shaheed testimony and prepared the new bomb, I learned that those who recruited me had lied. They had sworn by Allah's own name to find and care for my mother and sister, but it was only a trick. If they could lie about such a sacred trust, what other lies had they told?

"It was as though a woman's burqa had been ripped from my eyes, and I was no longer confused. The truth that could bring freedom was not their words but those of Isa Masih. And even to assure paradise for myself, I knew I could not kill others. I do not believe any longer that it is Allah's will for men to kill to attain paradise. I knew then what I was called to do. But first, I had to rid myself of the bomb. I borrowed from the Eid gifts to make a copy so those watching me would not know I had changed my mind."

Anguish was back in his eyes. "You know the rest. I . . . I thought I had killed you and the others when I saw the smoke rising above the walls."

"You didn't," Amy reassured quickly. "That's all behind us now. But now that it's all over, surely you can tell your story. I believe you. Others will too. If nothing else, Khalid deserves to be punished."

"No, no, I have only told you because I could not leave without knowing you understand. You do not know my people, our ways. The takings of battle go to the winner. I cannot prove what I have told you. And if I could find someone to testify to who I am, they will simply say again that it was battle, that my mission here today proves I was a Taliban."

Jamil's head shot up as the door creaked opened. This time Amy lifted her own to meet Steve's hard gaze that lingered on her tear-streaked cheeks. "Your time is long up."

"Please—just a few more minutes."

The door shut with a hard click. Amy turned to Jamil. "What are you going to do? You said earlier you had plans. Did you mean your mother and sister? That you're going to go search for them?"

"I do not know where to look," Jamil said simply. "Those who recruited me did not lie about their search, because I made my own inquiries. They have never returned to Peshawar, where we once lived. Nor are they listed in any camp or roll as refugees, at least not by their name. They had no male protector or money. They may have perished like so many others. Perhaps someday if the Creator of all is truly merciful, a Father to his children, as Isa Masih speaks of him, then I will one day discover what has happened to them.

Jamil spread his hands in acceptance. "Today—no, I have known since the moment I walked away from death to life what mission is placed before me. 'You will know the truth, and the truth will set you free.' But my people are not free. They have never been free, because they do not know the truth. As great a veil as a burqa is the veil of darkness and lies that has kept my people in chains. And now they must know the truth!"

"What are you thinking of doing?"

"I will go to give them the truth. As Isa Masih did. As his other followers have done. Did they not walk from town to town, telling the people the good news of a kingdom that is of the heart and not the sword? I cannot do miracles as they did. But I have some small gifts of healing. In the villages where there are no doctors, they will be grateful."

Digging into his pack again, Jamil brought out the infirmary's copy of *Where There Is No Doctor*. "I wished to ask if I might take this, to pay you from my salary to buy another. I can tell stories of Isa Masih and his teachings. If I do not have his words yet in Dari and Pashto, I can translate as I do for the children."

"No, of course you can take the handbook." Amy hurried into her room and returned with the Dari and Pashto New Testaments. "And Becky Frazer brought these this morning. I was going to give them to you—well, when everything blew up. But didn't you tell me it would be considered an insult to your country, to Islam, to teach the people to question the mullahs?"

"For you, yes, perhaps," Jamil agreed gravely. "Because you are a foreigner here and a guest. But another Afghan—that is different. You said once that freedom must come from within. That one country cannot give freedom to another but that a country must find it within themselves."

It was Steve who'd actually told Amy that. But she'd no opportunity to deny credit because Jamil was going on. "No, it is not the responsibility of a foreigner but another Afghan to carry the truth to my people. Even to the mullahs, because they too cannot have heard the truth. Perhaps when enough listen to the words of Isa Masih—not only listen but choose to follow his commands—then I may yet see the day when my country will rest on a foundation of justice and righteousness. And then my people will at last know what real freedom and peace can be."

"But you're acting like you can just walk out of here and . . . and start preaching about Jesus—Isa Masih—on a street corner. What happens if these villagers or the mullahs get angry for what you're doing? Are you even thinking how dangerous this could be?"

"Why should they be angry? Are Muslims not told also to do good deeds? Does the Quran not speak of Isa Masih as a great prophet? His teachings should have been told long ago to the people. But even if there should be danger . . ." His smile was the radiant one that reminded Amy so much of those media images of Isa Masih. "Don't you see? If I could die to avenge my family, should I be less willing to die to offer hope and truth and freedom to my people?"

Tears poured hot and furious down Amy's cheeks again. "I do see. It's just . . . oh, Jamil—"

This time the door slammed back into the wall. All three of the contractors were marching into the room as Jamil and Amy scrambled to their feet.

Stooping for his pack, Jamil said quietly to Amy, "Forgive me. I have lingered much too long. I must go now."

Amy made no further protest. She snatched up Jamil's pack and set it on the table. "Just one minute." Fumbling to open the knot that bound it, she swept all the remaining first aid supplies on the table on top of his scant clothing. "You may need these along the way."

The cash box was in the office, but Amy always kept an emergency stash of afghanis in her shoulder bag. Digging out the entire wad, she dropped it on top of the pile. "Your severance pay."

Then Jamil was moving away.

Dropping into the chair, Amy drew her shawl back over her face, lowered her eyes to the hands knotted in her lap.

"Get him down to the gate and off the property."

There was a shuffle of boots. A door closing. Silence reigned over the room. Amy knew she wasn't alone only because of boot tips intruding into her peripheral vision.

"You're in love with him, aren't you?"

The demand was so unexpected, Amy's head jerked up.

Then through gritted teeth, Steve burst out, "Didn't I warn you these people would break your heart?"

Amy didn't try to explain. Why should the former soldier believe a story too like tales fabricated by any number of real terrorists to talk their way past American interrogators? Her gesture was a helpless one. "You don't understand."

"Understand?" Steve paced a tight circle around Amy's rug before swinging about to face her again. A muscle bunched at his jawline. Then Amy saw impassivity fall like a mask over his face, heard formal courtesy take over his tone. "What I understand is that my men and I have intruded on you long enough. Especially since it would appear our interference was neither needed nor wanted after all. If you'll excuse me, we'll be off the premises just as soon as I can get everyone rounded up."

"Wait!" Amy leaped to her feet as Steve turned away. "I just remembered, my landlord down there, Khalid, your client—he said something about you remembering the day Jamil was captured. You were part of the Special Forces fighting with the mujahedeen. Were you here that day?"

He turned, and the grim blankness of his expression gave the answer even before he said curtly, "It was war. The battle to liberate Kabul. That piece isn't one I've cared to remember."

It was war. Just what Khalid had said. Then Jamil was right. There was no going back to the past, only forward to the future. But there was one other thing Amy had to know. "I sent a New Testament with that letter. Jamil told me one of the American soldiers was kind to him, even wrote a note in a New Testament to give to the interrogators so he wouldn't go to prison."

"One more piece of well-meaning interference that made no difference. Would you believe I even trotted up to Bagram on my next leave to make sure the kid was okay? But intel geeks don't talk to grunts like me. I always assumed the kid had been let go."

So there hadn't been a broken promise. "And now? Are you really going to let Jamil go, like Khalid promised he could?"

"Didn't I say so?" Steve took a long stride toward her. "Did you think I was lying down there? Or that I'm not capable of keeping my word?"

Something in the harsh demand hurt in Amy's chest as much as Jamil's own pain. "I didn't mean it like that. Please, you can't possibly be blaming yourself for all this. Like you said, it was war, and you were doing what you were trained to do. I'm sure a lot of things happened we'd all give anything to change. But at least you did what you could. Today, too. About Jamil, do you think I don't understand you did what you had to here? Or that I wouldn't rather know the truth—no matter how it's turned out?"

Amy broke off. How could she possibly speak to what was going on behind those stony features any more than she could sympathize with the horror of Jamil's narrative? "I'm sorry. I'm in no place to be handing out platitudes. I just—I don't want you to go without knowing how much I appreciate all you've done today. And all your men out there, too. If nothing else, at least we know someone's not targeting New Hope."

Swallowing, Amy lowered her head to wipe a corner of her scarf surreptitiously across her damp face before lifting her chin to manage an unsteady smile. "I hope you'll pass on my gratitude to your associates. And that I didn't totally embarrass your men by coming unglued like this. I guess I'm just not as brave as I hoped I'd prove in a crisis like this."

"Are you kidding? No Special Ops I've ever worked with could have kept their head and looked out for their troops under fire better than I saw this afternoon." His expression softened slightly. "In fact, Ian tells me he'll take you at his back in a firefight any day. You did just fine, Ms. Amy Mallory."

This time Amy's smile lit her whole face. But what she would have said, what he might have answered, Amy had no idea because just then the door opened. "Miss Ameera."

It was Soraya, an arm around her daughter, her husband hovering behind. The police below must have finished releasing the detainees.

Steve straightened, his body language withdrawing even before he stepped toward the door. "And now, if you'll excuse me, I'll let you get your world back to normal."

Then he was gone.

"Can you believe the perp turned out to be that kid we detained here on liberation day? I'd totally forgotten that little piece of action."

The CS emergency response team was pulling away from the curb, the last green pickup belonging to Jason Hamilton's police trainees just disappearing around a corner. Khalid and his convoy had left before Steve was ever downstairs again.

"What's really chilling," Phil went on, limping beside Steve down the sidewalk to where they'd left the SUV, "is that all our safeguards weren't enough. Like you always say, there's no way to rule out the traitor within. We're alive only because Jamil changed his mind. And for that alone, I can't believe Khalid let the guy walk out the gate. After all, we still don't have whatever MOI accomplice let him on the grounds. A few Pul-e-Charki tactics were bound to squeeze something more out of the guy."

Phil raised an eyebrow at Steve. "You think Khalid had an attack of conscience for what happened all those years ago?"

"Sure, maybe. Or maybe he's smarter than we're giving him credit. Look what he gets out of this. He's got it on record in front of Jason Hamilton, who has Waters's detail and his ear, that Khalid's not only a genuine target, but there's still unknown perps out there after his neck."

Steve held up his cell phone. "Cougar just called that as soon as Waters heard about our little adventure, he gave an immediate green light to extend Khalid's detail another three months. On the flip side, with Jamil out of the picture, Khalid doesn't have to worry about any embarrassing public testimony that might paint him negatively just when he's making himself very popular inside and outside of Afghanistan."

"You're right." Phil stopped abruptly on the sidewalk. "I can't believe I never caught that. Why that wily, devious—"

Steve dug out his keys to unlock the SUV. "Though maybe Khalid really does feel he owes the guy something, some sort of redressing the scales of justice, like they believe. You know, earn back some merit by showing himself merciful."

Phil shook his head as he got into the passenger's side. "I'll admit I don't understand how our principal's brain works. Or any of these people. They don't think like we do, not about what's right or wrong or anything else. And that's a problem. Because if we don't get what makes these people tick, even why this guy would change his mind today, we're fooling ourselves we can turn things around here."

Change his mind. Sliding into the driver's seat, Steve started the engine. He'd asked himself once what could make a suicide bomber change his— or her—mind. Was the answer so simple as it appeared?

Unlike Amy, Steve had no intention of so easily forgiving today's events. Whatever the justification—and too many terrorists had their own tale of tragedy—he despised everything Jamil stood for, every thought process, every decision that could turn a human being into a cold-blooded, calculating instrument of death.

And yet one thing Steve could admire about the man who'd been Amy's assistant. He'd at least been committed to a mission, a cause, enough to be willing to give his own life for it.

The passion Steve understood because he'd once shared it himself. As he'd witnessed such passion in Amy Mallory, who despite all evidence, insisted not just on considering these people worth saving but in offering her own self on their behalf.

And like Steve, when Jamil had deemed his cause no longer worth the sacrifice, he'd abandoned the mission. What would the other man do now with the new lease life had granted him?

And Steve himself?

Phil was still talking. "So with the contract extension, I guess we'll be in town a few more months."

Steve's reply was impulsive, but the decision had been months in the making. "You may. I'm out of here as soon as I can find a replacement."

Phil swiveled around to stare in disbelief. "Hey, just drop a bombshell, will you? So you've decided to listen to me, after all. Where are you going to go?"

Steve considered as he gunned the SUV down the street. "I don't know. Maybe in search of something to believe in."

Jamil had not expected to walk out a free man. So he wasn't surprised when his liberty lasted less than two blocks. This time the meeting place was not the ruined building but the police headquarters of the local precinct whose uniforms had shown up at New Hope the night of the break-in. The man training a weapon on Jamil's breastbone had co-opted the precinct commander's office. He wore the suit and Army parka in which he'd greeted Jamil that morning. But no longer was he making any attempt to conceal aquiline, hawk-nosed features.

As Jamil no longer had to pretend not to know the name that went with that tall, powerful frame. Ismail, deputy minister of interior.

"You did not complete your mission." The deputy's tone was flat, his calm deadly. "You betrayed your people and your oath. Why should I not shoot you like the lying dog you are, that you may offer excuses to Allah himself before you are banished to the farthest reaches of hell?"

Jamil's bundle was once again open and in disarray. Picking out a folded paper, he dropped it onto the desk behind which Ismail sat, his own voice no less flat and calm. "This is why I did not carry out my mission. You are the liar who will answer to Allah."

Surprise broke Ismail's cold composure. He unfolded the 8½ by 11 sheet. It was one of the photos he'd handed over the day before. Two women, one in a burqa, Jamil's female replica staring expressionlessly into the camera. "This? What is the difficulty?"

Jamil's casual relaxing against the doorframe didn't betray that he needed its firmness so that he did not tremble. "There are things it seems you have not bothered to find out about my family. My mother's tribe is Pashtun. It is said I look like her. My father was Tajik, a northerner much in appearance like the disguise you gave me."

The stillness that settled over the room told Jamil the implications of that conversational statement had sunk in. "Yes, my sister will have changed much over the years. But only Allah can change eyes the lapis lazuli of a Band-e Amir lake to black."

Ismail finally broke the silence. "You will not walk out of here alive."

Beyond the closed office door could be heard the precinct commander giving orders, the movements and voices of a dozen armed men.

Jamil shook his head as he straightened up from the doorframe, keeping his hands in sight as a trigger finger tightened across the desk. "I will—because of these."

He tossed two more photos onto the desk, close-ups of a man's bent head, one wrapped in a turban, the other not, but unmistakably alike. As Ismail's expression changed, Jamil took one more item from his pack. The portable DVD player he'd purchased with his Eid bonus for this very occasion. Opening the small screen, he set it to play. Before the recording finished, a gun butt had smashed the machine to silence.

"Then you did see me in the lightning. I feared so."

"I did not know who you were until you came by night to the place of employment you had arranged for me. My employer requested I take pictures of the men you arrested. When I saw your face among them, I thought to hide the camera among the fallen walls on our next meeting. Until you lied to me, I did not know to what use I might put it. But though your face cannot be seen there, your voice and movements are the same as the other taping, so that none will mistake the cameraman taping a testimony of shaheed or giving instructions to create a bomb. And believe me, I am not so foolish as to make only the one copy you have destroyed. If I do not leave here untouched, that recording will be on YouTube by nightfall, on your employer's TV screen tomorrow."

Jamil saw no disbelief as he gathered up his belongings, leaving only the smashed DVD player and photos. "I am not your adversary. If I will no longer be part of your mission, I will do nothing to aid your enemy and mine. But I have chosen another path, another mission. I ask only to walk away, to be left in peace to carry it out."

"But why?" His one-time mentor looked genuinely bewildered. "Your heart was set. To strike this blow for the freedom of our people was your vision more than mine. This—" he pushed away the photo of the two women—"was only a bonus. What has changed you so?"

Jamil shook his head. "That was your error. You compelled me to wait. And you told me as I waited to go forth and live. So I did. I went forth. I lived. And in so doing, I discovered that triumph lies not in death but in life. That freedom is not won through lies but in truth."

He braced for the bullets as he turned and walked out.

But they never came.

"There is plywood up on the broken windows, and I have hired two guards to watch with Wajid. The big doors can be repaired. The workers are making new hinges now. No, no, you must not offer payment. The bomb was against our landlord, and he will restore all damages."

Rasheed was being obsequiously helpful, his relief patent that the bomb wasn't on his conscience. That other confession, neither the chowkidar nor Amy had chosen to bring up. *If he's really learned his lesson, fine. If not, I've got my eyes open.*

Heading upstairs, Amy paused in the doorway of the extra suite that had been locked until now. Soraya, Fatima, and Ibrahim were moving around the empty space, discussing placement of belongings.

Catching sight of Amy, Soraya rushed over to kiss her on both cheeks. "We are leaving now. But we will be back tomorrow, and then you will meet my son." A glance at Ibrahim. "My husband's son, Fariq."

Amy walked past her own quarters to the office. Her conference call with Mr. Korallis was long overdue. *Soraya said Ibrahim's an engineer with the city water. We've been wanting to start a water project up the hill in that new neighborhood. I wonder if he'd consider working for New Hope.*

The electricity was still off, the only illumination in the hall a dwindling twilight coming through the office window as Amy opened the door, so it was a soft whine that alerted her to a silent figure rising from a huddle against the wall.

Farah raised a troubled face from the puppy she was clutching tight as though for comfort. "Is it true what they say—that Jamil-jan is gone? Who then will tell your stories or care for the children's hurts? Some even say it was he who tried to hurt us today. But that isn't true, is it?"

Amy sighed at the shimmer of tears in Farah's long-lashed, blue green eyes. Maybe it hadn't been wise or kind to introduce a young, undeniably good-looking man into the Welayat women's tightly proscribed world. Was this one reason the teenager had always been so eager to follow on Amy's heels? Jamil had never spoken to the women nor hardly looked at them. But to a young girl once sold off to a sixty-year-old, how could a man like Jamil seem anything less than an Afghan Prince Charming?

"No, Jamil would never hurt us," Amy reassured gently. "But it is true he is gone. Are you going to miss him?"

"I don't know." Farah's fair-skinned, young face looked as bewildered as unhappy. "I have always been afraid of men. My uncle was cruel, like the man he chose as my husband. But Jamil-jan, he made me feel safe. Like my father and brothers when I was small, though I remember them little."

Another life story Amy had not yet learned.

"We'll figure out what to do about story time tomorrow. You did such a good job the other day, maybe you'd like to tell some of the stories for me. As to the bandages and medicine Miss Becky left, how would you like to help me? Maybe even learn to do it yourself, like Jamil."

"You think I could?" Farah's face lit up. "Maybe I can become a doctor like Miss Becky." Then her smile faded. "And Jamil-jan? Do you think he will ever return?"

"I don't know. But we can hope and pray so."

As Farah disappeared with the puppy out onto the balcony, Amy entered the office. She was lifting the sat phone from its charger when she noticed a stack scattered by the explosion. Amy hadn't yet looked over the printouts and DVD Jamil had put together last night. One last service he'd left for New Hope. Picking up a thin package, Amy felt the shape of a DVD through duct-taped plastic. She'd started to rip it open when she saw the note taped to it in Jamil's neat printing.

Amy was reading the note when the sat phone rang. She tucked the package into her computer case before answering. Why Jamil had asked her to keep this small packet safe, she had no idea, but it was the least she could do.

"Amy, there you are! We've all been waiting here for your call."

Amy forced her voice to match the New Hope CEO's cheerfulness. "Sorry I'm late. We've had some excitement here—an explosion. No serious injuries, just some property damage. And it wasn't part of our rental, so New Hope won't have any liability."

"Good. Then let's get on to why we scheduled this call. I've got good news. Our original country manager slotted for Afghanistan back in September is available again. He's willing to make the switch to Kabul as soon as his visa clears. Certainly before Christmas."

Nestor Korallis sounded pleased with himself. "And just in time since your three-month interim commitment is up, what—next week? You want out of there to your original objective over in India, we've always got room there for leadership of your caliber. I've no doubt you'd find it more congenial working conditions.

"Or if you want it, the project in Afghanistan is still yours. You've certainly earned it. The new guy can come in as your deputy. Like I said, it's up to you. But I'll need a decision as soon as possible. Say, by tomorrow?"

The news was what Amy had been hoping for, praying for—a living, breathing deputy to take some of the load. Or even the possibility of an experienced country manager so she could walk away from this place without misgivings. *I could go home for Christmas and stay. Take on a project where I don't have to apologize for my faith or bite back what's in my heart.*

Talking to Becky just this morning, Amy had been frustrated enough with the whole system to storm away. After today's turbulent events, she'd even more reason to turn her back on the whole mess. It might even be for the best, the American nurse had warned her, if Amy wasn't willing to live with the conditions here. But now that the opportunity had been handed Amy, it no longer seemed so attractive.

After replacing the sat phone in its charger, Amy slipped down the stairs to the courtyard. Night had fallen during her conference call, but despite frigid temperatures, children were taking advantage of the darkness to play some variant of hide-and-seek up and down staircases and balconies, behind the fountain and empty planters.

Amy entered the kitchen quarters. Without the Hindi soap that usually occupied this hour, women were lying around on tushaks, chatting, their smaller children for the most part asleep in their arms. Farah sat cross-legged beside Najeeda, the sick woman's head lying on her lap. Despite feverish eyes and muffled coughs, Najeeda's son and Fahim were happily playing with Gorg. They smelled of Vicks, and on a nearby burner, Roya added eucalyptus to a steaming saucepan, a primitive humidifier that was nonetheless effective. Against the far wall, Aryana was sitting up straight, her baby clutched tightly. The young mother had been hysterical earlier, insisting the explosion was a conspiracy to steal her son away. Amy picked her way through sprawled bodies to her. "I'm sorry about the men who were here all day. Is everything well now?"

Aryana didn't relax her grip on her child, but it was with a fleeting smile that she shook her head. "As long as it is not my husband's brothers, I do not care who invades this place. My son is safe. What else matters?"

"You do not need to worry even if your husband's brothers do come," Roya spoke up. "Ameera-jan will not let them near you."

"None of us will," Farah said stoutly. "Together we are stronger than any man; is that not so, Ameera-jan?"

"Do not speak so foolishly!" one of the Hazara widows chided. "It is not proper for a woman to speak of opposing a man."

"I do not wish to oppose men," Farah retorted. "Only to live free as they do."

As the older woman started to respond, Aryana said suddenly, "Let her dream. What does it hurt?"

"Yes, let her dream," Roya agreed fiercely. "Maybe it is not too late for her dreams at least to bear life."

Roya turned to Fahim's mother on her other side. "You were telling how your family first came to Kabul. You were caravanning over the Salang Pass, and it began to snow."

As the narrative picked back up, Amy slipped out onto the veranda. *How can I think of leaving them? I don't want to hand Farah and Aryana and Roya and all these others to some strange man, no matter how competent a country manager he is. I love them.*

But was Amy willing just to show God's love where she couldn't tell it? To settle, as Becky Frazer had all these years, for making what little difference she could when doors were opening wide to go somewhere she could maybe make a big difference?

If I'm just going to hand out food and clothing and shelter, what difference does it make if it's me here or someone else?

Above courtyard walls, the evening sky was black, neither star nor moon visible through the mantle of smog and dust that had kicked up again once the snowfall had melted off. Amy focused instead on the night's sounds. Childish giggles, stifled laughter, and a slap of darting sandals against tile. The placid murmur of women's voices. A wail of wind across the balconies. The creak of those plastic panels along the back wall.

Still, is love alone really such a small difference to make? Amy asked herself suddenly and fiercely. Jamil as she'd last seen him—features passionately alive, grief-stricken dark eyes softened to tenderness, sweet smile—rose vividly to Amy's mind.

Love had been there. Maybe a little for Amy herself. She hadn't even dared to explore her personal response to Jamil's revelations. But above all, God's love. The love of a heavenly Father who'd reached down to his lost and hurting creation through the life of Jesus Christ. A love Amy had done her best to live out, however inadequately, among the women and children of New Hope.

And somehow, unbelievably, that love had softened murderous rage and hate to forgiveness and mercy. How many people had not died today because of the difference love had made in one heart?

I get why Steve is so bitter. I even get why Jamil would want to blow up the world. But, Father God, for all the ugliness, I see so much beauty you've created in this place, in these people. For one Jamil, it was worth coming here. To touch only these people within these walls, it's worth staying.

With that breathed prayer, Amy realized her decision was made. She leaned against a pillar, still listening to the night. Beyond the courtyard walls, the laughter and running feet, she could hear a distant rush of traffic, the blare of a truck horn. Out there on those roads, maybe in one of those trucks, Jamil was being carried away to a new life. Was his new mission as simple as he'd made it seem? Would Amy's path ever cross his again?

And what about Steve?

Amy stirred, straightening up from her resting place. Despite the companionable murmur behind her, she was acutely aware that she was standing on this dark veranda very much alone.

Soraya has Fatima, even Ibrahim. The women have each other. I know I have you, Father God, but just one other human being who really cares if I'm alive would be nice right now.

A chuckle gurgled behind a nearby planter. A small, dark shape wriggled, then stilled under the joyous illusion that night had cast a cloak of invisibility. With amusement, Amy watched two stealthy silhouettes creeping around the fountain bed.

There was a scurry of feet. Pouncing shadows. A screech. Then a small missile hurled itself toward Amy, arms clutching at her waist. As satisfied titters drifted off, Amy stooped to hug the clinging child, prepared for tears. "It's okay, Tooba-jan. They're gone."

But when an opening door cast a rectangle of warm, yellow light across the veranda, Amy saw only a smile on the face lifted to hers. The clinging arms rose to strangle Amy's neck. "Ameera-jan, I love you so much!"

As the girl darted back into the game, Farah stepped out the kitchen door and tucked an arm through Amy's. "Why are you here all alone, Ameera-jan? Don't you want to join us?"

Amy was smiling now as she let Farah draw her toward warmth and light and companionship. *And I love you too, all of you, so much.*

EPILOGUE

The sun was not yet high over the foothills when Jamil jumped down from a jinga truck bed. Walking to the driver's window, he handed in the afghanis that were the bartered passage. Jamil waited for a cloud of dust to settle behind the departing truck before crossing the dirt track. On the far side, a streambed snaked alongside a huddle of mud-brick houses, its water sustaining a narrow belt of fields and pastures. Here several hours south of Kabul, winter hadn't yet arrived. Leaves still lingered on mulberry trees, grass in pastures. In plowed fields, men were busy sowing the region's main crop—poppy. Burqas scrubbed clothes along the stream bank.

Tugging off his patu, Jamil breathed deeply of air that was clean and fresh, even the hint of animal dung preferable to diesel and smog. He hadn't expected to see this morning, and he felt reborn, light of feet and of heart, as he strode along the stream toward the village center.

A startled cry hastened Jamil's strides. A young shepherd herding his flock across the stream had slipped among the stepping stones. Jamil was there before the boy could scramble to his feet, lifting him from the water. A knee had slammed against a rock, a long gash bleeding profusely.

Villagers clustered around as Jamil carried the child up the bank. Dismayed wails told which burqa was the boy's mother. Opening his bundle, Jamil took out cotton, hydrogen peroxide, gauze patches. By the time he finished, the crowd had expanded to the greater part of the village.

"Who are you?" demanded a white-bearded man in the black turban of a Pashtun tribal elder. "What has brought you to our village?"

Jamil added a final strip of adhesive to his bandage before rising. He turned to the village elder and said courteously, quietly, "I am a healer. And a follower of the prophet Isa Masih. I come as he did to tend the sick, if you have any such among you. I come as well to share with you words of life from Isa Masih's own teachings."

The villagers showed neither surprise nor displeasure. Religious scholars, wandering mystics were nothing new. Did not the Quran's teachings command that such be treated with respect?

Some wandered back to fields and household chores as Jamil spread out his patu under a nearby mulberry tree. Far more remained, tugging up tunics to hunker down on their haunches. With curious eyes, they watched Jamil settle himself cross-legged on the patu. Children pushed their way in to squat down with their fathers. A cluster of burqas hovered on the outskirts.

Taking out the Pashto New Testament, Jamil leafed through its pages. Then he lifted his head, speaking clearly enough to carry to the back of the crowd. "The prophet Isa Masih promises in his teachings that the truth will set you free. He who listens to his teachings and obeys them will be like a house built on a foundation that cannot be swept away by the floods. Hear the words of life he has to say."

Slowly, measuredly, Jamil began to read.

"Blessed are the poor in spirit, for theirs is the kingdom of heaven.
Blessed are those who mourn, for they will be comforted.
Blessed are the meek, for they will inherit the earth.
Blessed are those who hunger and thirst for righteousness, for
    they will be filled."

About the Author

As the child of missionary parents, award-winning author Jeanette Windle grew up in the rural villages, jungles, and mountains of Colombia, now guerrilla hot zones. Currently living in Lancaster, Pennsylvania, Jeanette spent sixteen years as a missionary in Bolivia and travels as a missions journalist and as a mentor to Christian writers in many countries, most recently Afghanistan. She has more than a dozen books in print, including the best seller *CrossFire* and the Parker Twins series.

Visit the author's Web site at www.jeanettewindle.com for further information and a list of recommended reading.

Fires smolder endlessly below the dangerous surface of Guatemala City's municipal dump.

A politically relevant tale of international intrigue and God's redemptive beauty and hope.